Secretly Bound

Written by Jade

PURSUIT publishing

Published by PURSUIT Publishing
infopursuitpub@gmail.com

First published 2009

ISBN 978-90-5335-192-5   NUR 455

Dedicated To My Wife

She is ovulating. I can tell by the way she kisses me. Her lips are full and she kisses with intention. I know this means that after waiting patiently, I will have her.

She lies on the bed, naked and on her belly. Her legs are spread slightly, and her long, curly, red hair is flowing over her porcelain back. I come to the end of the bed and begin to undress myself slowly, while looking at her and longing for her soft skin. She has her own scent. It is a mix of her powdery perfume and the vanilla in her body cream. I am eager, but I want to take my time and savor the moment, because I know that it will be another four weeks before it arrives again. Four weeks is an eternity.

Crawling in between her legs, I am lost in her beauty. Her skin is warm and glowing in the dim light, as her long legs begin drawing me up her body. I run my hands over her calves and then slowly up to her inner thighs. She spreads her legs even further, as my hands reach the top. I am close enough to her swollen lips that I can feel her wetness on my fingertips.

I run my hand up and over the curve of her smooth bum. I squeeze it gently, while leaning down and placing soft kisses on the small of her lower back. Straddling her, I continue up with kisses, as I hear her moan in pleasure. This beautiful, sexy sound crawling from deep within her, escaping through her perfect mouth, ignites a burning sensation in me. My face reaches her hair and it smells like cherries. I carefully brush it to the side, so my lips can rest on the back of her long elegant neck. Kissing it lightly, first on the base and then moving around, I put her earlobe in my mouth. Blowing delicately into her ear, I feel goose bumps emerge on her skin. I lean down so my breasts are barely brushing her upper back. Placing my hands under her, I turn her over slowly so now she is facing me. She cups my breasts in her hands and places her lips over my hard nipples. She licks, sucks and teases them with her tongue, as I reply to her moan with my own sigh of intense desire for her.

As she spreads her legs behind me, I arch my back straddling just below her hips while my wetness is sliding over her protruding hump. Sitting up, I reach behind me, and place my fingers

5

between her legs. She is swollen and pouring warm, sweet honey. I rub her lips softly with my fingers as I stick my breasts out and she softly squeezes them. Moving on top of her slowly, I arch and throw my head back. My long, brown hair sweeps against my shoulder blades and provides a silky, soft tickling sensation.

Leaning down, I kiss her nipples, then her breasts as I carefully inch downwards, and bring my legs between her knees. Laying my cheek on her tummy, I bathe in the softness of her core. Lingering here for a moment, I breathe in her scent while enjoying her smooth skin. My hands move above to caress her ripe breasts and delicate nipples. Closing my eyes, I am lost in all things feminine. The moment is divine.

I begin to crave what is just beneath my chest, her soft, wet spot. Heat pulses through my body and pulls my face down just above her wetness, so my lips are just above her lips below. I breathe a long, hot breath and she squirms in excitement. "Put them inside. I can't wait!" she cries.

My fingers slide in easily. Massaging slowly the sensitive opening, while her nerves send signals all over her body, teasing her. I move deeper within and cup my fingers to reach her inner g-spot. Simultaneously, I lick just under her clit so softly, while I begin to move my fingers slowly back and forth. Her hips sway while she lets out short moans and then a longer one.

Stopping for a moment, I feel her heartbeat quicken, knowing this means she is ready to come to me. I move my fingers faster and faster in synch with my tongue, brushing her sweet spot, lightly teasing it. It grows very hard as she presses into me, while she arches and throws her head to the side. Her hips moving wildly, I hear her begin to release. Grabbing the steel bars of the headboard, she comes to me.

Hearing her makes me so swollen as my desire begins to peak. I slide on top. Her wetness combines with mine, as I spread my legs and rub over where my mouth has just been. She reaches down and slips her fingers deep inside of me. Straddling her, I lean back as she spreads her legs wide behind me, as I reach back longing for her warm wetness. I still feel the pounding of her orgasm as my body responds to her energy that sweeps over me. She is breathing hard as sounds of pleasure emerge from her mouth. Moving fast on top of her, I am losing control as she continues to explore deeper inside, softly massaging me. I cannot hold it any longer, and I lift my face high in the air, and come loudly for a long time. She pinches my sensitive nipples and it sustains my orgasm. For a moment, nothing else exists and time is frozen.

Collapsing on top of her, I place soft, wet kisses on her neck. We lay quietly in each other's arms and I feel connected to her again. I miss feeling close to her like this.

It has been one month since we last had sex, once a month is all it has been reduced to. This has been going on for two years and our relationship has suffered from it. The emotional connection has been stained with tears of defeat as we struggle to have another child together. The disappointment and frustration has been a constant darkness weighing on our every emotion.

She rolls over, turns off the light and I lie in the dark at her side. I should feel content and warm, ready for a deep slumber. Instead, I feel abandoned and desperate, longing for her. She is the only person with whom I've experienced such a deep and penetrating love. Just inches away, I can no longer reach her.

1

I lost my passion. I did. I lost it. It was gone completely and I was empty, walking through the motions without feeling. So, I thought about HER. SHE had flown away long ago, but SHE reappeared, when I called to HER subconsciously. I sensed HER presence immediately, looked up, and there SHE was, soaring high above my head, swooping down to get my attention. SHE had grown and manifested into a great presence since the last time we had seen each other.

SHE was tempting me, and I was unable to resist HER. I needed HER and SHE knew it. I could feel the fire SHE was breathing, because it was simultaneously burning inside of me. We have always been connected, but I guess I knew the moment I saw HER, we could no longer coexist. That is why SHE wanted inside of me, to penetrate deeper than SHE ever had before. SHE wanted to dig HER claws in and attach to me. There SHE would grow and expand, becoming more powerful than ever before, with each hot breath.

Held captive by the fiery eyes of the beast, I became lost between fantasy and reality. HER desires were stirred after a long rest. What satisfied HER hunger? What was SHE capable of? I got caught in HER trap, unable to escape, lost in distortion. SHE destroyed my life.

This is my confession.

MyLIFESeeker, it seems innocent enough. Many of my friends have accounts, why not me? It is a social networking site where people go virtually to stay in touch with old friends, make new friends, network, look for love...you name it. I have avoided MyLIFESeeker for years. Why do I need new friends? But that is precisely why I return to the website and consider joining.

I am an American living in the Netherlands and like most Americans I am really lousy at learning any language. I have been here eight years and I understand most Dutch. I can read local newspapers, watch television programs, and I think I understand about 85% of it. The difficult part is actually speaking the language.

Almost everyone in the Netherlands speaks some English. Many people are fluent. The Dutch have a gift for language and most people speak several. But I have found that since I moved away from Amsterdam, not everyone is as eager to speak English. This is a barrier for me to make friends. Even though I understand Dutch fine, not being able to speak it prevents me from feeling fully connected.

I moved to the Netherlands with my wife Jessica, who is Dutch. I first met her in Seattle, where she came to study for a year. We collided just two months before she had to return home, and we fell madly in love. It seems cheesy, and I don't think I ever believed in love at first sight before, but I do now because it happened to me. In fact, it still happens to me, sometimes, when I look at her. Her long red hair, pale soft skin, clear blue eyes, her plump lips, and her femininity are all things that attract me deeply to her.

Jessica and I have been together ten years and we have one child, a boy. At first, she was reluctant to have children, but after many discussions, we agreed it would be a great journey. As it turned out, being a mother was something that came very easily to Jessica. She was destined to be a mom and she is great at it. What a special gift she has given me, giving birth to our son. He is five now and he looks just like her. We are both crazy about him.

Having a child is a lot of hard work and it has been stressful on our relationship, but it has also made us stronger. Teaming up together to raise our son is our greatest accomplishment and makes our relationship impermeable in many ways. I love my wife deeply and admire the person she is. We are best friends. I am undeniably physically attracted to her. Simply put, I think she is hot.

She still has the ability to give me butterflies, goose bumps or chicken skin, as they call it in the Netherlands, just by a look or a kiss. We communicate well and hide nothing from each other. She knows everything about me and we are happy. Well, we *were* happy, very happy, but somewhere along the way things have changed between us.

Our relationship has been under a lot of strain. For the last two

10

years, we have been trying to have another baby. It is so difficult each month measuring ovulation dates to inseminate at the right time, taking temperatures etc, only to wait, then be crushed when Jessica's period comes. The devastation each month has overextended us. This, coupled with challenges of motherhood, has also affected our sex life.

We rarely have sex. Not because I don't want to, I try all the time. I think most couples with young kids tend to go through similar experiences. For me, it has been uncompromising and has created such a distance between us. I don't think Jessica has room to notice, because her thoughts have been consumed with expanding our family.

Last month was a turning point when we decided to stop trying for another baby. It has been very sad for me, but I can live with it; however, it has devastated Jessica. She can barely breathe, and fixing our sex life is the last thing on her mind. The distance between us has disconnected our natural flow. I find myself angry with her a lot and resenting the fact that she is neglecting "us". Emptiness is beginning to surround me and I don't know what to do anymore. Is this all there is left of us? I feel so alone.

One evening, while sitting on the couch, I say to Jessica, "I am going to open a MyLIFESeeker account to try to meet some new friends."

"Jade, we have lots of friends."

"Yes babe, but most of those are *your* friends. My friends are all in the US or other countries. I want friends here who speak English, and wouldn't it be great to have some lesbians around? All of our friends are straight. It also might be good, you know, to help us get over the disappointment."

"If you feel you need to, then sign up. It's okay with me," she says.

So, with a simple push of the button, I am now a MyLIFESeeker member. I open my laptop, log on and begin typing.

Screen name? Well, how about if I just use Jade. I'll use my real name, but not my last name, easy enough. I fill in my profile and make it available for everyone to see. Why not? What could happen? I can always change it to private, viewable only by my friends.

Personal Motto: "You Have To Say What You Want To Get What You Want."

I consider myself a woman who has always known what I wanted. My problem is I am not always satisfied with it when I get it.

Female
36 years old
Married
Lesbian
Gemini
University BA

I would like to meet those who laugh hard, challenge fear, promote change & live out loud.

Who am I?
International Woman of Mystery.

Femme, International Business Woman & Traveler, Euro-morph, Confessed Fashion Whore and Writer. I love women, dancing, traveling, Tamara Lempinka, Frida Khalo, the color black, Saturdays, dirty martini's with three olives, perfume, drag queens, Emma Peel, Japanese food, working out, high heel boots, old movies and movie stars (Garbo, Dietrich, Monroe), Italian wine, Marlies Dekkers bras, stale jelly beans & erotica. (not necessarily in that order)

My Favorite Music: Anything Madonna, Pink, Amy Winehouse, Ani DiFranco, Nirvana, Robbie Williams, Recent Britney, Prince, Old Glam Rock, Steve Miller, KISS, Guns & Roses, Queen.

My Favorite Movies: Thelma and Louise, The Long Kiss Goodnight, Anything with Angelina Jolie, Bound, The Women (1939), The Grand Hotel (1932), Gentlemen Prefer Blondes, The Sweetest Thing, Charlie's Angels

12

My Favorite TV Programs: Not much, L-Word, Grey's Anatomy

My Favorite Books: Anais Nin's Henry and June, Hemingway's A Moveable Feast, Anything Anne Rice, The Secret History by Donna Tartt, Most Nicci French novels, Steven King, The Happy Hooker by Xaviera Hollander, Blue Sleighty's Lesbian Erotica

Profile Picture? Oh, I have a picture I have converted to black and white. It is smart, not too sexy. I'll use that one.

Clicking on "Submit", I sit back and wonder what changes this will bring into our lives. Maybe we will find another lesbian couple with children. Or perhaps we will meet some interesting people. I put my hands behind my head, lie back, and I wait.

If only I would have known what would happen next. If only I had known about her.

2

Several days have passed and nothing has happened. In fact, I almost have forgotten my MyLIFESeeker password. I decide to log in and start taking our future in my own hands. Looking up people, I connect with some friends, and I find some old acquaintances through my friend's friends, but not too many. I get a few requests from different recording artists who promote their band and music by sending out friend requests.

I receive one friend request from a guy that had no friends, but wants to chat. His picture looks perfect, like a male model. Clearly it is a fake. He is probably just looking for a woman to have sex with. I guess it must be pretty easy to lie on any of the social networking sites.

I used to have a gay friend, Jonathan. While my girlfriend at the time and I were on vacation for three weeks, Jonathan stayed at our house. He scanned my photo in the computer and used my name and email address to pick up a straight guy. He had sex with him online from my computer, pretending to be me. I came back to several emails from a straight guy who lived in San Francisco. In the emails, he confessed his love for me and said he was on his way up to see me. My girlfriend asked me what was going on and I had no idea. Then, it occurred to me, Jonathan. Emailing the straight guy back, I apologized and told him that I had been on vacation and he had actually been having sex with my gay male friend. He never emailed back again, but it really grossed me out to think that Jonathan was virtually fucking some stranger, who was beating off to my picture. I guess you never REALLY know who is on the other end of the computer.

Tonight, I am scanning MyLIFESeeker, reading my friends profile pages, looking at their friends list and genuinely finding this whole world entertaining. I am fascinated with the fact that I really didn't know all of these things I am reading about my friends. I scan their friends and realize I don't know most of them. Lives are so complex. What you think you know about someone is such a small fraction of who they actually are.

Looking up at Jessica watching television, I become distracted by the hollow feeling that flashes through me. How did our relationship become so lifeless, and how have we allowed this distance to separate us? I think of when we met, and I ache for the "us" that we used to be.

We were full of passion and possibilities. The life we lived sustained us. We were each other's air, water and food. There was no other requirement, except sex. At all levels, our attraction to one another was so intense, that we could communicate without words.

From the moment we met, it seemed familiar, as if we knew each other. It was something that was just there, as if it always had been. When we spoke, I quickly found out she was smart, sweet and genuine. Over the years I have learned she is fiercely loyal, lives in the moment and has the occasional inspiration of goofiness like me.

Looking at her now, I daydream of the way it used to be between us. She appeared out of nowhere with the full package and caught me entirely off guard. I wasn't looking for love. Having just gotten out of my first long-term lesbian relationship, I wanted to play the field. But there she was, and she knocked me entirely off my feet.

I had my first girlfriend when I was 23 and it lasted three years. After the breakup, I met a Swedish exchange student named Kerstin. We had gone out a few times, but I was not ready to be in another relationship, so we were taking things slow. Kerstin was very cute, with long blond hair, and green eyes. She was shorter than I, and had a very loud laugh that made me smile. I liked her, but I was on the rebound.

One day she said she wanted to introduce me to her ex-girlfriend, who was dating a man again. She wanted us all to go out to dinner and also to invite a few other friends of hers. I was reluctant because I wasn't ready to meet the friends, and I certainly was not ready to meet her ex-girlfriend. But she was persistent, so I decided to meet her at the restaurant after work.

15

As I walked in, I immediately spotted a woman across the room. Her fiery, red hair and big, wild curls drew me to her. She was in heels, and taller than both of her dinner companions. Her very tight, dark orange turtleneck made her face pop out of the crowd. We noticed each other simultaneously, and that first stare lit me on fire.

Everything around me began moving in slow motion, the waiters slipping by, people chatting at the bar, everything. I broke my own trance, as I stepped toward the threesome standing at the end of the bar, waiting for their table. I had to get closer to this woman, who was she?

As I crossed the room, we continued to gaze at one another as the flames inside of me burned. She realized I was coming straight for her. My deep, dark brown eyes were drawing her in. Noticing that I had made her blush, she looked down for a moment, and then she instantly looked up and smiled at me. I playfully returned the gesture as I approached her. I was just about to say something that I hoped would be extremely irresistible, when I heard Kerstin's voice. She was standing next to the woman and before I could utter a word, Kerstin introduced me to her ex-girlfriend, Jessica. I knew at that moment, I was in very deep trouble.

I extended my hand, aching for her to touch me as she carefully placed hers into mine. I noticed her fingers were very long and elegant. The width of her hand felt so small and delicate, it fit perfectly in mine. I smiled and held it perhaps a little too long because the boyfriend jumped in and introduced himself. We were instant enemies.

Jessica and I sat at one end of the table. I had strategically placed myself across from her. The two other couples Kerstin had invited sat at the opposite end, and luckily they consumed much of her attention. Jessica and I chatted easily and I tried my best to charm her. Leaning in close, our conversation was animated as we flirted openly with one another. The blue of her eyes was clearer than the water in Jamaica, and I swam in them all evening long. They were partially outlined with a thick line of liquid eyeliner. Her long, thick lashes had a coat of black mascara, dramatically creating contrast to her light, baby blues that shown through. Her plump lips were the same color as her hair, and I could not stop watching them as she spoke. Back and forth from her eyes to her lips, I was

16

seducing her and she knew it.

Halfway through the meal, her very nervous boyfriend must have said something to Kerstin, because she directed her full attention to us and flashed Jessica the, "stop flirting with my new girlfriend" look, as Jessica's boyfriend shot me glances of jealousy. He seemed anxious and was shifting in his chair. Realizing that he was intimidated, I was cordial to him, yet I flirted with his girlfriend right in front of him. Yes, it wasn't the nicest thing to do, but I knew at that point, I was there to get the girl.

After dinner, we all went our separate ways, but I could not stop thinking of Jessica. I wondered if I would ever see her again, and I kept thinking of how or where I could randomly run into her. I had to see her. A strange feeling undeniably emerged in my tummy when I thought of her. It was love at first sight.

About a week later, fate took charge and brought us together. I had taken half a day off from work for no reason at all, which was rather unusual. It was a rainy Friday afternoon in November, and Seattle was cold and gray. Sam, my gay, male best friend, had called and begged me to play hooky from work and go with him to the movies. Because he knew I would always give in, he reserved his puppy-begging act only to those things that were extremely important to him. So, at the last minute, I rearranged my afternoon and accompanied Sam to the movies in Broadway Market.

When we arrived, Sam ran off to the bathroom. While waiting I was scanning the lobby. To my surprise, there stood Jessica with some of her friends. Shocked at my luck, I walked up to her. Standing behind her, I casually said, "So where is your boyfriend?"

She twirled around, smiled big and threw her arms around me. Her hug was warm and affectionate, and I was very aware this was the first time I had held her. I could feel her breasts press against mine. The fire from last week had started all over again, this time not only in my chest, but also between my legs.

She said, "Jade, I can't believe I ran into you here! I've been thinking about you. I had so much fun last Saturday. We have to do it again." I smiled flirtatiously and said, "Yeah, me too," I paused, "So where *is* the boyfriend?"

"He just got a page and he had to go to work."

I shook my head and said, "Hmm... That's too bad for him, but that can only mean one thing." I smiled as she looked at me very curiously. "I guess *I'll* have to take his girlfriend to the movies."

Her face lit up immediately, and I could see the excitement pour out of her. It was a quiet exchange, but everyone around us could feel the heat. She liked that I had confidence, and she liked it even more that I was being bad. She tilted her head and smiled broadly. What a flirt! I extended my arm and she reached around, grabbed my bicep and squeezed it, as she pulled herself closer to me. I led her over to the ticket office and bought two.

Sam strutted over to me and bantered, "You ho! I leave you alone for 5 minutes while I go to the bathroom, and you pick up some girl in the lobby!" He laughed and then leaned over and whispered, "She is fucking hot! Who is she?"

"Sam this is Jessica, Jessica meet my best friend, Sam."

Sam touched her hair and studied her up and down. He shook his head and said, "Girl, you are fierce!" He pointed at Jessica's outfit, "Love it!" and then the shoes, "Love those!" while snapping his fingers in the air.

"Oh I forgot to mention that Sam is also my hairdresser and considers himself the fashion police of Broadway."

"You go girl," replied Jessica. This was the phrase of the moment back then. Sam grinned and put his arm around her as we walked into the theater. He could not have given her a greater compliment. My picky Sam was so critical of the women I dated. He had never done this before.

During the movie, I was aware of the armrest separating Jessica and I. She was leaning toward me and I could tell she wanted me to touch her. So I reached down and put my hand over hers, while her friends watched every move we made and whispered back and forth. Sam sat beside me nudging me and making crude remarks.

"I bet that is a kitty you'd like to pet," he whispered and then laughed out loud. I chose to ignore him because reacting would only encourage him to further misbehave. Jessica seemed amused by him and that made me happy because I adored him.

I had my forearm on her leg, while her breast was just behind my tricep. I remembered feeling them against me when she hugged me in the lobby and the fire began to simmer again between my legs. I crossed them to contain the heat.

18

I could not resist moving my arm back a little, so I could feel it barely brushing the back of my arm. My heart was beating uncontrollably. I felt like a teenage boy trying to make the first move on his girlfriend. It was wildly exciting, and her energy was bursting through me in short pulses.

After the movie, I asked her if she would like to come to my apartment for dinner. Without hesitation, she said sweetly, "I'd love to." Well, we never made it to dinner. In fact we barely made it through the front door before we began ripping each other's clothes off. I pulled my thick comforter cover to the floor, lit the fireplace, and put on some soft music. Even though I wanted to throw her down on the bed and have steaming hot sex, I also felt something blooming inside of me, something deeper. She was precious and different than anyone else I had ever met. It was not long before we were both naked, facing each other.

She looked so beautiful. I could not deny my physical attraction to her. She had a flat tummy and the most perfectly placed breasts I had ever seen. I am powerless to breasts. That is my weakness.

She was a bit shy because I was only the second woman she had been with. She was so lovely standing there naked with the glow of the fire reflecting off of her skin. Her innocence captured me, as we stood very still, about a foot apart. Naked and exposed, we stared deeply into each other's soul. Our connection was paralyzed by the power of the moment.

We were communicating through an energy generated by our bodies that was greater than both of us. When I look back and think of that moment, a chill runs up my back and I can feel it, just as if it were only yesterday. I have never felt that way about anyone, no one before and no one since. That moment brought everything to me that I now love.

I moved closer, reached up, and gently touched her face as we kissed the most passionate kiss. Our butterflies exploded from our stomachs and came out to play together. It was the realization of true love.

We made love that night, over and over again, the next day, and the day after that. Making love with her was endlessly sensual. Our bodies had melted together and it was terribly romantic, but also unbelievably sexy. We were, and still are, very attracted to one another and so our lovemaking drips with passion.

19

Occasionally during that weekend, we surfaced for a breath of fresh air. We walked closely together to the Starbucks down the street, and we hung out in the second hand bookstore in my neighborhood. Everything between us was so natural. Even as we walked, we were still making love to each other by flirting and caressing one another. Our souls seemed to know one another, as if they had been waiting their entire lives for this very moment. We both knew we belonged together.

Her boyfriend kept calling my house all day on Saturday, then on Sunday night he showed up at my apartment with Kerstin. The doorbell rang just after we had gotten home from a short dinner down the street. It was great timing because in a few more minutes we wouldn't have been dressed. That entire weekend, while in the apartment, we had been naked.

I looked through the peephole and said, "Shit!" Opening the door slowly, I motioned for them both to come in. To say the moment was awkward would be completely understating the situation.

I had just asked Jessica what she was going to do about her boyfriend, and if she was a lesbian or bisexual. She said she was certain that she was a lesbian. Before dating Kerstin, she had been with the same guy since high school. She felt like she needed to try dating men again to make sense of what she was feeling for women. I thought that was perfectly normal since she had only come out about nine months before, and her first lesbian relationship was with Kerstin. Jessica said she had made a big mistake, and she was miserable with her boyfriend, both emotionally and physically. Sexually she hated being with men and knew for certain she only wanted to be with a woman. Just as she had finished the sentence the doorbell rang, and there we stood. Caught.

I suggested Kerstin and I go to the kitchen, and left Jessica in the living room with her soon to be ex-boyfriend, so we could talk to each of them privately. I grabbed two beers from the refrigerator and Kerstin and I sat out on the balcony with the door slightly ajar. I told her I was sorry, and that I had run into Jessica a few days ago. I explained that I had fallen for Jess. She said she expected that might happen because the sparks flying between us at dinner last week were obvious to everyone in the room.

"The two of you were in your own world. I knew that was

something that we didn't have... but you should have told me first before sleeping with her."

"I know. I didn't plan for it to happen. You're right and I'm really sorry." I was genuinely sorry for hurting her. She was a great girl, just not the one for me.

We had been on the balcony for about ten minutes when I could hear the boyfriend start to yell. Kerstin and I opened the door to confirm the voices were coming from inside my apartment and they were. We ran into the living room just in time to hear him raise his voice to a scream.

"You fucking bitch! You use people! You fucking used me, and you used her!" he said pointing at Kerstin. "I fucking wish you were dead. You deserve to be dead! You BITCH!" His face was red and the veins in his neck were popping out. Jessica was in shock and tears were spilling down her face as she kept saying, "I'm sorry."

She deserved to be dead? Those were pretty harsh (and rather childish) words. Based on his reaction, he must have been in love with her. Regardless, I had heard enough. I walked over to the door, opened it and said, "No one deserves to be talked to like that you asshole! Now, get the fuck out of my house!" He walked over to me and stopped just inches away from my face. He was slightly taller than I was, and he tried to use the height difference to intimidate me. Unimpressed, I held contact with his eyes and would not look away. He tried to muster up a forceful stare, but it came out more like embarrassment.

He said, "You just wait, Jade. You may be hot, but she doesn't care. She only likes you because you drive a nice car and will take her nice places until she has to go back home. Then she will leave you. In a couple of months, you'll be standing in my shoes. She'll do this to you too."

He was trying to scare me, but he only looked like a little boy who'd lost his favorite toy. He was throwing a tantrum and it was completely ridiculous. I laughed right in his face and said, "I am going to call you in a year and you will find we are still together."

"When you call me, maybe you will be ready to try out dick again too!" He smirked obviously surprised that he came back at me, if even with a cheap shot. His eyes moved down to my breasts and he was staring at them to annoy Jessica and me. Okay, he was going to get crude. I thought, Bring-It-On!

I took one step closer to him, coercing him to reconnect with me. "Even if I were, it wouldn't be yours. From what I hear it is far too fucking small for me," I said, lifting up my pinky, and bending it up and down, taunting him.

Kerstin started laughing loudly and he immediately directed his attention to her, "Stay the fuck out of this Kerstin. You should be mad too. You have gotten fucked over by these two." He turned to leave and then turned back around, "You two deserve one another. You will both get yours, karma always catches up!" He turned and stomped off with Kerstin following.

The boyfriend was right about one thing. Karma did catch up with us.

About a week later, we were driving downtown to have dinner, and I was flirting with Jessica pretty heavily from behind the wheel. I looked a little too long into her eyes and smacked into the car in front of us pretty hard. No one was hurt, but we were both pretty shaken up. I came within $800 of totaling my car, so they had to entirely rebuild it. I would rather have had it totaled!

The next round of karma came with the rental car company. I drove a rental car for a month, while they fixed my car. Having done a midnight drop-off on my way to the airport, the rental company called the next day and claimed I owed them $2000 for damages. The car was in perfect condition when I dropped it off, and I knew they were just trying to take advantage of the situation. After many hours on the phone and many threats of suing them, they backed off and dropped the costs. After that, I guess we were all paid up to the universe because the next two months were bliss.

Jessica and I were inseparable. With only two months together before she had to return to the Netherlands, we blew off work and school to spend as much time together as we possibly could. The end was slowly approaching and neither one of us knew what would happen. We didn't talk about it in those first several weeks together, but it was hovering above us. Every kiss became one less we would ever have together and eventually, it became the countdown to our last. As full as my heart was, I kept feeling I was drowning in those eyes of hers. I knew that I would not survive never being able to see them again. I decided there was only one thing to do.

I took her home to the Midwest to meet my mom and dad. It was Christmas and the snow was falling in our quiet, small town. I hadn't seen a good Midwest snow in years, and found that it made me feel nostalgic. It reminded me that there were still things I loved about this town, even though it was uneventful and in the middle of a cornfield. It provided me with the picture perfect background for what I was about to do.

On Christmas morning we woke at 9:00am. My mom had a habit of making a lot of noise in the kitchen on Christmas. She never admitted it, but I think she got more excited than anyone. She could not wait a moment past the hour, so she began clanging away on the pots and pans.

On the weekends, back at home, Jessica and I had gotten in the habit of staying in bed until ten or eleven o'clock. I was always up by eight and reading while I waited for Jessica to wake. After making love, I would wonder naked into the kitchen for two large glasses of juice and some fruit. I loved that we were creating habits together.

Jessica rolled over, looked at the clock and then looked at me. I had warned her of my mom's trick, so she smiled at me knowingly. I smiled back and scooted up close to her. I ran my hand under the covers and over her hips.

I kissed her and smiled, "Good morning, sleepyhead."

"Good morning," she said stretching her arms up and lengthening her spine.

She looked around the room and said, "I can't believe we made love all night long in the bed you grew up in. Why is that such a turn on for me?"

"You know you are the only one I have ever had sex with in this bed."

"Mmmm...I like it even better." She stretched and then paused to listen. "What's that noise?"

"It's mom in the kitchen. I'd better go out there before she hurts herself."

"No. The other noise. It sounds like a truck or a tractor or something."

I listened closely and I could hear it as well. "I'm not sure, but I have a feeling it must have something to do with my dad."

Jessica laughed. She loved it that I came from a small town in the middle of nowhere, where people did very strange things that seem perfectly normal to them. For example, the day before, we had been walking in town on our way to the pharmacy. She was wearing my high school letter jacket and within two blocks, five cars honked at her and waved. She found this fascinating, and she enjoyed just smiling and waving back. I explained that she was walking on the main cruising drag of our town. Yes, people still cruised. What else was there for teenagers to do in a small mid-western town, but to cruise? They would drive around to see who was out with whom, and if anything else exciting was going on. Very rarely was there anything interesting happening. We all grew up doing it, but after being gone for so long, to witness it again made it all seem funny. Everybody would just drive around, honk, wave and then drive on. Seeing Jessica's reaction made me giggle.

I got up and put on pajama bottoms and a long sleeve white t-shirt. Jessica watched me dress and kept reaching out to grab my bum. I loved the way we constantly had to have our hands on one another, always so physically aware of each other.

I walked into the living room and crossed over to the kitchen. Mom stood there with a look of surprise on her face. She always pretended not to play a part in my early awakening, and it was the same every year. I walked over and kissed her.

"Morning mom, where's dad?"

"Oh, Jade, you know how anal he is about the snow. He is out there on the backhoe clearing off our drive, the neighbor's drive and now he is working on the entire road."

I looked out the window and saw my dad sitting on the backhoe, with his leg dangling off to the side. He had broken his foot a week before that, and he was in a cast up to his knee. He kept shifting his leg back and forth uncomfortably. I could see his face turn red with frustration, and he was talking to himself.

He turned off the backhoe, inched his way off and jumped onto the ground. He was shaking his head as he hobbled up the drive. I opened the door, "Hi Pop," I said and gave him a quick kiss as the cold air and his frozen cheek stung my face. He didn't respond, because he was off in his own world. When he worked and things did not go as planned, he would be lost in his thoughts unable to

24

process anything else that was going on around him.

"God damn it, I can't stand this damn cast!"

Mom and I looked at one another. We knew that he was on a mission. We stood back as we watched him stomp through the living room and into the garage. I could hear him rustling through his toolbox. He was still talking to himself, and cursing at his cast.

"Where in the hell is my saw?"

My mom looked at me and rolled her eyes. "It's on the floor by your truck," she yelled back. I could hear tools falling on the concrete floor of the garage, and then I heard him sawing something. I grabbed an apple and bit through the skin to the crunchy, juicy core, as I poured myself a cup of coffee. I heard the sawing stop, so I walked over to the garage door and peaked out.

"Dad, what are you doing?"

He sat there with a crazed smile on his face, held up a piece of his cast and shouted in triumph, "How about that Jadie? HA!"

He had cut his cast off, down to his ankle. I shook my head wondering how he managed to avoid cutting his foot off in the process. Standing up, he tossed it in the garbage can, and walked past me into the house. He had already finished celebrating the battle he won against his cast, and he was off onto his next mission.

Jessica crept out of my bedroom. Hair all tousled from a long night of lovemaking and wearing pink pajamas, she had a cute sleepy look on her face. My parent's living room was white. The carpet, the furniture, the walls, everything was stark white. Jessica's red hair brought color into the room and immediately cheered us all up.

She looked down at my dad's foot, and then walked over to him and said, "Good morning." My dad looked up at her and smiled. "Have you ever been on a backhoe Jessica?" My mother interrupted "Not until after opening the presents." I looked at Jessica and winked. I knew she was wondering what a backhoe was.

We sat down, and mom brought Jessica a cup of tea and me another coffee. Warm, and cozy, I felt so happy and content to share my life and my parents with Jessica. They were both taken by her charm. She was genuine and we fit together. They saw it immediately. For the first time in their life, their restless daughter seemed at ease.

We started opening gifts. Smoked Salmon, blown glass Christmas ornaments, a Seahawk's cap and a few other local items were all things we'd brought them from Seattle. Mom had bought us sheets, sweaters and a Marilyn Monroe clock whose skirt went up and down every hour on the hour. Mom had the habit of getting me at least one unusual gift that she thought was "neat". It kept my dad busy, and he snickered every time the big hand hit the twelve and her skirt went up.

After we had all opened our presents, I stood up and said, "Wait, I have one more present." I pulled a small box from my pocket. My mom gasped and let out a loud Midwest "holler". She recognized the box straight away. It was the same one she had given me many years ago. Jessica had no idea what was going on, but she knew it was something big. Opening it slowly, she saw a ring inside. It was my mother's first engagement ring, and it had the smallest diamond I had ever seen. My father had replaced it decades ago with a huge diamond that he bought after he got lucky with a few of his investments.

I grabbed Jessica's hands and held them in mine. I could hear my mother sobbing on the sidelines, so I glanced over. She sat with mascara streaking down her cheeks, and her hand over her heart. My mother is always so dramatic. I smiled adoringly at her and teased, "Mom, don't have a heart attack just yet, and quiet down over there. I have a very important question for her."

I turned back to Jessica and I said, "Jess, I have loved you from the very moment I saw you in that restaurant, and I love you more every day. I can't stand the thought of living my life without you. Will you marry me?" Jessica lifted the ring carefully out of the box and looked up at me with her eyes all glassy.

"I love you too baby," she paused, as I sat on the edge of my chair. "You know I will marry you!" Jessica threw her arms around me, as my mom was jumping up and down hollering. I don't think my dad really knew what was going on, but he parted with the clock and hugged both of us.

"Oh, my baby is getting married!" Mom shouted as she squeezed us both tight. She spent the rest of the morning calling all of her friends and our family to tell them the good news. Jessica went on

26

her first backhoe ride, as I watched giggling at her bonding with my father. We were all so happy together that day.

Marry me...what did that mean? Gay marriages weren't legal in the US. Jessica was a student and her one-year visa was about to expire. So what were we going to do? The final month went by very quickly and she had no alternative but to move back home to the Netherlands. I was left with the scent of her perfume on my pillow and a promise that she would return to me, after she went home and made some money.

We kept a long distance relationship for six months. It was torture. My telephone bill one month was $600. It is hard to remember we paid that much money to talk on the phone before IP Telephony and Internet chatting.

We used to send love letters back and forth almost every day. It was wildly romantic and challenged my writing skills to come up with something unique. Some days I would send her diary entries, others I would make up a story or write a poem. Sometimes, I just wrote sex scenes between the two of us. My soul craved her companionship, and my body longed for every ounce of her skin. If I thought hard enough, I could still feel her long hair brushing against my skin, as she sat on top of me while I was deep inside of her. I could smell her scent and I could feel her spooning behind me, naked with her breasts against my back.

After a very long, torturous six months she came back to me. She flew into Vancouver. I remember, when I awoke that morning, my stomach was turning upside down with excitement. I could not wait to hold her and look into her eyes. Each second of that day seemed like eternity, as I waited for my girl to return.

Driving like a crazed maniac to Vancouver, I finally reached the airport. The moment is still so vivid. I even remember what I was wearing, a low cut suit jacket with a pair of beat up jeans. The airport smelled like cinnamon because there was a cinnamon bun stand just behind me, as I stood waiting for her. Trying to look cool and sexy, I was anxious, and the truth was, I was shaking horribly. When she walked through the doors, I stood there with my mouth open like a complete idiot. I had forgotten how beautiful she was. She walked gracefully up to me, smiled and tossed her hair back. She made me nervous. I had not seen those baby blues in six months. When she spoke, I remembered the voice that had been at the end of the phone for the last several months. Such a sexy, sweet voice that was occasionally a little scratchy. I had spent endless hours telling it my secrets, sharing my inner thoughts and planning our future together. So when she stood before me, I saw my future, our future and everything else melted away. I kissed her right there in front of about a hundred strangers. It was a long embrace and I will never forget it. I vowed that day to never be apart for more than a week.

After the kiss, she pulled back slightly, brushed my hair out of my face and then hugged me. Her hands went all over my shoulders as I felt the small of her back. We became eager to leave and get back to Seattle, to what would become our bed.

At the border, we had to go through immigration again. We flirted with the guy behind the counter hoping that he would not make it too difficult. He handed her a six-month visa instead of three, so clearly that tactic paid off. We went to the bathroom together before getting back into the car.

There were two empty stalls, and she went into one leaving the door slightly ajar. I took advantage of the opportunity, and followed her in. She twirled around in surprise, as I grabbed and pressed her up against the bathroom stall. Kissing her eagerly, my hands explored her body. We were giggling nervously, elated from seeing each other and for receiving the extended visa.

We heard someone make an "Ummm, Hmmm" noise. Looking at each other, we started laughing at the thought of getting caught. We straightened ourselves and walked out of the stall only to see a very hot, butch immigration officer wink at us and then enter the other stall.

Flirting the entire way back to Seattle, our conversation was flowing as it always had been, and the possibilities for our future were endless. By the time we arrived home that first night, it was late and she was exhausted from the long plane ride. We made love and then she fell asleep early. I held her all-night savoring every breath she took, knowing she was finally at my side.

Jessica and I were so happy living together. Our life was overflowing with passion, and our senses were completely stimulated. She was not able to work so she stayed at home, took care of the apartment, ran errands and did the grocery shopping.

She had dinner prepared when I arrived home from work, and afterwards, we made love or went out with friends. We were carefree and filled with laughter.

About four months after Jessica had returned, we ran into her ex-boyfriend. I didn't have to call him after all to tell him we were still together. Fate intervened once again. That darn karma, I just love it. It had been almost a year since he had been at my apartment saying those awful things to her. We had paid our karmic debt for cheating and now it was time for him to pay his, for making my girl cry.

We saw him at a party that welcomed international students every year. Jessica's professor had invited us there, so Jessica could greet the four women that were coming from the Netherlands. He had asked her to be a mentor to them. Her ex-boyfriend was there with all of his buddies, preying on the new women just like he had always done.

From across the room I spotted him watching Jessica. Clearly he was still infatuated, maybe even still in love with her. As she walked by, I saw him pull her arm and begin to give her a hard time. I made my way across the room just in time to hear him say something loud to his buddies about her being a "dyke" and that she "sucked in bed anyway". Jessica turned to ignore him, and she saw me approaching. I could see she was pleased because she knew that I was going to defend her honor and suspected probably a little more.

As soon as the ex-boyfriend harassed her, he too saw me walking towards him with fire in my eyes. At first he looked surprised to see me, then his intimidation resurfaced, and I intended to pounce on it. Maybe I made him nervous because he was attracted to me too, I don't know. I certainly was not going to let him get away with bad mouthing my girl again.

As I approached, I saw one of his friends tugging his sleeve and pointing at me. "Who is that, do you know her? You have to give me her number!"

The ex-boyfriend started to reply, but I interrupted him. I said loudly, so everyone standing near could hear me, "Now boys, don't believe a word he is saying. He is just jealous because I stole his girlfriend."

His friends' jaws dropped. I heard a few of them say, "No way," and I saw a couple of them high five. I had on a short, brown skirt and very high-heeled, brown, suede boots with my hair up in a twist. Jessica had on a long, tan sweater dress that hugged her curves, with brown high heels. I think they were pretty shocked at what had just rolled out of my mouth.

I walked over just in front of Jessica's ex-boyfriend and looked at him with a "fuck you" smile. I said sweetly, "You look surprised that we are still together?" I motioned for all of the men to come closer, as if I was going to tell them a secret.

"Oh and boys let me share something with you. I will give you a big hint...never, EVER, let your girlfriend sleep with another woman, especially one who is smoking hot in bed!" I smiled, patted the ex-boyfriend on the shoulder twice, and said, "No hard feelings." I grabbed Jessica's hand and strutted off. That ex-boyfriend brought out the worst in me, but I must admit, it was a hell of a lot of fun that night.

Jessica was unable to obtain citizenship in the US. We saw immigration attorneys, but it was impossible. Our relationship was a ticking clock controlled by US Immigration. Eventually her extended visa expired. So we started with alternative plans.

She had to fly back to the Netherlands every three months, stay a week or two and then return back to the US with a fresh three-month visa. After about six months, it started to get difficult when she tried to re-enter the country. Immigration officers grew suspicious of her frequent flights and began asking her a lot of questions. We always tried to charm the officers flashing smiles and telling jokes, but it was becoming more and more impossible.

Also flights were expensive and our savings was dwindling, so we decided to move to Europe. Gay Partnerships were legal in the Netherlands. We could live there uninterrupted and our relationship would be formally recognized.

The US prides itself as being the land of the free. Maybe it is for most, but it was not for me. Most people don't realize that I cannot live in my own country, with my wife and son. I soon realized that for me, the Netherlands was truly the land of the free. I was and still am very grateful to live in a country that does not discriminate against gay people. We are treated equally. Our relationship is legally and socially validated and society treats us respectfully. I don't care what anyone says, having marriage available to gay couples DOES make a difference. It is about equality.

I must admit, moving to another country excited me. I had always wanted to live in Europe. It was something I always thought I would do, though I had never been there before. So this made the decision to move quite easy for me. I was ready for a new adventure.

Amsterdam was a city of possibilities. It was alive and packed with new experiences. Similar to my move to Seattle, I was filled with fresh ideas, new desires and excited about our life in Jessica's home country.

The first few months were a bit stressful while waiting to land a job. I was, and still am, not very good at not working. I read all thirty books that I had shipped over, studied Dutch, painted every room in the house, and I shrunk a lot of clothes while attempting to do laundry. I was banned from using the dryer.

I wrote some. Over the years, I have also been a freelance writer for some gay publications. I don't make a lot of money doing it. It is just a personal desire that I fulfill in my spare time, but it does not pay the bills.

After a few months, I landed an international high-level sales job and luckily was able to make a lot more money than I did in the US. We moved from a small one-room apartment to a two-bedroom apartment in Amsterdam. A few years later, we moved into the house we live in now, a four-bedroom villa with a pool.

This house represented the life we had always dreamed of. It proved all things were possible. We just didn't realize that those things did not really matter. What mattered was holding on to our connection, not the dream.

3

A few days later, there are still no messages on MyLIFESeeker, so I decide to look up lesbians in the Netherlands, who have children. None. Revising my search to lesbians only, a lot of women pop up. While sitting on the couch with Jessica, I decide to browse through some of them. She is busy watching a program on television and I keep lifting up the computer saying, "How about this one? She has a girlfriend and they both look pretty nice." Jessica doesn't find it at all amusing because I am interrupting her while she is watching her favorite television show.

Jessica and I are both what I would call girly girls. We were L-word before the L-word existed. Many of my friends compare me to Bette, and Jessica to Tina. Like Bette, I tend to work hard and have occasionally been known to take my career too seriously.

Jess and I both wear lipstick, make-up, jewelry, and we have an extensive wardrobe. Jessica has a bit more eccentric taste in clothes than I, and she loves color. I have a fetish for high-heeled boots, designer sunglasses, accessories, funky suits, and strappy Marlies Dekkers' bras and underwear. I am not afraid of dresses, or skirts, the color black is my signature and I love heels. I am truly an unconventional lesbian in this sense. I own comfortable shoes, but rarely ever wear them, not even around the house. I wear my tennis shoes to the gym, to work out, or to play with my son, but that is about it. I'm almost always in heels with the exception of my biker boots, and I will sacrifice fashion for comfort any day, which makes me a true fashion whore. But my boots are comfy enough to run the length of Schiphol airport, Heathrow Airport, Heathrow Express into London, spend a day on the Tube and then back again all in one day, with my feet still feeling okay. This is as practical as I get when it comes to shoes.

You could say we are ultra-femmes in the lesbian world, I guess. We look straight, apparently. Not on purpose, it just has always been that way for both of us. No one ever suspects we are gay, not even lesbians. We are both very open about our sexuality, and we walk down the street hand in hand. In my professional life, when asked about my personal life, I am always very straightforward.

"What does your husband do?" I get this question often. I begin, "Well my wife was a stay at home mom to our little boy. But now that he is in school, she is going back to work again..."

Usually their mouth is dropping open and they have the "did I hear it correctly" look. I just keep talking so they can process it. It is a good way to bring it to them and it makes people feel comfortable.

Jessica and I have few lesbian friends. I don't know, I guess we just have more in common with gay men. When we lived in Seattle, we would go out to the bars and clubs mainly with a group of gay men. You would always find us favoring conversations about curtains, fashion or home decorating.

In Seattle, we wanted to have more lesbian friends, but it seemed that most of them never took us seriously. They were sure we were "temporarily gay" and that our relationship was an experimental fling. Things started to change about two months before we left Seattle, when I started playing flag football on Saturdays.

I showed up at the park and there were about twenty dykes standing in a circle getting ready to pick teams for the game. They did this every Saturday morning. My friend JJ invited me to play, but she didn't show up that Saturday. I strolled up in a tight, black tank and white shorts that looked like a skirt. I had my long hair tied back, full make up on including lipstick, which completely damaged any possibility I could have had to be taken seriously.

As I approached, I heard a couple of them snicker and say, "Who invited the prom queen?" I turned around and said matter-of-factly, "Actually I was the homecoming queen, but after I fucked all of the cheerleaders, they refused to elect me the prom queen." They laughed hard, and I had earned my way into playing, at least for that Saturday.

I was the last one picked. They would not let me have an interesting position and no one listened to a word I said. They kept calling me "The Homecoming Queen" and teasing me in a delicate way. I let them. I love attention from dykes. But they had no idea I was the quarterback and a running back on my high school flag football team. So I waited for the right moment to let my hidden talents emerge.

After our team was down two touchdowns and our quarterback was suffering from a jammed thumb, I said, "Jo, let me have a go at quarterback, what have we got to lose?" My teammates had grown to genuinely like me because I was holding my own, so they agreed. But the first down was no good.

One of the defensive linebackers broke through and got my flag. On the second down while in the huddle, I had instructed the wide receivers to go long. My team looked at me in surprise and then shrugged their shoulders. After the hike, I drew back and spotted my fastest receiver, well ahead of the defense. I drew back and launched the ball with all my strength, as everyone stood in astonishment. Yes, this girly girl can throw like a boy. It landed perfectly in the hands of the receiver, and it was our first touchdown. My team ran over and jumped all over me, and Jo kissed me on the cheek.

We scored a second touchdown as I broke loose and twirled my way down the field. No one could catch my flag. I may be shorter, but I move fast and strong.

After the game Jessica came running up to me and gave me a big hug. Jo said, "Let me guess, one of the cheerleaders?" Everyone laughed and it felt good to be around a group of women. Jessica had made brownies and brought bottled water for everyone. After they got to know us, they began to see we weren't so different. I think the L-word has made things a lot easier for us in terms of being taken seriously. Now, there are longhaired lesbians everywhere.

As I sit on the couch, I continue to look at all of these pictures of potential lesbian friends and find myself linking from one to another, then another. I find lesbians from all over the world. This could easily go on for hours. Flipping through screen after screen, I am beginning to grow a little bored, when I come across a picture of a very beautiful woman. I click on it. She has an interesting site with black and white shapes in the background. I open up the pictures and see more pictures of this very femme, very hot, long, blond haired, blue-eyed woman. She is striking. Her smile is warm and next to her in the photo is a woman who is very butch, with short spiky black hair, big strong muscles and a nice tan. Under the picture it says, "Emma and Eve".

34

Checking out her photos, I notice two other pictures. One looks like it was taken of them while standing on a canal in Amsterdam. There are a lot of people around and boats on the canal. I think maybe it was taken during Gay Pride in Amsterdam, when there is a parade of boats that journey through the canals of the city. The other picture is of them sitting on the couch playfully. But I notice there is something strange. The quality of the picture is strange, almost poor. Carefully studying her face, I am drawn to this woman, Emma. I find myself staring, and intrigued with this blue-eyed beauty. She looks very friendly, nice. Something in her eyes is calling me, and they are almost familiar, as if I know her. Do I know her?

Her profile says she is Dutch and from the Amsterdam area. Maybe I saw her while Jessica and I lived there? So without thinking and without reading anything much further on her site, other than a little of her profile, I decide to send her a message.

Date: September 26, 2008 8:45PM
Subject: Hello

Dear Emma,

Hello. I am new to MyLIFESeeker and I saw your profile. My wife and I are looking for other lesbians in the area. I saw you and thought I would message you. I want to be clear in that we are only looking for friends though, nothing more.

All the best,
Jade

I show Jessica the picture and read her the email I sent. She rolls her eyes and then says, "I still think this is silly." I turn back to my computer and I wonder what will happen. In a way, it is strangely exciting. Closing my laptop, I go get ready for bed.

I had no idea that waiting for me in my inbox the next morning, is the mail that will change my life forever.

35

4

Date: September 27, 2008   2:08AM
Subject: Hello

Beautiful, Sweet Jade

I received your message, thank you. I am a submissive. My girlfriend Eve is dominant. At night when she comes home, I am wearing nothing except black leather knee-high, high-heeled boots. She bends me over the back of the couch, she spanks me and then she puts on her strap-on and fucks me. She uses me.

I saw your profile. Are you new to MyLIFESeeker? You are very pretty. I read your motto. You are a woman who says what she wants and get what she wants, I believe? That is attractive and interesting. You can message me back if you would like. You seem like a nice person.

Your friend,
Emma

I read and reread the email over and over again. Why would she tell me such intimate details? Clearly she must be into S&M, and that is something I have never been particularly interested in, mainly because I never understood it, really. It reminds me of the first time I stumbled across it. I had a friend, JJ, who was a slave to several dominatrixes in Seattle. She briefly introduced me to a community that I never even knew existed.

I'll never forget the way that I met her. I was walking on Broadway alone, on my way to the bank. I had just come out as a lesbian, and did not know any hardcore dykes, let alone any that were into S&M. I remember seeing JJ from afar. She was walking with two other leather dykes and was talking and laughing very loud. Flipping her arms wildly in the air as she spoke, she was also looking to see who was watching her. She was desperate for attention, though would yell at anyone that stared at her for too long.

As she approached, her random conversations with strangers walking by entertained me. Moving closer to one another, I caught her eye and I flashed her a friendly smile. It seemed to surprise her, and she immediately reacted. She ran up and threw herself on the ground in front of me. Bending down with her arms extended in front of her, she raised and lowered them in an "I'm not worthy" gesture. I started giggling and said, "So is this how you pursue all the girls?" She looked up with a big grin and said, "Only the goddesses."

I loved that reply. So we became friends. We didn't hang out that often, usually we would just randomly run into each other. JJ was the first person I knew that was into S&M, and I asked her a lot of questions about it. She explained about dominant vs. submissive (D/S), and masters vs. slaves. Finally she said, "Maybe I should just show you?" I was curious.

One night, she took me with her to an S&M bar. The sight of JJ and I together was too much contrast for most to comprehend. She had a buzz cut and was probably the farthest extreme of butch I had ever seen. She was a badass. Nobody fucked with JJ and I loved that about her. She treated me with such respect and was such a "gentleman" to me. Opening doors, pulling out chairs, and she always stuck up for me. When anyone was slightly unkind, she verbally jumped on them and physically was always ready for a fight. She grew up on the streets and it had hardened her. Whenever she would over defend my honor, I would grab her leather coat and say, "It's okay JJ. Come now." She would soften immediately. I adored her.

So we entered the S&M bar. It was black in the corridor and I remember my heart racing. It felt like we were passing through the darkness into a forbidden world. After walking through a heavy baroque curtain, I saw that the well lit bar was in the front of the club. There were people standing around with drinks and most, but not all, had on black leather of some sort.

JJ wore a white T-shirt, a black leather biker jacket, black jeans with a silver studded black leather belt, and biker boots. She had a wallet in her back pocket with a silver chain connecting to her belt. Standing there in my tight bellbottom pants (the trend that summer), a frilly red shirt, and platform shoes, my hair was twisted up behind my head and I was carrying a purse. I looked like a fag hag ready to go dancing. When JJ and I walked in, the whole bar stopped and looked at me. I saw the bartender shoot my friend a stern look, and he shook his head as if scolding her. JJ bowed her head. She was still pretty low in the ranks of the Seattle S&M scene.

Looking around casually, I observed that farther back into the club, the lighting dimmed. There were people chained to the wall, whips, blindfolds and other scenes going on. Attempting to conceal my surprise, I tried not to watch or stare, but to look as if I had no reaction to it at all. It was very difficult, but JJ had already coached me on this; otherwise, I would not be allowed to stay.

Something intrigued me about the attitude of the bar. The control of some of the people walking by I found fascinating, almost innate. Enjoying being watched, they walked as if they owned the room and they seemed to get a thrill from it, yet remained in control. It was clear who the dominants were because they controlled the atmosphere. I sensed the power and I found myself bathing in it.

I didn't understand the S&M world though. I could not get around the pain and the humiliation part. It bothered me. There was one woman that I met through JJ, who must have been abused when she was younger. One week a year, she would go to a camp where she would color, play with toys, and act like a little girl. JJ said that the girl couldn't handle what happened to her emotionally when she was younger. She said S&M, and going to this camp to regain her childhood, provided her with a way of dealing with it. I could not wrap my head around it, though I tried.

Everything else was confusing. JJ explained the different colored bandanas, worn in either the right or left back pocket, indicted preference. For example, a light grey bandana worn in the left back pocket indicted Master interested in bondage, while if worn in the right pocket it indicated Slave. Yellow represented golden showers, light blue represented oral sex, red meant fisting, and light pink meant dildos. There were a lot of colors with different meanings, but I could not remember it all. I was speechless. It was very confusing, but JJ was my friend and I wanted to try to understand.

One night she invited me to a party she was hosting. I walked in the door and JJ threw herself on the ground in front of me like she did the day we met. I pulled her up by her shirt and gave her a big hug and kissed her on the cheek. JJ was the best hugger. Turning around, she introduced me to everyone.

The women there were all into S&M. At first, when I walked in, they all had the same reaction as the man at the bar. Who invited the girly girl? As the night wore on, we started talking, and I was open and explained that I did not understand S&M. We sat around the table for an hour and I hit them with question after question. Being used to most people forming conclusions prematurely, they were intrigued by my genuine curiosity without judgment. They essentially explained most of what JJ had, but I still couldn't wrap my arms around it. It wasn't for me, but it worked for them and that is all that mattered.

I never experimented much with S&M, not really, only playfully. One Halloween party, Sam and I dressed in leather and I led him around on a leash. That was actually a lot of fun. Whenever he got out of hand, I gave the leather leash a tug and he straightened up, of course that lasted only a couple of hours. I have tied lovers up before and have had role-played, but my experiences were only considered very mild in the S&M world.

JJ did want to be my slave. My apartment needed cleaning, so I seriously considered this, but only because stacks of books and papers lined my bedroom floor, and it was in desperate need of attention. I would not have known what to do with a slave. So I declined. Emma's email reminds me of all of this. I had almost forgotten about it. I haven't run across S&M since that short period so long ago.

The email Emma sent, I first feel shock and then curiosity. Why did she respond with an email about spankings and dildos? The second paragraph of her email seemed less rehearsed and almost written by her alter ego. Intrigued, I want to have a closer look at her site and then I see it, her blogs, there must be forty or fifty of them.

39

She writes them on a weekly basis and in journal format. They are filled with stories of dominance and submission, and the relationship she has with her girlfriend. Her life is ruled by being submissive. Her girlfriend, Eve, is running her life, both sexually and outside of the bedroom. Eve controls their sex life and everything in their daily activities, including what Emma eats and what she wears. Emma admits that she likes it that way?

She writes her private thoughts and describes the sex that she has with Eve. It is only mildly graphic, but she talks a lot about how spanking turns her on. Pleasing her girlfriend arouses her sexually, so she enjoys surrendering control.

I feel like I am reading someone's sexual diary of their innermost thoughts, and I cannot stop reading. It makes me slightly uncomfortable, but it is so intriguing that someone would write so freely, and is unafraid to be so openly submissive. I used to write often. I kept a diary until I was about 25 yrs old and wrote poems, short stories and a few articles. I have started three books in my lifetime, reaching page 50 and stopping. I always felt my words were compromising. I dreamt about writing a book, but I always struggled with writing openly, in fear and in admittance that I was, in fact, not perfect. Over the last several years, I have grown to embrace my flaws. I wonder how that would change my writing?

Emma writes stories of how she hates men. Despising them because they always hit on her, she essentially avoids them altogether. She likes that her girlfriend protects her by dealing with them on her behalf. I don't think I have ever met a lesbian who has spoken so blatantly about having a hatred for men. I have no problem with men, well most men. I am taking the assumption that she must have possibly been hurt, maybe even abused?

There is something slightly unsettling in the way she writes. There is anger in her prose, almost masculine, direct. I have to remember she is Dutch. Dutch is a harsh language. It is extremely direct, almost shockingly so, and most Dutch people say exactly what they are thinking, no sugar coating. It is clear, some of the words in her writing are translated to how you would normally say it in Dutch.

I look at the pictures again. Something is odd about them, almost as if it they are scanned. They don't look digital, do they? Maybe the pictures were taken by a low pixel, digital camera? I am not

40

certain. I hover above on the response button. Should I reply to this? I move my mouse down...Delete?

A quiet force pulls my hand over. I click on 'Reply' and begin to type.

Date: September 27, 2008   8:31AM
Subject: RE: Hello

Emma,

Thank you for your reply. I must admit I was a bit surprised by it. Actually, I am not sure how to respond to it. I am not into S&M. While I consider myself a strong businesswoman succeeding in a man's world, and while I am dominant to an extent, it is something I am not into. I respect the S&M community to the degree I understand it. I am sure you have no interest in continuing our conversation. But I am curious, I read some of your blogs and you seem very angry with men? Can you not coexist with them? I can, and I do, all of the time. I have no problem with it. Maybe it is because I know who really holds the power. :o)

All the best,
Jade

I logout to do my work, and at lunchtime I log back in to MyLIFESeeker. I could get addicted to this if I am not careful. Nothing is there, and I don't think much of it. I am sure Emma would not respond back to me, which is okay. I am still surprised by the blogs that I read. They are posted for everyone to see, and by reading them I feel like I have done something I shouldn't have. Maybe it is the diary format that makes me feel this way, but she writes blogs as if she is speaking to someone, intimately telling them a story, her story.

After dinner, I sit on the couch with Jessica. As I tell her about the email, she acts disinterested. Logging in to read it to her, I see that I have "New Messages", how exciting. I click on my Inbox

41

and see it is from Emma.

Date: September 27, 2008 4:36PM
Subject: Co-Existing with Men

Beautiful, Sweet Jade,

This is a man's world, Jade. You can get along with men.
You are successful in this world. That means you are a strong
woman. Women are only welcome for one reason in a
man's world. To be looked at, hit on, told what to do or to
fuck. I cannot stand men. They hit on me all the time. They
are only thinking with their penis and I wish they would leave
me alone.

I find successful women very attractive and dominant. Of
course I want to write you back. Eve controls my life. That is
how I like it. I like her to use me.

Your friend,
Emma

I am not sure again what to do with this email. Her English is
good. Is she even Dutch?

When I read the email to Jessica, she is simple and
straightforward. She says, "Why are you even emailing her?" I
pause for a moment, thinking she has asked a good question. Why
am I still messaging her?

"I don't know, I think it is interesting," I say while studying
Emma's picture. I still wonder why she looks so familiar. I search
my memory unsuccessfully to see if I have met her before.

"Well, I think she is very odd," she says and turns back to her
newspaper.

I close my notebook and go to bed. Three words echo in my
mind and bother me: "She uses me." What does that mean? I am

also wondering if she has been abused. She hates men and she is into S&M. I hear JJ telling me some people approach S&M to deal with abuse and the emotions that result from it.

Why am I so curious? And why, when I look at her picture, does it seem like I have met her before? I need to reply to her because my head is full of questions, but it can wait until the morning.

Date: September 28, 2008 7:22AM
Subject: We live in a man's world

Dear Emma,

I have been thinking and I have some questions. I don't know you very well, but I am curious. You say your girlfriend uses you and that you hate men. Have you been abused? I wonder why you hate them so much. I just don't understand and am trying. If I am being too forward, please tell me, I know it is inappropriate of me to ask.

I agree with you, to an extent. The business world in many ways is still very much a man's world, but there is room for women and it is changing. It is more of a woman's world than you might think. Maybe you are just in the wrong situation?

Are you into hard core S&M? What does submissive mean to you? I am just interested. I am in a relationship with my wife and I love her. I could never use her. I guess I do not understand what you mean when you say she uses you and why it bothers me.

All the best,
Jade

Date: September 28, 2008 4:32PM
Subject: Submissive

Beautiful, Sweet Jade,

You have so many questions for me. If it pleases you I will answer them. I think you are curious about me?

I have not been abused. I am also not into S&M. Yes, I like to be spanked, no more. I am into dominant and submissive (D/S). It is not just sexual, for me it is a way of life.

I don't know much about S&M but I have met a few people that have explained it to me. In the S&M world the dominant partner is a mistress and the one in control. The submissive person is the slave and the one being controlled. It is consensual, this is very important.

Some have basements or a special room called a dungeon so they can tie their partner up and "torture" them. The dungeon is where they keep all of their equipment. It is about trust and mutual pleasure. They have safe words so that if it becomes too much, their partner knows to stop when the safe word is used.

Why are people into S&M? Some say they use it to relieve stress, some say it helps to deal with emotions. Some just enjoy it. It is different for everyone.

In D/S the submissive person submits power to the dominant. There are different degrees of this. How did Eve and I get into D/S? It all started several years ago. We were sexually exploring things in the bedroom and she spanked me. I liked it, WOW! It gets me very excited. The spanking is not hitting, and it does not hurt me. I enjoy it.

This led to many other things. It brought out Eve's very dominant side. I found that I enjoyed pleasing her so it worked for both of us.

I submitted all power to Eve. She is in charge of our life together. I like her deciding everything. It is not only sexual, but it is in all aspects of our life together. For example, every Monday and Friday I do the grocery shopping. I ask her what we should have for dinner during the week. She names

44

a few dishes and I buy the ingredients. I always call her before I cook to make sure it is what she wants. I enjoy pleasing her and want to always make sure she is happy. I can only submit to her. This is the way that I feel comfortable.

When we go out for dinner, she orders for me. She buys my clothes and tells me what to wear. It pleases Eve and is satisfying to me, also sexually. It is a turn on for me to see her happy with me. Sexually she is also in control of the relationship and is always in charge. I cannot initiate sex. I can only be ready for it. She decides when we have it.

We never have fights and we get along great. There is nothing to fight about. There is no power struggle. She allows me my freedom to live my life how I want because I am good to her. Most people would not understand this. I can live how I want within our agreement. It works for us. She takes care of me. Does that make sense to you?

I am an attractive woman. I am not bragging but I am attractive. It is something I have been told my whole life. Eve likes it that I look good. She likes to own me and to show me off but she is very jealous. Sometimes, she scares me a little because she gets so jealous.

She doesn't allow me to speak with men unless I have to. This is okay with me. You see, together we have worked out our relationship. We have defined it.

There are also rules...Eve calls them The Pussy Rules.

1. Hands Off Rule: Eve owns my pussy and no one else gets access to it. Including myself, so no masturbation.

2. The Rule of Convenience: She likes me to wear crotch-less underwear. According to Eve, taking off underwear is too distracting and it takes too long.

3. Wet and Ready Rule: I don't think I need to explain this one.

4. No Men Allowed: She does not allow men in our house unless they are colleagues or friends of hers. I am not

allowed to have any male friends.

5. Her Way or the Highway: Her decision is final. Always.

She is in charge of my body and everything else in our life. I like the rules. They work for us. I think you are curious about dominance, am I right? If you want to be dominant with me, I will let you. I can show you instead of tell you. Maybe that is easier?

You tell me you love your wife. Be good to her. Is she good to you? I see on your profile you are a parent? Take care of your children and do not abuse them.

Your friend,
Emma

Don't ever abuse my child? What does that mean? I am confused because I thought she had not been abused. What an odd comment. This is getting more bizarre by the moment yet, strangely, I am growing more fascinated with finding out more about her.

I am also trying to understand the D/S world. I mean, when I think of it, I guess every relationship has a degree of D/S. There is always a more dominant partner. When one does not agree with the other, someone needs to submit. I have always seen it as a balance. Both partners share bits of each, but there is one partner that tends to be dominant in making the decisions and taking care of certain situations.

In looking at my marriage, I am the more dominant one in providing financially for the family, making decisions, and my wife counts on me for certain things. She likes that sometimes she can just ask me what we should do and that I will decide. I make decisions quickly everyday in my business and then I move on.

My wife is strongly opinionated, and she can be very dominant as well. When we argue we both submit. We know instinctually, whatever the topic, which one of us will need to give in based on the level of importance it represents to the other.

I try to imagine a world where I would tell her what to wear, what

46

to eat, and what to do. I would not like that. I think of some relationships I have observed. There are men that do this to women all of the time and vice versa. Some women enjoy submitting and others fight it. I do understand there is a degree of comfort one feels knowing that they are taken care of. My wife takes care of us too, and I rely on it, I like it.

I think of my mother and father. My dad was always jealous and accusing my mother of trying to attract other men. He struggled to control my mother, who fought submission on a daily basis. He responded by emotionally or psychologically punishing her for not obeying him. This caused resentment and a slow dissipation of their marriage.

I wonder what D/S, and the upfront agreement has given to Emma? She says that she never fights with her girlfriend and they get along fine. Is it fulfilling? It bothers me that her girlfriend is jealous and she describes it as "scary". Is their relationship as strong as she thinks? In my experience, jealous people are not dominant. They are controlling and manipulative.

If she is content, why does Emma want to know if I want to be dominant with her? Does she mean sex? She contradicts herself by saying be good to my wife. What does she mean? The biggest question that I cannot seem to escape is why do I find it oddly exciting that she is submissive? Or is it that she is so fearless in writing about it? I'm not sure.

Jessica comes down after putting our son to bed, and we are sitting on the couch. She lays her head in my lap and I caress her back and face. She is so gentle and beautiful. I love to touch her. And the way that she smells, I miss her so much. We have not had sex in over a month. Not since we decided to stop trying to have another child.

I haven't pushed her. I want to give her the time that she needs, but I am getting to the point that I need sex or I am going to break. After reading all of those blogs and listening to Emma talk about sex, I can't keep my mind off of it. Plus something hormonal inside of me has intensified over the last several years. It has further enhanced my sex drive, and this is only magnifying my desire to make love to my wife.

Smiling coyly, I say to her, "Maybe we should go upstairs a little early tonight?" Jessica immediately withdrawals, "Baby, not tonight...I am so tired."

Boom. Big blow. I know that she is tired. She takes care of our son all day, but she is always tired. Most of my straight girlfriends say the same. At the end of the day after taking care of their kids, they just want to curl up with a good book, but their husbands want to have sex. This is where I side with the husbands. After a hard day of work, I come home and want to make love to my wife, but all she wants to do is read a fucking book!

Her words defeat me. I am loosing my strength to fight for her. My beautiful Jessica is slipping away, slowly, through my fingers. I can do nothing but watch as our intimacy dissolves. This combines with my new friendship, and I can feel myself changing.

5

I wake up early today, 6:30am. The chill of the early morning darkness makes me shiver, as I creep down the stairs and enter the living room. My son runs to me and gives me hugs and kisses. He is just like a little puppy, all bright and shiny with a smile on his face. I love to start my day with him running up to me eagerly. It is a ritual I cherish. Inevitably it will end one day. I know he will grow up and be gone, so I will enjoy it every single day that it lasts.

I turn on the coffee maker and then prepare breakfast for him. Afterwards, I get him dressed while Jessica is getting ready. She brings him to school each day, and then she goes to work three days a week at a shop in town.

After they leave, I retreat to my office to workout and then work. It is a small house in my garden, and it is my sanctuary. I have a desk, chair, a computer, workout equipment and a television. It is my space where I can be creative and the silence allows me to work uninterrupted. All things motivational and that financially provide for our family, are born in this room.

Shivering, I step inside and walk over to turn up the heat. After taking a few sips of my hot coffee, it begins to warm me. I sit down at my desk, log into MyLIFESeeker and begin to write to Emma.

Date: September 29, 2008 7:30AM
Subject: RE: Submissive

Dear Emma,

I am sorry about linking S&M and your hatred of men to a history of abuse. That was really an ignorant thing of me to ask. I am glad you were not abused though.

So you are not into hardcore S&M. I have never gotten the hardcore stuff, not that there is anything wrong with it. I actually find it a bit fascinating.

It sounds like Eve is good to you in the ways that you need it, and you are in a relationship that works for you. She has your best interest at heart, doesn't she?

I have never thought about it, but I am more dominant, and my wife is more submissive. I guess I do make most of the decisions, and she does what I decide. I have never really thought of it like that because we do talk about everything. I don't think I could be with someone without an opinion. I love that about her.

I work and have the traditional male role. My wife holds the traditional female role. I provide for the family, while she is a stay at home mom, who has just reentered the workforce part-time. Essentially she keeps it all together.

To think of it though, don't most relationships have a degree of dominant vs. submissive? Maybe not as openly as you admit to it, but I think most relationships do. Most people subconsciously put themselves in one category or the other, or both. Maybe I am wrong. I wonder if because you are so open and have an upfront agreement, is that why there is no power struggle between you and your girlfriend?

Your English is really good. Do you live in the Netherlands? Spreekt u Nederlands? (Do you speak Dutch?)

You made a comment about being good to my wife and kids. I want to be very clear. I would never hurt my child intentionally. I am a parent and we make mistakes. Sometimes things we say come out wrong and our children are hurt, but I would never do it intentionally. I am not sure I understand why you made that comment?

As for my wife, I am very good to her. I spoil her all the time. I try to make a good life for us. We are struggling at the moment because we cannot have a second child. It has been a real strain on us for the last three years and certainly on our sex life.

Tell me more about your life, where did you grow up? Do you have

50

a family in the Netherlands? Do they accept that you are gay?

All the best,
Jade

Date: September 29, 2008   9:01PM
Subject: About Sex

Beautiful, Sweet Jade,

You are a very nice person. May I ask you, are we becoming friends? I should like very much to be your friend, if it is okay with you?

I work with kids. I am an assistant in the children's psychology ward of a hospital. I see so many parents who hurt their children by not listening to them, but also who abuse them. Sometimes it is physical, but more often mental. Their parents are not there for them. Both parents are involved in their own lives. They ignore their children. I can relate to this.
I am glad you are good to your child and your wife. Always show them love. Take care with your words. They listen, very closely. It affects them. More than you will ever know.

Natuurlijk spreek ik nederlands. Why do you ask?

You say you and your wife have problems sexually. Do you want to talk about it? It must be hard that you are unable to have more children. Can you adopt?
Eve and I had problems sexually, several years ago. That is why I decided to try new things in the bedroom. She really liked it. Then it grew from there. She made rules for me. I told you about those. Foreplay can be many things. It is not always just sexual.
We have more agreements. We defined our relationship so there were no questions. I stopped trying to resist her dominance. We stopped fighting. It worked for us.
When Eve comes home, I stand there naked or in some sexy

lingerie. Sometimes she cannot wait and we do it in the entryway. Or sometimes when she comes home I clean or work outside in our garden and she watches me. She likes to do this.

Eve is always working in the evening. She carries a lot of stress with her business. So I do what I can to help relieve her. I offer myself to her. Just waiting for her to touch me makes me wet. Last night she put me on top of her desk. All of her papers were spread out and I sat on them with my crotchless panties. She had me on top of her work contracts.

Did I tell you? I like sex. A lot.

So you are dominant. How dominant are you? Have you ever spanked anyone? If not you can spank me. Just tell me you want to spank me and you can. I will help you learn more.

Your friend,
Emma

I read Emma's email and find myself visualizing the relationship she has with her girlfriend. I imagine coming home to my wife wearing something sexy. I would not be able to keep my hands off of her. I think of Jessica coming to me in my office. I put her on top of the desk and have sex with her. Just thinking about it begins to drive me crazy. I think I would quite like to see her doing something around the house in something sexy. Hmmm... This would not happen. We have a child so the days of wild sex, at random times and places, are gone. I feel like everything is on a schedule, except for sex.

Emma is inviting me to spank her. Telling me she loves a lot of sex, she is tempting me, but I will not bite. While things with Jessica are not going well, that is not what I want out of this friendship.

But, what do I want?

I have a business trip to attend to. I will be gone a week to the
UK, then to Brussels, and finally to Paris. I enjoy traveling for my
work. Though I see a lot of hotel rooms, it is a space that has
become mine, and I have a few hours to spend alone. Everyone
needs that. I am not gone very often maybe three or four trips a
month, for one or two nights. But this week is very busy because
we are in the planning cycle for our next fiscal year.

Being away allows me to stay busy and get a lot of work done. I
also get to connect with colleagues that I am otherwise on the
phone with. We have worked together over the years, and I have
become good friends with many of them. Sprinkled throughout
many major cities in Europe, I have many friends or acquaintances.
When I am in town, we go out for dinner or meet up for lunch. We
talk business, but also have a few drinks and laughs.

I am working in a male dominated industry, so often I am out to dinner with a group of men. I don't mind it at all. In fact, I love what I do, and the men are always very respectful to me. They all know I am gay. I never hide it, unless I feel my safety is in jeopardy, or I am in a country where gay people do not have any rights. Then I play it safe, I steer the conversation in other directions.

It is also good for me to be away from my wife and son. Jessica gets to have enough time away from me, to miss me, and I miss them too. When I come home they are so happy to see me. I feel like the luckiest woman on earth. My family is everything to me. Jessica is my rock.

I just wish she would come around and come back to me. As each day passes, we drift further and further apart. The intimacy and magic is fading to a humdrum existence, and I cannot go on like this.

While on the flight to the UK, a man sits next to me. He is desperately trying to get my attention. I travel so much that random conversations on airplanes are not something I look forward to. Always pretending to be focusing on something very important, I consider myself a master at avoiding plane chit chat. Putting on my iPod, I escape into my own world of music.

I see out of the corner of my eye, the man sitting next to me is looking over at my legs. I have a nice trendy suit on and my black pants are tucked into boots that come just below my knee. Men look at one of four things: my boobs, my legs, my ass, or my eyes.

The man tries to catch my attention the entire flight. I am of course, very busy reading, listening to music and keeping my eyes in my own business. At the end of the flight, I make the mistake of looking out of the window where he is sitting. He leans over in my line of view, smiles, and motions for me to put my earphones out. Pulling one down, I look at him with a raised eyebrow.

He is part of the men's rugby team that is on the plane. Very well dressed, his arms are cut and popping out of his tight white t-shirt. He is wearing nice cologne, but also smells a little sweaty, not bad, but like a man. Male pheromones have never affected me, but most of the women on the plane are stealing glances at him. Confident, even a little cocky, I know his type.

54

He says, "I am sorry, I don't usually do this. I cannot believe I am going to ask you this, but I am afraid if I don't it will be one thing that I look back and regret. Is there any way that you will have dinner with me tonight? I am staying at the Hilton at Heathrow and there is a very nice sushi restaurant there. Do you like sushi?"

Shooting me his million-dollar smile, he is handsome and relies on his dimples to charm women. I notice that he ends his question with a distraction. Do I like sushi? Crafty. I am sure he does, in fact, do this a lot.

I study him for a moment and then say, "I don't think so."

He volleys back, "What? Not a fan of sushi? They have fish too, do you like fish?"

I snicker a little to myself and say, "Oh, yes, I do love fish and sushi too."

"What is the problem then? You have such beautiful eyes," he says, trying to distract me as he searches for a different strategy.

"Look, while I am flattered, there is an entire plane full of women that would love to have sushi with you, and you have managed to pick the only lesbian in the crowd. A married lesbian at that," I say, holding up my finger where my wedding ring rests.

He seems a little shocked, judging from his silence. I put my headphones back on and start packing my things into my bag. He waves at me, and motions again for me to put down my headphones. I pull one earphone out and nod for him to speak.

"You are kidding me right?" he says with a smirk.

I know what he is thinking. He is getting the whole slumber party and pillow fight visual that most straight men get when they think of two women together. Oh no, here we go again.

"I'm serious. Dead serious," I say a little annoyed while continuing to pack up my bag.

He pauses and says, "Well..."

Oh no, here it comes. I can feel it. Here it comes. Don't say it. Please don't say it! I cannot be held responsible for my actions if you say it...

"Um, can I watch?" he says eagerly looking me up and down.

If I had a dollar for every time I heard some stupid idiot say this to me, I could have retired years ago. It is the same as the whole whistling at women thing that men do. Why do they do that? What do they expect, whistling will make a woman swoon? Come on. It really does show how sometimes, men can be so, so stupid. Can I watch, really? REALLY? As I said, I cannot be held responsible for my actions.

I look at him, pause, give him a very naughty smile, and I say in a deep, sexy voice, "What, you have never seen two woman together? A stud like you?"

"I slept with two women once, but they would not...you know."

He looks at me to fill in the blank. "Carpet-munch?" I say.

He laughs a nervous, anxious laugh. "Yeah, that is a good one. Carpet Munching."

"I'll tell you what, today is your lucky day. My partner and I will meet you at the sushi restaurant at 8:00 tonight. Afterwards, let's go up to your room. Bring condoms, lots of them!" I whisper. I see his eyes growing very big in surprise.

"Really?"

"Sure, you're handsome enough." I stand up, gather my things and walk off, while I shout over my shoulder, "Don't be late."

I am disgusted and shaking my head to myself while walking through the airport wondering how many men actually show up, believing that I will let them watch! I don't mind being noticed by men or even having their attention. But the whole "can I watch" reaction has got to go. Probably not the nicest thing to do, but you know what? I'll bet he will think twice before saying it again.

I take the cab to my hotel, and the first thing I do is check MyLIFESeeker to see if Emma has messaged me. I am finding her responses more and more intriguing. I must admit, I am missing sex and in a strange way I look forward to our conversation. I am not longing for the same kind of sex she is having, but at this point *any* would do. I open up MyLIFESeeker and wonder why I am more interested in checking my personal rather than work email. Strange.

Date: September 30, 2008   9:32PM

56

Subject: My Mother and Father

Beautiful Sweet Jade,

You don't want to discuss sex with me. That is okay. We don't know each other very well yet. If you want to discuss it, I will listen.

Do men really pose as lesbians for sex? That is a little scary don't you think?

You ask if I grew up in the Netherlands. Yes. My father is American and my mama is Dutch. I grew up speaking English with my father. That is why my English is so good.

Let me tell you about my parents. Growing up my mama and father mostly ignored me. They never wanted to have children. Before I was born they could go to parties with their friends and could spend more time with each other. After having me, all of that stopped.

My mama and I don't get along. She hates that I am a lesbian. It is against her religion. She is very religious. I told her when I was 18 that I was a lesbian. She ignored it at first. I told her again. She still ignored it. Then she started leaving me scriptures everywhere. Saying what I was doing was bad.

I grew up feeling very lonely.   My mama disowned her own daughter in a way. Do you understand what it is like having parents that don't speak to you? I don't know your situation. For me it was terrible.

My dad was always gone working as I grew up. I never really spoke to him much back then. He was always talking on the phone when he was home. He did not have time for me and he was very stern. He never got involved with me.

My father got bored with my mama and their marriage. My mother is very traditional. So after having me and after father began to ignore her, she became very religious. My father was not. He could not deal with it. He had an assistant. She was 10 years younger than my mama, and she was a very beautiful Dutch woman. My father was tempted. He divorced my mama when I was 19 and started with his assistant. Or maybe he started with her before that. I don't want to know.

He married her when I was 19. My mother hates her. I wanted to but I couldn't. My mama didn't accept me being a lesbian, but this woman didn't care. She said it was okay.

She was very outgoing and eccentric. She threw big parties at our house and would invite me. I came back from college during the holidays and it was so fun. Our house that was so quiet and dead came alive. She had a lot of friends that were in the arts. They would come over and talk all night about things I never knew existed. I was shy and I didn't talk so much. These people made me feel more comfortable.

My father was very attracted to her. I thought she was fantastic and he was happy. Overnight he changed. He taught me how to play golf. I played a lot of golf with him.

We still play together. We always talk when we golf. He puts his arm around me when I play well. This lets me know he loves me. But, sometimes I think that he wishes he had a boy, someone who could take over his business.

My mama and I don't speak too often. She recently got a computer and emailed me. Do you think she could love me again? Can people change?

Before my dad remarried it was awful for me. I felt like an unwanted and unloved child. I was always seeking their approval. I wanted to be a good girl.

This is why I say be good to your kids. They need to know they exist. They need to know no matter what, you will always love them.

Your friend,
Emma

This email makes me so sad. It must be awful to have to deal with a mother that does not accept you are gay. I have friends who have had a lot of issues when coming out to their parents, but I never had a problem. I am in the minority.

Her words also put my mind at ease. She shared a personal story with me, something that is painful for her. I feel her emotion and vulnerability, and it transforms any doubts that I had about her.

For some reason, I feel like I can open up a bit and begin to trust her. Let me send her an email. Her writing to me is bold and I wonder if I can I do the same? I want to. I want to find that passion in my writing again. Maybe this is a good chance for me to do that, by writing to Emma fearlessly. She is inspiring me to be more daring.

But how daring am I willing to get? Do I have it in me?

6

Date: October 1, 2008   6:30AM
Subject: About Me

Dearest Emma,

You have shared some secrets with me. You have told me about your relationship with your parents. It must be difficult not having your mom support you, and it must be frustrating having her leave scriptures everywhere.

Do I think people can change you ask? Not really, but that doesn't mean they don't want to. I do think they can recognize when they make mistakes and try to fix those. It is part of getting older and wiser, and it is a subtle change that evolves over time. It is a positive sign that she emailed you. Maybe this is the first step.

Your father remarried and it had a positive impact on you, I think. It is better they got out of a bad marriage than set a bad example for you. You got to see a good side of your father and it changed him for the better. Your father was in love and it brought life to your house.

The relationship with your father is better. Treasure it. I grew up not knowing who my father was. Don't get me wrong, he was a good provider for our family and he was there physically, but I did not really know him.

ABOUT ME

I grew up in a small town in the middle of the USA, where there were lightening bugs and tall cornfields in the summer, and snow piled high in the winter. Back then I did not know I was gay. There weren't any openly gay people around, and as far as I knew, it was not an option. Having the straightest life you could imagine, I went to dances, had boyfriends, went to college, and was in a sorority. I say that I did not know I was gay, but looking back I did, I just didn't understand it. There was no opportunity for me to comprehend it.

I had one friend when I was 7, maybe 8 and we used to play a little game called 'See What Happens'. She would spend the night. At night when the house was still, we would turn off the lights and get in bed. I would stay awake and she would go to sleep and we would both agree to "see what happens" after she fell asleep. She would only pretend of course. After a few minutes, she would roll over into my arms and I would hold her.

I remember the first time she rested her head on my chest. Her hair was silky and smelled like strawberries. I remember touching her face and it being so soft. She lay in my arms with her head on my chest, tilted her head up, and put her mouth on mine. I would kiss her and she would kiss me back. She was my first kiss.

She would wake up and I would tell her what she did. Then it was my turn to fall asleep. I would of course kiss her back. It was all very innocent. This went on for a year or so and then it stopped.

When I was sixteen, I stayed at her house. The lights went out and she once again pretended to fall asleep. She rolled into my arms and I caressed her face. She tilted her head up, and she gave me her mouth. We kissed. This time I got very excited. I felt something twinge inside of me.

We kissed for a very long time, as I caressed her face and neck. My stomach was in knots, having never felt like that before. I had kissed boys by then, but never did it make me feel like this. Her lips were so soft, her skin so beautiful. I wanted to find the courage to go further, like my boyfriend was trying to do with me, but I did not. We stopped. She rested her head on my chest and went to sleep. That was the last time we played that game, and the last time I stayed the night with her. Maybe it scared us both, I don't know. Had I known then that I might be gay, she might have been my first girlfriend. I'll never know.

In high school, I had boyfriends but was mostly uninterested. When I kissed them, they did not make me feel like I felt when I kissed my girlfriend. I basically ignored the boys in that way. I never flirted with them. They were like brothers to me. This of course made me unattainable, so I was the focus of many a quest for some boys. My mom could not understand why I was not interested. My sister had been boy crazy, but my mom realized this daughter was very different.

She told me, every single day of my life, that I could be anything I want to be, and that I did not need a man. She said I should provide for myself, and not depend on anyone ever. This would give me freedom. What she meant was I would have the freedom she never had.

My senior year I had a boyfriend, Jamie. I was elected homecoming queen that year. Jamie and I were part of the popular crowd. Everyone loved him. He was the star of the football team and the most charming guy in our senior class. I was the star of the tennis team and we were the perfect couple, according to everyone. I knew differently though. For me, it was not perfect.

Every night, I would lie in bed, and my mom would come up to tuck me in. This was our moment alone, when I was not the stubborn teenager. Instead, I was vulnerable. I was always reading poetry when she came in. Poetry calmed me, it still does. Some nights we would chat a bit, and I was whimsical, happy-go-lucky. Other nights I wanted to be alone. There were many nights when I was depressed or upset. I would ask her to lay with me and hold me. I would cry and tell her that something was wrong with me, but I did not know what it was. I told her I wanted to do great things one day, and that there was something I was meant to do. But I did not know what that was, and it tortured me.

She would hold me until I calmed down and fell asleep. My mom took that much time with me. Can you believe it? Being a mother now, I know there are some nights that I just want to fall into bed instead of reading bedtime stories, but she gave that much time to me. She is amazing. She gave so much to me, and she still does. It always bothered my mother knowing that I was terribly upset, and that she could not understand why. On the surface I had a perfect life, I was a carefree bird, flying high for everyone to see. Below the surface though, was someone terribly unhappy, that bird was really in a cage.

About Jamie, I told him when I went to college we would break up. He was going to a college on the west coast, so we would not see each other anyway, except maybe for summers and Christmas. I knew I had a few things to figure out. The night before I left, we went to a field and had sex for the first time. It was pretty horrible, as first times usually are. I lost my virginity to him, but he was a good one to lose it to. He was very sweet to me, but I was the one that was not interested.

The next day my parents drove me to the university. I cried most of the way to college. Saying goodbye to my childhood, I was now a young woman starting a new life.

xoxo
Jade

Date: October 1, 2008   4:30PM
Subject: Your childhood

Beautiful, Sweet Jade,

You have confided in me. I think that means we are good friends. You have told me what happened when you were young. I feel so good that you are sharing things with me.
You told me about your mother. It has really affected me. Actually it made me cry. She was there for you. I wish my mama would be there for me. Sure I have my stepmother there for me. But it isn't the same when your real mother doesn't know you are alive. Or respect it. You see I have a good relationship now with my father. You have a good relationship with your mother. Two halves make a whole. We can support one another.

You told me about Jamie. You didn't love him. He took your virginity from you and he did not deserve you. I shouldn't say that to you but I want you to know. I say what I feel.

So you knew that you were gay when you were very young? I did too.
I was a tomboy. I played soccer with the boys. My mom always tried to get me to be interested in all of her friends'

sons. We would end up playing golf together or something like that. Just friends.

Boys didn't look at me like that. I was skinny and I wore my hair like a boy. When all the girls were growing up and wearing makeup and lipstick, I wasn't. I was still a tomboy and I was glad the boys didn't look at me.

One summer we had a clubhouse, a boys club. I was allowed in because I was considered one of them. One boy stole a magazine from his father. It had naked women in it. The boys looked at it and made comments. They would always go to the bathroom. I knew what they were doing.

I would get to look at the pictures by myself. I was so attracted to those women. I wanted to kiss them. I ripped out a picture and kept it under my mattress that whole summer. One day it disappeared. I think mama found it and was too embarrassed to say anything.

I kissed a few of my girlfriends when I was little. I looked like a boy so when we played school or house, I was always the husband and I kissed them. As I grew up, I only kissed one boy. After playing golf, we were standing behind a bunch of cars and he leaned over and kissed me. I could see it made him very excited. He reached over to touch my breast and then I hit him in the eye. No boy ever tried kissing me again.

I never had sex with a man. I slept with a girl for the first time when I was 18. I went away to college in America. I had a roommate who had a best friend that would come to visit us. She had long, dark brown hair and I was attracted to her. One weekend she arrived to visit but my roommate had gone home for her mother's birthday. I said she could stay even though my roommate was not home. She wanted to go out with a guy that she had been seeing on and off when she came to visit. I gave her a key and told her she could come and go as she pleased. I was always home though, studying. I didn't have any friends.

When she stayed with us I always watched her undress. She had the most beautiful big tits I had ever seen. I would look at them whenever I could.

64

That night she arrived home at 3:00am. She was acting funny and she said she had done ecstasy. She was mad because the guy she was seeing had wanted to stay out with his friends. She said his friends were very stupid and were acting like jerks, so she came home.

She was flirting with me. I never tried ecstasy before but she explained that it increases your senses. Everything looks and feels great. You love everyone. She also said that sex is amazing on ecstasy.

She told me to sit on her bed and she sat beside me. She reached over and felt my hair. She said it felt so good. She saw me looking at her big tits. I wanted to touch them. They reminded me of the girls from the magazines we used to look at. She opened her blouse and I touched them. She leaned over, I lifted her bra and I sucked on her nipples. I was so excited. I felt so wet between my legs.

She started kissing me and she put her tongue down my throat. She was pretty wild. She told me to undress her and she took off my shirt and bra. She rubbed her big tits on mine. I think you know by now. Yes, I like tits.

Then she rolled over, took off her underwear and spread her legs. It was the first time I had seen a pussy. She was so wet. I could not handle myself. I went down with my tongue and had no idea what I was doing. She liked it though. I think she was embarrassed or regretted it because the next day she got up early and left. I experimented more during this time.

Later I will tell you more about my life.

Your friend,
Emma

Emma wrote to me and she was confiding about her sexual experiences. Something in her language bothers me. She uses the word "tits" and it sounds so masculine. I know in Dutch, "tieten" means "tits". "Tieten" is used much more casually by women and is a normal word to refer to breasts, so this would be the normal translation. Some Dutch people even say "kut" meaning "cunt" the way Americans use the word "shit". I really do not like the word "cunt". It feels degrading to me, but since I have lived in the Netherlands, I don't react so strongly when I hear someone saying it.

I feel like we are sharing secrets, our deepest secrets. Her first sexual experience with a woman sounded very exciting. As I read it, I found myself visualizing her with her roommate's friend. She does not have many friends and it sounds like she leads a very lonely life. I feel sorry for her in a way.

Writing so honestly, I feel carefree when I am messaging with her, while thinking about her and how her life must be. I sense something emerging inside of me. I was sitting at dinner tonight with my colleagues, and I found myself drifting, thinking about her. More and more I find that I am thinking about her and wondering, who is she?

I want to share more with her, more secrets that very few people know about me. Getting home late this evening, I start to draft my next letter to her that I will finish and send off in the morning. I decide to be even more daring and revealing.

Date: October 2, 2008 8:30AM
Subject: Growing Up

Dearest Emma,

You are sharing a lot with me. It makes me break down my barriers and I want to share my secrets with you. Why is that? I am not certain, but there is honesty in the way that you write that I like very much. I will try to do the same. But first I want to say, your first experience with your roommate's friend sounded very...well, hot. I want to hear more about you Em, you make me curious and there is so much more I want to know about you.
Now I will continue with my story...

UNIVERSITY
I went to university where I met more boys. One in particular came

66

along shortly after I arrived. He was so adventurous, the bad boy who no one was able to capture. He was a playboy and we started dating. Different than most of the girls he met, I would not have sex with him right away. I tamed that bad boy with my innocence.

We became friends, really good friends. He was falling in love with me. I loved him. Was I in love with him? I thought I was, but looking back, no. I loved the fact that he drove a motorcycle, and when I got on the back of it, I felt like I was going somewhere. I felt reckless and carefree, just like him.

He was in a fraternity, but he was not really active, he just showed up every now and again. One night he invited me to one of his dances in a beautiful hotel, and after the dance we would stay the night together in our own hotel room. I had never done this before spend the night with a boy.

I wore the most unbelievably sexy, sleeveless black dress and high heels, showing off my legs. Always the gentleman to me, I got ready in the bathroom, and he got ready in the hotel room. When I finished, I peeked out and didn't see him. Noticing the balcony doors ajar, I slowly approached the sliding glass doors and saw him standing alone outside, just looking out into the darkness. He was quiet and in deep thought. I stood behind him and made an "uh, hum" sound.

He turned around and looked me in the eye, as his mouth fell open. He shook his head and looked down for a long moment. It surprised me and I began to think something serious had happened. Then his eyes slowly rose to meet mine and he stared at me for a very long time. I felt very touched by how gentle he seemed. It was a side he had never revealed to me. He said, "I'm sorry, I'm speechless. You look beautiful... you... You Jade." Then he grabbed my hand and kissed it. I was surprised by his gesture. Who was this guy? And where did my bad boy go?

After dancing and several drinks, we all ended up in the room of one of his fraternity brothers. All lounging around, there must have been ten couples in that hotel room. I genuinely liked the laid back crowd, as we all sat around drinking beers and talking. I was sharing a big chair with a girlfriend of one of his frat brothers, and we were deep in conversation. His frat brothers were trying to get him to smoke pot. He knew I did not like it when he was high, but I tolerated it.

I heard him say, "No thanks man". The room fell silent, everyone stopped talking. His frat brothers were harassing him saying,

"Smith not smoking pot, what the fuck man? You of all people, why not?"

I turned to him at the same moment he looked at me. He reached over, pulled me up close to him, grabbed my face and in front of everyone said, "Jade, I'm so in love with you. I don't need to smoke pot anymore. I only need you."

The room fell silent. No one could believe what he had just said. The bad boy had fallen in love with the good girl. (Well the good girl part was about to change but more on that later.) All the girls were looking at him with dreamy eyes, and wishing he had said that to them. I smiled, grabbed his face and kissed him. He knew with that kiss, we would make love for the first time, and we did. And you know what? It was pretty great. He was a very good lover. He taught me how to have sex...and we did...have sex, lots of it. On top of a bar, in every room, in his car, wherever we could.

One night we were at an Indian reservation, this is where people would go to "park". We were the only ones there. I was somewhat undressed and on top of him, when I got a great idea. I looked around and saw no one.

"Come on," I said opening the door and pulling him out of the car. He had his shirt off and jeans on. I walked in front of the car about 15 feet and I lay down on the grass. A broad smile covered his face as he ripped of his jeans. He was so excited (it was obvious). He ran over and jumped on top of me. Before we knew it, we were both completely naked, rolling round in the grass. All of a sudden, a bunch of cars pulled up and the headlights reflected off our naked bodies. Searching for my English schoolgirl-looking blazer, we could not stop laughing at the situation. Finally I found it and put it on, as we grabbed the rest of our clothes and ran to the car. I was wearing only the blazer. Smith was naked. The cars were honking and flashing their lights. Someone was even yelling out of the window, "Yeah baby!"

We ran to the car laughing. It was thrilling and so unbelievably exciting. I jumped on top of him in the car, and we finished our business. It was unbelievable, sex out in the open, even getting caught.

Smith and I would go out together. He was a party animal and together we had a lot of fun. Living carefree and without boundaries, we did wild and crazy things. He was so adventurous and he brought out the bad-girl in me. Every day was so exciting.

Sometimes he would just show up out of the blue and sweep me away on his motorcycle, me not knowing where we were going. We were explorers, and mostly best friends who had sex.

We broke up because he made out with my best friend. I had warned him, if he ever cheated on me, it was over. And it was, just like that. By that time, I was ready to move on anyway.

This started a random set of sexual activity with my new found freedom and my bad-girl evolving. There were several more men, but not another serious boyfriend until my senior year at university. Along the way, I knew that there was something not quite right being with men. It didn't feel like what I thought it was supposed to, but I kept trying.

Michael was a businessman. I met him while playing a game of pool. Having graduated a few years before, he was in town for a college reunion. After several attempts of getting my attention, he wrote a check for one million dollars, handed it to me and said, "You can cash it if you will let me take you on a date." Of course on the bottom of the check he had written "Void", but I thought it was pretty clever.

He became my boyfriend and would come and stay with me from Friday until Sunday. I genuinely liked Michael, and we got on well. He was a kind, very nice man, but I was not really that interested in him. As I said, there was still something that was not quite right to me. And I realized, something strange was happening. Michael had become my cover...listen closely, because here is where it gets interesting.

I had become friends with a woman named Cameron. She was a blond-haired, brown-eyed beauty, and she was quickly becoming my new best friend. She was a sorority sister, and we hung out on spring break of my junior year. One night during break, while everyone else was sleeping, we went and got a bunch of beer. We spent the whole night on the balcony talking and drinking. It was an instant collision of two people who were destined to meet. She made me laugh, and she was the first person that I'd ever met, that actually got me. She really understood me.

Coming from large families and being the youngest by several years, we had a lot in common. We had a similar outlook on life, and we were dreamers. Our imaginations came together and played endlessly, this was our dance. That night we discovered

69

one another. We were genuinely attracted to each other's souls. She had no limits, and neither did I.

My senior year, a group of us moved out of the sorority house, and got a house on campus. Unbeknownst to us, Cameron and I just happened to choose rooms next to each other. We started our senior year off together and became inseparable. We inspired one another. We played together, hanging out, working out, and going to parties. She was loud and random. Adventurous. All the men loved her. They felt like she was one of the guys because she could belch louder than all of them. Somehow it was charming, endearing really, and they all wanted to fuck her.

We were together all of the time and were physically very close. She would come and lay with me on the couch, when I was watching television, resting her head in my lap. She would also put her arms around me or climb into bed with me. We would spend hours discussing the possibilities after graduation. We talked about our dreams, what we wanted to do and who we wanted to be. We discussed traveling to Europe, and opening a clothes store together in some exciting city, far away. It seemed like our lives would always intertwine.

Sometimes she even slept in bed with me or I in her bed. As she lay next to me, I remember feeling her breasts press against me. It drove me crazy, and eventually I found myself beginning to want her, but I had no idea what I was feeling. Of course it all makes sense to me now.

We gave each other back massages. She would take her shirt off, and I would unsnap her bra and rub her back. I remember wanting so badly to reach around, grab her boobs and pull her back into me, so I could kiss her neck and shoulders. It took every ounce of strength that I had not to. It was punishing.

She hung out with Michael and I all the time. She was our third and was always with us. Michael was fine with it. He loved Cameron. She was gorgeous, entertaining and he loved how happy I was when she was around. What I began to realize was that Michael had become my decoy and this is how I discovered it.

One day Michael and I were in bed. We had just had sex and Cameron came in wearing a t-shirt, underwear and no bra. She jumped on top of me.

I put my arms around her and hugged her tight. Separating us was a very thin blanket. We would always sleep closely together, but this time she was on top of me. Her full body weight was pressed

70

against me, and I remember the rush of excitement this sent through my body. I wanted her on top of me. Through the thin blanket, I could feel her large breasts, her hipbone pressing into my tummy, and her legs wrapped around me. Her inner thighs were squeezing my leg and I could feel her crotch on my upper thigh. It was warm and inviting, and immediately my entire body was full of desire for her.

I wanted Michael and the blanket to disappear. I think Michael sensed this immediately, because he called us carpet-munchers, jokingly. I really did not understand what that meant at the time.

All I knew is that I was incredibly excited, and she was the one that I wanted, not him. I wanted Cameron! I felt sure that my heart was pounding so hard that she could feel it through the blanket. That was not the only thing pounding, as I imagined her naked on top of me, and it drove me mad. I was crazy with desire for her, and I needed to figure out a way for it to happen.

Cameron and I were asleep one night. It was rather warm and we were laying in our bra and underwear. Our friend Kris came in and asked us if we were lesbians. She said everyone in the house was talking about it because of our open affection and our flirtatious behavior towards one another. Cameron laughed and said, "No." I hesitated. Were we? Was I? I wondered.

The following weekend Michael, Cameron and I went to see the movie *Basic Instinct* with Sharon Stone. In the movie she is a bi-sexual woman and writer who is a murder suspect. During the film she kisses a woman. I am sure you have seen it Emma, haven't you? It was the first time I had ever seen two women kiss.

I was sitting there, Michael on one side, Cameron on the other and Sharon Stone was with this beautiful woman. It was a long kiss, and it was…very hot. The three of us grew very still. My palms began to sweat and I felt like everyone was watching me fall apart. I realized they were as enthralled with the kiss as I was. I wondered if they were thinking what I was thinking? I imagined Michael was thinking of watching me kiss Cameron. I was thinking I wanted to reach out and grab Cameron's neck, pull her over and kiss her. Maybe Cameron thought, hmmm…that is something I would like to try?

Nothing ever happened with Michael, Cameron and I. Michael and I broke up because he got a job out of state. I was fine with that because, though he was a nice guy, I was no longer interested. I was too busy discovering something that began to make sense to me, my love for women.

Cameron and I took things a little further. She and I used to play pool and we were a great team. Playing for drinks or food, we almost always won. We would have a night out playing pool, and it would not cost us any money. Together we could charm any team of men who would try to beat us, and they ended up having to buy us a beer or a shot of Tequila. It was amusing. It was our game, and we were good at it.

After one very successful night on the tables, we were walking home around 2:00am. We'd had several shots of Tequila, and we weren't quite ready to go home. So we were jumping around being very playful, laughing and joking. We stopped at our friend's house across the street from where we lived, a house full of boys. Most of the party had left and gone to the bars, except for two guys who were getting ready to lock up the house. Cameron and I were on the sidewalk, arguing about whose boobs were bigger. She touched mine, and I touched hers. We tended to do this, see who could be more shocking. We were just playing, but there was something behind the play. At least I sensed it. Watching in disbelief from their porch, they called out to us, and we walked over to them. We decided to let them settle our dispute.

Cameron ripped her shirt over her head, threw it on the ground and said, "What do you guys think?" I took my shirt off too. Cameron likes to be looked at. She likes attention and I do too. It is something we have in common. We complimented each other at the surface and at a very deep level, still do.

There we both stood with our shirts off, and the rain came pouring down. The two guys had no idea what to do with us. Cameron and I were dancing around in the rain in our bras, laughing. Soaking wet and cold, we decided to go inside and we hung out in one of the bedrooms. We played music, and we were just being goofy, jumping around reacting to one another's energy.

Cameron and I started dancing together. We have always danced very well, together. Our movements are in synch, they always have been. Still to this day, we are perfect partners and I love dancing with her. We can naturally feel each other's rhythm. They say you can tell the kind of sex you will have with someone by the heat that you have on the dance floor. I have always found this to

72

be true.

She and I were grinding, our hips moving together. Looking back, I know for certain that Cameron and I would have made great sex partners. It would have been intense and playful, passionate, yet adventurous. We would have fought for the top and the bottom. That never happened, but it almost did.

We broke out of our trance to see both guys watching us. It was clear what they were thinking and it came down to who was going to make the first move. Cameron walked over and started kissing the cuter guy. Then she grabbed me, and started moving my hands over her body. The second guy freaked out and left. I think he must be the only straight man I know that would leave while watching two women together. I guess he was afraid it was going to turn into a foursome, I don't know.

Me, I stood there with butterflies, trembling with the excitement of touching her sexually. I was right there, clearly ready, and the moment had finally presented itself. So the guy started kissing us both. Pants flew off and before I knew it, Cameron was on top of him having sex with him, and I was behind her kissing her back. This time it was okay for me to reach around and grab her boobs as I kissed her neck. I think she was surprised how turned on this made her. Kissing and touching her provided such a deep sensation. I knew, at that moment, there was something new emerging, a truth. Her skin was soft, beautiful. The way she arched while on top of him was so sexy, and I wanted to kiss the small of her back. Seeing her on top of him only made me want to be the one inside of her. My feelings were very overwhelming and clouded from all of the tequila. I didn't understand it all, so I just let myself dive into the moment and feel it. And I did, throughout my entire body.

The guy came quickly and then rolled over and fell asleep drunk on the floor. What an idiot, he had no idea that the woman he had just fucked was so wonderful. It was all over too quickly for me. I didn't want it to end.

Cameron and I climbed up in his bed. Naked in each other's arms, we were talking and laughing as we always did. Laying in the dark and caressing one another under the moonlight, our bodies became exposed with the first ray of morning light. We realized we had better get out of there before we were discovered.

We got dressed and crawled out of his window. You know, why use the door when you can use a window? At that early hour, we were the only ones awake. We ran laughing and giggling playfully, all the way home. Our clothes were still wet from the rain dance earlier that evening, so when we got home we undressed and climbed into my bed. It was so warm and I nuzzled up into her arms this time. She was touching me with her eyes closed and I returned the gesture. My hand wandered down to her crotch. She spread her legs, and I ran my fingers on her inner thigh then over her underwear brushing her clit. It was so exciting! My heart was pounding.

Her breathing was growing heavier. I knew I was turning her on. What was I supposed to do now? I had never been with a woman. I tried to find the courage to continue, but my fear prevented me. I removed my hand, and she rolled over and we spooned and fell asleep. I could not stop thinking of what I SHOULD have done. A few nights later, I found myself with another chance.

We were out playing pool again. We had had several shots of tequila and she was flirting with me. Usually she was flirting with the men, but this evening her attention was fully on me. I leaned over and said, "I think you were very turned on the other night." She leaned even closer looking me directly in the eye and said, "So why did you stop?" A challenge. She always had a way of trumping me, and I loved it.

We went home earlier than usual that night. She anticipated I would act on her invitation and I planned on doing just that. We got into her bed knowing this time something would happen. We started messing around again, this time I found my courage. I ran my fingers over her tummy and down between her legs and I stuck my fingers inside of her. She was so wet and her heat sent such a rush of pleasure over my body, it overwhelmed me. I got very nervous, and she sensed it. I think she saw in my eyes that this was no game for me, so we both looked at each other and started laughing. We left it at that.

We continued sleeping in the same bed, but no sexual touching. Going out with her became a slight torture because I longed for her to flirt with me again. But she knew that there was a line she was able to cross and come back again, and I could not. She cherished our friendship enough to stop what we had started. Even if it meant hurting me a little, rather than letting it go further and hurting me a lot.

After college I moved in with her and two other roommates. Cameron and I started leading separate lives, and it became clear to everyone that I was, in fact, a lesbian because of my utter lack of interest in men. I felt trapped and depressed, and needed to leave to follow my dreams. I desperately wanted to escape the Midwest and go west, but I had no money.

My first job out of university, I worked selling vacuum cleaners, $1200 vacuum cleaners. This was honestly the first job I had and it was something I said I would never do...sales. Well, I sold more vacuum cleaners in the first month of employment than anyone ever had in the history of the company. I received a bonus for my efforts. Thirty $100 bills were placed in my hand in the sales meeting. I had never had this much cash that was actually mine.

That night I was in my room working on an oil painting for our roommates who were getting married. I always had heavy curtains in my paintings during that time, and they were always done in grays and heavy purples. In addition to coming out of the closet, I needed to come out from behind the curtains. Weighing down upon me, they were no coincidence. Cameron came in, looked at my painting and said, "Jade, you are very talented. Have you ever thought about art school?"

Those words changed my destiny. They really did. I looked over at my stack of $100 bills and those words opened the door for me to move on. And I did. I quit my job the next day and I drove home and told mom and dad I was moving to Seattle. I wanted to go to art school.

I knew I had to leave Cameron. Our friendship would not survive me falling in love with her and her not returning it. So I left. Heartbroken.

xoxo
Jade

Date: October 2, 2008 9:32PM
Subject: College

Beautiful, Sweet Jade,

You told me a lot about your college days. You found your first woman Cameron and maybe your first love?

Can I say this to you? Please do not take it the wrong way. I read your story and found myself wishing that I was Cameron. I felt a little jealous of all 3 of these people who got to make love to you, but I mustn't say that. I saw your pictures on MyLIFESeeker. You are very attractive. I have to say something. I saw your big tits in the pictures and I cannot stop thinking about them when I read your messages and visualize you. I should not be saying this to you though.

You said the sex was not bad with Smith. That it was great. I could never have sex with a man. I have no desire. Let me tell you about my college days.

I told you I went to school in America. Just for my last year but it was good and that is where I learned to speak better English.

I told you I slept with my roommate's friend. This time at college for me was only to get my degree so I studied a lot. I did not have many friends at all and I did not sleep with anyone else during that time. I didn't have as much fun as you did. I wish I could have met you during my college days. I think we could have had a lot of fun together. I think you would have taught me a lot. You are so outgoing and carefree, that excites me very much. I am not. I am actually very quiet.

While I was at college I tried hundreds of times to call my mama. She would not take my calls. By then she was living alone. I think she must have been miserable. I told you mama could not accept that I was a lesbian. It meant her daughter was committing a sin. I would never be forgiven for it in God's eyes. It meant she would never have grandchildren. She didn't tell me this, but I knew it because my father told me one day when I asked him about it. I also think she hated that I was going to college in America. She saw it as betrayal because I was attaching myself to my father's culture. I would see her during holidays only. She barely acknowledged me.

After college, I came back to the Netherlands and I went to work. I also started going out to lesbian bars. During college

I blossomed and turned into a woman. But like you at first I could not meet anyone.

Then I started meeting a few women but none of them were exciting to me. I told you that I am shy. But I am smart and I was looking for someone with a little more to offer me. Someone exciting, adventurous. I would still go home and visit my dad and step mom. My step mom always encouraged me to not be so shy. She said I needed to put myself out there and be open.

So I did not have a serious girlfriend until I met Eve. I will tell you more about this. Jade, if you want, please tell me more about you. I love to read about you and your life. I love when you to tell me stories. It is so exciting. It makes me get to know you better. I think you are very special. I think about you a lot.

Your friend,
Emma

Date: October 3, 2008 6: 26AM
Subject: Mom

Emma,
I am still on my business trip. But this trip is different. I have such wonderful messages from you. You are opening up to me and are saying such nice things. It makes me feel good to read those, I must admit. Although you say you are thinking about my big breasts. You are also jealous of the men I slept with and of Cameron, why? You have a girlfriend. You should not be thinking of me.

I am sorry to hear you tried to reach your mother and she could not accept you. I told you my relationship with my mother, a very strong bond that mostly goes unspoken. Mainly because of me, but I will talk more about that in a minute.

MOM
My mother and sister were always best friends. My sister is fifteen years older than me, so they are much closer in age. They would

always sit holding hands, talking, crying and talking some more. They would cry so hard that each would sit with thick streaks of mascara running down their faces. I would come home and my sister would be over, telling about her latest crisis. I would walk through the door and tease them. I would pretend to cry along with them, sometimes dramatically falling to the floor crying so hard until I would clearly die of a broken heart. This made them laugh.

I was not jealous of my sister and my mom's relationship. I didn't want my mom to be my best friend, though my mom certainly wanted to be mine. I kept my feelings very quiet. She did not know if I had boyfriends or anything about my private life. My sister told her everything and I was exactly the opposite.

As for my sister, we could always talk about anything. She wasn't around much because she was older than I was, but if I ever needed her, she was always there for me. Growing up, I loved spending time with her. She could tell the funniest stories and she always made all of us laugh.

My mom always tried to get my friends to tell her information. She would ask them if I had a boyfriend, who my friends were, you know all of those things. But I kept things quiet from her. Those nights I told you about, when I would cry and she would hold me. She, I think, liked it in a strange way because she knew that she was witnessing a secret side of me that no one got to see but her. It made her feel close to me, and I was lucky she had the time for me. She would hold me on those nights that I needed her, and she would tell me what I needed to hear or sometimes nothing at all. She instinctually knew when I just needed to talk. In return, I trusted her with my biggest secret, but I would rarely voice my real feelings for her openly.

Then occasionally I would surprise her. We won a tennis tournament and I was recognized in front of the entire school. I had to give a speech. Now realize, my mom came to every match, and she took me from town to town to play tennis. She loved going with me. It was a social activity for her, but also I was doing some of the things she had always wanted to do.

She would get up early with me in the summer and stay all day with me, while I trained into wee hours of the night. She gave me so much of her time. She did that for me. I didn't always say "thank you", but she knew I appreciated it. On a rare occasion, I would make grand gestures to her.

78

So, I had to give a speech in front of the entire school when we won the tournament. I stood up and talked about the match, and then I said, "There is one person in my life who has made this possible. This person has given me more love and support than she will ever know. Her words of advice have helped me get up everyday and strive to achieve my goals. This person is my mother. So in front of everyone I want to say thank you mom, I love you so much."

For a week, she cried each time she told that story to her friends. It meant a lot to her.

I am coming to the part about when I come out to my family, but I will have to write about that tomorrow. I have a meeting to prepare for.

xoxo
Jade

I arrived in Paris today and for some reason, I feel so romantic. I manage to survive the Parisian taxi driver who drives like he's training for Formula One. A car moves quickly in front of him and cuts him off. Throwing his hands in the air, he grips the steering wheel hard and maneuvers around pulling up next to the culprit. He rolls down his window and starts yelling at the unsuspecting driver, who then rolls down his window and begins yelling back. I have missed Paris.

Yes, even among the chaos, I feel fresh. Writing about my sexual awakening has reminded me of my youth and of the passion that was beginning to emerge inside of me during that time. How could I have let something so precious slip from my life? Striving to write has disappeared from my day. I hardly write privately at all anymore. An unexpected surprise, Emma is helping me discover it again.

I am staying at a hotel near the Eiffel Tower. In the morning, I will get up and go for a run around that area. The magnificence of such an architectural wonder baffles me as she quietly stands tall watching over the world that moves around her. Someone actually created this powerful beauty. So many sites are like this in Paris, and it is one breathtaking structure after another. The city is alive with beautiful people sitting in cafes, lost in their deep conversations. I get wrapped up in it, and I love to go every chance I get.

Arriving at my hotel and entering my room, I carefully place my suitcase in the closet. I am eager to check my messages before heading off to dinner with clients. I think of Emma and I find it strange how a virtual person is becoming such an important friend to me. She mentioned in her last mail that she was feeling more for me than just friendship. I don't feel so lonely anymore, and a secret part of me is unsure where this will lead.

I wonder what I am doing? What am I looking to discover or rediscover. I am wondering if it is possible to uncover that innocent passion again and bring it back into my life? I feel it beginning to grow and it feels like electrolytes feeding my sexual dehydration. I am alive again.

When I phone home, I speak to my son. Jessica and I exchange a few words, but there is a distance growing between us that is becoming unkind. When I think of her, I feel stagnant and lost. Anger continues to grow inside of me. It is new and unwelcomed, but is it? It is forcing me to consider other paths.

All the while, Emma is writing me, and I am becoming more involved with this friendship that we have. I find it exciting that she is looking at my picture and thinking of me, as I reveal more and more secrets.

Date: October 3, 2008   4:26PM
Subject: Crying

Beautiful, Sweet Jade,

I am crying right now. You made your mother very proud I think. You told her you loved her in front of everyone. I wish she could have been my mother. I wish my mother would hold me and love me the way your mother did. You are very lucky. I have my stepmother but it is not the same. She is more like a big sister to me.

The wrong women always picked me. This was the problem until I met Eve.

Eve came to the hospital where I worked. I told you she is a very powerful woman. She had read an article in the newspaper about a little girl who came into our psychology ward. This little girl had been beaten by her father and then raped. It was such a horrible story. It had moved Eve so much that she wanted to help. She wanted to visit the little girl and bring her presents and just brighten her day. She came to us and said she wanted to give this child a friend. She wanted to do nice things to brighten her spirits. She did so many things for her.

She started talking to me a lot after her visits and asked me to go to lunch with her. Then we went out on several dates. I began to realize, Eve was very different. We have been together 3 years. Yes, it took us time to figure it out. We experimented in the bedroom a lot. Our sex life is great. I told you I am a very sexual woman. I always want sex and this keeps Eve very happy. She has a big dildo and she loves to use it on me.

I would keep you very happy too, I think. How big is your dildo? Sorry, I know I must not say that. Why am I jealous of those people that got to be with you in college? Because I think you are sexy and you are also interesting and exciting. You tell me stories and I love them.

We are both in relationships now but in college we were not. I must say no more but I cannot help it. If I am too naughty you can spank me and maybe something else?

Your friend,
Emma

Saturday is the day I spend with Jessica and our son. Holding hands as we walk through the park, I love to flirt with her while our son jumps around and explores. He needs to be busy and to get out and run. He needs freedom to discover the world, of course with his watchful mothers. Laughing playfully, I run beside him as Jessica smiles at us. We are content. I love Saturdays. At least I used to.

When I am away for so long, they always miss me terribly. Jessica and I used to make love the night I returned. We felt so happy to be in one another's arms again. On the airplane home, I am yearning for her, for her touch, and her femininity. I want and need her. My entire body is aching as I try to push away the resentment. I think of the fullness of her lips and her tongue caressing mine. She is such a fantastic kisser. My body is responding to these thoughts, and I need to cross my legs. I smile knowing that people surround me, and they have no idea what I am thinking about.

But something hovers above, weighing down on me as I remember the last several months of business travels, and how my returns have been different. When I come home, Jessica is very tired. She kisses me, and then goes to bed. This has become normal and when I think of it, I feel the darkness creeping inside of me. A sudden realization comes over me, and I grow very angry. Did she not want me anymore? Where has the passion gone in our relationship? I have felt it resurfacing all week in my conversations with Emma and I miss it. I long for it to come back into my life.

A relationship is constant work. There are the fundamentals like communication, respect and compassion. And there is the physical, which is a critical component. Sex makes me feel intimate, loved and in love. It is a need that is almost masculine in physical requirement, but feminine in the sense that I need passion driving it. No sexual desire leads to failed relationships.

What do I feel building? Resentment? It cannot be. I have never resented Jessica. But I feel it growing inside, and it is black and cold. Then there is Emma, who wants me and is bringing energy back in my life again. She is warm and full of color.

Date: October 4, 2008 7:45AM
Subject: Seattle

82

Dearest Em,

You had trouble finding the right woman at first. So did I. I had a lot of one-night stands. My choice. But the serious relationships I have been in are only two, lasting three and ten years. The foundation of a good relationship is good communication and genuinely enjoying each other's company.

Let me continue on with my story. So I left for Seattle... heartbroken.

SEATTLE

On a cold, rainy November day, I packed up my car and drove by myself to Seattle. It took me seven days to get there, driving eight hours per day, mainly because I ran into snowstorms and drove through a blizzard. The drive was breathtaking. Before leaving, I felt like a butterfly trapped in a cocoon. With each passing mile I was evolving into someone else. I was inspired by the newness of creating my own path. When I drove into Seattle, the first sight of it made my chest open up. For the first time in my life, I felt like I was exactly where I was supposed to be.

I got my first apartment that I lived in completely by myself. It was a tiny, one room studio with a small kitchen, a living space, an entry way and bathroom. It had a beautiful view over looking Capitol Hill, the gay area of Seattle. I remember those sunsets. I used to sit on the windowsill in awe. After the sun disappeared behind the mountains, I would run a bath and listen to Tori Amos. The space was so small, but I LOVED this apartment. We belonged together. This is where I began to come out of the cocoon and spread my wings.

When I first arrived, there was a man who came around to fix some electrical problems in my apartment. His name was Jake. He owned his own company. We talked the entire time he was there. He was such an honest person, smiled a lot and genuinely wanted to know about my life. After he finished his work and was leaving he said, "Maybe I'll stop by sometime." I said, "Sure," thinking I would probably never see him again.

I filled my days with buying things for my empty apartment, shower curtains, silverware etc... I needed everything and I was making it my first very own home. I didn't have much money so I just bought the basics. Then I discovered something very unique to Seattle, second-hand bookstores. They were everywhere and I quickly realized I'd rather have a room full of used books than furniture. Lingering for hours, it reminded me of my love for old books. My parents would buy them by the boxes at garage sales, and then put them in storage. I never understood that. As a child, I would sit for hours in the dark, enclosed storage room, opening up each book. Reading the names of the people that had signed them and wondering how far they had traveled. They transmitted me to unknown worlds. I loved those books.

I read so many books during my first several years in Seattle. Especially since I lived alone. I read everything I could get my hands on that could possibly be of interest to me, a book about Greta Garbo, Katherine Hepburn's autobiography, books on vegetarianism and a book about Kandinsky and Der Blaue Reiters. You name it, I was open and in discovery mode.

One night I came home, and there was a guy sitting outside of the apartment across from mine. He sat alone in the hallway reading. I asked if he was locked out, and he said he was visiting his friend who was asleep inside. Not wanting to bother him, he had come into the hallway to read. So I asked what was so enthralling that compelled him to sit in an empty hallway. He was reading *A Joseph Campbell Companion: Reflections on the Art of Living* by Diane K. Osbon. This boy asked me if I had read it. I said, "No." So, he gave it to me. He said he had read it a hundred times and he wasn't kidding.

Oh, how this book changed the way I was thinking. It basically explained concepts and quotes from Joseph Campbell. Campbell talks about "the hero's journey" and "following your bliss". He said "Oh that's what destiny is: simply the fulfillment of the potentialities of the energies in your own system." I felt like I was fulfilling my destiny. I knew it. And this book just appeared by random circumstance from a boy who wanted to pass on his favorite book. Years later, I passed my copy on to a stranger who was in need. I love thinking about that book traveling and helping people who need it.

On Thanksgiving night there was a knock at the door. Jake stood there with a plate covered in aluminum foil, a bottle of wine and a friendly smile on his face. He said, "I thought you might be alone on Thanksgiving, so I brought you some food."

What a very sweet, thoughtful gesture, I was moved by it. I invited him in and we sat on the floor. I didn't have a couch yet, so we sat and talked for hours. He told me he had just gotten divorced and was a bit devastated. I told him about myself and a bit of where I grew up. We were two rather lonely people on the same path of finding a new self. That was our connection.

He left around midnight. He said, "Would you like to hang out sometime, let me take you to see some bands play. I can be your official Seattle tour guide." And he was.

He introduced me to the music scene. It was the end of the grunge rock phase, so it was a very exciting time in Seattle. He took me to microbreweries, we drank wheat beer, and he took me to dive bars, where we played pool. He loved that I was a woman who liked to do guy stuff. Quite the seafood specialist, he taught me the different kinds and how to cook it to perfection. We genuinely loved each other's company.

Christmas time came around and he called and said, "Come with me to the coast. Let's go spend Christmas on the beach." This is the first time we had sex. I thought he was a very nice guy and we had a lot of fun together, but something was still missing.

In January, I started art school. I already had my B.A. and it felt like I had taken several steps backwards. Many of the students came straight out of high school. One day the professor pulled me over after our speech class and asked me what I was doing there. I had given a speech the previous day on Neuro-Linguistic Programming or NLP. It was a 30-minute speech. It blew everyone else's away.

I told him I was hoping to be a creative director in an ad agency and thought I needed to learn a bit about artists. He said, "Jade, you could teach this class." I left art school shortly after that.

Things with Jake were based on a solid friendship, not a sexual relationship. We could talk about anything and we did. One day, I decided I had better tell Jake that I thought I might be gay. He looked down, a bit disappointed, and then looked up and said, "I'll take you to the gay club. You can dance with some women, and then you will know."

Well, I found out that, yes indeed, there was something going on with me. The gay bar was new and exciting for me. I had never been to one. I saw women dancing with women and men dancing with men. The pounding of the music was exhilarating and I felt like I was entering into a world where I belonged.

I thought this was a bold move from a guy who was in love with me. I think Jake knew he would lose me regardless, because I wasn't as invested as he was. I thought it was a grand gesture on his part. To put someone else's happiness before your own, it was selfless. I haven't met that many selfless people in my life. Jake was one of them.

Around this time, I wandered into a hair salon and got my hair cut by a gay guy named Sam. He was the first openly gay man I had ever been around for an extended period of time. From his Doc Martins and his trendy Broadway underground look, to his black art tattoo on his arm, he was the picture of flawless. We became close friends very quickly, and soon he became my best friend in Seattle. He loved having a girly girl to play with.

I told Sam I might be gay, but I was not sure. Around this time his best friend was coming to visit from Alaska. Her name was Amy and she was a stripper. He told me about her repetitively and how he thought we would really get along. Then he smiled and said casually, "Oh, and she's bisexual." I stood very still. Bisexual? Why did I feel excited and yet so nervous to meet her?

Oh, how this one person would impact my life. She would change everything for me.

AMY/ANAIS

Over the next few days, anxiety had overcome me and curiosity had built. Finally the day came that Amy arrived at Sam's apartment. Sam had invited me to go out dancing with them. So after changing my outfit twelve times, I stood outside his apartment. Knocking my signature knock, he opened the door with a big grin. I shook my head and said, "Stop!" He scanned my outfit and nodded in approval, "You may enter."

I pushed by him, pinched his butt and then looked around the apartment. No one was there. Sam giggled at my obvious impatience. "She's in the bathroom," Sam said carefully eyeing my reaction.

86

I sat on the couch, looked through some music and managed to fill what seemed like eternity by pretending to be busy reading a magazine. Sam could see I was nervous.

I heard the bathroom door swing open and in walked this power, this force, this woman that made my knees weak. She was tall with long, deep red, curly hair. She had a long face with strong features and the most beautiful eyes I had ever seen. They were yellow. She wore heavy makeup, and it suited her. She was dramatic. We locked eyes, and she was coming right for me.

She sat down next to me, very close, and pressed her leg against mine. Instantly a warm rush went through my body. She was wearing Sam's cologne, Egoïste by Chanel. Still to this day, when I smell Egoïste, I think of Amy.

She entirely overwhelmed me. As she talked to me, she looked into my eyes, and she touched my leg as she spoke. With each touch, her energy shot through me, calling me to her. Her unusual eyes and long stare were mesmerizing, and she openly flirted with me, as she spoke in a deep, raspy voice. She oozed sex and I was sitting there entirely exposed.

We went to the club, and she was dancing alone on the dance floor to Prince's "Erotic City". I could not stop watching her, as her hips swayed with the music. Her eyes closed and the beat of the song led her into another world. She didn't care she was dancing on her own. I studied her, lost in her rhythm. Sam leaned over and whispered in my ear, "I think you like her...GRRRR!" I looked at him realizing I had been caught. Sam winked at me. He saw me as the little innocent girl from the Midwest, who was about to become a lesbian.

All night, Amy sat close and spoke with me. She leaned in close, pressing her breasts on my arm while bringing her face just inches from mine, as she spoke in a raspy whisper. She kept looking at my lips as she spoke to me, as if she wanted to kiss me. I had never had a woman entice me like this before. Every action and movement was so sexy that I could not resist her.

After we went dancing, Amy said she was not tired. Knowing exactly where I wanted this night to go, I asked her if she wanted to come to my apartment. I wanted her lips on mine. I wanted her and every inch of her beautiful body.

In the apartment, she looked at my pictures scattered around, in my closet and at every little detail. She was so curious about me. I think, being so naïve about so many things, I fascinated her and in turn, her curiosity intrigued me. She opened up my photo album and she wanted to know everything about me. She sat on the floor across from me and asked me questions about each photo. She told me tidbits about herself. We spoke for hours on end. The conversation was easy and flowing, and I realized this woman, who sexually attracted me very much, also mentally fascinated me.

After awhile, we began speaking very softly. By this time, we were sitting close on my new futon. Again she was pressing against me as the heat between us was building. She was seducing me and I found myself lost in her. I was drowning in her eyes as we spoke. Her words, her worldliness made my heart pound. Our faces were getting closer as we spoke, and I was longing for her lips.

This was the moment that I asked her if she had ever been with a woman. I already knew the answer. I had been waiting all night for the perfect moment to ask her this. I knew this was also my chance to ask her if I could kiss her. But she was one step ahead of me. She had been waiting for the question.

She smiled and paused, looking me deeply in the eyes. "Yes, Jade," she replied softly. I asked her how it was. She wondered why I asked, but I knew she knew the answer. I was certain Sam had told her. I looked at her with an innocent expression and said, "Because I want to kiss a woman. I think I might be gay."

She smiled and leaned into me putting her mouth just before mine. She touched my face and then she said, "Okay." She stood up and went to the bathroom. After a few minutes, I could hear the shower running. I sat there wondering if I had said something wrong. I heard the water stop and a few seconds later she came back into the room. She was standing before me naked and I knew *this* time I was more than ready.

She looked so beautiful in the early morning light. Her long hair fell down covering most of her breasts, but I could see their curve. My eyes wondered up and down her body and there was no hiding my desire for her. I realized she was observing my reaction.

I slowly looked up at her. Novice was written all over my face, and she understood immediately that she needed to guide me. She came over to me and smiled, looking at me in a kind and gentle way. She knew this was a defining moment in my life and she honored it.

She slowly leaned in. Her lips were just above mine and I could feel her breath. This time she leaned in further, closed her eyes and kissed me. It was a long soft, deep kiss. The perfect first kiss.

As she sucked on my bottom lip, everything inside of me quivered and then exploded. Wetness poured between my legs. My insides were blazing and I was smacked full force by a new reality. Everything all at once made sense to me.

At that very moment, I was certain that I was a lesbian.

Oh, that kiss. My heart was racing. I was burning inside. I wanted her, but I was afraid. She grabbed my shoulder and said, "Don't worry, I will show you." And she did.

I cannot tell you how liberating this was, being able to touch a woman in this way. I had private access to her body and I was free to kiss her breasts, suck her nipples, and kiss her soft neck. Her skin was so pale, beautiful. I kissed her hips, her legs, and inner thighs.

When I got between her legs, I was uncertain. Don't get me wrong. It was exactly where I wanted to be, but I wasn't sure where to begin. She helped by telling me exactly what to do and how. I knew she could teach me, and I would get better. I remember the first taste of the honey between her legs. I wanted to inhale that very moment and keep it inside of me forever. I wanted her to show me the way, again and again.

On top of me, her body fully pressed against mine, just like Cameron had done, only there was no blanket separating us. She was rubbing on me and I could hear her breathing begin to quicken. Her hips were grinding, pushing down on me. When she came, the noise she made, God! It turned me on so fucking bad! It was so unbelievably sexy. I almost came just watching her.

Afterwards, I lay next to her, holding her, running my hand of over her soft skin and wanting the moment to last. She smiled at me and said, "Now do you know?" I looked at her, touched her face, smiled and said, "Everything is clear." Crystal.

After that, we hung out together a couple more days. We shared a love for literature. She is the one that brought me to Anais Nin's writing. We would talk for hours and hours about literature, art, and poetry. We romanticized everything. I started calling her Anais. Did you ever read *Henry and June*, Em? Anais falls in love with Henry's wife, June, and then also with Henry. She is madly in love with her. Bringing out the masculine side of Anais, June is the first woman she falls in love with. She held such a burning passion and desire for June. I called Amy my Anais, but she was really my June.

As suddenly as Amy appeared, she disappeared before my eyes. She ran away, back to Alaska. Just like that, she was gone. I hopelessly walked the streets of Seattle seeing her everywhere, or thinking I did. Any woman I saw with long, red hair, I had to look at her face. Sam saw how devastated I was and gave me her address. I wrote her a few times, but I knew I had to move on. I always felt that one day she would be back. She was not someone who would be temporary and I always knew she would remain in my life, if even at a distance.

Em, I am telling you a lot. I have a lot more to tell. This will be in my next mail. I look forward to hearing more of your story.

Oh and Em, you are being naughty and no, I am not going to spank you. Although, if we were in college, I think I would have.

xoxo
Jade

_____

Date: October 4, 2008 5:32PM
Subject: A Soulmate-Amy

Beautiful, Sweet Jade,

You told me about moving to Seattle. I can feel you miss it terribly. You make me want to visit there. I wish I could go there and you could show me around. Take me to all of the places where all of these stories happened.

You told me about Jake. He was selfless if he let you go? My beautiful Jade, if you were with me, I could never let you go. I would submit myself entirely to you.

You met another man in the hallway who brought you Joseph Campbell's work. Can you tell me more? It changed your life? How?

Then there was Sam who brought Amy to you and it was your first time with a woman. I think you loved her. Maybe she was your first real love? I think you still love her. In a way, just the way you write about her. I think Amy made it safe for you and she is the one that ultimately deserved your first

90

time. Thinking about it, she actually took your virginity. She was the first woman you slept with and the first person you truly loved. Am I correct?

I get the feeling that Amy was not on course. Maybe she was not following her bliss. She was a stripper, but did she want to be? You talked with her about literature and shared the same passions with her. It sounds to me like she was meant to do something else and was stuck.

I feel how you loved her, just by the way you write about it. I find myself jealous of Amy. I should not be but I am. I am jealous of everyone in your life that got to have you, knowing that I never will. I really should not be saying that, I know.

Jade, you live your life. You are an adventurer. I know there is a lot you can teach me. I think there are some things I can teach you, but I cannot say. Tell me more. Were there more women?

In college you would spank me, what else would you do to me?

Your friend,
Emma

Date: October 6, 2008   6:42AM
Subject: Awakening

Dearest Em,

I am writing so much to you Emma. Now you must know, I don't do this. It is hard for me to completely reveal myself and my inner thoughts or my story. You are a very special friend. I will tell you more.

Amy did not want to be a stripper. She needed the money and it was the only avenue that was presented to her at the time. So Amy had to go back to Alaska, that is where she could make money. I will talk more about her in a minute.

91

Let me tell you more about that Joseph Campbell book, the one that helped me realize how to follow my bliss or, should I say, helped me better understand what it was that I was doing. It put words to my thoughts and actions and made sense of it. The book changed my life. After I moved to Seattle, I unknowingly lived by his words, well, most of them. I followed my bliss. It brought me to Seattle.

Essentially the book is about not being stagnant. Not being afraid to shake things up. If you are too set in your ways and do not explore other paths that present themselves to you, you will not grow. The opposite, you will disintegrate. It is about living without fear.

For Christmas, I bought my mom and dad a book about Seattle, and I wrote some of my favorite passages in the inside cover. After the passages I signed the letter:

"Thank you both so much for giving me such a wonderful gift...the opportunity to discover my potential. Here are some beautiful pictures of Seattle. I just wanted you to see where your little girl is. Missing you and sending all my love and gratitude,
Jade"

That book helped me understand why I needed to go to Seattle. I was destined to discover my life, the one I was suppose to live. It gave me the tools I needed to understand what I was doing and to continue without fear.

MY STORY CONTINUED

So Amy left me and I had to move on.

There were a couple of straight girls that I dated or went out with. There was one that I had known from art school, she was Latino and very, very hot. Her name was Veracruz. She had big brown eyes, long black hair, luscious lips and she was a little taller than me. Very fit, she had curves in all the right places.

To say that I found her attractive was an understatement. She had caught my eye the first day I walked into class. She had smiled at me, and I was sure everyone was watching me melt right there in the front of the room.

I often caught myself staring at her. A flawless face and silky smooth skin, she was a bright light and everyone wanted her

92

attention. She seemed wild and rough around the edges, which contradicted her looks and this made her even more attractive to me.

To my surprise, I saw her out one night with a friend at a lesbian bar. We caught each other's eyes at the same moment, and she smiled invitingly. I had left school, so we hadn't seen each other in awhile. That smile made my legs move quickly, until I stood directly in front of her.

She hugged me and then grabbed my shoulders and said, "I wondered if you were gay, you used to hang out with Randi. She is gay right?"

"No Randi has a boyfriend." I winked at her and said, "But I don't have a girlfriend...not yet anyway."

She grabbed hold of my shoulders even tighter and without wasting time she said, "Will you come home with me?" Then she leaned over and in her low, sexy Spanish accent she said, "I want you to fuck me, can you handle that?"

I leaned over putting my lips right in front of hers. Looking straight into her eyes, I smiled naughtily and heard myself reply, "First, I want to lick your lips... all of them. Then, I will fuck you all night long. And yes, I can handle it." She seemed surprised, but pleased with my reply, and frankly, so was I. My words must have created immediacy in the situation, because she grabbed my hand and led me through the crowd. Out front, we flagged a cab and then made out in the backseat the entire ride to her house. She was so sexy.

Well, I found out she was not gay. She was straight, occasionally bisexual. The sex was hot though. We were entirely attracted to one another and she had a magnificent body. We ravished each other all night long, and then drifted off to sleep, as the morning light began to creep into the room.

Only a couple of hours later, a little girl about four or five years old walked into the room. She seemed un-phased by a stranger in her mom's bed, but I felt extremely uncomfortable. She didn't tell me she had a kid! Oh my god, we were really loud when we were having sex. Veracruz kissed the little girl and told her to go watch TV while she made her some breakfast. Just when I thought it could not get any worse, a guy wondered into the room, apparently he had been sleeping on the couch. Veracruz smiled as he walked into the room. She stood up naked and gave him a kiss on the

93

cheek. I was shocked, but entirely distracted by her perfectly round bum, gorgeous figure and soft skin reflecting the beam of sunlight that shone through the window.

"Pablo, this is Jade. Isn't she hot? She is a fantastic fuck!" I lay naked and mortified. He looked at me, and then glanced down at my boob that was peeping out from below the covers. He smiled and said, "Maybe if you are not busy later I can find out?" I pulled the covers up high and shot him a very clear, "I don't think so" look.

"Jade don't mind him, this is Pablo, my ex-boyfriend," Veracruz said casually. "He knows I occasionally sleep with women. Pablo, stop teasing her."

Pulling the covers up higher, I reached my hand out and he shook it. Veracruz left to go to the bathroom. He stood there, sipping a cup of coffee and looking around at our clothes scattered all over the bedroom. I broke the uncomfortable moment by asking him if he always slept on the couch. He told me except for when "the crazy-ass motherfucker" was around.

"Who is the crazy ass motherfucker?" I asked reluctantly. After I spoke, I knew I probably didn't want to know the answer to that question. Could things get any worse? Veracruz re-entered the room still naked, smiled and jumped on top of me, kissing me playfully.

"It's my boyfriend," she said. "But don't worry, he is in jail for stealing a car and assault. I would never have brought you home with me if he were here. He would have killed you if he caught us in bed together," she said so nonchalantly that I suddenly began to feel like jumping out the open window behind me.

I had no idea where I was and no cash for a taxi home. What was I thinking? I got up, showered, dressed, and said that I had to go to work. I asked where I was and she gave me directions to the main road that would take me home. It was a long, long walk. I smiled the whole way at my ignorance. I was learning a lot about women. I needed to take better care of my choices, but I was feeling more and more confident in the bedroom. She was very hot. The sex was raw and undeniably fantastic, but clearly there was way too much drama. I could not see her again. It was too weird.

She called a few times and I told her I was not going to play third wheel to some guy. She understood. I saw her one other time at a gay club. I was dancing, and the next thing I knew she grabbed my hand and pulled me into the restroom.

She pushed me against the wall and said "Baby I remember that night we were together, and when I see you dancing like this, looking so sexy, you know what I am thinking!"

She then proceeded to kiss me, as her hands ran all over me. All the women in the restroom were staring at the obvious heat between us. She had on a tight shirt that showed off her flat tummy. Her boobs were bulging out of her low cut shirt and her jeans showed off her curves. I remembered that perfect bum on top of me, and it was very difficult to resist. Yes, she was beautiful, wild and unpredictable, but I did resist this time.

She was one of the many straight women that came and went during that short period of time. I always ended up with a straight woman. I seemed to be a straight girl magnet.

There were about four others that I dated after that, and then I met my first lesbian girlfriend, T. She owned a business on the 14th floor of a high rise downtown that was adjacent from the office that I worked in. One day, I saw her in the canteen. I knew immediately, by her appearance, that she was a dyke. She had short, dark hair and no makeup on. She styled it with a hard gel, so that it looked messy but still very professional. Taller than me by about three inches, she had broad strong shoulders and a very sporty figure. She wore a suit with a tie and had on men's shoes. Classy and sophisticated, she smelled like men's cologne. Men's Obsession, if I remember correctly.

I found her completely attractive, and so I smiled at her sensually and she responded immediately by flirting with me. Everyday we would get coffee at the same time, and she would speak to me. She was so charming and her smile was incredibly sexy. Confident and strong when she walked, she commanded every room that she entered.

After a few weeks of this, I ran into her while working late one evening. She asked me if I wanted to have lunch with her the next day and I accepted. The lunch lasted three hours. We talked about everything. She was surprised to hear I was a lesbian. She was certain that I was a straight girl flirting with her.

We began having lunch together at least three times a week. We developed into very good friends, who sat very close and playfully teased on another. T had a girlfriend at the time, but things were not going well with them.

One day at lunch T asked me, "Will you have dinner with me

tonight?"

"I thought you had a girlfriend," I said tauntingly.

"I do, but I want to take you out on a date. My girlfriend and I are on a break."

"What does 'on a break' mean," I said.

T laughed, looked down, shook her head and said, "We can see other people. You have a lot to learn about being a lesbian."

"That is why I have you to teach me!" She smiled at me for a very long time, which confirmed her intentions for that evening.

So, I went to dinner that night with T. It was a small Chinese restaurant on Capitol Hill. This was the first date I had been on with a woman. Sure, I had met women at clubs and through friends, but this was a date. I remember being so excited and nervous. I changed my clothes at least five times. I settled for a very low cut, tight black shirt. The sleeves were tight and around the wrists it extended with a long frilly cuff.

She picked me up at my apartment and we walked to the restaurant. She laughed at me as my cuffs kept falling into my meal. I remember she reached over and pulled them back as her hand brushed my naked wrist. It was electrifying. I also caught her looking at my boobs on several occasions throughout the evening. Clearly I had made the right choice in what to wear.

We had a great dinner. I really liked this woman. She had a sense of humor that was off the wall. I loved that about her. T was very butch. She had very strong arms from lifting weights and a very muscular back. Her legs were rock hard. Cocky in a good way, she made me feel comfortable, even though I was so ignorant about the gay community. I found her very charming and extremely sexy.

During dinner, she mentioned that she had just gotten the keys to her new apartment that afternoon. She wanted to give me the grand tour and seemed very excited about it.

On the top floor of the building, just a few blocks away, her apartment was huge. She gave me the tour ending in the room that would become her bedroom. This was pretty clever, I thought. It had a balcony wrapped around the entire front and side of the apartment, and overlooked downtown. When I think of it, the Seattle skyline still makes my heart sink. I have never encountered a more beautiful site. Sunset was always my favorite time of the day, when the sky turns a mix of reds and oranges. You can see the outline of black mountains off in the distance behind the water, as the space needle quietly gazes on the last few moments of the day.

As we stood silently on the balcony, I could feel the attraction building between us. The moment was incredibly intense. I realized it was the first time we had ever been completely alone. Over the last several weeks, I had imagined what it would be like kissing her. So, I stood there waiting for her to make a move. She was the one in charge of the situation. She had all the experience.

It was cold, so we stepped back inside. As I turned around after closing the door, she came up to me, pressed me back against the glass and kissed me so passionately. I could feel every strong muscle in her body tighten. Her tongue massaged mine and it made me so excited. I never had a woman kiss me like that! Straight women certainly did not. A completely new experience for me, I wanted her to teach me everything that she knew.

She took my breath away. I stopped kissing her and grabbed her shoulders and a fistful of her leather jacket. I pulled her in closer to me and whispered in her ear, "You have to stop because you are making me so wet. I get very wet, but right now I'm so fucking wet." She looked at me a little shocked. That was all she needed to hear. She pressed into me and I wrapped my leg around her pulling her even closer. My arms exploring her muscular back, I could feel her strength. Pulling her coat off, I ran my hand up around her neck, followed with my lips and then I blew in her ear. This drove her crazy. She placed her face in my neck and inhaled my perfume.

We broke in her new bedroom that night. She threw me down and we had raw, hard sex. She was so sexy and she knew how to fuck. She knew just how to handle the girly girl in me.

Afterwards, she walked me home and we agreed to see each other again. We did, for almost three years. T was very special to me and taught me a lot about lesbian sex, the gay community and about a lot of things really. I'll come back to that later.

COMING OUT

After meeting Amy and before meeting T, I came out to my mom. One day my friend asked to borrow my car. He needed to drive across town to pick up a curling iron. He was a hairdresser friend of Sam's, so I thought it would be okay. While driving across the bridge, the license plates fell off of my car. A police officer happened to be at the intersection and pulled him over. What are the odds? This guy was not very lucky. The police officer found he had so many outstanding parking tickets, that he took him to jail immediately. My car was left under some bridge in Seattle.

The police phoned my parents and told them they had found it abandoned. Why? I have no idea. Maybe they forgot to call it in, and some other officer found it thinking it was abandoned. I will never know. Meanwhile, I was out hanging out with friends, but wondering where my car was. Remember these were the days before everyone had mobile phones. I got home at about 8:00pm.

The phone rang and I answered it. It was my mom and she was crying hysterically "Jade is that you? Thank God, I will call you back." She hung up. That was strange, I thought, and I panicked slightly, wondering what was wrong with her. About ten minutes later, she called back and explained what had happened. She was still crying but was no longer hysterical. She told me about the phone call from the police and said she had thought I was dead.

I said simply, "No mom, I am not dead…but I am gay."

Silence. Long Pause.

"You're not bisexual," she asked still crying from before.

"No." I said. I still think that was a funny response.

"Well, okay (pause) I am just happy you are alive," she said in a weak, weepy voice.

We talked more about it over the days to come. She decided not to tell my father right away. She would also wait in telling the rest of the family, she needed to process it. I thought for sure my father would fly out, take me home and send me to some wacko who would "deprogram" me. Boy, was I wrong about that. My mom handled it well. She was happy to finally see me take an interest in dating.

My mother eventually told my sister. She called me crying because I would never be able to have children. People react in such different ways. My mother told my brothers too, who all had a difficult time with it. Mitch had it the worst. He is my middle brother, the protector, and he was anti-homosexual. After losing a bunch of weight over it, he came around. My eldest brother's wife was mean to me at first, saying I looked wicked in the pictures that I had shown them of Seattle. I think she even told that to her kids because they seemed to be afraid of me. She wouldn't let her daughter see me unsupervised, when T & I went home for a visit. Eventually, she came around and we get along now. She just needed time to process it and I understand.

They all realized when I was home visiting, I was not wicked and I was not any different. My youngest brother for the most part was okay with it, but a little surprised. He said that he stopped using the word "fag". He has used that as long as I can remember. His family was accepting and genuinely interested. My mom told my dad. He just looked at her funny, and then said simply, "Okay."

T was the first girlfriend I took home. I wasn't sure how my dad would react and I have to say he completely surprised me. One morning while both of my parents were at work, T and I were alone in the house. I sat on the couch, and T was lying with her head in my lap. I was stroking her face and hair when my dad came in, unannounced, and walked through the living room. T sat up very quickly and looked down as if she was doing something wrong. He walked right by and left the room without saying a word. Then, he immediately came back in. He looked at T very sternly, and my heart fell, guessing what he might say to her. But he said, "You shouldn't move when I come in. You are with my daughter and you love her, I can see that. You can show it. You don't have to jump up. Be yourself."

That was the most my father has ever said to me that came from his heart. He loved T very much because he could tell dirty jokes with her. He still always asks about her.

My mother and father came to visit T & I. We took them on a trip to the Oregon coast, and my father got to wade in the ocean for the first time in his life. He and mother walked along the beach poking at starfish and holding hands. It was the closest to love that I'd ever seen them achieve. They were like two little children, so curious. Looking out over the ocean my father said, "There sure is a lot of this world to see." That was the second most profound thing my father has ever said to me. Unfortunately, he never ventured much farther than the Midwest after that trip. I thought maybe he would, but he did not.

My parents got a divorce about ten years ago. My father was having an affair with a woman who was only a couple of years older than myself. He and my mother were sleeping in separate rooms for nearly a year. When she came to visit me again, I told her to get a divorce. Everyday, when I was in high school my mother would say, "The only reason I stay with your father is so that you are taken care of." I told her she didn't have to take care of me anymore and there were no more excuses. After building up the strength, she went home and filed for a divorce. After 43 years of marriage and at 60 years old, my mother was divorced. It was the best thing she ever did.

After telling me he was having an affair, my father's lover called to tell me he had asked her to marry him. She asked that I give them my blessing, so I went home to see my dad. Giddy and happier than I had ever seen him, I forgave him for cheating on my mother because ultimately they were both unhappy. I said, "Dad what you did to mom was wrong. You really, really hurt her. But, you have always accepted everything about me, so I forgive you and I will give you my blessing. I hope you are both very happy."

They did get married years later and it didn't last more than a few weeks. After she took most of his money, she left him and is now with another man. My dad is alone and unhappy.

My mom moved south with her sister-in-law and they live in a tight elderly community that supports one another. She is very happy there. It is funny because they are all dating, having dances and yes, having sex. It is like 90210 for older people. Unfortunately, after she divorced my father she lost all of her money in a bad investment, so I support her now financially. Social security provides her with very little and she cannot live on it. She feels guilty, but I remind her of all she has given me. She gave me her time and whatever I give her will never be enough, but I try to do what I can.

My parents are friends now. Talking on the phone all of the time with dad, Mom has gotten over her anger. My dad is so lonely. She checks in on him and he likes to hear from her, he misses her. I think Mom wishes he would be the man she had hoped he would be. She doesn't want him back, but taking care of dad will always be a habit. She will always be trying to change him. It is something she has always done. Some behavior is difficult to change, but it makes me so happy that they are friends.

Now about T, she was older than me, and I was still in my party girl phase. I was only 23 when we started dating. While she was focusing on her business and ready to settle down, I was going out all of the time, discovering my new life. This was a bad mix when trying to build a relationship. It didn't last. It was my fault.

T accused me of cheating all of the time. I didn't for 18 months, though she thought I did. When she would leave me at the dance clubs, there would be women hitting on me. Yes, I was flirty, but nothing happened. Lesbians did not often hit on me, mainly straight or bisexual women would. I only danced with them, at first.

I was working with a girl who was bisexual, named Lisa. She had gone to college and had been in a sorority as well. Bright and bubbly, we had a lot in common and talked endlessly. She had long, light brown hair and a contagious smile. I flirted endlessly with her. Actually, T and I both flirted with her. One night after work, Lisa and I went and got a six-pack of beer. We sat in a park and chatted and I told her how T always accused me of cheating, but that I never had. I had never even kissed anyone else. She said her boyfriend did the same. He always thought she was out kissing girls and was very insecure about her bisexuality.

For some reason we thought it was a good idea to kiss, since we were being accused of it and so we did. We kissed and talked on and off for about 2 hours. I regretted that kiss. Though she was very sexy and a great kisser, it was the first time I cheated on T...with a kiss.

This led to two other kisses with straight women. One woman I met at a dance club. She was there with her boyfriend and I was there with a friend of mine. Very petite with a cute body and long, dark, curly hair, she danced like a stripper on the dance floor, and she kept looking over at me. Finally, she made her way behind me and started dancing with me. She was incredibly sexy and I was in a frustrated moment of weakness. So, I kissed her and my friend kissed her boyfriend. He owned a nightclub in downtown Seattle and we went there after hours. The club was closed, but he turned on the lights and music, and the four of us danced some more. Afterwards, we went into the back room and drank a few beers and talked. Nothing else happened just kissing.

Now I did dance with a lot of women. I danced very sexually, but this did not mean I wanted other women. I just really loved to dance. Usually I didn't mean anything by it. Sometimes people thought I did, and tried to hit on me. The dance floor has always been my world where I could let go and let the music penetrate my soul. My body would take over and guide me without thought. It always felt so good. It still does. I LOVE to dance.

The other straight girl I kissed, I kissed her several times when I would see her out and about. She was a woman that I met through work, a friend of a friend. I figured, for some reason, it was okay since it was only kissing. It was only in the last year that I was with T, that I actually had sex with someone else.

I cheated on T with Amy...she came back to me.
I must go.

xoxo
Jade

Date: October 6, 2008   4:42PM
Subject: Amy is Back

Beautiful, Sweet Jade,

Maybe I should buy Joseph Campbell's book. I've been thinking about what you said about it. Maybe I waste too much time on hating men when I really should be living my life. Like you do.

You told me about coming out to your parents. That is a bit of a funny story really. You make me laugh the way you told your mom. I am smiling now just thinking about it.

So T was your butch. I wondered if you ever dated butch women. You were a party girl and she was a businesswoman. That was a bad match. And she accused you of cheating which then actually led you to cheat. Amy came back to you. I cannot wait to hear how this story ends.

102

You learned a lot from T. What exactly happened between the two of you? You were kissing straight girls and very feminine women and yet you had a relationship with a butch. You liked being with a butch, someone in control yet you kept kissing straight women where you were in control. Did that tell you something? I find butch women very attractive. I know you are girly but maybe you are butch too?

Could you be my butch in the sheets? Maybe you are thinking about exploring this side of yourself more. I know that you would make me feel so safe and protected. Having you take care of me would be all that I would need. Can you tell I have been thinking of you? About being with you?

Am I being naughty for saying this? Do you want to spank me? What would you do to me if we could be together? I asked this already but can you handle it? Am I pressing you to go too far? If you want me, I am yours.

Your friend,
Emma

I read and reread Emma's words over and over again. She wants me to be her butch in the sheets. Femme in the streets, butch in the sheets, that was a song from Fem2Fem that I used to listen to years ago. Sam and I loved it.

Emma wants me. I need to be wanted right now and it feels so good, but I cannot. She is my friend. Revealing so much to her, for some reason I trust her, but she wants to be more? Can I give more? I close my computer, gather my bags and leave the office. I had to drive in today to drop off my expenses and I had a few customer meetings. After a very long day, I am looking forward to the journey. It will allow me time to collect my thoughts.

On the drive home, I am thinking about Jessica and I. I feel my anger begin to build. The lack of sex, I cannot face yet another night of feeling bitterness towards her. Something is growing and starting to surface. The seeds have been planted and it is starting to spread undesirably, like Poison Ivy.

Jessica and I have spent the last week not interacting. My anger is apparent and she is dead inside. She cannot get past not having another child. Or is there something else that she is upset about? Always angry with me, she never touches me. Her sweet kisses are a distant memory.

Last week, I told her that the no-sex between us is becoming a huge problem. I suggested I should find someone to have sex with, a fuck-buddy. Not taking me seriously, she just laughed and walked out of the room!

Arriving home, I find my son waiting at the window. Walking in, he grabs my legs and hugs me tight. I feel my bitterness dissipate with his chatter and laughter. Sitting down on the floor in my suit, I tickle him and his giggles fill my empty heart. He brings light to my day.

Jessica, entirely unaware of my discontent that is now hiding in the shadows behind our son's voice, comes in and begins with a laundry list of action items for me. "Jade, can you please take out the trash? Oh, and I need a red pepper. I forgot a red pepper, can you go get one?" Just hearing her voice makes me feel distant. I need five minutes with my son. Finally, she asks if I have had a good day.

"Yeah, it was alright," I say slightly annoyed.

She begins to tell me about the day she had. Listening half-heartedly, I withdraw. She stops speaking mid-sentence, turns and walks out of the room. I would typically follow her, come up from behind, kiss her on the neck and apologize. But not today, I don't want to.

After putting our little boy in bed, Jessica comes into the room and sits down. I move over and look at her very seriously. Before I know what is happening I hear myself utter the words that ultimately would change everything.

"Jessica, we have discussed this before. Do you think I should have a fuck-buddy? I need to have more sex and you know this. We have been over and over it. I need more sex. I need to have a fuck-buddy because this isn't working for me." I say it very firmly and she sees that this time I am entirely serious. Recognizing the spark in my eye, her body grows very tense, and the frustration explodes.

"Then have one Jade! Have a fucking fuck-buddy," she yells uncontrollably.

She storms out of the room and I sit very still in astonishment. I realize I now have what I wanted to hear, her consent. But is this really what I want?

As I go to sleep that evening, I think of the last words Emma wrote. They are engraved in my head as I drift off into a dream world. Could I be her butch and dominate her? Would I spank her? Do I want to? Dominance. It is something I know, but how well?

Earlier, I was not sure how to respond to this. Now my answer becomes very clear to me.

7

My alarm buzzes at 5:30am. Jumping out of bed, I welcome a full day of meetings as a distraction. I love going into Amsterdam, it reminds me of when we first moved here and how new and exciting everything was. Feeling very awake and in a good mood, I am ready to go this morning. Creeping down the stairs, I try not to make too much noise so I can relax in the stillness of the early moments.

My son and I are both early birds and love the first hours of the day. Jessica wakes up a "grumpy butt", as we like to say. She always needs a few minutes to lie there and wake up. It always baffles me how people can sleep in because I have never been able to, even as a teenager I was always up early. My son and I open our eyes and hop out of bed before we are actually awake. Our minds move quickly and our bodies do their best to keep up. Usually, he is downstairs when I come down, and he is bright-eyed and watching television. He always gives me a big hug and kiss, and feeds me some very fascinating piece of information he has either read or seen on television. Not today though, it was too early and he was still sleeping.

Negative thoughts of my discussion with Jessica begin to fill my head and anger takes over, covering everything, including her. Yet, there is a clarity that pushes them away, I have a new mission. I now have her consent, so my thoughts are simply focused on one thing: find a fuck-buddy. And that is what I intend to do. I make a cup of coffee, pour a cup of Acaí juice, and I turn on my laptop. A rush of excitement tricks it's way into my mind.

Date: October 7, 2008   6:46AM
Subject: Amy is Back

Dear Em,

You said a lot in your last message. I will come to that in a minute. It is important, but first I want to finish my story about Amy before I can answer your questions.

I am reading Anais Nin's *Henry and June,* once again. I think I mentioned that book before, in one of our conversations when talking about Amy. In fact, that message prompted me to buy it again because I had given away my copy to a friend of mine. I ordered it straight away, and it arrived yesterday.

It has been years since I have read it, ten or twelve? I don't remember. I am falling in love with it just as I did the first time I read it. The first chapter captures me, and I am taken in once again by Anais Nin.

The way she writes, a simple sentence is such a profoundly passionate thought. They come one, after the other, after the other. It is like multiple orgasms of the mind and heart. Poetic. I am having a love affair once again with this book. The first time I read it, it inspired me to write and she showed me how to use specific words or thoughts in a more intricate way. I am reminded of the silence I felt from its absence.

I like to read poetry before I go to sleep. So resting on my nightstand, it calls to me every evening. I am rereading it very slowly, page by page, savoring every word and marking my favorite passages with a yellow marker. Now I can quickly reference the sections that move me, and go to sleep with a fire, an infatuation brewing in my thoughts as my body rests. Her words transform that infatuation into something physical for me, which influences my daily life. No word could fully describe the sensation her writing brings to me. Discovering it again awakens the desire I once had to be a fearless writer. It reminds me to take risks and to tap into that raw place, deep inside, where my emotion has been quietly simmering.

The book is about Anais Nin's sexual awakening, when she meets a couple Henry Miller and his beautiful wife June. Though she is married, Anais falls in love with Henry's writing, and she falls madly in love with June. Though liberating to her sexually, she finds herself imprisoned by this couple and the love she has for them.

I read it in Seattle, when I first came out as a lesbian. It was very much a parallel to my own sexual awakening in a way. Seattle was my mistress, and women were just then an option for me. It began just after I met Amy; she brought this book to me. I told you she was actually my June, though I choose to call her Anais, even to this day. Perhaps I didn't want her to know, but she knew. Oh yes, she knew.

I told you, Amy left me and returned to Alaska, but she came back when I was with T. We had a love affair. Amy said that we would be lovers for the rest of our lives. Regardless if we were both in relationships, we would be unable to resist one another, and I believed her. I could not imagine it any other way. Our passion for literature mixed with our lovemaking, and we became wrapped up in an illusion, a beautiful illusion.

Now, about the woman to whom I gave my copy of *Henry and June*, we shared a very special night together. This book was a precious treasure to me. But that night brought a very unusual experience, one that moved me enough to part with my favorite book. Let me tell you why...

Amy and I were out at a gay bar, and as I mentioned, we used to cause quite a stir. I told you she was rather tall with long, red hair with yellowish eyes. Her look was dramatic and her features were almost drag queen-esque, especially with her naturally thick eyelashes. Striking. When she walked, she commanded the room. Her quiet stare intimidated most people. She was with me, girly girl lesbian in very high platforms, smoky eyes, and my dark red lips glowing against my pale skin. We were an unusual couple.

Everyone tried to figure us out. Were we lovers? Were we not lovers? The sexual energy between us was scorching. When we were together, nothing else existed around us. We fascinated and challenged one another and would easily get lost in our infatuation. Our conversations felt secret. No one else could possibly understand us, and oh, how we flirted. But we could not touch in public because our affair had to be discrete. Our fervent, mysterious world filled up each of us and we were completely captivated by one another. There was no room for anything else.

We would sit in the booth staring across the table at each other, telling stories, talking about books and sharing secret confessions. We spoke about everything that could possibly have been inspiring to us at that time. We were entirely attentive to one another. There were no two people who were more interested in listening to what the other had to say. She understood my deepest passions and desires and how sometimes they tormented me, because she was the same.

When she spoke of something very important to her, her voice was deep and soft. I was one of the few that got to see her vulnerability. After listening to my thoughts, she would always pause and internalize what I had said before replying. The way she analyzed a situation and translated it into something so profound baffled me. She was wise beyond her years and I wanted her across the table and through every intense word between us. Aside from our verbal conversations, our eyes were always silently engaged, having an entirely separate dialogue with each other, and gently pulling us closer and closer to one another.

That night, Amy and I were out at a bar and we ran into my friend Rain. Rain was this beautiful straight girl with long, very dark brown, almost black hair. She was a fag hag like me, and I always saw her out dancing, which is how we became friends. She had exotic, green eyes that glowed against her silky, olive skin. Her body was curvy, her boobs mid-sized, and she had pillowy lips. Tall and elegant, she walked with such grace. Rain and I shared a love for dancing, and we were always excited to see each other, so we could hit the dance floor together.

When I introduced them, I saw Amy look at Rain the same way that I did. Rain's unusual beauty was inescapable. I think the obvious connection between Amy and I intrigued her, so she sat with us. We both flirted with her all evening, and she became wrapped up in our energy. No one had ever broken in before. Amy and I were always caught up in each other, but that evening, we let Rain catch a glimpse of our undisclosed world.

Afterwards, Rain invited us back to her house. She resided in the attic of a beautiful mansion on Lake Washington, owned by two doctors that also lived in the house. She babysat their daughter and cleaned their house in exchange for room and board while she finished college. Lush fabrics draped from the walls and ceilings. Rain had created a room where a concubine might live. It was a work of art, a phantasmagorical room, which transformed us to another time and place.

Rain was a drama major and had a clothes rack in the corner with all of her outrageous outfits that helped bring the room to life. She dressed over the top. Many of her friends were drag queens and she shared a love for boas and heels. Drawn to the rack of costumes, we started undressing and trying them on.

109

Boas, hats, scarves and high heels, you name it, and we had it on. We were all three dancing around, giggling and running the boas and scarves over one another. I was wearing red, lacey underwear with a long, fake pearl necklace around my neck. A red boa thrown over my shoulder hiding my naked breasts, I towered in the most ridiculously high heels I had ever seen. Amy had on a black bra, underwear, and a short black scarf tied around her neck. The black boots she had on came just above her knee. We were dancing together and clinking our martini glasses, while feeding each other olives. Laughing as we spun around, we both stopped and stared at Rain. She was completely naked dancing in the middle of the room. Her dark hair was flowing over her body as she turned in circles.

Amy and I were both stunned and allured. Her movements were hypnotic and we paused, speechless. Our eyes moved all over Rain's body, devouring each perfect curve. She was a goddess traveling in her own moment with a sensual, feminine aura that glowed softly from her body. We stood admiring a private, almost spiritual, moment.

I grabbed Amy's hand, and we walked over to Rain. She looked at us while she continued to dance, and invited us in to enter her universe. We began to move together in one ball of sexual energy. Running our fingers softly over each other's naked flesh, Rain's skin, oh...softer than any other woman that I have ever been with. Amy and I were indulging in her ripe breasts and full lips.

Floating to Rain's bed, we began moving all over each other. My hands stroking all over both of their bodies, while I received many soft kisses back over mine. Multiple hands caressing and exploring, sensuality was overflowing. Our bodies melted together, and we were lost in the experience. It was an all female, extremely erotic moment. This, my friend I can tell you, was a beautiful night for the three of us. We were all concubines that evening, for each other.

The next day was Rain's birthday. I gave her my copy of *Henry and June*. I wrote something in it, but I don't remember what I said.

SERIOUS BUSINESS

You asked about T. Yes she was my butch and I was her girl. We had very straight sex. She liked to fuck the girly girl in me. She did teach me a lot as I said, let's leave it at that. Then you asked me something. Can I be your butch? By this you mean dominant, I

110

assume.

While I am a very femme lesbian, I consider myself rather dominant sexually. Even when I had sex with men, I was always in control of most of the sexual relationships I had. Except maybe with Amy. But was that a relationship? Then there was T. She was very dominant as well and I loved that about her. But there were two in control of that relationship.

Am I capable of being a dominant? The answer is yes. I am already. I do have this girly girl side that has needs though. This side is still dominant, very much in that I know what I want, but this part of me likes different things.

Do you want a virtual fuck-buddy? What is a fuck-buddy? We have sex virtually with no chance of us ever meeting. Will that work for you? I will show you my dominant side and then you can teach me how it should be. I am ready to explore it. Now can you handle me?

Send me a picture. I want to see more of your body.

xoxo
Jade

I arrive home this evening at 6:00pm after a full day of meetings. It has been such a long day. Coming through the door exhausted, I discover Jessica is beyond mad at me. She has taken our son to McDonalds and left me a note saying "at McDonalds". That is it. There is no dinner, and no smiling little boy waiting for me to come home. She is punishing me. An empty house, everything is dark. She has never done this before. She always calls me, and we discuss dinner plans. Anger must be consuming her, or maybe she is realizing the consequences of our words.

It is October, the days are getting shorter, and there is a chill in the air. We haven't fully cranked up the heat yet, as we normally do for our winter schedule. Taking my suit jacket off, I put on a tight black sweater and walk over to the refrigerator. Not much is inside, and I don't feel like cooking. I have no desire to go back out into the cold, damp weather, so I grab a few carrots and make a tea. Warming my hand on the cup, I wonder if Jessica and I went too far the other night with our discussions. And then I remember the message I sent to Emma this morning.

What was I doing? I thought I wanted to challenge my writing, which I have, but how did *this* happen? Is this even what I wanted? Is it so bad? A virtual fuck-buddy is better than having a real lover, isn't it? There is no chance of us meeting, ever, and I can end it whenever I want. She doesn't know who I am. I don't know who she is. It is harmless really. Isn't it? I have no intention other than having sex. It isn't even sex, it is virtual sex. It means nothing because it is only a fantasy. Is the writer in me driving my actions?

Opening my computer, I check my email. Emma has sent me a picture of her on the beach with a drink in her hand. It looks like it might have been taken in the south of France. She is wearing a very skimpy bikini, her body is tall, lean and her breasts are large, round and inviting. She has beautiful curves and contours. The picture has dissolved my doubts as my desire for her builds. I want this woman. Opening my Inbox, I have a new message. A rush of excitement comes over me and I read.

Date: October 8, 2008   4:32PM
Subject: Fuck Buddy

Beautiful, Sweet Jade,

I sent you my picture. Did you receive it? I know you like big tits. Yes, I have them. It makes me shy to send my picture especially one this sexy but I know it is what you want to see.

I must answer you right away. You are dominant. I knew it! All along I have known. Do I want to be your fuck buddy, your virtual fuck buddy? Yes, yes, yes! YES!
You can spank me. You can use me.

I have been thinking about you for so long. About if we were in university together. I have been fantasizing about it. We would be roommates and we would tell stories, secrets. Then we would fuck all night long. I am fantasizing about you looking at me the way you looked at Amy.

You have decided for me, you want me as a fuck-buddy. You decide everything and the power is yours. I enjoy it. I will do what you say. I have been listening to your stories and I think I have a good idea how to please you. I have been tempting you. Yes, I admit that. I am so naughty, maybe a spanking?

Your friend,
Emma

A craving rushes throughout my body and everything begins to tingle. I feel alive, as wetness builds between my legs. I am compelled to reply quickly.

However, I am not certain I can spank her and dominate her the way that she needs. It is not something that I fantasize about, spanking someone. It is challenging my imagination and I am certain my writing ability will be too. I will try to create something I think she will like. The thought of creating a whole world that is entirely new to me is exhilarating.

My heart is racing as I hit "Reply" and begin to type.

Date: October 8, 2008 6:00PM
Subject: Fantasy

Dear Em,

Tonight I will be your dominant Jade. I want you to know, I am a lover, one that you can trust. I will not hurt you in any way. I will certainly not use you either and I will never humiliate you. Tonight we will fuck, and understand, this is not making love. I do not think

113

you know the difference. Am I right? I will tell you about it one day. You and I will only fuck. I only make love to my wife. Now, come with me on a journey....

A man arrives at the hospital where you work with an envelope and one red rose. Everyone around you wonders who sent you the special gift? It must be from your girlfriend they think, but you know it is from your secret lover, me. You open the envelope and a plastic key falls out along with a card. It says:

The Lynn Hotel

Openstraat 26

Amsterdam

Room 2728

Be there at 9:00pm sharp. Wear nothing under your long coat, and wear high heels.

After work, you go home, shower and put nothing on but a long coat and heels. You take a taxi to the hotel, enter the elevator, and press the button to the top floor. The doors open revealing a long corridor where the lighting is dim and the walls are dark gray. You begin to search for room 2728. It is the last room at the end of the corridor and you notice the word "Suite" is above the room number. Fumbling in your the pocket for the room key, you open the door and walk inside. A huge bed with fluffy black pillows and a stark, white comforter cover greets you. The lighting is soft and mysterious, the walls are dark grey and there is a certain smell that is familiar to you.

The secrecy excites you, and I think you are smiling in anticipation. Wearing nothing under your long coat, you are unprotected and about to meet me for the first time. Noticing a red rose with a note on the bed, you walk over, pick it up, and begin to read. It says, "Turn around and walk."

Spinning around you see a connecting room. Walking over, you peak inside. It is an office with an oversized black executive chair facing the desk. The desk is facing the window, exactly opposite of the entrance to the room where you are standing. Through the window you can see the tall, connected residential homes across the street. Some of the windows are dark and empty, while others are glowing with life. Looking around the room, it appears empty. You speak quietly, "Hello?"

At that moment, the big chair spins around, and I reveal myself to you. I am wearing tight black pants tucked into tall, black, high-heeled boots. I have on a wide, black belt, a low cut, black jacket and a black tie around my naked neck. My legs are crossed and my head is tilted down looking at the ground. Slowly lifting my eyes up, it is the first time we make a connection. My eyes are dark brown with smoky eye-makeup accenting their intensity. They are famished. I smile a naughty smile, raise a contoured eyebrow, and lift my chin up so now you can fully see my face and features.

Standing up, I say in a low but firm voice, "Remove your coat, I want to see all of you."

Looking down at the floor, you drop your coat in a pile around your ankles. You are standing naked before me, wearing only heels. Your eyes are lowered? Are you shy? As I walk over, I see you are taller by several inches with your heels on.

"Remove your heels," I command. We are now at the same level. As I walk around you, you sense me studying your body. My fingers run over the small of your back and brush the curve of your ass.

"Something is missing," I say. Stopping in front of you, I lift your chin. Startled by the magnificence of your beautiful face, my lips curl into a smile. You know that you are safe.

Still connected, I loosen my black tie, and lift it over my head. Holding it up in front of you, you lower your head as I place it around your neck. It is not too tight but loose and comfortable. I lift your chin again as I observe the tie approvingly. Leaning my face into yours with my mouth just before you, I look at your lips calling them closer. Moving my mouth to your ear, I whisper, "Bound."

Removing my jacket, I expose my tight, black shirt with a low neckline. You notice that I have large tits. You are very naughty for looking at them, and I am going to spank you for that. Grabbing your tie, I lead you over to the desk and push the big black chair out of the way with the bottom of my boot. You put both hands on the desk and bend over. Anyone outside could be watching us and this heightens your awareness.

I spank you on the ass several times, firm but not too hard. "I will spank you five times later for being five minutes too late. Now, turn around."

As you do, I see a fire in your eyes. You like to be spanked very much. Interesting. Seeing the spark makes me want you even more and I yank a little on the tie and say, "Come with me."

Again you look at my tits. You crave them. I lead you over to the bed. "Take my shirt off." You lift my shirt and see a very strappy, black Marlies Dekkers bra.

"Turn around and bend over with your hands on the bed," I say. Spanking you again with my hand, the stinging sensation ignites the flames that now begin to rush through your veins. "Now turn around and sit down."

You sit down on the bed. I see you, hot and bothered by the spanking, as I walk up, spread your legs, and step between them. Your face is right in front of my breasts, and you desperately want to put it in them. I shake my head, not yet. Running my fingers over your face, down the side of your neck, lightly brushing below and above your tits, your nipples grow very hard. This pleases me. "Unbutton my pants."

I turn around and you see the back of my bra has many straps. Unhooking it and taking it off, my back faces you. I take off my boots, my pants, and my black underwear, and I grab my strap-on. Putting it on and turning around, you see it is big, but not too big, just right.

Grabbing the back of your neck, I pull you close as I place your lips over my nipples and nod. Licking and sucking on them eagerly, you are making them grow even harder. You hear me let out a long, sensual sigh.

I touch your face and bring my mouth down to yours, my lips lingering just centimeters from yours. Feeling my breath, you are releasing to my command. I open my mouth and kiss you. It is a very passionate kiss. Tongues touching for the first time, I run my hand down and touch your wet pussy. I caress your swollen clit, as my tongue plays with yours. You are ready for me.

"Lie back on the bed and spread your legs."

Playing with the dildo on the outside of your lips below, I rub it lightly on your sweet spot. You swell even more. I can see you growing very excited, so I pull back and come up to lick and kiss your breasts. Working my way down to your tummy, your hips, down further to your legs, and inner thighs, I see you are soaking.

Pouring with desire, I need to be inside of you. I lift back up, and I stick the dildo in slowly. As I go in further and further, you see my face begin to change. I like being inside of you and it shows. My body tenses as I moan lightly in your ear while pressing on top of you. You feel my strong arms, as I am unable to control myself. Slowly moving the dildo in and almost out, while I move my hips in a circle. I continue to push into you as I press harder against you. In and out of your pussy as I continue deeper still. You feel my body on top of you and my tits pressing against yours.

Your moans tell me to move a little more quickly. As your hips move faster below me, you press hard against the dildo and begin to respond loudly, as I move wildly on top of you. Feeling my breasts rub against yours, you tremble uncontrollably and you come. I love watching you come to me.

Surrender to me, Emma.

Hearing you and watching you in pleasure, I am almost coming. Quickly, I move my hand down and rub my clit only a few times. I cannot hold it back. My body tenses and then releases several times as my orgasm pounds. You are intensely studying me. Are you looking for my approval? You have it.

Our breathing slows as I look into your eyes and kiss your cheeks. I lean down and whisper in your ear, "Now you are mine."

xoxo
Jade

The words flow. How was it that I could write this? I don't fantasize about spanking and dominance? What has Emma put into me?

I press "Send". Closing my laptop quickly, I look at the clock as I hear a car pulling up outside. They are home. I sit there very still and guilty. In shock, I wonder, where did this come from? Even more surprised, why am I so wet?

Date: October 9, 2008   6:14PM
Subject: The first time

Beautiful, Sweet Jade,

Oh Jade. You said two things to me. You said, "Bound" and "Now you are mine." I am yours Jade. I have always been yours. You are dominant in a much different way than Eve. I

117

feel safe with you. I was nervous about the evening but then I knew it was you.

This fantasy is so exciting to me, I cannot even explain. I got to see you and be with you for the first time. I must not say, but I have been thinking of this for so long and now it is happening.
You spanked me right in front of the window so everyone can see me? You are turning me on Jade. I cannot believe this.
I was making you so excited. I could see on your face that you like fucking me. Pleasing you makes me come for you and I want to scream your name.

You asked me if I know what love is. I think I do because you just showed me. Eve does not give me flowers or is not as adventurous as you are. She does not do what you do with me. Maybe you just showed me making love? You said it was fucking but it seemed like making love to me.

I am yours. Fully yours. Jade I will give you everything that you want, as much as you want and I hope you are pleased with me. I have always wanted you. My dominant lover, you are taking over my world.

Your friend,
Emma

Date: October 9, 2008 11:36PM
Subject: I want you again

Dear Em,

You enjoyed what I did to you. We will explore each other much, much more. I am glad that I am dominant enough for you.
Notice I will not use you. You will be safe with me. You say that you have always wanted me. You are so bad Emma. You have

been trying to tempt me all along, haven't you? I will spank you for that.

I understand more and more about dominance and submissiveness. I told you I have always been this way. I have never met anyone as submissive as you though. I am surprised that you want Eve to run your entire life, to make every decision. Can I handle that? Yes. Does it stimulate me? Immensely. Am I still learning? Yes. But you are taking the dominant side I already have and magnifying it. Am I enjoying this? Oh, yes. I think I am discovering something new.

No, I did not show you making love. Making love involves romance and one day I will tell you about it because I don't think you understand. I get the feeling that you only know fucking and associate that with romance. They are two very different things. But first, come with me, I must have you again.

Arriving at your house, I ring the doorbell and you open the door. I smile very seductively. Taking your hand, we walk inside to your bedroom. "Undress," I say.

Completely naked, you lie on your tummy so I can torture you with kisses. I kiss your calves, your knees, your thighs, your bum and your back, working my way up to your neck. I grab a handful of your long hair. Firmly holding it and giving a little tug, you are not afraid because you know that you can trust me.

I reach down and spank you twice before taking my pants off. "Get on your knees."

You are on all fours as I put the dildo on. Reaching down between your legs, I can see the beautiful curve of your ass. Honey pouring all over my hands pleases me. You are so wet, as I slip the dildo inside of you slowly. Very gently, I am a gentle lover Emma, as I told you.

I hear your moans grow as I move so slowly. Grabbing your ass tightly, I spank you while the dildo is going in and out. Is this new for you? You begin to push back against me harder and harder.

"Touch your clit. Though Eve doesn't allow this, I will. It pleases me to watch you come."

You move your hand over your clit, while I continue moving a bit faster pushing the dildo further into you. Hearing that you are

119

about to come, I pull it out. I touch your back and your ass as I see you squirming for more.

I don't want to torture you, so I enter you again. Immediately you come to me, as your body is moving wildly and shaking. Collapsing, I lay down on top of your back while kissing your neck then rolling over on my side. You turn on your side and we face each other. We stay like this for a while, learning how to recognize one another.

Tonight you will not touch me and I will not come to you. I want to show you that I am in control, always, and I will take care of you Em.

I kiss your lips softly. Em, you have such beautiful eyes.

Next I will tell you about romance.

xoxo
Jade

Date: October 10, 2008 6:16AM
Subject: Confession

Beautiful Sweet Jade,

The way that you are with me is something I have never experienced, ever. I think maybe it is the same for you, although you are being dominant in such a unique way. At least it is different for me based on my experiences.

You say I do not know making love and romance. I think you might be right, but I am realizing that maybe I have nothing to compare it to.

Yes, I am yours. At the moment, I am only yours. I want you Jade. I told you I have been fantasizing about you for some time. Your stories and our friendship have made me have very strong feelings for you. Eve is not in my thoughts. Your light shines so much brighter. You, Jade, are the only one I want to be submissive for. You really are the only one for me. And I will say something to you, if I can, but only if it pleases you. I know this is risky for me to tell you this.

120

I love you. I cannot believe I said it. I want you Jade. I not only love you, but I have fallen in love with you. I don't know what else to say. I know that we can never be together. And I am crying.

Maybe it sounds sudden to you? I knew several days ago. When you were telling me your story. With every email, my feelings grow for you. I have been visualizing myself in place of each of the lovers you told me about. So it is not new for me.

I should not have told you this. I have been very bad, I know. I want to meet you so bad. But I cannot.

You see. Eve works all of the time. She has no time for me. Only on the weekend, or to show me off to her business associates. Several times a week we fuck. I understand this now. She has no love for me. If she does I don't know. I do not ask her this because I cannot. She will punish me if I push her.

Your story. You feel things, Jade. You have such passion. I want to learn passion and making love. I know I can learn all of this from you. Your wife is so lucky to have you. But you do not want me because I am not good enough for you. So, I am writing this. Wondering if I will ever send it to you.

I will say no more. I will only let you respond. Whatever you say. I will still love you.

Your friend,
Emma

She is in love with me? What? Has this been building all this time? We have traded so many emails and so many secrets and we message each other every day. She has grown to know more about me than most of my close friends.

But I never wanted her to fall in love with me. I was certain she just wanted to have sex with me, and maybe she also needed a

121

fuck-buddy. This is way too deep. I have taken this too far and now I must do something about it.

I pause a moment before replying. While this is my initial reaction there is something else that I feel. Elation? She is beautiful, accessible, and she is saying exactly what I want to hear. She is in love with me. I cannot seem to completely overlook what she is making me feel again. She is eating away my numbness and replacing it with something new.

And I wonder, she says she must not ask Eve if she loves her because Eve will punish her. What does this mean? Is she being honest to me about her relationship with Eve? Is she being forced to submit or is there a dominant side to Eve that is growing into something "scary", someone that will "punish" her. It bothers me. Is she in danger?

Date: October 10, 2008 8:46PM
Subject: Too Far

Dearest Em,

Your mail, oh Em, this has gone too far. While I am so flattered that you have fallen in love with me, you know my situation. I am married, love my wife and I have a child. I am happy. You have a wonderful life together with Eve and I never wanted this to happen or to come in between the two of you.

Here is what we will do. We will end our fuck-buddy world. You will love me ONLY as a friend. We will be friends that share secrets, support one another and inspire each other. The way it used to be between us. We will not breach this agreement and I will make sure this does not happen. I will protect you and you are safe with me. You do not need to worry about this any longer. We will not meet.

Work on your relationship with Eve and make things better between the two of you. I am bothered by the fact that you say that she will "punish" you. Is there something you are not telling me?
I will work on my relationship with Jessica. You are a great person

122

and dear friend. Let's continue as friends. I am so sorry things have gone too far and that you are crying. The last thing I ever wanted to do was hurt you. Forgive me.

xoxo
Jade

Date: October 11, 2008 5:32AM
Subject: Friendship

Beautiful Sweet Jade,

I will do as you say. We will end our fuck-buddy relationship and I will focus on working things out with Eve. You say this is your fault. You ask me to forgive you. No, this is my fault. I ask for your forgiveness. I know that I am protected and I am safe with you. You protect everyone around you. They are so lucky to have you. Everyday.

Last night Eve noticed something strange about me. She asked me if I was interested in someone else. She said that she knows me very well and she could see something was going on. I could not hide it. I told her about you. She was very angry and she punished me. She said that I must not meet with you ever.

Then she said she loved me. She rarely ever does this. I told you she is a strong woman. She never lets her guard down and now she feels threatened by you. We made love last night. I am finding her again and I am ignoring my love for you.

So you will take care of this. You will not allow it to go any further. I trust you Jade. I know that in a different situation, you and I would be together. I know this. But we cannot and we will not. I believe this is the right thing to do as well. Thank you for taking care of me. There is no other like you.
So let's continue as friends as you say. I hope to still hear

from you often.   Otherwise, I would miss you. Can you recommend any good lesbian movies?

Your friend,
Emma

I read this message, over and over. I should feel relieved, but I don't. As quickly as her love for me surfaces, it disappears in one message. How has Eve punished her? Enough for her to dismiss her love for me. How is that possible? First she confesses, and then less than 24 hours later, Eve confronts her. She feels threatened by me, and I wonder what Emma has said to her. I did not mean for this to happen, yet...

I am not a jealous person, but I cannot deny that I want Emma back. I feel something for her, yes. What is it? I cannot name it yet, because it is not full. It is undeveloped. But I do know instantly that I want her back.

No, I cannot think of this. I must act selflessly. I need to think of the best interest of my family, but something has crossed over in me. Unable to step back, I want more from her, but I will uphold my promise. Keeping it only at the friendship level, I must honor my integrity and uphold this promise.

I am struggling. My relationship with Jessica is also getting worse by the day. Resenting her more and more, it is eating everything good inside of me. I find myself often thinking of Emma. Why? Earlier she was not real to me. Now that we have had sex virtually, it feels different to me. Picturing her vividly as I wrote the fantasy, I could smell and taste her. I could feel her breasts against my warm skin.

My heart, which is always in place, is now pulled. Emma is yanking at my heartstrings, and then retreats as if it were a mistake. She moves, and she slips away from me. Leaving, but not really leaving me, it is almost worse. I sit here only with desire for more, longing for something that does not exist. Repeating my old patterns, I am aching for the illusion. Jessica has no idea of the complexity of my thoughts, and for the first time I cannot tell her. I am hiding from her intentionally.

I think of my son. How can I be taken away by this illusion? This building desire, I am beginning to feed off of it. Is this becoming an obsession for me? Emma is just an infatuation, and I admit that I am trying hard to deny the feeling that I want to win her back. I cannot do this, I promised her. I need to focus and stay away. Can I keep my promise?

I keep thinking of what she has brought out in me. This thing that was sleeping inside of me stirs from a long rest. SHE is almost awake. Can I soothe HER back to sleep? I feel SHE is becoming stronger than me and is certainly stronger than my rational self. Fed by my denial SHE grows. SHE is awakening. SHE is becoming.

And I know it.

8

Last night we went out for dinner, and Jessica and I hardly spoke. The silence was excruciating. We busied ourselves with entertaining our son by telling stories and reading books. When we spoke, it was in low, mumbled voices. Emotion was absent. The words that came were only words of decision: where to go, what to eat, and what to bring, but nothing more.

Friday nights after our son was in bed, we used to sit together and talk about the week or about the weekend. We would make plans. We used to laugh and enjoy each other's company. Tonight I feel the distance. Gradually we have been drifting night after night, until I direct my attention to this enormous gaping hole between us, made wider by our lack of intimacy. Our once happy relationship has turned into a ghost that stands watching us, unable to speak. Incapable of communicating, she can only stand quietly observing, helpless. Though we cannot see her, we both know she is there, stuck and longing for the impossible, to live again.

After dinner, Jessica was watching a movie, and I was on the computer typing away to my new friend Emma. She came to the table where I was sitting and said flatly, "I am going to bed Jade." I glanced up at her.

"Okay." I caught her eyes for the first time all day. She looked at me for a long time, bent across the table and came closer to me. I knew she was very serious and that she was about to say something I did not want to hear.

"I don't want you to come with us tomorrow to the birthday party. You and I are having problems, big problems, and I think it is best if we stop pretending that everything is okay when it isn't. I think we need to spend sometime next week discussing what we're going to do." She waited and studied my reaction.

"You don't want me to go tomorrow," I said flatly.

"No, I will be there with all my friends, and I just want to be with *them*. It's obvious...there's something wrong between us...I don't want them to see it," she said moving back to a standing position,

126

crossing her arms and looking decisive.

I took off my glasses, closed my laptop, and took a deep breath. "You have never just left with our son before. The other night when you went to McDonalds, you didn't call. You just left. We have hardly spoken all week. Are you punishing me? For the fuck-buddy conversation?"

"Yes, I am. You've left me, Jade. I don't know where you are right now," she said quietly.

I looked blankly into the distance and then to her. "You left me too, a long time ago. I'm so confused right now. I feel so far away from you. Have we reached a place where we aren't recoverable?"

"Not from my point of view, but I think you feel differently."

"I don't know... I don't know what I feel right now, let's just step back and we will discuss it tomorrow or Sunday night, okay?"

"You are running away. I feel it," she said, as tears welled up in her eyes.

"Let's just talk about it tomorrow." I couldn't look at her or her tears that were about to overflow. They would poke at me and ask me to give in to her. I felt a hardening and my emotion retreating, so I reopened my laptop. She looked at me, hurt and angry, then turned and went to bed.

Is it already too late?

Today is Saturday and I am still wondering if our time has passed. I am hollow when I think of it. Jessica and our son have gone to an indoor kids playground for a birthday party without me. Alone in a big quiet house, I reminisce about how this used to be my favorite day of the week. Needing to escape, I decide to drive to Haarlem and go shopping.

After parking in the garage, I walk down the narrow shopping streets into the town square where there is the "Grote Markt" or the "Big Market". I love Haarlem's town square. There is the "Grote Kerk" or "Big Church" that is standing proudly over the busy Saturday scene. Restaurants line the square and people sit eating or drinking coffee. Usually big heaters allow everyone to remain outside, even as fall arrives.

The Dutch love to drink coffee and people watch. When I first moved here, I was accustomed to grabbing a coffee at one of the many coffee carts in Seattle, and drinking it on the go. Sitting, having coffee, and people watching, was something I had to get used to, along with the very, very strong Dutch coffee.

Walking around aimlessly, I am enjoying the distraction of the busy market. You can buy fish, cheese, flowers, nuts, shoes, clothes, etc... The random smells and noises collide and isolate my senses. It reminds me to breathe on my own, without any other thoughts.

I love people watching as well. The typical Haarlem woman is very tall, blond hair, with blue-eyes and a flair for trendy clothes. It is a city filled with beautiful women.

They look like the Emma that I picture in my head, and I wonder if one of them might be her. Standing next to a woman that physically looks like her, I think to myself, "Could this be Emma? Is she that tall?" I wonder what it feels like to react to her smile, in person. Speculating about all of this, what is happening to me? I am looking at other women, and I am thinking about what it would be like to be with them.

One woman in particular continuously enters and takes over my mind, Emma. What do I do with this feeling though? It is consuming me and I am losing myself to this new person that is emerging. Who is it now that begins to inhabit my skin? I don't recognize HER. I am not sure I like HER, yet I cannot deny SHE is growing and expanding inside of me.

I admit that I want to win Emma back. SHE wants to win Emma back. SHE must always win. I made a promise to Emma by saying we would be only friends, and that she could trust me. I am about to break that promise. My competitive nature is enhanced by a realization that we have moved forward in our relationship. We have begun to meet at the edge of the abyss, and I am not certain I can return. Emma has tried to retreat, but SHE will entice her to come back. I am aware that I am losing control to HER, yet I am frozen.

SHE is the sleeping dragon inside of me. SHE has stirred, is now fully conscious and is moving forward with full intention. SHE knows exactly what SHE wants.

And SHE has no guilt.

Date: October 11, 2008   7:59AM
Subject: Gia

Dearest Emma,

I am glad that we agree. You will stay with Eve and I will stay with Jessica. We will love each other only as friends and will no longer be fuck-buddies. We will forget that ever existed. It is our agreement. I will keep it, and I will make sure you do too. So now, let's be friends.

You were asking me about lesbian films.
Gia is based on a true story. Have you seen it? Angelina Jolie stars as Gia and won a golden globe for her performance. She is outstanding in the film. It was on TV last night and I watched it.

It is about a wild, beautiful, young girl from Philly, who just happened to fall into modeling. Living out loud, she was wild and unpredictable. Haunted by loneliness, her random nature was her greatest strength and ultimately her downfall. Everyone was always leaving her, who could keep up?
On her first shoot, she meets a female make up artist, Linda, who is the only person that is nice to her. After the shoot is finished, the photographer asks if anyone wants to stay around and create art, naked.
Gia says she will stay if Linda stays. Linda agrees. During the shoot, Gia is jumping against a steel fence, untamable, while flirting with the camera and her new friend. The photographer asks Linda (straight-laced blond with a boyfriend) to join her. Mesmerized by Gia, she undresses and slowly approaches. It is a very sensual shot, two naked women attracted to one another but separated by a cold, steel structure. They reach out and touch each other, but cannot completely embrace (you can watch this online and also a very hot clip of them making love). The fence is a metaphor for all things that separate them. There are many.
Gia becomes addicted to drugs. When Linda is available to be with her, Gia struggles to overcome her addiction.

129

I won't tell you the rest, in case you want to rent it. The ending is very, very sad. Gia experiences the extremes, the best and the worst of life. Linda is the only thing that matters to her, aside from the drugs, but it isn't enough. It is a great movie. I could not stop thinking about it during the night. I think it gave me nightmares.

I saw this movie the first time about ten years ago. You see, before I met Jessica I was a bit of a wild child, after I moved to Seattle. I told you my bad girl began to emerge after Smith. Boundaries, what were they? Well, of course I did have some, but I did live a bit in the fast lane for a while. I am not referring to drugs. Sure, I briefly experimented a few times with some drugs. It was recreational, and infrequent. I never had the interest really. Drugs were around though in the party scene. Yes, I was a party girl, but not like that. I knew too many people that destroyed their lives with drugs and my experimental phase ended quickly.

In my wild child days, I loved hanging out with drag queens and going to dance clubs. I was coming out, and it was unbelievably exciting to me. Drag queens tended to gravitate towards me and I adored them. A couple of them lived with Sam and I, for a short time. It was entertaining, always over the top and we lived in one big funhouse.

During this time I was also ambitious, but did not know what to do with my energy. It resulted in me being anxious and occasionally self-destructive. I could go out all night, on and on I would go. The faster I moved, the more I felt like I was doing something important. I was not though, other than learning some very valuable things about life, people, about trust and deceit, life and death. Maybe I will tell you some of those stories one day.

After I saw this movie last night, I wondered what would have happened if I had not stopped moving so fast. I always felt that I was rushing through life. Dreams, big dreams as a child fed me and drove me as a young adult, yet tormented me. I was never satisfied with where I was and so it became a habit to move on, so quickly that most people could not keep up. I left where I grew up partially because of that reason.

The innocent girl from the Midwest was safe. Wild child in Seattle was not. I am very lucky that I met my wife who helped ground me. Could she keep up? Oh no, but she made me want to slow down a little, just enough. She was the one who could bring me

130

back. She helped me to learn to move more slowly with intention, rather than quickly and out of control. She helped me find a balance.

Anyway, I recommend *Gia*. I wanted to tell you about it.

xoxo
Jade

_____

Date: October 12, 2008   6:34AM
Subject: Gia

Beautiful Sweet Jade,

I am so glad we are still friends. Thank you for sharing this story about Gia. She was always moving fast, like you but in a different way. You relate to her. I can see that. You said you are always running very fast.

I went online. I saw the clip of Gia making love with Linda. You are right. That was a very hot clip. Gia looks like a girl who could handle me. She looked like a girl who knew what she was doing.

You say that you learned a lot in your days with drag queens, and you loved hanging out with them. Why? I don't know any drag queens.

You moved fast. You learned a lot about life and death. How so? What happened? Were you in trouble?   I hate to think of you in trouble. Although even at your weakest, you could handle yourself. You are a strong, smart woman. You could handle anything, this I am certain. Including me. Were you afraid that you would lose yourself? I am not. I know you well enough to know that you would not do that.

I never did drugs or go to parties. I missed out on all of these things. If I had met you in your wild days, I would have fallen.

You would have told me your adventurous stories and I would have fallen for the reckless side of you.

Things with Eve are going better. She is still getting over what I told her. I want to stay with her. She is good to me.

I spoke to my mother the other day. She actually took my phone call. She invited Eve and I to come and visit her. Eve will be fucking me with the bible beside the bed condemning our actions.

We will also visit my father and stepmother. I want to go golfing with my dad. He wants Eve to come too. Eve is good at golfing. We played a few times together but I usually keep this activity only for my father. It is not the same if I golf with someone else. Even Eve. I let her win. It keeps the peace. My dad taught me all of his tricks. How to hold the golf club, how to measure the wind, and also about practicing my swing.

Tonight I will have a special treat for Eve. I bought some new lingerie. She will come in the door and be unable to wait. I think she will fuck me on the living room floor. Maybe she will say she loves me again. I wonder if she could even one day lead me around with her tie. She has one. She wears it with a crisp white shirt and suit jacket.

You asked me how Eve punishes me. Silence. The silent treatment is so difficult for me. I feel so guilty because when Eve is silent it is because I have done something outside of our rules and our agreement. I have not been good and she punishes me. I deserve it. Sometimes she does other things.

Maybe she will bring me a rose one-day, like you did. Maybe she can learn these things, even how to make love. I need to think of how I can bring this thought to her. It needs to be her thought. I cannot come to her with it. I can suggest things in a way that it makes it her idea.

What do you think?

132

Your friend,
Emma

Date: October 12, 2008 11:18AM
Subject: Drag Queens

Dearest Em,

You have asked me what I think about Eve. I think you need to do what you need to do in order to make that relationship stronger. You know how to do this already. You don't need me to tell you. You will do just fine. I believe in you Em. You want her to do the things I did with you? Yes, I noticed this. You are learning. I do not like the idea of her making you feel so bad though. I wonder how else she punishes you. She had better not be hurting you.

That is nice you will visit your mother. This could be a real breakthrough Em. I am so happy for you.

DRAG QUEENS

You asked me about the drag queens, why did I love hanging out with them? Drag Queens are fun, dramatic and full of power, but deep down many are sensitive and sometimes insecure boys, who have found their voice by doing drag. Contradictory as it may seem, this is what I found in those that I knew well. Drag Queens scare the shit out of a lot of people, and they have a laugh over it. They are funny, smart and incredibly witty. Hearing my two friends banter on was like watching a verbal tennis match. You never know what they are going to say or do next. I love this unpredictability about being around them. Even when they are not in drag, they are still unpredictable.

I adored the two that lived with Sam and I. I loved to go shopping with them. At night, we did facials and masks, they taught me how to shape my eyebrows and all kinds of make-up tricks. Spending about four hours getting ready for a show, I loved to sit in on the bathroom countertop, drink martinis with them and observe as they transformed. Trust me, you have never learned anything about make-up until you have watched a drag queen in creation. Their face was their palette. Every evening they performed, the bathroom door would dramatically fly open, and a new work of art would emerge. I was in constant awe of their flair and immense talent.

One night, I was out dancing and this gorgeous woman came running up to me, hugged and kissed me. I had no idea who she was. She was a drag queen, but at first glance it was really difficult to tell if she was a real woman or not. As it turned out, she had been at our house the night before, but was not dressed in drag, so I did not recognize her. While everyone else had been getting ready to go out, she and I were lying on my bed talking. Only one night later, I did not remotely recognize her. I had an immediate crush, but I knew her boobs were not real and there was the body of a man underneath, so my crush ended quite quickly.

Another night, Sam and I threw a party and a bunch of queens and gay boys came over. We had the most fun that night. One of them, in from out of town, stole all my costume jewelry though. It was okay, because I didn't need it anymore.

After that time of bliss, I did see some things happen though. Things that were dissonant; harmony turned to cruelty. These things stole my innocence. I became jaded and streetwise very quickly.

My two favorite queens moved out and a gay guy moved in. He was a part time club kid and full time drug dealer, unbeknownst to us. After a month or so, he ended up in a bad situation, I think he started doing too much of his own drugs and had eaten away his profits. Eventually he could not pay rent to Sam and I. We let him get away with this for several months. By that time, I was not living there anymore because I had moved in with T, but my name was on the lease and he owed us $2000. We were forced to kick him out, and Sam suggested we should keep some of his things and sell them in order to pay the rent. This made the guy very angry and he threatened to kill us, no joke, and for a while I was afraid he would. Walking home late at night, I would feel like someone was following me. Who knows, maybe they were. I was cautious. Eventually it all blew over, but that was pretty scary.

I saw so many people around me disintegrating because of hardcore drugs. They make people do stupid stuff. They took over so many lives, people I cared deeply about.

One other friend of mine who only occasionally did drag came to me and asked if he could stay with T and I. He was homeless at the time and didn't have anywhere to go. He was giving up drugs and wanted to get his life back on track. I said he could stay, but if he did any drugs, there would be no questions, he would be out. He promised he would not and in the back of my mind, I always knew eventually he would again. I was entirely unprepared to handle the reason that drove him to it.

I loved this boy dearly. He was so, so sweet and I felt very motherly towards him. T and I used to tell everyone he was our houseboy. He loved this because it was a term of endearment and he desperately wanted to be loved. He ran errands for us, cleaned the apartment and some evenings, I would go with him to drag shows or out to the clubs. One night, I painted him silver for a performance and it was SO much fun!

Six months later, he was clean, still living with us and doing really fantastic. I thought perhaps he had proven wrong my initial assumptions. He was so full of life, and he was beginning to respect himself. Entirely transformed, I saw the change, and I was so proud of him. But then it all fell apart.

One day he went to the clinic and he found out he had AIDS. His family had turned on him a long time ago because of the drugs, so he had no one but us. He was so down, and he could not cope. We were unable to reach him and he started doing drugs again. One morning, he showed up after having been out all night, and I saw by his eyes he was tweaking. It broke my heart, but we had to kick him out. I cried for two days after he left. I felt so guilty, but I told him in the beginning there were no second chances in this situation. When I am burned once, the walls go up. Even though he was dying, I could not have a drug addict in the house, especially since T had some problems with drugs when she was young.

I didn't see him again, until about six months later. Walking on the street wearing rags, he was a homeless junkie by then. I was driving home from work, wearing a business suit, and I pulled up next to him in my shiny, new, black car. He was dirty and smelled of urine. The contrast only six months created was horrific.

I asked him where he was going, and he said he on his way to buy syringes. I looked at him with sad eyes and I said, "It's cold. Get in the car and I will take you where you are going." Sitting next to me was the shell of a boy I once knew. He was hopeless and his eyes were entirely dead. My heart was broken, but that was nothing compared to what he was. He was irreparable. He was dying, but I bet the drugs killed him before the disease actually took his life.

I hugged him before he got out of the car. I told him that I loved him and that I was sorry the way things turned out. He said he was sorry too. That was the last time I saw him. Before he had left my home, he had given me a poster-sized picture that was taken of him. It was his favorite and it captured a boy lost in life. When I looked at it, it reminded me of how I failed him. I regret, to this very day, I was unable to keep that picture, because it was too painful. I have no idea whatever happened to him and my heart drowns every time I think of him.

xoxo
Jade

Date: October 13, 2008 6:35AM
Subject: Amy and Rain

Beautiful, Sweet Jade,

Your life with the drag queens sounded so exciting!
Then you told me about the drug dealer who threatened your life. You tried to help him by letting him stay even after he owed you money and then ended up threatening your life? What a dick. I cannot stand to think of someone doing that to you.

The gay boy that you tried to help, I feel your pain. I think you know he must be dead by now. I think you still feel guilty about it. You should not. It was not your fault. You cannot be responsible for someone else's addictions. Jade, it is not your fault.
He lived with you and T. Do you still see T?

I was thinking about Amy. You told me a few messages back about Amy and Rain and that night of the threesome. I never responded to you about this. It was so erotic. I can envision it. What a very special moment in your life. You think of it when you read *Henry and June*. But I think you think more of Amy. She is still in your life, right? Are you

136

friends? Do you still see her?

I also would like to read *Henry and June*. You make it sound so appealing. Her words were like multiple orgasms. I like having multiple orgasms over and over. I wish you could have me in this way. I would give myself to you over and over again.

But I cannot say that or think it. So I will stop being bad.

Please tell me more.

Your Friend,
Emma

Emma is coming back to me slowly. Trying to resist me, she cannot. She will return. I will keep denying her and this will make her want me more. My sleeping dragon is tricking her.

Has this become a game for me? What kind of person would do that to someone else?

Date: October 13, 2008   8:03PM
Subject: The Illusion of Amy

Dearest Em,

Yes, you are being bad Em. Let's stick to what we have agreed okay?

I do still see T often. We are good friends, the best. I absolutely adore her, and I am so thankful that she returns my affection. T & I discuss business a lot, and we tell jokes. We accept each other's flaws. She is an amazing businesswoman and has achieved a lot in her life. I look up to her in this way, and she has taught me many things. Not taking myself too seriously is one of the lessons I learned from her. A lifelong friend, she comes to visit me or I go to see her when I can. I am so lucky she is still in my life. We are family.

137

As for Amy, do I still see her? No, she is too far away. But we do still keep in contact. Our conversations are the same, always passionate, always about life, books and other things. Did we honor our agreement to always be lovers? No, that ended when the illusion ended. Let me tell you more.

Amy had moved back to Seattle. I saw her often and we were lovers. We had our experience with Rain, and we would go out together. I would sneak downtown to see her. She lived in a terrible apartment that she hated and struggled to afford. I wonder if she was embarrassed about it? I don't know because we never spoke about it. I didn't care. Much like June, Amy could do no wrong in my eyes. I was attracted to everything that she was, especially the flaws. I wanted to save her and protect her, but I could not.

We did not have sex every time we were together. Actually, most of the time we did not. Just being with her was enough for me. You are right, looking back I thought I was desperately in love with her, or was it the illusion of her? From the moment we met, she captivated me, but I could never tell her. I could not let my heart get too involved. I knew she was straight, she had a boyfriend, and ultimately she would always leave me. As for me, I wanted to possess her, maybe because I knew this was impossible.

We were trapped in this illusion that we had both created with our passion for writing, reading and being with one another. We ignored everything else going on around us. When we made love, actually it wasn't making love, and it wasn't fucking. It was something different, something euphoric, erotic, and beautiful. It wasn't real, it was a consensual illusion created by both of us. And it was exactly what we both needed it to be. Similar to Anais and June.

The move back to Seattle was her break away from stripping. She wanted to better her situation but was not sure how. I encouraged her to go back to school. She was extremely bright, but she did not have the money. Amy could not pay her rent, and she could not make good money unless she got back into stripping. Desperately wanting out, she did the only thing she could, she ran away again, to California this time.

Again, I was left to pick up my life without her. It seemed empty to

138

me. I had no one to share my thoughts with, my dreams, or my inspirations. I longed for sitting across from her, her eyes burning into my soul, making me want to be everything and nothing at the same time.

You see Amy and I were so afraid of disappointing one another. The over intensity that we created, a life on the edge, we both knew it was merely something we invented. I don't think either one of us could face the reality. I wonder if Amy was afraid I would discover that she wasn't the person I thought she was. On the contrary, she *was* the person I thought she was. I just knew that she could never be with me. I was okay living in this illusion. I thirsted for it.

It reminds me of a few passages from *Henry and June* by Anais Nin:

"When we were together June said, 'You will invent what we will do together.' I was ready to give her everything I have ever invented and created, from my house, my costumes, my jewelry to my writing, my imaginings, my life. I would have worked for her alone."

"To think of her in the middle of the day lifts me out of ordinary living. The world has never been as empty for me since I have known her. June supplies the beautiful incandescent flesh, the fulgurant voice, the abysmal eyes, the drugged gestures, the presence, the body, the incarnate image of our imaginings. What are we? Only the creators. She *is*."

"Because I am not always just living, just following all my fantasies; I come up for air, for understanding. I dazzled June because when we sat down together the wonder of the moment didn't just make me drunk; I lived it with the consciousness of a poor poet, not the consciousness of the dead formula-making psychoanalysts. We went to the edge, with our two imaginations."

--all above passages taken from Anais Nin's *Henry and June.*

You see Em? She created her own illusion of June. Had I done the same with Amy?

Yes, I was still with T, but I knew I had created far too much damage in our relationship. It was ultimately getting close to the end. I felt guilty and ashamed for letting her down. It was hard to even look at her because I could only see how I had disappointed her. I still feel this way and I need to tell her I am sorry. I am so scared she will never forgive me. She is such a good friend and I am terrified to lose her.

A couple of months had passed. I was still with T and one day Amy called. She was in town with her boyfriend, the one she went to see in California. Would I come and meet them, she wondered. So, I did. I decided right away, he wasn't good enough for her. I hated him and I left them both at a bar downtown. I am not often a hater, but I despised him.

Another passage in Anais Nin's book *Henry and June*:
"Everything with me is either worship and passion or pity and understanding. I hate rarely, though when I hate, I hate murderously. For example now, I hate the bank and everything connected with it. I also hate Dutch paintings, penis-sucking, parties, and cold rainy weather. But I am more preoccupied with loving."

I can relate to this Em, I AM more preoccupied with loving.

How did T and I break up? Again, this is something I am not proud of. I was out with a colleague. She was a tall, leggy, semi-supermodel, who was smart as hell, and I found her incredibly attractive. She had the most beautiful brown skin and toned arms. She could out perform anyone in our office by pure intelligence alone. Straight but going through a divorce, she wanted to go out all of the time, and so we became really close friends in a very short time.

One night, we had been out at a bar for dinner and drinks. Afterwards, we went dancing at a club near my house. She and I never slept together. We never even kissed, but we skated very close to the line, but never crossed over. This particular night we both had a lot of drinks at a club close to my house. So I said she could sleep on our futon. When we got to the apartment, I gave her a shirt to sleep in, and she went into the bathroom to get ready for bed. I rested on the futon while waiting for her to finish cleaning off her makeup, so I could get ready for bed as well. I was almost asleep when she came out of the bathroom. She drowsily walked

140

over and climbed beside me, gently placing her head in my arms. Once again, here I was with a straight girl that I had a crush on, in my arms and wearing my t-shirt, and ONLY my T-shirt. No underwear, nothing else. I did nothing though. I did not even try to kiss her, not even after T and I broke up. I am not sure if she ever wanted me to, but I think she did.

Anyway, we were lying on the futon, she in my arms, and both of us almost asleep. T came out of the bedroom and tapped me hard on the head. I knew it. This was the end. I had no emotion, and neither did she. The "us" we knew had fully disintegrated. I got up and walked into the spare bedroom with her. She looked at me, or maybe she looked through me. She said, "You have to leave." I said, "I know."

And that was it. After three years, that was all we said. The next day I looked for an apartment and several days later, I left.

I moved into a tiny apartment and was single for a short time. I did not see Amy again until during this time. She came to me. She was single but dating, and so was I. This was the first time we had both had been available since the first time we met. Something was different, and was changing in her. Amy was beginning to settle down and had decided to go to school. She had taken a lease out on an apartment and had found a job. No longer the illusion, she was becoming real, figuring things out. She was making plans and had stopped running away. I liked what I saw in her.

We both knew we were on the edge of crossing over from our intense love affair that was so passionate, an illusion we both would cling to forever. We were bridging over to reality and we wanted to be together one last time. We said this would, in fact, be the last time we would ever to be together, and it was.

We made love this time. It was not erotic or euphoric. We made love, it was real, and it was fantastic. Touching her skin, looking into her eyes, seeing something so different made our connection even deeper. I kissed every ounce of her body and savored every last moment. I wanted it burned into my memory. Licking her soft breasts down to her tummy and hips, I moved my face in between her legs and tasted her for the very last time.

141

After she came, she smiled and said, "How can you keep getting better every time? Where did you learn to do that?" We both laughed. Reality had set in.

We went from an innocent Midwest girl & a stripper--- to a whirlwind perfect, beautiful, passionate, elusive love affair...our illusion...to reality, two friends laughing.

After I met Jessica, we visited Amy and her new boyfriend before we left for the Netherlands. She had moved to a small town in Oregon and met someone special. Amy and I talked about real things. We can always talk and there is a huge degree of passion still in our conversation, but now it is always something within grasp.

Josh was the first boyfriend of hers that I actually liked. He was and still is a nice guy. They fit together. He smiles a lot and jokes around. I like that very much about him.

Whatever happened to Amy? She got married to Josh. She went to school, got her degree, and she now has a very good job. She has a very high level of respect from her colleagues and has moved up very quickly in her company. She is proud of her accomplishments, but she entirely underestimates herself. She is an incredible woman that I know will do anything she sets her mind to. I am very proud of her. She is a true friend to me. I know that we truly understand one another, and we are still connected by the complex layers of each other, at a level far deeper than we ever imagined. I cherish her friendship.

I still covet the illusion though. I keep it in a very special place along with our friendship. I have a few individuals in my life that still have a little space in my heart with their name on it. Amy is one of the few.

That is my story of Amy, my Anais, who was really my June.

I will write you tomorrow about June. I will take you on the journey with me.

xoxo
Jade

Date: October 14, 2008 6:55AM
Subject: Lucky Girl

142

Beautiful, Sweet Jade,

Your story of Amy, is so heartfelt. You lived in an illusion with her and you both broke through that. You are still friends.

Amy was a lucky girl. First to take your real virginity, then she won your heart, now your friendship and a special place in your heart. Could I too have a special place in your heart? I should like to live with you in an illusion, one where we could be lovers, together. You could show me making love and many more things.

I am listening, waiting for more.

Your friend,
Emma

Date: October 14, 2008   9:22AM
Subject: June

Dearest Em,

So now we will begin the journey of Anais and June. Get lost in the words. I do.

"A startlingly white face, burning eyes. June Mansfield, Henry's wife. As she came towards me from the darkness of my garden into the light of the doorway I saw for the first time the most beautiful woman on earth."

"Her beauty drowned me. As I sat in front of her I felt that I would do anything mad for her, anything she asked of me. Henry faded. She was color, brilliance, strangeness."

"She poses for me as she leaves. I want to run out and kiss her fantastic beauty, kiss it and say, 'You carry away with you a reflection of me, a part of me. I dreamed you, I wished for your

existence. You will always be a part of my life. If I love you, it must be because we have shared at some time the same imaginings, the same madness, the same stage.'"
--Above selections from Anais Nin's *Henry and June*

These are a few pieces from the book. Do you see why it is so special to me? The poetic words, so many of my favorites, reach in and pull at my tummy. They tug and press on the spot that houses my creativity, opening the door and allowing my ideas to escape. I relinquish all power to her words as they penetrate every single secret crevice.

Do you understand Em?

xoxo
Jade

Date: October 15, 2008 6:33AM
Subject: My June

Beautiful, Sweet Jade,

You have shared Anais describing June, meeting her for the first time. I am not sure I understand it in the same way that you describe. The words are powerful. You say you lose all power to her words. I feel the same way.

When I read these words, I think of you. You are the one and I can no longer deny my feelings for you. I am trying to be good but you make it impossible. Eve would punish me if she knew how I really felt. I know what we have promised. But I don't care about the promise anymore.

Could we live in an illusion?

Your friend,
Emma

144

Can we live in an illusion? A thrilling rush of excitement pours through my body, she is back. She came back to me! She has no idea that, yes, I do want this! Now I want her more than ever.

Jessica and I spoke last night. She said that she wanted to "take a break". Now I have heard these words many times with T, taking a break is usually the beginning of the end. These are words I never thought I would hear Jessica pronounce, ever, not from her. She is always the grounded one. The one that is always figuring me out, working out how to handle me in ways no one else could. She knows me, and most of my many dimensions. Yes, she must know that "taking a break" would be the words that would make me leave.

It doesn't necessarily mean seeing other people, but it does mean separating. It means exploring if you want to see other people, and figuring out where to go next by having the space to decipher the issues on your own. Was she testing me? I didn't think so, but hearing this made me down, very down. Taking a break is defeatist. What am I going to do? There is Emma and she is back. She wants to live in an illusion.

But can she? Is she capable and deserving of the illusion?

9

Date: October 15, 2008   9:36PM
Subject: More June

Dearest Em,

More about June...

"We went to a sandal shop. In the shop the ugly woman who waited on us hates us and our visible happiness. I held June's hand firmly. I commandeered the shop. I was the man. I was firm, hard, willfull with the shopkeepers. When they mentioned the broadness of June's feet, I scolded them.   June could not understand their French, but she could see they were nasty. I said to her, 'When people are nasty to you I feel like getting down on my knees before you.'"

"When we walked together through the streets, bodies close together, arm in arm, hands locked, I could not talk. We were walking over the world, over reality, into ecstasy. When she smelled my handkerchief, she inhaled me. When I clothed her beauty, I possessed her."

"June who judges, selects, discards people with severity, who knows, when she is telling her endless anecdotes, that they are ways of escape, keeping herself all the more secret behind that profuse talk, Secretly mine."

"The intensity is shattering us both. She is glad to be leaving. She is less yielding that I am. She really wants to escape from that which is giving her life. She does not like my power, whereas I take joy in submitting to her."

"We went on talking. She is as affected by my eyes as I am by her face. I told her how her bracelet clutched my wrist like her very fingers, holding me in barbaric slavery. She wants my cape around her body."

"I have discovered the joy of a masculine direction of my life by my courting of June. Also I have discovered the terrible joy of dying, of disintegrating."

--All above selections from Anais Nin's *Henry and June*

Em, I will live in an illusion with you. I will be your June and you my Anais.

xoxo
June

_____

Date: October 16, 2008   6:24AM
Subject: June!

Beautiful, Sweet Jade,

My heart is racing. You signed your letter June. You will be my June! I am yours and I will submit entirely to you.

Anais writes like she is tormented by June. Is she? I don't think it is so. How can June leave her? And why does Anais feel like a man? But she says she enjoys submitting to June. I am very confused. Anais is the submissive one? I could never leave you. I am not capable of that because you do possess me. I cannot resist any longer that you are changing me. I am thinking of new things. You make me feel so romantic. You make me more passionate. I am lost in you. And I want to be your Anais.

How should I sign this?
Your Friend,
Emma (Anais?)

Date: October 16, 2008 10:13PM
Subject: Parallel Universe

My Anais,

You want to know if Anais is submissive. Yes, she is submissive to men, but June brings out a masculine side of her. Longing to posses June, Anais finds only anguish when she cannot. Instead, she can only submit to June. It is an internal dichotomy that exists deep within her heart and mind.

June leaves. She always leaves and runs away. Wanting to stay, she fears Anais will discover she is not the wonderful person she feels Anais has created in her head. She needs to go back to her world where she will feel comfortable again, the place she feels she deserves. In her mind, she is not worthy of Anais, but what June doesn't realize is that Anais *does* see her, accepting and adoring *all* of her.

June doesn't understand that by leaving, she actually provokes Anais's thoughts to develop into something far worse than if she would have stayed. Anais would have loved her, including her flaws, and they would have been lovers. Leaving changed everything. Anais moves on to Henry and in trying to figure out June, she finds something else with Henry. She begins to relate more to his terrible stories of June. Her adoration of June becomes tainted and this further plagues her thoughts.

PARALLEL UNIVERSE

You wonder if we can do this. Can we create an illusion? Yes, I can. Keeping our agreement, we can create a pretend world that only exists between our messages to one another. Emma and Jade are just friends. We will create a parallel universe, an illusion, where we are Anais and June. You will call me June and I will call you Anais. We will live an illusion through them, but you must understand one thing, these two worlds must never cross. We must keep them separate. Can you? I will.

You say that I am touching your heart. Do I want you? Anais, yes, I must have you. I have been resisting for some time, while in my mind I cannot stop thinking of your lips and your naked body. I

148

must have your breasts pressing against me when I am deep inside of you, making love to you. Your soft skin I want to inhale, so the scent of you will stay with me wherever I walk. I have this feeling for you. I have not named it, but it is there and it is developing.

A parallel universe will allow us to live an illusion, and then it will end. Are you prepared for that? I must know this before we continue.

And yes, I am changing you. I am showing you passion and if you are prepared, I will show you romance. And yes, I will spank you...it has been far too long.

xoxo
June

Date: October 17, 2008   6:48AM
Subject: Prepared for the Illusion

Beautiful, Sweet June,

You want to know if I am prepared to live in an illusion. That we will never cross over. Yes! This is a good option for us to stay in our real worlds and keep focused on our relationships. But we can be together as Anais and June.

You say you must have me. You make me love you. You command me to love you and you do not even say the words. But you speak deep inside of me. You enter inside of me in ways that are so new.

You will bring me so many things. What you say, it makes me feel love. It makes me want to submit to you and your desires. You make me feel romantic already.

You will make love to me. My pussy is yours. My clit is yours. My tits and my ass. They are all yours, June.

I am ready and waiting for you to make love to me.

Your lover,

149

Anais

Date: October 17, 2008 10:22AM
Subject: Making Love vs. Fucking

My Anais,

You are very curious about making love and are beginning to understand or feel those feelings that go along with it. Submit yourself to me and you *will* feel it. Let me first explain more about it.

Mental and Physical attraction must come first, then emotional. A related passage from Anais Nin's *Henry and June:*
"There are two ways to reach me: by way of kisses or by way of the imagination. But there is a hierarchy: the kisses alone don't work."

I relate to this, oh yes. There must be both kisses and imagination present in order for me to begin with a lover. I have found when one is absent it never works out for me and is a short-lived relationship. I realized this in Seattle. Both must be present, but equal amounts of each make for a perfect match for me. This is when I begin to feel connected to someone. In order to achieve making love there *must* be an emotional connection (and romance).

"I have seen romanticism outlast the realistic. I have seen men forget the beautiful woman they have possessed, forget the prostitutes, and remember the first woman they idolized, the woman they never could have. The woman who aroused them romantically holds them."
--This passage is from Anais Nin's *Henry and June*

FUCKING VS MAKING LOVE
Fucking is physical, and mental.
Making love is physical, mental and very important, emotional.

150

The acts are very different. There are two separate ways that we will be together. We will fuck a lot. Making love, not so often...remember it is powerful, sacred and it will be romantic, yet erotic in a different way. There will be no spanking, or fantasies...only a deep probing connection.

Fucking has a beginning and an end. The acts are raw, animalistic-pure physical attraction, and mental stimulation. To fuck well you must have physical attraction, but to fuck very well you must include mental stimulation. Hot! You already understand this, I think.

I only fucked men; I never made love with them. I am not physically attracted to men, so I only dated those whose minds, or something about their personality, allured me. Sex was mostly fine and occasionally great. I can come with a penis inside of me so it was functional for me, but I missed the physical connection. Fucking a woman opened up a whole different world to me because of the undeniable physical attraction I have to the female body.

In high school, when I would go shopping with my mother, she never understood why I never returned attention to the men or boys that would look at or flirt with me. I was not remotely interested. I think it worried her. She didn't notice that I was far more excited about going into my favorite clothing store where the very beautiful college girls worked. They gave me attention and pawed all over me, helping me try on clothes and checking how they fit. I flirted with them endlessly, although I did not understand it at the time.

After I came out, my mother and I were walking down Broadway and a pretty woman walked by and smiled at me. I stopped talking and turned around to look at her, as she walked past. My mother jumped up and down saying she had waited to see me react to someone hitting on me, and finally I did...to a woman.

So yes. I am completely physically attracted to the female body. Acknowledging this brought fucking to a whole new level for me, and I finally learned what making love was all about.

Fucking is raw...we use harsh words to describe it like pussy, tits, and ass. This is where we can also bring in fantasies like ties, spanking etc. When we make love, we will not use these words.

Making love begins with physical and mental attraction, but to entirely achieve love making, the way that I know it, there must be the emotional connection. The feeling builds deep and lasts. It does not end when one comes, it continues, sometimes forever. The emotional connection reaches far down, deeper than any other feeling, and creates this ache in your heart and tummy that explodes. There is no better sensation, an aching elation combined with a tender exchange between two souls. It is when two people connect at a level, without words, only feeling. This can lead to beautiful things, but it can also lead to a degree of craziness.

I don't think you have ever experienced it Em, am I right? I will say no more because it is almost time for me to show you. You have been so patient and I will reveal to you, if you are still interested? But first, I have to ask you one more thing. Emma is with Eve, and when Eve asks you something you must tell her, I respect this.

But with June, you belong to June. Only June. If Eve asks you to tell her, you must not. Ever. Em, can you do this? As Anais, can you belong to June and only June? I must know this one last thing. Can you lie to Eve if she asks you about me? Are you still interested?

xoxo
June

Date: October 17, 2008   4:32PM
Subject: Am I Still Interested?

Beautiful, Sweet June,

Am I still interested? Of course I am! I will submit to you June. I will lie to Eve for you because I am in love with you already, and I will do anything you ask me to do.

You will show me the difference between making love and fucking. You describe it, but I think to understand it fully you will need to show me. I cannot wait! I am sitting here just waiting for you to show me this. I am writing this to you while I am at work. You are all that I can think of right now. I mustn't say this. I am ready for you to make love to me.

I am ready for our parallel universe to begin. Where I belong only to you.

152

Your lover,
Anais

The dragon is rearing HER head and HER desire is overcoming me as I ask Emma to lie to Eve. I have made this request of her because, like Anais, I want to possess her. Although, I am not sure my intentions are the same.

She will lie for me. I wonder what else she will do for me?

10

A few days have passed since Jessica has told me she wants to take a break. Strangers living under the same roof, unable and unwilling to speak, the silence is stifling. Sleeping in the spare bedroom, I can hear her late at night on the telephone talking to someone, low so I cannot hear. I don't know with whom she is speaking. Maybe she has a lover? Is that why she asked for a break? I don't think so. It could not possibly be because she is not like that. It is most likely a friend that she is talking to, about our problems.

Our son does not suspect anything, although I think he has picked up on our negative vibes. He has been acting out a lot lately, and I sense he is aware of the distance. I cannot believe that love is escaping us.

After he is in bed, I go to my office and I am lost in my parallel world that is about to begin. I continue to obsessively think about Emma and I begin to wonder who she is. I wonder if I can find her? Will she ever agree to meet me, if I ask her? What would happen if we met? Would it ruin everything? Do I even want to? Or would I rather just keep this parallel universe, and cling to the fantasy? I don't know anymore.

And what about Jessica? My Jessica. I must not think of her right now, first I have to figure out what my intentions are. Emma is bringing something new out of me that I like very much, yet when I am conscious and lucid, something also scares me. She is putting something in me that is spreading and quickly covering every part of my life uncontrollably. Creating desires that I never realized could possibly exist, and yet, they only exist with her. No one else has ever generated this type of craving in me and that is why I am so afflicted by her. I don't recognize myself and I am not sure I like it. Do I actually feel these desires or am I simply writing a story that will entice her? I am fascinated by this journey, but in the back of my head it feels like watching a train wreck. I feel outside of my body looking through someone else's eyes, just watching to see what will happen next.

Date: Oct 17, 2008 11:22PM
Subject: Romance Begins

My Anais,

I am glad you are interested. You make me feel confident that we can live in a parallel world together as Anais and June. You will never tell Eve of this world, and you will belong to me and only me. Now it is time to show you romance and making love.

MAKING LOVE

Sitting behind your desk at work, a woman walks through the door carrying a large vase of red mixed with white roses. I choose your favorite flower because I will represent all things favorite to you. I mix my favorite flower in, because I possess you, and you belong to me. Tonight we will become one.

There is a note with the flowers and it reads:

My love,

I am thinking of you today. I am longing for the softness of your inner thighs, to lay my head there after making love to you. Yearning for your beautiful blue eyes, I will spoil you tonight.

When you return home from work, I want you to put on your short black dress. The one that is low cut, so I am able to see the top of your breasts peaking out. I will know they are mine, and you will see me admiring them all evening, burning to caress them. My desire will build, as I steal little touches when I can, and when you least expect it. I want you to wear black panties and a delicious bra that you will eventually reveal to me, when I ask you to.

Now inhale the flowers, inhale me inside of you, so you are full of me and there is no room for anything else, no other thoughts... only of me.

Xoxo

June

A NIGHT OF ROMANCE

I pick you up at 7:30 and you have on the dress that I asked you to wear with high heels. They create distance between our lips, but I find them, as I find you and everything about you, irresistible.

Walking through the streets of Paris, I am holding your hand to my chest, showing all those that walk by us that you are with me. You feel very safe. I can tell by the look on your face, you are not worried. The men, that would otherwise attempt to approach us if we were alone, stop and stare at us. You need not fear; we have silenced them. Feeling my breasts on the back of your hand creates a heat between your legs and a hunger for the moment that they will be uncovered.

We arrive at the restaurant, one that I have carefully chosen for you because they serve your favorite food. Our table is slightly hidden in a cove in the back. Here is where we can see the world, but they can only get a glimpse of us.

Sitting close, I reach over and pull your dress higher, well above the knee. The tablecloth covers you so that I am the only one that can see your bare, toned, upper thigh. I cannot see your inner thigh, but I am thinking of it, my favorite spot. Knowing that it rests above the end of your dress, just above where my eye can see, makes me shift in my chair. Mesmerized by your features, I smile, returning the warmness you exude. Putting my arm around your chair, leaning over, and whispering in your ear, "You look beautiful." Those words have made you shy and I find it adorable.

Throughout dinner, my speech is animated and dances around your heart, as I dive fearlessly inside of you. I have turned my chair around the table so we can look at each other better. You are slightly out of my reach and it enhances my senses. I am forced to reach you with my eyes. Dark and presiding, you cannot avoid them as we discuss travels and the book I am reading by Hemingway, *A Moveable Feast*. We discuss all things inspiring to us, foreplay of the mind.

During dinner, I present you with a gift, a small token of my affection. I had been walking through the streets of Paris one day, and I saw a necklace. The large round pendant caught my eye, in the same way that you did. Shimmering and astounding, I had to own it. I bought it for you, to find comfort that we are destined for each other in such a special way. The circular shape reminds you that making love has no beginning and no end.

You open it, and the emotional reaction across your face melts my heart and boils my blood. Walking around behind you, you lift your hair in acceptance of my gift. The elegance of your long, bare neck arouses my perceptions, and reminds me of the soft flesh

156

Anne Rice's vampires would feast upon erotically. I want to kiss it, gently in the back to give you goose bumps, and to make your nipples erect, ready for me later. I cannot resist as I place a soft kiss at the base, where it merges with your sculpted shoulder.

Sitting down, I pull my chair close to you again. Resting my arm around the back of it, I am admiring the fact that the beautiful necklace is lost beside your bright aura. You like that I give you the attention that you deserve and anticipate what the rest of the evening will bring.

After dinner, we leave the restaurant arm in arm and again your hand to my breast. Secretly bound... to me.

The rest will come to you in a message tomorrow.

xoxo
June

Date: Oct 18, 2008 6:01AM
Subject: Romance Begins

Beautiful, Sweet June,

I have never felt this feeling, ever. Again you bring so many new emotions to me. Your words are so enticing. Thank you for the flowers. You said something new to me in the note. You want to lay your head on my inner thighs after making love to me. I have never had anyone do this. I think it would be so romantic. You make me crazy with anticipation!

We are walking in Paris. I do feel safe with you. Bound. I feel the fullness of your breasts under my hand. Have you seen me looking at them? But I mustn't touch them until you tell me to.

I have never considered inner thighs so erotically as you describe them. I will spread my legs to give you access, so you can see. We talk. Your eyes are commanding me. I am defenseless. Knowing how much this pleases you makes me even wetter. I feel it seeping down onto my inner thighs. Where I know later you will lay your head. Near my pussy.

After you have taken me in every way that you want to. My pussy belongs to you.

Thank you for the gift. It is very special. I never want to take it off. You stand behind me. You can see down my low cut dress. Do you see my tits and nipples? They are so hard knowing that you want to feast on my neck. They grow even harder thinking of being naked with you. I am thinking of your mouth and your tongue sucking on them.

Your blood is boiling? This is so erotic! How exciting!

Your lover,
Anais

Date: Oct 18, 2008 10:46PM
Subject: Romance Part 2

My Darling Anais,

As I mentioned, first we will make love. We will fuck again later. When we do, I will replace your tie and the pendant with something new. I will have a very special surprise for you and I will ask you about your fantasies. I want to know them. I am thinking of your wet pussy and your big tits, and yes, we will fuck again soon.

But first, we make love. Do you see how my language is different when I talk about fucking? Remember, when we are making love, we don't use words like pussy and tits. It is more romantic than that. The words should be soft, gentle.

Before we continue, I will allow you to have something very sacred to me. Because you have been good and you deserve it. But you must understand, even in our parallel universe this is something no one takes from me, it is something I grant the few and chosen in my life. Yes, I have had a lot of sex, various people, random places, men, women, men & women, women & women. But making love, I have only allowed a very few carefully chosen ones into this world of mine, protecting my heart because it becomes involved with this act. If I give it to you, cherish it my Anais, be

158

devoted and covet it. I trust that you will. I am giving you the chance.

ROMANCE CONTINUED

After leaving the restaurant, we weave through the streets of Montparnasse. Hand to breast, bound to me...

I anticipate that you have a growing excitement surfacing between your legs and smile knowingly to you. The thought of your warm wetness, existing because I bewitch you, is so exciting to me. Knowing that I cannot touch you yet, forces my body to continue to respond to the thought. The fire is beginning to burn inside of me.

The fall breeze is chilling us, so I hold you tight as we walk. We are laughing and enlivened. Seeing your coat is too short and the wind whipping up your legs, I stop and give you my long, warm coat. I take yours. This exchange is gentle, as I help you on with my coat that embraces and protects you. My hand brushes against your breast as I close the coat, feeling your hard nipples...waiting for me. The flames are extending throughout my body. All the while I am yearning to undress you, for your softness, and for you to release to me. Seeing you with the pendant around your neck, wearing my coat, I stop for a moment and face you. You are my love, no one else's. Secretly.

It is just beginning to rain as we reach my apartment. Come, you will stay the evening with me. I knew that you would not be unable to resist my heart, my commanding eyes, and my desire for you. It reaches in and pulls out a passion that has been resting in me like a sleeping dragon that has reawakened. I feel your flame ignite, looking into your eyes, through the windows of your soul. I intrigue you because there appears to be no bottom. Once you think you understand, I will show you something new.

Tonight you are deserving of something very sacred to me, my heart. Our first night of lovemaking, yes, we have fucked twice before, as fuck-buddies, but this is very different. This is far more serious and my heart is now involved.

I have bought you new clothes, new makeup, a new bra and panties. When you leave my apartment tomorrow, I will have fully clothed you. You will spend the entire day in an outfit that I have

159

chosen especially for you. You will feel my warm embrace and tremble at the remembrance of the evening.

Standing in my apartment in Montparnasse, I turn on the dim lights uncovering my tiny hideaway, an apartment you have never seen. This is where I come to be inspired, and is where I run away to when I want to write. You didn't know? I love to surprise you. This place is sacred to me.

Two rooms and a bathroom, the place is small, but to me it is one large playground for my imagination. It allows me to grow and expand, filling this small, quiet space with life. You see a desk and notes written feverishly on post-its hanging on a board next to it. In the corner, by the desk, is a small bookcase with my very favorite books, writers that inspire me, ones you have often heard me mention.

Clean and tidy, the room smells like fresh flowers. You turn and see my bedroom, all white except for the artwork and pillows on my bed. Sprinkled throughout my room, German expressionism, Lempicka, Frida Kahlo prints and other small paintings I picked up along the way. There is always something emotional in them, sometimes dark or mysterious, and all pictures of women. A vase full of roses is on the table beside the bed, and I have put some of the petals on your pillow, just a few...calling you, all connected to me. Music is playing softly, all of my favorite romantic songs I would have given to you, speaking to you through the lyrics.

I tilt my head down and look up slightly. You cannot stop looking into my eyes that have now become fiery. You are spellbound, as they command you forward, and you move to me with no knowledge or control. I continue to call you with the flame that is burning and expanding deep inside my soul. Grabbing your face in my hands, I blink slowly and whisper in your ear. "I want to make love to you." The words seem gentle, new and profound to you.

Slowly taking off my coat, I admire your body. I reach down to where your dress meets your thigh and lift it carefully. I adore uncovering your treasures. Lifting up your dress, I run my hands over the beautiful curves of your bum and then over your hips. Further up your sides to your arms, you then raise them over your head as I ease off your dress. Placing my head between your breasts, I unhook your bra with one hand and it slips to the ground, finally revealing your precious, naked breasts.

160

I lift my arms as you carefully pull the shirt over my head. Standing in my strappy bra, our chests meet. Placing soft kisses on your nipples, you hear me moan in pleasure. I have been craving you all evening. This sudden release of intensity fills up the apartment and enters you.

I lick and suck your nipples as I find my way up to your face. Holding it in both hands, I look deeply into your eyes for a very, very long moment. The windows of your soul are clear, and your inner beauty is astonishing. You feel me communicating through the expressions on my face. Something funny in your tummy begins tugging, wanting to grow. Looking down at my chest you feel the wetness pour between your legs.

I pull your chin gently back up so your baby blues are now connecting to mine. Raising my eyebrow, I whisper in your ear, "You may kiss them." Moving your mouth down my neck to my full, ripe chest, the fire in you is glowing, red-hot as you kiss them. Running your tongue over my nipples, they are harder than ever before.

I grab your cheeks with my hands again, gently as you continue to devour me and I moan in ecstasy. Warm, oh... so wet between my legs, my body responds by dripping warm honey. Pulling you up slowly, I must kiss those beautiful lips. Mine are full and swollen, ready to take what belongs to them.

You open your mouth for me and I stick my tongue in slowly massaging yours. We are now scorching. And oh, those lips. A long, perfect kiss reaches the funny feeling in your tummy and allows it to grow. It will show that feeling inside a way to escape its captivity, releasing it to roam and explore. Butterflies, uncontrollable desire, fire, flames, we have entered each other's madness.

Looking at me, you see I am very serious. I am calling you, but my heart is retreating. You sense the inner turmoil and that I need to reveal something to you. You want to hear me speak those words... but will I? Can I? The rest of our clothes melt away into a pile on the floor.

Lying down on the bed, you spread your legs for me. Your naked body is submitting to me, and your trust makes me ache, as I see the growing anticipation in your face. Something is surfacing and it is very gentle and feminine, escaping from the depths of your soul. It is a feeling that you are unable to control, so freeing it allows you to fully surrender to me.

Your heart is twittering as your sweet spot is swelling at the thought of me entering you. The hunger you see inside of me consumes you. Studying every inch of you, I reach my hand between your legs. You are more than ready and the fire between us is raging.

I lean down and kiss your inner thighs. The skin here is so thin and it is the path to one of your treasures. I move up to where it meets your lips below. Pressing my tongue against your thin skin, I make you swell even more. I move over, just above your smooth lips, and you feel my hot breath teasing you. I lean down and place my mouth over your sweet spot. Licking the honey, I indulge in fully tasting you and reacting to your energy that is now pulsing with every touch of my tongue, as your hips twist from side to side.

Sitting up, my knees move between your legs. I have a special dildo for us, so we can both enjoy, called a Feeldoe. There is no harness. The small end goes inside of me and the other end has a larger dildo that will slide inside of you. It is wide and not too long.

Slipping the smaller end inside of me, I sigh loudly. The large end I rub slowly on you applying pressure as I massage you with the tip. Sliding it in, the vibrator pulses throughout the Feeldoe, representing our emerging energy that now connects us. I love this dildo because I feel like I am truly inside of you.

Savoring the moment, I rest just inside of your lips where you are so sensitive. Pressing further in, you immediately see the expression of both pain and pleasure. The pain is not physical. It is emotional. Inner turmoil. You feel my heart exploding as I continue to slowly slip inside of you, further bearing down, as our breasts press together. I moan loudly. You have never seen me in such ecstasy. Leaning down, I close my eyes and press my face in your neck. Inhaling you, I become intoxicated.

Pressing deeper still, I move my hips in a circular motion to touch all of your sensitive spots, as the vibration massages your g-spot. With my face above yours, you see something building, this time without fear. Diving into each other's windows, we are fully engaged. You arch your back, as I slowly move up and down with my hips continuing in a circular motion, all the while remaining

162

connected.

Our bodies are one. One beating heart, one burning fire, raging beyond control. Leaning down to your ear, I whisper without hesitation, "I love you. I am giving you my heart. Now, release yours to me." You feel that funny feeling expand throughout your entire body, it is love, and it is everywhere within you. This is the sensation that will last, long after we make love. When we separate tomorrow, this will stay with you, and will always link us.

Moving faster, every movement is intensifying. Continuing to look at one another, we are fully exposed and releasing. A bit faster, it is building. My breath growing heavy, my moans quickening, and my face showing you every emotion. Faster, moaning, breathless. My body is out of my control. Love has taken over and leads my every movement.

My back arching and retracting, you feel a power come over me as your every muscle absorbs it. Having wanted you in this way for so long, you are mine and I am fully giving myself to you. Hearing you come to me, cries of pleasure and the expressions on your face release me. We explode for the whole world to hear and take part in our pounding ecstasy.

Still coming, I rest my hand on the side of your neck gently but firm. I lean down and put my face on the other side of it. My lips are touching your delicate skin precisely where I kissed you earlier this evening. I pound intensely for a very long time, because I am inside of you, physically, mentally and emotionally. Holding me close you feel a vibration between us. It brings me more pleasure than you will ever understand. You feel my body tremble and react to the fusion. We are entering a new universe, one that only we have created.

You feel love more deeply than you have ever felt before. New and exciting, yes, it is our love. As I lie on top of you, I press softly, deeper inside a few more times to feel the remaining pulses of your orgasm, pure pleasure from you, translating to me. Bringing your hands to my heart, you can feel our new beat.

"I love you June," I hear you say. I see something change in the way you look at me. You are so vulnerable. I sigh once again. Hearing you say those words fills my heart and I place my lips on yours. Enjoying the pureness of the moment, I ache in such a good way. In the middle of this feeling, as I kiss you, I transfer it to you. It is now the aching elation that only we share.

I pull myself down and lie horizontal with my head on your inner thigh, as I told you I would. On my side looking up at you, I place my hand over your warm wetness that has now completely become mine. I play with your slippery lips, and I can smell your sweetness. The vibration continues to exist, powered by love.

You are defenseless to my touch and my senses. I will now take care of you and everything that surrounds you. I want you to sleep in my arms and together we are fully satisfied with this new feeling, this new us. Oh, we will play, we will fuck, and we will do many other things as well. But this has changed us; it has changed everything.

You should know...

My love for you will only grow and I will show it to you in so many ways. You submitting to me feeds my passion. I will do great things with it. I am committing to you, and you will have a place in my heart for eternity. Your eyes have branded your name in the space that is now yours and so sacred to me. Now, my love, I cannot wait to have you again and again, always with me, loving you with both "kisses and imagination".

This is what love and making love is.
Do you feel it Anais?
Confess to me.
June

Date: Oct 19, 2008 7:02 AM
Subject: Confession

Beautiful, Sweet June,

You have given me your heart. I will cherish it. I will covet it just as you have told me to do. And you have told me something very special. You have told me that you love me. I will never hurt you. Impossible.

Jade, I mean June, this feeling in my tummy. The one that you said has expanded. You are right. It has lasted long

164

after reading your message. I cannot escape it. What you have shown to me, I have never known love like this. I understand what love is now, thanks to you. You have taught this to me. And you have no idea how this has freed me.

You are dominant in a very, very different way. In a better way than anything I have ever experienced. I feel close to you. Closer to you than anyone. You do possess me. I cannot think of anything or anyone but you. You told me to keep this separate. I try, but I keep thinking.

I think of how you gave me your coat because I was cold. You take such good care of me. I think of your apartment in Montparnasse. I want to go there with you. You are a writer? Well, your messages to me, yes I can see that, but I did not know you write. Maybe one day you will write about me?

The roses, your artwork and the books are all romancing me. They are a part of you. I want to be there in that apartment with you so they can become part of me too. I want to take care of your needs. I want to lie on the bed reading your favorite books. I would look up and watch you writing. I would be there in sexy lingerie, spreading my legs and tempting you to come to me when you were ready. I will be waiting for you to make love to me again and again.

If only you could touch me, my Jade. I feel you dominate me but you are so gentle with me, my lover. I feel your love. I do feel love Jade, for the very first time in my life! We come together, and I have never experienced this. You are all that is inside of me now. You have given me an orgasm that I never had before.

You say you love me. If only. Your pleasure is all that I seek. But I feel the way that you love me and it feels so good. Just thinking of the way you made love to me makes me all wet right now as I write this message to you. I am sitting here with my colleagues. They are inches away from me. My patients are all around me. I am pretending to work. I am instead

165

squirming in my chair with my panties wet. I keep thinking of your beautiful ripe breasts. I love them so much.

In fact, I think only of you. I feel love, real love for you. I cannot feel anything else at the moment. There is no room for Eve. There is no room for anything or anyone but you. But I mustn't say this to you.

You say confess to you. I just have. But maybe it is time for a spanking.

Your lover,
Anais

I told Emma to confess to me because I sense there is a secret. She divulges that she loves me, and she is having difficulty keeping our relationship a fantasy. She is crossing over, yet, I still wonder, is Emma who she says that she is? Is there something more to her relationship with Eve that she is not telling me or is there a bigger secret? Some things don't add up, but I cannot pinpoint it. Maybe her flipping from a love confession, back to Eve and now back to me is concerning me. Is that normal? Is she playing a game with me?

There is more she has to confess. I know it. I want us to continue as we are; yet, my curiosity is digging from the back of my mind. It is seeping through and driving me to continue to challenge her commitment to me. Part of me wants to press her to reveal everything. Maybe she is already?

Can I try to find her? Maybe I can look her up on the Internet? I will need her last name to do research.

Her language is becoming softer as we are romancing. Is she really learning love? She says she felt love, and I believe her because I can feel her thinking about me. I am sure she never knew passionate love before. I expected that. Giving her my heart in the fantasy, does this mean I really love her? I have a strange feeling in my tummy, and the sensation from making love with her has lasted. Even if it was only in my mind, it has lasted. It seems so real! I have missed this connection with Jessica. Maybe I am transforming that love to Emma, because she is there for me. But where is the line between fantasy and reality? They are blending, and I am not sure I can recognize either any more.

What is happening to me?

Date: October 19, 2008   11:47AM
Subject: Remarkable

My Darling Anais,

I want to share the most remarkable story with you. I had been writing last night to you, Anais and June making love. While writing, I felt you enter every part of my being. I cannot possibly explain this to you. You see my heart does strange things. That is why I am careful with it.

This morning while waking up, yet still in a dreamlike state, I felt you behind me, and it seemed so real. I felt you wanting to touch my breasts. I imagined grabbing your hand, you spooning behind me and putting your hands between them. They were soft and warm. I was sleepy.

"Touch me, everywhere you want," I said. I told you to kiss me on my shoulder and neck, and to run your hands all over my body. My back arched, as I responded and pulled you close. You ran your hands over my muscular legs, up over my hipbone and around squeezing my bum. Feeling safe you rested your head on my back. It seemed so real to me.

The time was 7:02 AM, the very same moment your last message came in. I felt you Anais, I felt you thinking of me. Isn't that extraordinary?

And your message Anais, you confessed to me. I think you quite like disclosing to me. I love it. Little secrets, our secrets. I have a feeling there is more you have to reveal, but I do not need to hear anymore, at least not right now.

You will take care of my heart and only think of me. All are things I want and need right now. It makes me fall for you even more, but we must remember when we write, to write only as Anais and

June. Remember that Emma, so you mustn't call me Jade.

Knowing you are sitting at work, thinking of me, and getting all wet while no one around you knows what is happening, is very hot! Next time that happens, I want you to do something for me. Now, I know Eve does not permit you to touch yourself, but I also know that she says that no one else can have your pussy. You have given that to me, so I guess you are also prepared to break the rules for me?

Show your love for me Anais. Next time you think of me, masturbate, and when you do, think only of me. Do it at home, when you are thinking of me. If you do it at work, you risk getting caught. Someone accidentally catching you would humiliate you. I could never humiliate someone that I love. My emotions would never agree to this, never Anais.

ABOUT HENRY

Anais to Henry "Please understand, Henry, that I am in full rebellion against my own mind, that when I live, I live by impulse, by emotion, by white heat. June understood that. My mind didn't exist when we walked insanely through Paris, oblivious to people, to time, to place, to others."

"I am trapped, between the beauty of June and the genius of Henry. In a different way, I am devoted to both, a part of me goes out to each of them. But I love June madly, unreasoningly. Henry gives me life, June gives me death. I must choose and I cannot."

"He asks to see me again. When I wait in the armchair in his room, and he kneels to kiss me, he is stranger than all my thoughts. With his experience he dominates me. He dominates with his mind, too, and I am silenced. He whispers to me what my body must do. I obey, and new instincts rise in me. He has seized me."

--All Above Selections from Anais Nin's *Henry and June*

My darling, perhaps I am also your Henry?

xoxo
June

168

Date: October 20, 2008 6:35AM
Subject: I don't understand

Beautiful, Sweet June,

You tell me not to let our illusion cross over to reality. I will not, because you tell me not to.

You say that you thought of me when I sent the message. Well, I was thinking of you too. What you described, I would love to spoon behind you and to touch your breasts, bum, and kiss your naked back and neck. I would love to sleep next to you.

I feel so safe with you June. So safe that I did what you said. At home, Eve was busy talking on the telephone while I was cooking. I was thinking of you.

I went to the bedroom and grabbed Eve's dildo. Then I went into the bathroom and locked the door. I imagined you above me and stuck it inside of me just as you would do. I imagined you on top of me pressing inside of me. I came so quickly. I was so loud that Eve came to the door.

She wondered why it was locked. I told her it must have been an accident. I had been playing with the doorknob because it was loose and I must have locked it. I told her I stubbed my toe on the bathtub that was the moan she heard.

I tossed the dildo in the closet and hoped she would not see it. Later I went back, washed it off and returned it to its place. Eve would be very angry if she knew I broke her rules. I lied for you Jade. I masturbated just as you told me to do. I did it to please you and to show my love for you.

You ask if perhaps you are my Henry too? June, you are not a man or do not want to be a man do you? I do not understand. I am not sure, but maybe I misunderstood you? I could never sleep with a man.

Your friend,
Anais.

169

She went against Eve's rules and masturbated for me. I tell her not to let the parallel worlds cross over; yet, I am pushing her to do just that. She masturbated while thinking of me, and Eve was in the next room. How far is she prepared to go? I have been trying to create an interesting illusion, yet I feel something else crossing over in me. Am I trying to control her? Am I testing her love? Am I falling for her? Do I love her?

I am teaching her about love and in return she is falling in love with me. But why do I sense that I am slowly self-destructing? All I know right now is that I want more.

The Dragon is rearing HER head and breathing fire. SHE needs more.

Date: October 20, 2008   11:31AM
Subject: RE: I don't understand

My darling Anais,

I use Henry metaphorically. As Anais says in the quote, he represents life to Anais, and June represents death. Henry is domination in a different way. Anais is in love with June physically and she wants to be mentally, but there is nothing there, other than female understanding. So Anais creates her own interpretation of June, in her writing, where she magnifies her. It is mental, physical and emotional. Anais always makes love with June (in her imagination). She never fucks June.

She is in love with Henry's mind and his writing. He represents fucking, passionate fucking, but she makes love with his mind. If only she could combine the two, that is her struggle.

No, I am not a man, nor do I want to be a man. You know I am far too girly for that, but I do have a masculine side. I also have a very feminine side. There is no in-between for me, it is one extreme or the other. I also have a mind. I think you are physically, mentally, and emotionally attracted to me, and that I can both fuck and make love to you.

170

I want to represent life and death to you, the full picture. Do you understand? You will call me June, but you will love both the "Henry" and the "June" in me. You masturbated for me, and you proved your love. You lied to Eve for me. I think you love me even more than you say.

I am going to take you on an adventure so get ready for it. Oh, tell me a fantasy you have. Don't be shy.

xoxo
June

Date: October 21, 2008 6:48AM
Subject: An adventure, I am ready

Beautiful, Sweet June,

I understand now. Yes you are my "Henry" and "June". But I will call you June if that pleases you. I am very excited because you will take me on an adventure. I know I will learn something new. My stomach is in knots.

You want to know a fantasy of mine. Well, I really should not say, pleasing you is all that I need. But you have asked me to tell you. There is something I am curious about. You know I like to be spanked gently, not too hard. I also liked you tugging me around with a tie. Maybe if you tie my hands to the bed? I would never allow anyone else to tie me up but with you, I am curious. I trust you.

I am wet and ready for you. Take me, take me!

Your friend,
Anais

Date: October 21, 2008 11:38AM
Subject: Someplace Exciting

My Darling Anais,

You are so naughty, telling me what to do to you. Keep telling me as you are, but I will have to spank you. That will come later.

First, I want you to put on your a low cut dress, a new one I bought for you. It is revealing more…much more. It is also backless, and it clasps around your neck. It is bit shorter and high waisted, just under your breasts. What a beautiful, flowing fabric, it falls just below mid thigh. It is elegant, perfect for your curvy body and beautiful breasts. I will pick you up tonight. I am taking you someplace new, exciting, and erotic.

You open the door and I am standing holding one red rose in one hand, and in the other I have a small, wrapped box. This is the gift I promised you, if you were good. Opening it, you find a collar with a silver ring on the front of it. I bought it for you, and tonight it will replace my tie. Pushing the boundaries a bit, I wanted to see if this is another fantasy you might have?

I smile at you and raise my eyebrow. Are you ready for this? Putting the collar on you, you see I am dressed in all black and very dominant. My makeup is harsh, very dark, and my smoky eyes look straight into your windows. Now, lets go play!

We walk to a very strange part of town, where you have never been before. At the end of a dark street is a leather bar. I have never been here either, not to this one. Whips, chains, or the hard-core S&M stuff does not interest us. But there is something about an S&M bar that I think you will find interesting, erotic even. I want to show you. You will go with me to many places you have never been before. I will show you new things, and you will discover something unfamiliar all the time. Now, come with me and don't be afraid.

We walk through the door and are completely out of place. The regulars stare at us and shake their heads like we should not be there. Doing something I should not be intoxicates me. All eyes locked on us, we are outcasts.

A butch, leather dyke, with a whole array of silver contraptions attached to her belt, walks over to us. She looks us up and down, as if she is going to eat us. Then she says loudly trying to humiliate us, "Honey, I think you two are in the wrong place, you

172

better go back to mommy and daddy or the disco around the corner." She smirks as the regulars sitting at the bar all have a laugh.

I do not flinch, not one blink. Catching her eyes as she turns back around, I stare unaffected, with no reaction, and this intrigues her. Breaking the silence, I say with a very confidant air and inviting smile, "Oh, really. If you are so sure about that, play me in a game of pool. You win and we leave. I win, you buy us both a drink, and then leave us the fuck alone." Yes, this girly girl with big tits has a mouth.

Responding with a look of surprise, she becomes aware that she is supposed to be the one in control. She chuckles, scans the room at everyone watching our exchange, and says, "This is going to be fun." I pay for the round of pool. It is my pleasure. She racks them confidently and thinks, "A piece of cake!"

I help you take off your coat. You look fucking hot! I am entertained as they stare at your collar. Taking off my coat, it is clear you belong to me. The leather dyke shifts as we surprise her again.

After I break and nothing falls, she gets one shot, only one, and she misses. I run the table with ease as you watch each ball fall. I am enjoying constantly teasing her with my eyes after every shot, reminding her, I am not like any other girly girl she has ever met. Enjoying her becoming hyper aware that she has underestimated her competition, I confidently knock in ball after ball. She is realizing I am someone completely unexpected, who is capable of taking her power.

In between each shot, I feel you gazing at me. As our eyes meet, we lock into a silent exchange. You find a new level of my inner dominance growing and surfacing for everyone to see. As my last ball sinks, the bar falls silent. The toughest, leather-daddy in town just got whipped by a girly girl. I love surprising people, but I actually think you are enjoying it even more.

She buys us a drink, shakes my hand showing a sign of respect, and then she does leave us alone. We have now earned the respect of the bar, and are free to roam.

I have another surprise for you. Reaching into my purse, I pull out a leash. What, a collar without a leash? You didn't think I forgot that now did you?

I attach it to the ring of your collar. Leading you, only occasionally do you feel a gentle, loving tug as we move through the room looking for a place to sit.

Before stepping in to the bar, you felt uncertain about coming here, but I have shown I will always make it safe for you. You will find something interesting in the most unexpected of circumstances and unpredictable places. Being afraid of the unknown is wasting opportunity to grow. Venturing past your paradigm is where you will find the greatest gifts. Together we will do this. I am not afraid.

There are all kinds of attachments on the wall. It is not too hardcore, but there are some gentle whipping, tying up, and spanking scenes being played out. As we walk through the middle of the bar, people observe us. While we initially looked like we did not belong here, we have proven ourselves, and continue to raise the level of curiosity surrounding us.

Walking through the center of the bar we find a table in the middle of all the activities as we survey the scene. No staring, it is not allowed. Watching is okay, if done in the right way.

After a few minutes, I pull your barstool closer to me. Tugging on your leash gently until your lips are next to mine, we kiss. You are mine, but not so secretly in this place. I sense eyes all around us, engaged in our display of affection. Standing, I spread your legs, and step between them. Running my fingers over your cleavage and down around your waist, I kiss you again, our tongues playfully teasing one another. You reach up and touch my tits, which is not allowed. You are so naughty. I will take you home, spank you, and then I will tie you up. I will be gentle.

Back at my apartment I undress you, but I stay fully clothed. I bend you over the table, spank you and then spin you around.

"Take off my shirt Anais." You do, and I turn around and lift my long hair. "Now take my bra off." I lead you, by your collar, over to the bed. Gentle tugs only.

"Lie down," I command. You do and eagerly await my next instruction.

"Place your hands above your head."

Tying your wrists to the steel bars on the headboard, I see that, indeed this is a fantasy of yours. I tie them, not too tight, but tight enough that you cannot get away without my help. Pulling on them, twisting from side to side, this is tormenting you in an erotic way. The only torture that I will give to you, is that of pure pleasure. That is all that I am capable of. I am ravenous tonight.

174

I kiss and suck on your neck sliding down wildly to your nipples. Pulling you to me, I move my mouth down, and I can see how wet you are. I hover above your pussy as my warm breath makes you squirm. Brushing my tongue against your clit very lightly, you twist under me. I notice you can no longer take the teasing, and you must have my lips on your hard, swollen sweet spot. Pressing harder against it, I hear your heavy breathing and moans grow stronger.

Moving up your body, I place my breasts just before your mouth. I see you pulling, attempting to release. You want to touch my chest but cannot. Moving my mouth just above yours, I lick and suck on your bottom lip. I love to kiss you when they are puffy and soft, reminding me of kissing your lips below.

Rubbing against you, this time there is no strap-on. Spreading your legs wide, you wrap them around me. Cupping one arm around your ass, I lay two firm spanks on it. Immediately I see the fire in your eyes. Sliding my pussy against your warm wetness feels so good. Untying your arms, "I want your hands on me!" I say. You immediately explore all over my silky, smooth back, moving down to my ass, as you press me harder against you.

Lying back, I want you to lick me. Put your fingers deep inside me, and suck on my clit. You hear my moans, and feel my body moving with the rhythm of your fingers. They are long enough to reach my spot of pleasure, while touching my hard clit lightly with your tongue. I begin to move uncontrollably, as I grab a handful of your hair. My body becoming strong and tense, I release loudly and come as you feel the rapid pulses of my orgasm with your tongue. Pulling you up, I kiss your lips, your cheek, your earlobe and your eyelid.

"Get on top, I want to lick you," I whisper.

Straddling my face, you press against my lips. Your honey is running over my chin, while I am gently massaging you, tightly holding your ass. Pushing against the wall, while your hips are moving in a frenzy you come in my mouth, as I suck on your sweet spot, then I press my tongue far inside of you.

This is only the beginning. We will have many more adventures.

xoxo
June

Date: October 22, 2008 6:01AM
Subject: What you do

Beautiful, Sweet June,

June, my feelings for you continue to grow. How can that be possible? Even when we are fucking I feel such love for you. The new place you brought me to was such an adventure.

You got me a collar! How exciting. You are right, I watched you playing pool the whole time. I found it incredibly sexy. When you bent over the table I could see down you shirt. You know how much I love your big tits. You made me feel so confident. Usually I am shy. I would never wear this low cut dress except for you. I know you will not let anything happen to me. I feel protected when I am with you. I do like people watching me, but only when I am with you and I feel safe.

You took me home and you did tie me up and fuck me. Your teasing made me squirm. It made me want to please you even more. You had me lick you. If only I could taste you. Thinking of feeling the pounding of your orgasm in my mouth makes me so horny. And vice versa, I have been thinking more and more about this.
What are you doing to me Jade? I am not sure I can keep the parallel universe separate. I am trying. I am really trying, but I don't know anymore.

Your friend,
Anais

Date: October 22, 2008 12:23PM
Subject: Trust

My Anais,

176

You liked my "new place". I thought you might. It is a good place to experience and explore. You don't have to be full on S&M to enjoy the attitude of the bar. We will go many places together. I have a full imagination, and you have nothing to fear.

You say that you have deep feelings for me. My feelings for you are growing too. You are becoming a bigger piece of my life, and I am giving you a bit more of my heart than I ever imagined, which is okay with me, it feels okay. You are afraid. Do not be afraid...we can keep our parallel universes separate from reality.

Reality: We inspire one another; we are great friends. I love you as a friend. You are moving me to create stories that bring passion to my daily life. Our friendship inspires us to be better people and do great things.

Parallel Universe, our illusion of Anais and June: We explore our desires for one another, we make love, we fuck, and we have an amazing love affair. We are madly in love. This world is a secret to everyone but us.

We can keep these separate, and you can trust this. I want you to know that you can trust me, I have nothing to hide, and I will keep these lives separate.

Strange, I just realized I don't even know your last name. Are you allowed to tell this to me? I would like to know.

A LITTLE RENDEZVOUS

Let's do a little shopping and go to dinner, shall we? I drive you to a little shopping street that I know in Amsterdam, the PC Hooftstraat. This is where the wealthy shop and lunch in small cafes. It too is a place with attitude. Let's break it in.

Walking hand in hand, we pass restaurants where people are sitting outside, under heaters, having a drink. Wearing my tie today, I can give you a little tug whenever I want, and I will. My tugs are playful and I do it with a smile. Holding your hand, whispering to you, we smile as we walk. There is no question we are lovers.

I see a dress in the window of one of the shops. Try it on for me. Sitting in the middle of a large open room of mirrors, the dressing room is quiet. You walk out wearing the most beautiful, flowing dress, turning side to side to model it for me. Raising my eyebrow and smiling naughtily, you know exactly what I am thinking.

You walk over as I stand up and tug on your tie. Pulling you over, I kiss you. Only the gay guy behind the counter can see us. He watches, unable to avoid the heat. I ask him for scissors and I cut off the tags to the dress. You will wear this to dinner.

You return to the dressing room to gather your things, and I follow you. Coming in from behind you, I reach up under your dress and grab your bum. Turning you around, I stick my hand down the front of your underwear and play with your pussy. You are so wet.

All of those people watching us, as we walked by, excited you didn't it? I turn you around and pull down the top of your dress exposing your tits. Pressing them against the cool mirror while standing behind you, I reach one arm around and massage your lower lips. I still have my other hand underneath you, and I stick my fingers inside. Your body is beginning to remember me. It knows my touch and responds to it. My desire for you is full and you are incredibly excited by the possibility that someone can hear or discover us. Pressing hard against the mirror, you let out a moan.

You turn around and face me. Passionately, I grab you and push you backwards so your bum is pressing against the mirror. I bend down on my knees with my hands cupping the curve of your ass. You spread your legs slightly, as I lean forward and move my lips over your wet pussy. I lick your clit lightly as I pull you in to my mouth. It only takes a minute before I feel you come. I stick my fingers inside of you as I suck on your pounding clit. You come again quickly, this time on the inside. You make me so fucking hot! Standing, I move my mouth to your ear and whisper secrets. My voice is deep, soft and sexy. You smile in ecstasy, while finding comfort in my words.

Slipping out of the dressing room, I approach the counter. I still have your scent on my fingers as I pay for your dress. You emerge looking beautiful and we walk smiling, as everyone is unaware of what has just happened.

xoxo
June

178

My desire for Emma intensifies. I feel something new growing in me. I can no longer deny it.

I want to meet her.

11

Date: October 22, 2008   10:45PM
Subject: Seeing Your Eyes

Beautiful, Sweet Jade,

You say that we are great friends in reality. Yes, I want that.
But is that all that we are, just friends? I know the way that I
am feeling. I want you more and more. But am I allowed to
say that?

Jade, your fantasy was so hot. I must admit it made me so
horny. Oh, how you surprised me when you came in the
dressing room and what you did to me was so sexy. My hot
nipples were pressed against the cool mirror and I could see
your reflection. Behind me, fucking me. I moaned. I know
other people could hear. You say that I am fucking hot?
Well, you are so unbelievably sexy.
I am sitting here so wet. My clit is throbbing. I read it three
times! I am blushing as I write this.
Also, I want to tell you a secret. May I tell you these things? I
want to meet. I need to look into your eyes. Is this possible?
What would happen if we were to meet? I know you say we
are only friends. But could you keep your hands off of me? I
know one thing for sure. You are beautiful, so stunning. You
make me feel love like I never have before. Do you want
me? Can I ask you that? When we meet, I will be ready for
you. I will want to be yours. I am powerless in your presence.

My last name? Of course I will tell you. My full name is Emma
Simone Whitmeyer. I was named after my grandmothers.
My father's mother was named Emmie (American) and my
mother's   mother   (Dutch)   was   Simone.   I   loved   my

180

grandmothers very much. They are both dead now. But that
is why I have always loved my name.

Your friend,
Emma

She wants to meet me! She had to say it because I never would.
My heart is pounding as I read this email. Noticing she no longer
calls me June, she is no longer Anais to me. This is not a game. If
it ever was, I don't know anymore because I am consumed by it.
My virtual world and reality are crossing over. I am losing control.

Telling me her name, she is now real to me, and she wants to
meet. My earlier concerns have faded, and new possibilities begin
to emerge. Fighting them off, they continue to return, feeding on
my denial. Tonight I will look her up on the Internet, and see if I
can find out more about her. Putting herself out there, she is
risking her relationship with Eve, for me.

What are the consequences? Jessica has disappeared from my
thoughts. I cannot find her. Something in the back of my mind
continues to search for her, but I am compelled by an entity that is
far stronger. It muffles her voice, as I become more overwhelmed
by Emma. Jessica is a distant memory, and the dragon has hidden
her where I cannot see her any longer. SHE has only one vision,
and that is meeting Emma.

Am I prepared to carry through with this?

Date: October 23, 2008 7:33AM
Subject: Crossing Over

My Emma,

You ask me if I want you? You already know the answer to this. Of
course I do. There should be no question there. I want you. But
are we crossing over?

You are confessing your love for me. You are romancing me with your words, and I notice you growing more passionate. You are also giving more of your heart every day. You have learned making love. The feeling that lasts is beginning to make sense to you, and I see it.

You have been torn these past few days between reality and our parallel universe, and, I must admit, the edges are beginning to blur. You have written so many savory things to me.

The story in the shop made you very excited and swollen. This makes me long for you. I am in my bed right now, typing this message, thinking of you and wishing you were here beside me. If you were, I would type while occasionally glancing over at you with love in my eyes. I would brush the hair out of your face and wink at you. While writing, I would take your hand and put it on my breast.

Putting my computer away, turning on my side, and running my hand all over your body, I would admire every curve. I would take the dildo, and slowly put it inside of you while we are lying side by side with your leg over me.

Wrapping my arms around your hips and resting my hands on your bum, I draw you in to me. Slowly, we would make love. Putting your mouth near mine while holding my face, we would find our vibration again.

Afterwards, our souls unite, and we are unable to tell where one begins and the other ends. I grab your cheeks and I kiss your beautiful lips. I love you Emma. I love you so much. In my arms you drift slowly to sleep.

Reality. I am sitting alone in my bed. Feeling you. Think of me touching myself, thinking of you and writing this. Can you feel me?

CROSSING OVER

You say you want to meet. I have been waiting for you to say this to me. I want this to happen, but I am not so sure we should. You want to know what will happen when we meet? The truth is I have no idea. I am venturing into unchartered territory. I have never been in love with someone I have never met. Is it love? One of two things will happen. We will find we do not have a physical connection, and we will be friends. The other, we will find there is an intense connection, and we will need to decide how to handle it.

Either way, I do want us to meet one day. Not being able to fully picture you when I think of you is difficult. I have your pictures yes,

182

but it is not the same as meeting in the flesh so I can access you with all of my senses.

You are being very sweet and soft with your words. I like this surfacing in you. Our connection is intensifying because of it, and it draws me closer to the possibility of us.

You must realize that I also have a girly girl side to me, and I need to introduce you to it. The part of me, that likes to dance, is playful and is a sex kitten. I need to see if you can handle this side of me.

Get ready for our next adventure.

Before I go, you told me your name. Emma Simone Whitmeyer. It is a beautiful name and even nicer to know that it came from a combination of both of your grandmothers. Did you get to see your American grandmother often? You said your father ran a business. Did he get to go home to America much? What kind of business was it? Surely he could take some vacation?

Also I forgot to ask, but how did it go when you and Eve stayed the night with your mother? Did it go well? Did she put a bible by the bed?

I like that you told me your real name, it makes me trust you even more.

xoxo
Jade

_____

Date: October 23, 2008 4:33PM
Subject: RE: Crossing Over

Beautiful, Sweet Jade,

Oh Jade, if only I could be in bed beside you. It is so sexy to think of you next to me, typing away on your computer. Maybe you are writing a story about me? I could lean over and put my head on your perfect breast and play with your nipple. But, only if it pleases you. What you have written is

183

very romantic and it makes me fall deeper in love with you.

You are unsure how it would be if we were to meet. I am not. I told you the way that I feel about you. You feel us crossing over as well. I want so bad to see you in the flesh and feel your touch.

But I cannot meet you. Eve will not allow it and I have promised you I would not see you. If I did she would punish me terribly. Maybe even forever. But I am crossing over and I don't understand what to do about it.

You say that you have another side to you, a girly girl that you will show me. The sex kitten that likes to dance, interesting. I have never really danced very much.

I cannot wait to see what our next adventure will bring. What you bring to me Jade, with your stories. I love them very much, as I love you.

My father did not go home to America very often. You are American. Do you go home often to see your family? My father was always working. He owned a business, a factory. He did very well and then he sold it about 20 years ago. He made a lot of money when he sold it.

You asked about Eve and I staying at my mother's house? My mother changed her mind. She called and said we could not come because she was sick. It made me sad.

Your friend,
Emma

_____

   She says she cannot meet with me? She is being fickle again, just like when she confessed her love to me and then retreated back to Eve. What control does Eve have over her? It bothers me again that she describes Eve as punishing her "maybe forever". Is she in danger, or am I just reading too much into this. Maybe she is feeling guilty because I am married and have a family?

   There is something, I can hear it whispering to me. It is trying to catch my attention. What is it trying to say?

184

She is on the edge and is afraid to jump with me. She is conservative and not so adventurous so maybe this is why? I have taught her love for the first time, yet she is still resisting. It doesn't make sense to me. I thought she was powerless to me? What is she hiding?

I wonder if she can handle my Girly Girl side. Can she resist?

Date: October 23, 2008   10:29PM
Subject: An Adventure with Girly Girl

Emma,

I am so sorry to hear about your mom. I really am. Maybe she really was sick? Keep your chin up. Even small steps eventually lead to significant movement. It might be slow, but it will improve. She has a lot of years of negative thinking to overcome.

Your dad was a successful businessman. It must have been hard being over here and running a business as an American. He must have learned how to speak Dutch really well.

You say we cannot meet, you promised Eve. I understand. We will keep our Parallel Universe separate. It is better this way. Now it is time for an adventure. I want to cheer you up. Get ready to meet the girly girl side of me.

My Anais,
AN ADVENTURE WITH GIRLY GIRL
I call you on the telephone. I am working late tonight, but I have a surprise. I will pick you up at 10:00pm and take you someplace fun. Wear something hot; I want you to stick out. You will stay with me tonight in my apartment in Montparnasse.

As you open the door, you see a very girly girl tonight. I have on a dress. Short and tight, you can see my curves and I have on high-heeled strappy sandals and big clunky jewelry. When I walk, I strut, and I am tempting you to touch me. I want you to look at my ass and desire me in a different way. You have more freedom with this side of me that is more playful. "Ready to have some fun?"

We walk through the streets of Paris, and I hold your hand. We are talking and laughing, in our secret world, where no one else exists. I see people observing us, wondering if we are together. As we walk, I wrap my arm around your waist and move it down over your bum and squeeze. They know now, don't they?

We enter the dance club where there are both gay men and women pressing against each other as they dance. As we enter, the gay men flock to us, giving us a lot of attention. We chat them up and then leave to go get a drink at the bar. Finding a table next to the dance floor, it is on a platform so we can see everything and everyone. The chairs are high like barstools. You sit and I stand. Leaning over, I whisper in your ear while you feel my breast press against you. You have been looking at them all night, I see you looking.

"I am going to dance. First I want you to watch." I take a step back, wink at you, spin, and prance off.

I am always comfortable on the dance floor. The beat of the music enters my body and I am in a trance. People begin to move around me, some trying to catch my eye so they can dance with me. I avoid eye contact. I am looking only at one person. You are studying my body as it moves, my hips and my legs. Glancing at you and then away, I am tempting you. Do you want me yet? My energy is playful, yet commanding, as you begin to relax and enjoy this new place.

Coming up behind you, I press my breasts on your back, lean over, kiss your neck, and blow in your ear. I whisper, "Come play with me". You seem unsure because you don't dance much. I will teach you. On the dance floor, I put your hands on my hips so you can feel the movement. Our bodies know each other's rhythm very well by now. You sway with me as I run my hand over your stomach around to your bum and pull you closer to me. You are releasing your body to the music and begin to feel comfortable.

I can see your tits, moving slightly beneath your blouse. I take off my scarf and tie it around your neck, as I lean over close to your face and give the scarf a little tug. I have claimed you. You see this girly girl does things a little differently.

A woman approaches us. She has thick legs, a round bum, curvy body, big luscious lips, and beautiful brown skin. I grab your hand

186

and hers. I place her in front of you, and I move behind you. You seem uncertain, but I whisper in your ear, "It is only a dance so enjoy it."

She is with her bum grinding into you. I am behind you, pressing into you with one hand just under your tits and the other on your ass. She is a good dancer. "Touch her."

She turns around, leans close to you, and puts your hands on her hips. I begin kissing your neck and you close your eyes tilting your head back in response. When you open them, she moves in to kiss you, but I step in between and say to her, "Only dancing." She complies. As the music changes, I thank her for the dance.

Face to face, I run my hands up your body. Kissing your chest, I make my way down the top of your breast peaking out. The heat between our bodies creates a movement that is hypnotizing.

Looking at my boobs, I see you want to touch them. I raise my eyebrow and you know that with my girly girl side, you may touch them without asking. My very hard nipples show you just how much I want you. NOW!

Moving through the crowd, we see there is a line at the coat check. Waiting, I lean up against the wall and pull you in close, pressing your hips into my crotch. I wrap one leg around you and pull you even closer, as we kiss wildly. The woman behind the counter interrupts, "Ladies you best give me your tickets; otherwise, I am going to jump over this counter and join in!" She chuckles to herself.

As we walk home, I am burning for you. Escaping into a doorway, I slip my hand inside your dress and pinch your nipples as you moan. Your lips, your tits, your hips, your bum, and your legs...I am touching it all now. I slip my fingers up your dress and then inside of your underwear to feel how wet you are. Very. I open my coat and you know I want your hands all over my body. You suddenly get the urge to fuck this girly girl. Your desires are changing aren't they? You have never fucked a woman before? I will show you the way.

Rubbing against each other in the doorway you wonder, will someone walk by? The moment is heated and intensely erotic. My mouth over your ear, I whisper, "When we get home I want you to fuck me with the big dildo. Watch it go in and out of me." I see by your reaction, you are more than ready for this, and you will begin to crave this part of me too.

We get back to my apartment, and can barely make it through the door. I need you to fuck me, but first, "Bend over." I rub your bum and hold it tightly, as I spank you. Yes this girly girl can spank you too. But guess what? I want one too, playfully and just a couple firmly on my bootie. "Now, fuck me baby. Slow and soft at first, and then I want it very hard."

We tear our clothes off. Beginning to understand, you enjoy having more freedom to touch and be spontaneous. I like it very much when you let yourself go and submit to your own desires. You put on the harness and reach for the big dildo as I bend over on all fours on the bed.

"Put your hands on my ass." You do.

"Put it inside," slowly, this dildo is huge, no lubrication needed though, I am doing just fine without it. You put the tip of it inside of me and can hear me moan as my back arches and I press back hard on it. As I move my body, you see it going in and out, and you feel a tingling just below where the harness is. You feel like you are inside of me. You are fucking a woman for the first time, how does it feel?

Moving back and sitting on my knees, you are still behind me and inside of me. I lean back against you while pressing down hard. You are almost fully in. I feel your breasts pressing against my back and it makes me crazy with desire for you. I move up slowly so you are almost fully outside again, and then I come down hard and press you even deeper.

Your hand wraps around grabbing my chest. This turns me on, you holding my breasts while I can feel your boobs against my back. It is making me so, so hot.

"Kiss my neck, in the special spot." You will find my secret G-spot on the back of my neck just below where it meets my right shoulder blade. You know this erotic zone well. When I am kissed here, I lose all control. I cannot resist anyone who finds it. It is a pleasure-zone, but also a danger-zone and that is why I never reveal its location to anyone but my lover.

You are growing very excited by my movements, feminine and sexy, but still dominant in a different way. My back arches, I lean back and grab the back of your neck and hair. Pulling you close,

188

your chin rests on my shoulder. I put my cheek against yours and you feel my nipples harden as I am moaning, moving quickly, and grinding hard. "Fuck me. Fuck me harder!" My body shakes wildly, and my muscles tighten as I come to you, loudly, intensely, making a different sound than you have heard before. My body releases and I lean back against you, limp.

Sex Kitten. "You just made this pussy puurrrrr..."

Turning around to face you, you immediately know to suck on my nipples. They are so hard as you take them in your mouth and I moan once again enjoying the pounding of my orgasm. I lie down on my stomach and you lie down on top of me.

You spread your legs and rub your wet pussy on my bum. You think of how you just fucked me. Your clit remembers and you envision being inside of me. You are rubbing harder and harder while imagining your clit deeper inside my pussy. Grabbing a handful of my hair, you tug on it, gently. You lean down and kiss my neck and cheek hard. You see with my girly girl, you can discover new things.

You move beside me and are now on all fours. I spank you again and then I give you a love bite on your ass. Just a little one as I spank you again. Now I am going to make you come.

I want to lick you. Lying on your back, I open your legs, slip on top of you and offer you my nipples. You lick them anxiously. My tongue slips inside of your mouth and massages your tongue. Kissing your lips makes me want your other lips. I want to taste you.

I run my big tits down over yours, over your tummy and hips, down to the wetness between your legs. Rubbing my hard nipple over your clit several times, pressing your wet pussy with my tits. I can hear the noises you are making. Faster and faster I am moving as your clit moves over and between my tits.

I feel your body tense. Moaning and twitching, you come to me. As your breathing slows, I lift my body up, lie on top of you and spread my legs. Smiling at you. Naughty. Purrrr. I kiss you sweetly. You can handle the girly girl side of me.

And you know what else? I think you are surprised how much you like it, and how much you will think about watching the dildo go in and out of me. You want to fuck me as bad as you usually want me to fuck you.

And you will again and again.

xoxo
Jade

Emma Simone Whitmeyer. I am very nervous and my heart is racing as I open up my search engine. What am I doing? She trusted me with this information and now I am going to take advantage of her trust. I cannot believe this. What kind of person am I? What kind of friend? Is my obsession for her taking over my morals?

Darkness moves me forward, and I am aware of the dragon. SHE is here hovering above my shoulder, watching. HER eyes are glowing.

I want to know everything I can about her, this person on the other side of the computer. The one who says she wants to meet me, then retreats. Why? I have to have the answer to this. I type her name in Emma Simone Whitmeyer and click "enter".

The little ball is turning for ages as the search engine is thinking. It will not come up fast enough to satisfy my anticipation. The page populates but finds nothing. Then I type in, Whitmeyer, Fabriek (factory), Nederland.

I am shocked at what I find. I can barely breath.

12

Emma's father Christopher Whitmeyer was not a businessman at all. He was an artist. He and his wife lived in Amsterdam, but traveled all across Europe together painting pictures of beautiful women in Paris, Rome, Barcelona, Ibiza, you name it. Series after series of his paintings are displayed. They are exquisite.

His wife, Isabella was a sculptor. Christopher's paintings did not begin to sell until he was in his thirties. Their artwork was popular in the trendy New York art scene and sold for quite large sums of money. Selling all except one, Christopher kept his favorite painting of his wife, standing naked on the street in Paris, holding one red rose.

In her thirties, Isabella became pregnant and gave birth to twins, Emma and Erik. She and Christopher continued to paint and sculpt and were very famous in the Dutch underground art world. After having children, they settled down in a grand house they bought in Amsterdam-Zuid. The upper floor was their "Floor of Birth" inspired by Andy Warhol's "Factory". So, this is where the factory that Emma mentions comes in. In the summer, they would spend time in the south of Spain where they had a home close to Marbella.

I continue to read the biography of Christopher and Isabella in disbelief. Emma really is who she says she is! But why did she lie about her parents? Regardless, relief and a new brightness begin to emerge. I am thinking of the possibility of actually meeting her. Then I find it, the missing link perhaps. Overwhelming sadness and compassion spreads over me, as I continue to read in disbelief.

When the twins were fifteen, tragedy struck. Christopher and Isabella were hired to complete a series of paintings in India. The trip would be too far and too long to take the children out of school for so long, so they left the kids with their grandmother. Having finished the paintings in Bombay, they traveled south to Goa to hang out with the European artistic crowd. While there, they rented a motor scooter allowing them to easily explore the area on their own. The day before flying home, they were riding down a winding road. Isabella was on the back and Christopher was driving. As they sped around a bend in the road, they were hit head on by a car that was going too fast. Both were killed instantly. Emma, and her twin brother Erik, remained in Amsterdam with their grandmother. That is all there is online, nothing more.

Looking up Emma's name in the Amsterdam directory, I find nothing. But there is a listing for Christopher Whitmeyer and an address. An address! Perhaps the grandmother still lives in the house. No, Emma said that her grandmother was dead. Emma lied to me about her father's profession and again about the entire story of them being alive. Why would she lie about these things? To protect her identity? She has told me her name. Maybe she is in denial? That was a long time ago though, and if she is in denial, then she emotionally hasn't dealt with the loss. Is she afraid to leave this dominant/submissive relationship with Eve, who "uses her", for something more emotional? Would that force her to deal with her issues around her parents? Perhaps Emma still lives in the house?

I must go to see her. One look is all I need. Maybe it will end all of my uncertainties. Is what we have far more powerful than what she has with Eve, or I with Jessica? The question burns inside of me and I have to do something about it.

She said in her last message that she could not leave Eve. Giving her my girly girl side, I am curious how she will respond. I must also give her something exciting and romantic, more than an adventure. Something that grows from the depths of my imagination and that will capture her heart, compelling her to meet me.

Excitement pulses though my bloodstream, and I have a funny feeling in my stomach. I cannot eat or sleep. Oh God, I *am* falling in love with her.

Date: October 24, 2008   6:58AM
Subject: An Adventure with Girly Girl

Beautiful, Sweet Jade,

You have shown me something very special. Can I call your girly girl, GG? I should not ask. You might have to spank me? When I am with GG I can be adventurous too. Oh, and GG is such a flirt. She gave me a love bite. She is outgoing and unpredictable, this is so exciting. I have never done this before. Let me say, you are right. I like GG very much. Especially when she purrrrss in my ear and rubs her big tits all over my body. She makes me shiver.

Fucking GG from behind, this was new. I have never had such an experience. Pressing her back into my breasts and letting me fuck you from behind while grabbing your tits and kissing your cheek. This was also very romantic, fucking GG and kissing your neck. Jade, I want to...I have to say... I cannot resist GG. I love the other side of you too. You are right though. I like to fuck GG as much as I want you to fuck me.

I think you are a fascinating person. I can explore so much with you. You once said, just when I think I understand you, you will surprise me and there will be more. I understand what you meant. I see the dominant side of you, and I see the complete opposite in GG. Well, GG is different. You are showing playful, passionate and raw sex. Am I right? What more could you possibly have?

Jade, I am so in love with you. I cannot say that out loud, because it hurts. We have to keep it secret, I know. I wish I could see you, look into your eyes. I need to touch your skin. I cannot say such things. It is about pleasing you. But I do feel myself changing.

Your friend,
Emma

Date: October 24, 2008   11:59PM
Subject: Missing You

Dearest Emma,

I feel the distance between us and I am missing you tonight. Come to me, I am sending you a taxi. I want you to lie in my arms, cheeks against my breast with my hand on your hip. Sleeping, all night long with you in my arms.

You will always be safe with me. I will take care of you. Always. You know my love runs deep. My heart is vested. You are beautiful in so many ways. My feelings come out through my eyes and transfer in through the windows of your soul. They go deep down inside of you. I do find you a very special person, more than special actually, unique in so many ways.

What you say in your last message is inspiring. I see such inspiration and passion blooming inside the fabric of your words and thoughts. I see you opening up to me and to other things. It is a gift to watch you change and discover.

Now, I want to say something about what you said that pleases me very much. It reinforces my love for you and my trust in you. I know you love the dominant me. Good. I told you I am dominant. It is a side that has always been there, now magnified.

But my girly girl, or GG, as you have named me, (I like that by the way) is also dominant, but in a very different way. You are thinking about GG too now and I think you are falling in love with that part of me too?

I will always keep you guessing. Sometimes you will see the dominant side of me, and sometimes GG. Other times you will see one, but get the other. You will travel and do many things with both sides of me. Wait until you see our next adventure. I am writing it now. I know that you are smiling when you read this. You are beautiful.

More from *Henry and June*
"---but Anais, when I think of how you press against me, how eagerly you open your legs and how wet you are, God, it drives me mad to think what you would be like when everything falls away."
Passage from Anais Nin's *Henry and June*

194

xoxo
Jade

Date: October 25, 2008   6:46AM
Subject: Two for One

Beautiful, Sweet Jade,

I told you before you have a dominance I never knew existed. You make me feel so special and you are so nice to me. You love me in an entirely new way that is so much better than I ever imagined.

But you have said something very disturbing to me. The passage, from *Henry and June,* you included in your message scares me. The last sentence, "God, it drives me mad to think what you would be like when everything falls away." I don't want this to end Jade. Surely you don't mean that? Am I just reading too far into this?
I want to confess something to you. I have been thinking of GG lately. I have been thinking of how she took my virginity in a way. She is the first woman that I have fucked with a dildo. I liked it. Yes, I loved fucking her. You say that I can do things with GG. I cannot wait. I have more freedom with GG? It has made me fantasize about that side of you.

If I would have come over to you last night, and GG was there I can tell you what I have been thinking. I would have been lying on the floor. GG would bend down and kiss me upside-down. She would rub her big tits in my face. She would climb further and then press down rubbing her tits against mine. Then she would put her face over my sweet spot. She would rub hers all over my face and she would come when I stick my long tongue deep inside of her. She would make me come this way too. Sucking hard on my clit upside down.

I want both. I have two for one in you Jade. Thrilling!
And you are so right. I am smiling.

Your friend,
Emma

I find it interesting how she is responding to GG, and I find it ridiculous that I am referring to myself in third person? Am I bringing out a more butch side of her? It seems so because her language has a much different tone to it. It is also quite exciting to take her virginity, if only virtually. She said she is changing. Maybe I am teaching her love and giving her freedom? Is this what she is resisting? Why does she cling to Eve? Am I now fully involved? And what has she done to me?

I give her freedom while every day I am imprisoned, driven by the obsession of feeding the dragon. I cannot stop because SHE pushes me to the extreme. This has brought great things to me in the past but also great losses. It is a risk and SHE thrives on it. SHE forces me forward.

I have Emma's address programmed into my navigation system. She is exactly 27 minutes from my house. Tonight I will go to her. I anticipate she would arrive home from the hospital and would be getting ready to cook dinner for Eve. She must get home around 5:00pm. I will sit there, in my car, and I will watch. Hidden, but perhaps I will get a quick glance.

Will I knock on the door and surprise her? Maybe I should. Confidence fills my body, I know if she looks into my eyes that will be all she needs. Before I go, I will send her one more adventure that I wrote last night. She will read it at work, just before she goes home. She will be thinking of me. When she sees me, she will not be capable of resistance.

But, when I see her, will I want to be with her?

Date: October 25, 2008 3:30PM
Subject: Our Last Adventure

My Darling Emma,

You are scared by the last sentence that refers to when this all falls apart. I realized that if you can never leave Eve, as you say you cannot, then our illusion will end one day very soon. I cannot go much further with a virtual love affair that will never come alive. I too will move on. Let me be clear, this will end if I can never see you. As I said from the beginning, you must be prepared for it. Not now, let us have one last adventure.

First, let me make a few comments. Keep confessing to me. My GG likes the fantasy you had, yet is crushed because I know it will never materialize. GG will have to go away, she doesn't stay long. She runs away. And yes, you did have two for one.

Another passage from *Henry and June*

"By living as I do I am preserving our love from bitterness and death. The truth is that this is the only way I can live: in two directions. I need two lives. I am two beings."

Oh, how I understand this Emma. I am truly a Gemini. I have written another adventure for you, possibly our last.

ONE LAST ADVENTURE

I have rented a limousine and driver for the evening. Ringing your mobile phone, I ask you to come outside of your house. Happy to see you, I grab your face and kiss you. You look amazing. Walking over, I talk to the driver while you remain on the sidewalk. You like the way I walk and you can see my ass in my tight black pants. I know you are thinking of how you fucked my GG from behind last night.

Driving for about an hour out of town, I am taking you to a place more obscure. It is hidden in a woody area at the end of a long driveway. When we arrive, you see a very large building that is lurking darkly in the shadows of the woods. There are dim lights in the windows that produce a red glow, and it makes the house look like it's alive. You look at me, intrigued, and I hear your heart pounding. I take your hand to my breast, as I always do, to ease your excitement.

A man with a tuxedo and top hat opens the door. In a thick French accent he says, "Madam, so nice to see you," he nods, "and who is this lovely creature?" he smiles at you.

"This is Emma, she is only with me tonight. We are exclusive, Pierre." He nods. He will take care of everything for us.

The doorman opens the heavy wooden door and we walk inside. A beautiful woman, dressed in a flowing, deep red sari, comes up to us. Her big eyes are inviting.

"Nice to see you again madam, may I take your coats?"

"Yes, you may take hers, I will keep my suit jacket on for now," I nod.

She helps you remove yours and steps back, clearly stunned by your beauty. Your neckline is cut so low, revealing the curve of your breasts that is hidden underneath your dress. Catching her gazing at them, I make her shy and she looks down at the floor.

Approaching the end of the corridor, you see heavy doors that open, and a big man with a small list stands waiting for us. As soon as he sees me, he smiles in recognition and gives me two kisses, one on each cheek. "Jade, so nice to see you this evening."

"Michel, it is always a pleasure. Tell me, on a scale from 1 to 10, how is tonight?"

"An 8 maybe 9."

"Good, good." I look at you and wink.

"How are you tonight madam?" he nods at you.

You smile, "I'm very excited!" You have a twinkle in your eye that instantly charms him.

"I have picked out the best place for you both, one where you can see everything," he pauses, looking over his glasses directly at you, "and if you want, where everyone can see you best."

I nod approvingly, and slip him a large bill for the courtesy of the best seat in the house. He opens the thick, heavy, red curtain and we step in.

"You may notice that everyone here knows me." I see concern surface on your face. "The reason is because I wrote an article on this place last year. I interviewed everyone and spent a couple of days uncovering all sorts of secrets. You're the first person I've brought here…it's a very special moment for me."

198

You see my sincerity. You had thought you were one of many women that I brought here, because I knew everyone, didn't you? Now you realize, you are the only one to be my guest.

I offer you my hand to pass through the curtains into a very new world. Once a woman enters a harem and passes through the Gates of Felicity, there is no returning and the outside world ceases to exist. While we are here, reality will transform as we relinquish ourselves to a fantasy. It will disappear once we pass back through this heavy curtain, our gate. And, I assure you. We will depart.

You step through very carefully, and your eyes grow wide in astonishment. The room looks like the inner sanctum of a sultan's harem, the Hall of the Sultan. This is where he is pleasured and entertained. It is a huge square room and everything in it is covered with lush silk fabrics in deep reds, oranges and blacks. Even the ceilings and walls are draped in bright, dramatic fabrics. They cover the entire space.

I am watching you innocently discovering a new world.

In the center of the room, you see a circular stage. Surrounding the stage, you see a wide ring of canopy beds with sheer curtains that can be opened or closed. They all face the stage.

A woman greets us, and we follow her, circling the stage as she leads us to our bed. You notice some curtains are fully closed, some partially and others are wide open. The people are well dressed in mostly suits and dresses, all having taken plenty of time to prepare for this evening.

We are taken to the bed exactly opposite of the entrance. Everyone that walks in will see us. Standing at the front of the bed and scanning the room, we can see everything very well, just as Michel had said. We remove our shoes and climb up onto the firm but cozy, cushion. We will leave the curtain draping completely open, for now. I want them to see how exquisite you are. They will want us, but they will all know, by the color of curtains and by the rules, that they can look, but not touch.

Beside you is a list. Every bed has specific rules. Orange curtains mean the occupants are inviting others to come and speak to them. Deep red curtains, like ours, signify our exclusivity. No one is allowed to come to us. They can only speak, if spoken to.

We rest comfortably against the large plush pillows. I have my arm around you and my hand is on your naked shoulder. You are sitting beside me, leaning close with your legs bent to the side. I feel you looking at me, so I turn to you. You are stimulated by the thrill of the environment seeping into you. I am completely in control of this situation and you are again in a very unusual environment, yet safe and protected.

Leaning over for a very soft kiss, I touch my tongue on the inside of your top lip. You imagine how it feels on your clit when I kiss it. "We are being watched," I whisper. You become aware the room is full of people observing us, the newest and last to arrive.

There are women dancing in front of us. According to the rules, the dance is called Raqs Sharqi, translated it means "oriental dance", but we call it "belly dancing". Though you see their breasts and hips moving slowly and enticing you, you must not touch them, it is not allowed. Breaking the rules means expulsion.

Belly dancers have always intrigued me. They are so sensual yet hold a silent power through one mesmerizing dance.

The waitress comes to us, lays a silver tray down and places a bottle of still water on it. She also brings a basket with something wrapped in a red handkerchief.

"As you requested, madam," she bows.

"Thank you," I nod and I put it to the side.

The drinks are delivered along with hors d'oeuvres. Our waitress opens the bottle of champagne and pours us each a glass. All of the food served must be eaten with your hands, so they provide us with steaming hot towels that smell of lemon. I open one and gently wipe your wrists, palms and fingers. After cleansing mine, I feed you a piece of fruit. Taking it in your mouth, you bite down, and the juices trickle down your chin. I run my finger across your soft skin, scooping them up. Offering you my fingers, you take them in your mouth and lick off the juice. I feel my sweet spot immediately swell as I watch you suck my finger. I think of how you suck on my dildo.

I motion to the guard who stands near us. All exclusive beds require a guard, to ensure the rules are followed and that no one approaches. I ask her to draw our curtain so that the sides are closed but the front remains open. Looking forward we can see the stage and those across the room from us.

The lights begin to dim and shadows emerge onto the stage. Sitting back against the pillows, I spread my legs. You know to sit in between and lean back against me. As the show starts, my arms enclose around you.

The stage brightens revealing belly dancers, fire-eaters, contortionists, and heavily tattooed individuals, all moving together to the beat of a drum. There are two women with piercings and one is sensually tugging at the others nipple rings. It is one beautiful, fantastic work of art.

I whisper in your ear, "I see you looking at the women dancing and tugging the other's nipple rings. I think you like it?"

Resting my chin on your naked shoulder, I stick my hand inside the top of your dress. I cup your breasts and squeeze your nipple, as you watch the woman tug on the other's protruding ring. Your eyes close and the sensation of the moment shoots through your body down between your legs. Pinching it again, I kiss your delicate neck.

The music begins slow and then starts to quicken. As it does, the movements of the dancers become more animalistic, moving faster with the beat. The music grows louder as the dance becomes more intense. Swaying together as a tribe, you are mesmerized by the movement, as you indulge in my kisses and pinches.

Snatching the blanket beside me, I place it over your legs and hips. I slide my hand under your dress and between your legs. Massaging your inner thighs, my fingers then move over your wet lips softly. The music intensifies as their bodies are frenzied. They press against each other, licking and sucking. Moving wildly, they look like a rhythmic orgy. Intensely engaged, you are growing more and more aroused. Across the room there is a couple watching us. They can see my hand move underneath of the blanket, and the pleasure emerging on your face.

The men and women on stage begin arching their backs uncontrollably, pressing their hips forward, simulating an orgasm onstage for everyone to watch. The music stops. The light dims. I feel your hips moving, pressing your clit against my fingers and your breathing going deeper and faster.

I motion to the woman to close the curtains of our bed. One of the tattooed dancers approaches and says, "Madam, are you ready for me?"

"One moment," I say as I turn to you. "Lay over my legs."

With your bum just over my warm, private area, I lift your dress and spank you. Your bum is red, but it does not hurt. It is the perfect repetition of love taps. The people around us might even be able to see our silhouettes through the sheer curtain.

Sitting in front of you, I grab the red handkerchief. "Hold out your hands my love." I place it carefully in your hand. "This handkerchief is red. It represents passionate love," I say in a deep voice. "If it were torn, it would represent dying from heartache, but you will see this one is perfect, and there is something for you in it. Open it."

Placing it in your hands that are cupped together, you receive it as if accepting communion. Sharing intimately on a mental and spiritual level, you look at me with your curious eyes. Eagerly you open it and find a tiny ring with a stone on it. You look confused.

"What is it?"

"It is a nipple ring." You look up at me and I see the love in your eyes. They soften and become glassy. I have touched you. We are deep inside connecting, feeling the vibration of one another again. I speak to the tattooed woman waiting just outside of our curtain. "Now we are ready." She comes in with all of her tools carefully bagged in sterilization pouches and resting on a surgical steel tray.

I pull the top of your dress down exposing both of your breasts and I smile reassuringly.

"Which one shall I do?" the piercer asks.

"Her left. It is my most sensitive nipple and now it will also be hers."

Holding your hand tight, I see you are a little nervous. Watching her carefully, looking at her tattoos and drinking in the moment, it is overwhelming you.

"Are you ready?" she asks you.

You look at me for approval. I kiss your hand that I am holding and you nod. The needle punctures your nipple. Two emotions visibly emerge on your face, first pain, and then pleasure from the relief of the needle exiting. The piercer cleanses the area, then, provides you with instructions on how to care for it.

202

Once again you are mine, with something more permanent than a necklace or a collar. Every twinge of pain you feel in the first few months as it heals, you will think of me. Thinking of me, and our love, will take the pain away. The woman pulls out a mirror for you to see. You look at the permanent piece of jewelry that has become a part of you. Representing me.

The curtains are closed completely now and I pull the Feeldoe from my purse. Pulling up the bottom of your dress, I see your wetness glistening. You are partially sitting, leaning against the pillows. Removing my jacket you can see my breasts popping out of my shirt, as I unzip my zipper, and pull my pants and underwear off.

I lean over to your face. "Open you mouth and stick out your tongue just a little."

As you do, I gently touch my tongue on yours, while simultaneously touching your clit softly with the head of the dildo. Each time I touch it, I give and retract my tongue. Your whimper is so sexy.

I rub the dildo on your lower lips as my tongue moves around in your mouth. I slide the dildo inside of myself and then into you. You lay all the way back and I move on top of you. Pressing deeply, it only takes a few slow pushes for you to come to me. Your whimper turns to a moan, as I lie on top of you still inside. After a moment I roll over and lie on my back.

"Get on top of me."

You come down on the dildo and the other end presses deeply into me with the shaft massaging against my sweet spot. The vibration is hitting my clit and I can come easily like this. You surrender your un-pierced nipple to me as I lick and suck it. Sitting up you arch as you move wildly up and down on the dildo. I watch it slide in and out of you.

Leaning slightly back, your movement pushes the other end up inside of me. You see in my face, I am about to come. I grab your ass with my hands, pressing you down harder onto me. I release to you once again. A balance between power and sensuality emerges. You lay on top of me as we kiss passionately. I see you are in love, and I am loving you right back.

Reaching into my purse, I have brought underwear for you to put on, because I anticipated yours would be far too wet. I wipe your sex with another steaming towel. Then mine too. After dressing myself, I help you on with your underwear and pull up your dress. I kiss each body part softly as I cover it.

Opening the curtain the guard nods at us. "Are we ready to leave now ladies."
"Yes," I say, looking over at you. Your smile is big.

As we leave, we know the other people have been watching our silhouettes. They saw you on top of me, arched back with your beautiful breasts in the air, and a little ring dangling from your nipple...

We escape through the gates as our coats are returned to us. Opening the door, we meet our driver who holds a very large umbrella over our heads and takes us to our limo. The rain is pounding down hard. The smell is so fresh. It is cleansing.
In the limo on the way back, you lay in my arms, your head against my breast. Soft music is playing, as you drift off to sleep. I hold you gently, close to me. And I smile as I look down and run my fingers through your long, flowing hair.

xoxo
Jade

P.S. If this is our last adventure, know that I will miss you.

I click "send", put away my computer and go to my car. I have told Jessica that I have a business dinner in Amsterdam and it could be late. How late will I be? I wonder. I know I will return, but I have no idea how it will change me.

The car ride is relentless. A constant anticipation dances in my stomach. As I inch closer and closer, I run through different scenarios in my head. I think of seeing Emma walk up to her house. I will be seeing her for the first time in the flesh, a woman that I have had in so many ways, yet have never touched.

Fluttering butterflies in my stomach creep up through my body, when I think of knocking on the door. Will she recognize me?

204

What will she say? Will I get to kiss her for the first time? Will she invite me in? Will I take her there on her living room floor, on the table, and again in the bed she shares with Eve?

Just a few minutes away, I envision her eyes, claiming their spot in my heart. My love for her is expanding so quickly. Sober and lucid, yet, I am uninhibited. The dragon is flying high, breathing fire, and searching for HER prey with no regret.

Reaching my destination, there is an open spot on the canal. I am parked only a few cars away from the address. Initially I scribbled it on a loose piece of paper, but now it permanently resides on my navigational system. Permanent, just like my actions. I am baffled by my luck. Parking spots like this, in the center of Amsterdam, are impossible to find. Fate has created an opening, tempting me to claim it. It is 4:46pm and my anticipation pecks at me. I sit and I wait. SHE is waiting.

At exactly 5:15pm, I see movement in my rearview mirror, and my racing heart startles me. There is a blond haired woman crossing the road then she walks on the sidewalk across from my car. I crouch down and turn around to catch a glimpse. She passes, but I cannot see her face very well. I am hiding. If she were to glance over, she could see me. She walks past and now I see only the back of her. Fumbling in her pockets for her keys, her body shape is exactly as in the beach picture she sent to me. From the back, I am certain. It is Emma.

She opens the door of the very house with the address of Christopher Whitmeyer. "It's Emma! It is MY Emma." I am instantly elated to finally say those words out loud. This makes my fantasies real and my inner dragon's eyes are penetrating her. As suddenly as she appears in my reality, she disappears behind the door. My Emma, I did not get to see her face.

My heart is racing while my hands are shaking. Now is the moment of truth. I must decide what to do. What the fuck am I going to do? There she was, just before me, and I did not even get to see her. I have come this far. SHE compels me to open the car door.

I take a deep breath and I grab the package next to me. Inside the square box is my black tie, a gift. I get out of my car and move forward deliberately. She belongs with me and Eve can no longer have her.

Walking across the street, up the steps and standing before the heavy door, I ring the doorbell. Immediately, I hear footsteps coming closer and closer. I am about to face the woman that is in my every thought and movement. My heartbeat is rapid, but I am in control. I am prepared.

The door opens and I gasp. Standing before me is an extremely beautiful woman, far more attractive than I had imagined, most certainly the woman in the pictures. In person, her face is creamy and her skin, flawless. She is taller than I, but not by much, just a few inches. It is her smile, her lips, oh God those full lips, her body and the part that stuns me the most, her crystal clear blue eyes. Finally I can see her windows and I am lost in them. Oh Emma, it IS YOU! I explode from deep inside. My love is confirmed and she hasn't even spoken. I am standing here exposed and speechless.

Staring at one another, we share an intimate moment. Then she smiles at me, it is friendly, inviting and it melts me. It is one from someone you can trust and undeniably one of recognition.

Lost in her windows my inner dragon begins to command her. I curl my lips flashing her the naughty smile that I have told her about so many times. This is so familiar to me now.

"Hello Emma," I say in a deep, sexy voice.

Her broad smile fades to a look of confusion. Taken aback by her reaction, I realize I am about to hear her voice and the first words she will say to me.

"I am sorry, but do I know you?"

"Don't you recognize me?" I smile again knowingly.

She studies my face closely. "No, although you do look familiar to me," she says, "but you should know that I am not Emma."

My heart sinks. Fully confused, I tilt my head and say, "Emma Whitmeyer?"

"Oh...oh no..." she pauses, "you don't know do you?" She stumbles over her words and stops. She has a look of compassion on her face and her eyes grow very soft. "Yes, I look a bit like Emma, people used to confuse us all the time. I am so sorry to tell you, but Emma died about this time last year."

My heart falls into the abyss. I have jumped and fallen into the darkness. Tears immediately well up as my face begins to burn. I

206

want to speak, but nothing comes out. I am without a voice.

"Did the two of you used to date?"

I see how she is looking at me, studying my face, searching for recognition. She is so feminine and her genuine concern distracts me. She is worried about me, just the way Emma would be. But my Emma is gone. She is dead. But who have I been writing to every day and who has been responding to my messages?

Before I realize what I am saying I hear myself begin to talk. "Yes, I used to be together with Emma, but that was a long time ago." I lie.

"Oh my...I...I am so sorry you had to find out like this. Would you like to come in? Maybe have a cup of coffee and talk about it?"

"No, I can't stay." Fighting back the tears, I hear myself speaking again, but unaware of the words that are coming forward.

"But Emma used to live here? If you don't mind my asking, who are you? You look so much like her, are you a relative?"

"No, I am her brother's wife. My name is Eve."

A spear has fallen from the sky and landed through my chest. I am crumbling right before her. Snapping into reality, I see her reacting to the shock on my face. I struggle to hold back my emotion.

"You must know Erik, her brother?" she says.

"No, I'm afraid not." I barely manage the words. "I'm sorry, but I must go, I am sorry to have bothered you. I'm so sorry, I am very upset and I must go. Thank you so much for being so kind. I'm so sorry, Eve. You seem like such a nice person." Backing down the stairs in denial, I turn and run to my car. I hear her in the background, a small voice echoing through the fog in my head. She is asking my name.

As I reach my car, tears pour down my face. Jumping inside, the keys fall to the floor. Frantically, I pick them up and try to find the ignition. I need to leave before Erik comes home. Erik. Oh... OH MY GOD! I start my car and tear out of my parking spot, driving like a mad person. My overflowing tears are shielding my view, and my thoughts are flooded with only one statement. Ultimately, I now know the truth.

Erik IS Emma.
And Eve reminds me of her.

13

I don't remember the drive home. Unsure of how I made it out of Amsterdam, I only know that I was shaking and crying the entire way home. My thoughts were clouded and I was disoriented.

Managing to compose myself about ten minutes away from my house, I become hyper-aware of my appearance. I must look a mess. Pulling down the mirror, I cringe at the reflection. Streaks of mascara running down, my face is red, swollen and my eyelids are puffy. I can never deny crying, my eyelids always expose me. Forced to compose myself, I know Jessica will want to know what the hell is wrong with me. I have nothing to say, but the truth.

I pull into the drive and Jessica's car is gone. A sense of relief washes through me as I stumble out of the car. Turning off the wireless house alarm, I open the door. Hearing the alarm disarm, it is safe to go inside. We recently got the system and it is extremely loud, so I try to avoid setting it off at all costs.

The house is quiet, dark and there is no note. I check my messages and I hear Jessica's voice saying she will spend the night at her parent's house with our son. With very little strength left, I am relieved because I am entirely unprepared to tell her tonight.

In the kitchen, I open the refrigerator, pour a glass of white wine and guzzle it halfway down in one big gulp. Picking up my laptop, I decide to go upstairs to my bedroom. It is only 7:30pm, and my insides are beaten and bruised. My heart aches as every inch of my body is pummeled by denial. I lie on the bed, on my back, and stare blankly at our high ceilings, trying to process all that has just happened. Everything has changed.

My anger swells remembering that Emma promised me she would take care of my heart. She lied to me. She lied about everything! Why would a person do that to another human being? This has all been just a game to her. She was never in love with me.

I have to stop saying "she". Emma is dead. How can someone who never existed be dead? That is the worse part. I thought I was creating this illusion where Emma and I could be together. I was tricking her to leave Eve and come to me. Only as it turns out, the joke is on me. Emma *is* the illusion. The ultimate illusion, and she, I mean he, played me.

Emma has to be replaced with Erik in my mind. I can barely bring myself to even think of his name. It seems so foreign to me. It doesn't belong in my vocabulary. He has been misplaced here in my world and is someone I do not know and never want to.

The virtual sex, I feel nauseous, sick. I have been having sex with a man. Virtually, but nonetheless, all of those fantasies disintegrate with the thought of a man entering the picture. I think of all the times "she" said "she" was wet, *he* must have had a hard on. Running to the bathroom, I throw up in the toilet, an expulsion of toxic truths.

Anger continues to build at the thought of him taking advantage of me. He used *me*! I detest him. What a sick motherfucker! And yet, I cannot help but wonder...why?

Habitually I open up my laptop and log in to check my messages on MyLIFESeeker. My heart races at first, wondering what Emma will say. Wait...there is no Emma. I am filled with sorrow because I know that she will no longer be there. Actually, she will be, but never in the same way.

I see that I have one new message. It is from her...him.

Date: October 25, 2008 4:46PM
Subject: Meeting You

Beautiful, Sweet Jade,

My sweet Jade. You have taken me on this adventure. It is so exciting, romantic, sexy, all of these things. Everything you have done to me is such an amazing experience. I feel it is real. You took me to such a special place. You made me feel so safe.

You gave me a nipple ring to further bind us. I am bound to you already.

210

Yes, you are right. I did enjoy this very much. It was completely erotic. Is it a real place? I would love to go there with you sometime. I am the only one you chose to bring there? I am so grateful for all the things you do to me. You spoil me.

You made me so excited that I am sitting here so wet. I have to message you back. Immediately. Let me tell you why.

Because you said something so serious to me that it scares me. You will leave me because I will not leave Eve. This is our last adventure together? My heart is breaking and I am holding back the tears as I write this. I can only think of you and how I want you now, more than ever.

Jade, you are consuming my thoughts. I am torn inside. You do represent life and death to me. You give and teach me so much. With you I live. Not being able to be with you is death to me. We are Anais and June. But I have something very important to say.

I will meet you because I can no longer deny you. I cannot lose you. I am so in love with you. I would do anything for you, including leave Eve. I know I will risk a lot by meeting you. It terrifies me actually. The thought of losing you is unbearable. You will see what a naughty girl I have been when you see me.

I am so afraid. Losing you would be death and I know meeting you will also be death. You might not want me, you said it, you are unsure. You tell me when and where we will meet. I will be there. Know this. My love for you is real. More real than you could ever imagine and as for me, I want only you, but it isn't up to me.

Let there be no doubt in your mind. I am ready to give myself entirely to you. I want to please you and only you.

Your friend,
Emma

_____

I won. She says she wants to meet me, and she will leave Eve. Bittersweet triumph flows through my body. The game is mine, and I can leave this mess behind. Though ultimately, I have lost more than I can admit. She is terrified that I might not want her, really?

He has got that right; I will never meet him. Pulling at me, I wonder if this is Erik talking? Does he really want to meet me? Is he really in love with me or is he still playing the game? This is so fucked up. Unable to distinguish the two, Emma and Erik are somehow one in my mind.

The email was sent at 4:46pm this evening. Strange that this was the very moment I arrived at Emma's house, Erik's house. It still makes my stomach turn to think "she" is really "he". Emma is dead and I need time to mourn. I must give birth to Erik as a separate person, and be able to separate the two in my mind. Disintegrating into my bed, I am certain there will be nothing left of me in the morning.

Drifting off to sleep, the evening's events surge through my mind. I am fading into my subconscious when it happens. Sitting up very straight in bed, it is completely black outside, and the house is silent. My heart is racing, pounding out of my chest, as sheer terror encapsulates my body. One piece of information that I have overlooked: my box, with the black tie. The one that I carried to the door to give to Emma, I must have left it in the car, didn't I?

Hurtling down the stairs, I grab the keys on the table, and force myself through the front door into the pouring rain. The crisp air stings my face, as I open the door and search my car frantically. The box is not there.

Sinking into the passenger seat and denying my carelessness, I attempt to replay my actions. I must have dropped it as I was leaving. Think Jade, you must remember! I don't recall putting it back in the car. It must have fallen to the ground as I turned to run to my car! What have I done? The magnitude of my actions suffocates me, as I am forced to face a new reality.

In the box, along with the tie, I included a piece of paper. The paper contains my full name, address and phone number.

It was part of the gift.

14

I wake to the sound of my son's voice. Disoriented, I look at the clock. Ten o'clock? I must have fallen asleep around 4:00am, after staying up late, trying to figure out what I was going to do. I fear for the safety of my family, as my secret world is crumbling into a nightmare.

I went online last night and booked a three-night getaway at a resort a couple of hours away from my house. I had to figure out a way to get my family out of the house to safety. I need time to clear my head and figure out a plan. I don't know who Erik is and more importantly what he is capable of.

Luckily it is fall break this week, so we can get away without taking my son out of school. I just need to get Jessica on-board and agree to the mini vacation without telling her what is going on. We are essentially strangers right now, who are "on a break", so I know this will not be easy. Jumping out of bed, I run down the stairs as Jessica is just coming through the door.

"Take off your coat and hang it up please. Shoes off too and put them nicely in the hallway," Jessica says. I come to the end of the stairway and I connect to her with an "I'm sorry" smile. She looks surprised. I think it is the first time I have sought her attention for weeks.

I watch her as she is taking off her coat, quietly admiring her while she is unaware. "Hi," I say relieved to see her. She turns to me in surprise and she smiles with uncertainty.

"Hi," she replies. "Did you miss us or something? I hope you don't mind that I went away to mom and dad's house because I could not bear being home alone."

"I understand," I say grabbing her hand. "And yes, I did...miss you...both. I've been doing a lot of thinking and I have a surprise for you. I know you don't like surprises, but it will be good for all of us."

Following me into the living room, she pulls our son on her lap as she sits on the couch. He is eagerly waiting to hear what gift is about to come his way. Jessica grabs his hand enthusiastically. They always know when I ask them to sit on the couch, that an exciting surprise is coming their way, usually involving spontaneous travel.

"It's fall break, the weathers bad, and it has been raining for weeks," I say. "I thought it would be good for us to get away and have some fun together. Now, I will have to do some work while we are there, but I have booked us three nights in a resort where we can swim, play and go out for dinner every night. It also has an indoor playground for kids and a lot of other things to do. What do you guys think?"

My son immediately jumps up on the couch and starts bouncing on it. "Yeah, yeah, yippee..." he is screaming with joy. I look at Jessica, "What do you think?" She looks at me seriously and then breaks into a smile.

"I think it is a great idea. I suppose we leave this afternoon, if I know you and impulsive ideas?"

"Yes, we can check in at three o'clock this afternoon, so we had better start packing."

"I'm on it!" Jessica says as she jumps up and starts to walk outside of the room. "One last question, how many bedrooms are there?"

"Only two," I say wondering what her reaction will be.

"So we will be sleeping in the same bed?"

"Yes, if that is okay?"

"Yes, but you must know, I might not be able to keep my hands off of you."

We connect for the first time in weeks, and it feels good. Though I am surprised that she is so agreeable. I thought for certain there would be a long discussion first.

After we pack our bags in the car, I grab my laptop and papers from work that I need to review. I leave a message with my vice president informing him that I have had something come up, and I will be taking the next three days off. My agenda is fairly clear this week, because I am catching up on office work and preparing my plan for next fiscal.

Our son is jumping all around the room singing. He is proud that he packed his own suitcase. Though filled only with toys, he beams as he shows me the contents of his bag.

Jessica prepared some sandwiches, crackers and fruit to eat on the ride up. It is a couple of hours we have to drive. It has been so long since we have had a road trip together.

It feels good to be behind the wheel. I push Emma and Erik to the back of my mind and deny the fact that I am retreating. I have been beyond stupid and have put my family in danger. That is completely unforgivable.

In the car, we are singing songs, eating our lunch, and enjoying the anticipation of a few days away. It feels familiar to me, real. I feel myself again and deeply connected to our family unit. We are laughing, telling jokes, chattering just like it used to be on other long trips we've taken. Life away from our house always brings us closer. It is a journey where we all grow together, in the same direction, bonding us further together.

Arriving at the resort, I go to check in. Jessica and our son walk around. The entire property is built to look like a Dutch city. Connected houses, two stories high, form a ring around the town center where there are shops and restaurants. We pull up to the two-bedroom townhouse we have rented. It is a good size.

Jessica looks over at me. "This is perfect. It is so cute!" she beams. It warms my heart to hear the excitement in her voice, melting away all the darkness that has spread in the last 24 hours.

Opening the door reveals a big entryway, stairs that go up to the next floor and a door to the downstairs area. Our son busts through it to discover a living room and a full kitchen with dining table. He zooms past us, and we can hear him barreling up the stairs, as Jessica and I look at each other and giggle. Her eyes are so kind and full of life.

We follow him upstairs to make sure there is nothing dangerous he can get into. There are two bedrooms and a large bathroom. Looking out the bathroom window, I see a small man-made lake with little pedal boats in it. There is a tiny back yard that leads to a walking path around the lake. Jessica is right. It is perfect. We unpack as we explore our new little house. Excited to have a little vacation, we quickly get settled and decide to take a walk and explore.

Surveying the streets, we walk towards the town square, as

Jessica and I peak into the different houses looking at the sizes and layouts of each one. It really does look like a small Dutch village and feels like we moved to a new town for a few days. As we approach the town square, we see an ice skating rink in the middle that is surrounded by restaurants, a grocery store, and a few shops. Our son runs over and wants to skate. "We can do that tomorrow morning. We need to go back and start getting ready for dinner," I say, "but first let's buy some groceries."

The grocery store is small, but has all the essentials we need. We buy bread, cheese, sandwich meats, yoghurt drinks, juice and wine. As we check out, our son has the job of putting the groceries on the counter. Taking his role very seriously, he is looking at the cash register lady to see if she is watching how carefully he places each item on the counter. He proudly stacks the contents of our basket up on the counter and the woman behind it watches him and smiles.

"He's cute. Is he yours or your sisters?" she asks Jessica.

I lean over and say, "Oh, I am not her sister." I put my arm around her shoulders and kiss her cheek. "He is ours." Jessica looks over at me clearly affected by the first kiss I have given her in weeks. The woman behind the counter smiles back, "He is a very big boy now that he can help with the groceries."

We grab our groceries as our son waves at the cash register lady. He has made a new friend and no doubt will want to look for her each time we go by. Running ahead, he is peaking into windows, jumping on and off steps, and picking up rocks from the ground. He is our little puppy, running and exploring. I love to watch him. It reminds me to not move so fast, to appreciate the moment and notice the light on the flowers. I look over to Jessica and feel happy.

As we are getting ready for dinner, I contemplate digging in to a little work. No, tomorrow morning, it can all wait until tomorrow. I don't want to be tempted to log on to MyLIFESeeker. I want to deal with that tomorrow as well. Tonight, I want to remember a life before the madness.

Jessica comes down in a trendy suit and a very low cut tank top and I can see her breasts very well. She has accessorized her outfit with heels and jewelry. My wife is stunning. I know she has an agenda and is tempting me. Admittedly, I am powerless when she

216

looks so sexy.

I dress in a pair of jeans with artwork on the back pockets. I have on a trendy jacket with a low cut shirt underneath, a belt and high-heeled boots. I catch Jessica looking at my breasts. She is a boob girl as well and is being very obvious with her glances. I welcome them.

At dinner, our son is an angel. Ordering his food nicely all by himself, he eats all of it. Jessica and I have a couple of drinks, and we joke and flirt with each other as we entertain our son with a variety of games. It's good to feel close to her again. I find myself catching glances of all my favorite things about her, her eyes, lips, breasts and her neck. Her curls fall over one eye, and when she glances up, I can see her clear baby blues inviting me to join them. I adore most that she is a wonderful mother.

After I pay the bill, we go to the cloakroom. Helping Jessica with her long coat, I am close enough that I can smell her hair and perfume. It is intoxicating. My body responds to her scent, she always smells so good. It reacts as if on automatic pilot and craves every ounce of her. She has this affect on me. She always has.

On the walk back to our little house, it is dark and the air is crisp. Stars fill the sky and the moon is full, as are we. Our son is chatting away with us, asking questions about the stars and planets. Stealing a glance at my girl, she is open and alive. I reach for her hand and hold it tight.

As soon as we get in the house, we discover it is way past our son's bedtime, so we take him upstairs. We put his pajamas on, and I tell him a bedtime story that must include all his favorite obsessions and action heroes of the moment. I make up an off-the-wall animated tale that inevitably ends with, "And then everyone went to sleep, because they were SO tired." We kiss him goodnight and go downstairs.

Opening a bottle of red wine, I pour each of us a glass. It feels warm going into my body and I find myself releasing the lurking gloom, submitting to the light. I turn on the iPod that I brought. It contains all of the romantic songs that we have loved throughout our years together. Jessica notices immediately.

Sitting together on the small couch, I flip on the electric fireplace. The lights are low and romantic. I sit at one end of the couch, leaning against the arm, turned towards her. She sits against the other arm facing me. We each have one knee up and I am aware they are touching.

We are laughing as we tell stories of when our son was younger, remembering all the funny things that he did. It reconnects us. Our very favorite song comes on and our smiles turn to stares. Love. I am relieved and elated that our connection is still there.

"Well, we should go to bed, it is getting late," I say.

"Yeah, our little man will be up early."

"I know. I need to get up early so I can finish my work. Then we will go swimming and afterwards skating. How does that sound?"

"It sounds perfect. This all...is perfect." I linger on her beautiful clear, blue eyes, as emotion fills the space between us.

After going upstairs, I wash my face and brush my teeth in the bathroom. She takes her turn, as I undress to my black t-back underwear and climb into bed. She emerges from the bathroom wearing a very sexy red nightgown. Slipping beside me after turning off the light, I can hear her breath and see her pale skin, as the moon softly lights the room. Captivated by her scent, and by knowing her warm body is lying next to me, my senses crave her. All of these weeks without her, I have missed her so much.

Moving my arm towards her, I brush her exposed skin. She reaches for my arm immediately and caresses it. So gentle, her touch sends chills throughout my body. She runs her hand up my arm, pulling my bicep, and pressing against my naked breast. My breathing is growing heavier as I struggle to resist her. But I cannot. I touch her cheek as she lies on her back looking at me. Running my hand down to her neck delicately, I move it further to her chest and then over the top of her breasts.

Slipping my hand inside the top of her nightgown, she squirms then lets out a gentle sigh. I feel a wetness pour between my legs, as I run my hand down farther. She opens her legs slightly and I move my hands up to the delicate skin on her inner thighs. She twists and softly whimpers. A beautiful song that makes my body rise, reach up and pull down the sheets. Moving between her legs, I rub her thighs, as I lean down I kiss them passionately. My heart is opening and I am softening. I am submitting to her body. Bending down, I rest my head between her legs. Putting my arms around her bum and running my hands up to her hips, I pull her

218

close. Emotions overtake my body. God, I love this woman. I love her more than anything. All of the feelings that have grown for her over the last many years swell up inside of me.

Lifting her nightgown up, my cheek moves over her bare skin. I continue moving higher over her tummy, then between her breasts. Straddling her torso and sitting up, I pull her to me. The nightgown slides over her head as I place her face on my breasts. Resting my hand on the back of her neck, we hold each other and drink in the energy of our emotion.

She lies back and I ease down placing both of my legs in between hers. Resting my head on her chest while stroking her soft skin, I run my lips over her nipples. Jessica, twisting below me, whispers, "I've missed you...your touch. I want you to come back. Come back to me baby." The strength of her sentiment fills me. On top of her, I gently hold her face and look into her eyes. I kiss her cheeks, her eyelids, and then finally I kiss her lips, swollen and wet, as I stroke them with my tongue.

Softly holding my back, she pulls me in to her while wrapping her legs around me, giving me a full body hug. The heat between her legs sizzles on my warm naked skin. Her breathing merges with mine and once again we become one. Two puzzle pieces that fit perfectly, we belong together.

Rolling on my side facing her, she does the same. My hand brushes down the side of her body, over her hips and she instinctively spreads her legs. Her wetness tells the extent of her desire for me. She does the same with me, and my honey pours all over her fingers. We move deep inside one another, as the fire between us begins to heat the room. The bed, the sheets, everything is beginning to burn.

Pressing against each other, our bodies find their common rhythm. They know each other so well. Faster and faster we both begin to moan, as we are pressing deeper inside of each other, ready to come.

"I want you inside of me. Make love to me baby," she whispers.

I get up and find the Feeldoe in our suitcase. Returning, I slip the smaller end inside of me. The shape of it allows it to stay inside as I press the vibrator on. The buzzing sensation runs throughout the entire dildo intensely. Slipping the other end slowly inside of her, I move passionately, and I press down, moving my face just above

219

hers. The connection between us, we speak without words, in our own language. Our bodies follow the familiar flow and create one beautiful movement. Our tongues reunite, as I sway my hips. My heart is full of love for her and I can no longer hold back my emotions. My clit swells, as does my heart, and both explode in and outside of my body, as I let a loud moan. Jessica releases at the same time.

Fully unified. I kiss her softly all over her face. She smiles at me caressing my hair and returning the soft kisses. Lying in my arms, her head is on my chest and her hand on my breasts. Emotion fills my veins and penetrates my muscles, as I tremble through my orgasm. She holds me, as tears stream down her face. She knows I am full. I am home.

15

It's very early. My work is calling me, so I force myself to begin to register consciousness. Jess is sleeping naked by my side. Still dark in the room, the streetlamp creates barely enough light for me to see her. Lying on my side and looking over at her lovingly, the memory of every touch from last night fills me. Longing to remain by her side, I allow myself a short interlude of deep contentment. I have found my way back again.

Getting up, I put on a warm sweatshirt and yoga pants, then creep downstairs and flip on the coffee machine. Switching on my laptop, while yawning and stretching, my iMac greets me with its familiar start up sound. I don't want the serenity to leave, but I know there is a pressing matter that must be taken care of. First, I need to get my work done.

Sitting down at my computer and opening up my business plan, I begin typing away while sipping on my coffee. Within the hour, I finish my work. Jess and our son are still sleeping. I'm surprised the two of them are not awake yet. It is so quiet here, so perhaps they will indulge in a long slumber.

Now it is time to face Emma...Erik. With the dark cloud hovering above my head, I contemplate going back upstairs to Jessica. I long to crawl into bed behind her and put my hands over her warm skin. I would kiss on her neck and listen to her as she begins to wake. Snapping back to reality, I know I have to handle this situation and put my family, my relationship and myself out of danger. I have to protect my home.

Logging in to MyLIFESeeker, there are several messages from Emma in my inbox. I expected this. Opening the first one that was written the night that I left Erik and Eve's house, I reluctantly begin to read.

Date: October 25, 2008 10:35PM
Subject: Please Don't Leave

Beautiful, Sweet Jade,

I am sitting here tonight and my thoughts are only of you. Wondering if you will message me and when we will meet. I have submitted to you, Jade. Fully. I am yours. I love you. I mustn't say it, but I do.

I hope my last message pleased you. Please don't run away from me. Please. I sense that you are. Am I right? I beg you, please do not leave me. Not now.

Your friend,
Emma

Date: October 26, 2008   9:33AM
Subject: Where are you?

Beautiful, Sweet Jade,

My love, where are you? I am worried. I have not heard from you. It has been the longest time, since we have started messaging, that I have not heard from you. I fear that you have gone away and I am crying. I cannot bear this.

I have given you what you wanted, just as you have asked me to do. I have agreed to leave Eve and more. I have agreed to meet you and to risk everything.

Do you still want to meet me? You have not read my last message. I can see that they are still unread. Are you okay? I am becoming very worried about you. Did something happen? Where are you? Please come back to me, Jade. I miss you so much.

Have I done something wrong? Is there something that you have found in my last messages that you can no longer live with? Did I misbehave in some way?

Where are you?

Your friend,
Emma

I feel nothing as I read the mails. Dead. I only wonder, does he not know? Did Eve not mention that I stopped by? Maybe she did and he did not bring it together. Why would he think it would be me that arrived at his house?

I need to message him back and press to see if there is anything that he knows. Stalling him is the only way to get him to message me more. Searching for a crack, I know I need to be careful. The missing box still haunts me, where could it be? My intuition sends warning signals that he is still playing the game. If he is, I need to be smart and careful with my words.

Date: October 27, 2008   6:45AM
Subject: I'm Okay

Dearest Emma,

Thank you for your messages and for your concern. I am here. I am just very busy at the moment. I cannot write right now. Don't worry about me. I am fine.
I must go and spend time with my family right now. I am sure you understand.

xoxo
Jade

After sleeping in until eight o'clock, Jessica comes downstairs with our swimming clothes and a small bag. While I'm standing at the counter making breakfast, she comes up behind me and moves my long hair to the side revealing my neck. Kissing it lovingly,

223

she reaches around, fondles my breasts, and whispers in my ear.

"I am still wet from last night."

Smiling big, I turn around and put my hands on her hips. She slides her arms around my shoulders, and then rests them behind my neck. We kiss, sensually and full of love. Enjoying the moment, I hug her tight. Placing my face in her neck, her sweetness captivates me. Inhaling, I am filled with her and the love we share.

Tugging at the back of my pants, I look down and see my son beaming up at me. I pick him up and we kiss him, one of us on each side, as he puts his face in between us. It is a "Mama Sandwich" kiss. "Good morning little puppy," I say. He makes a yapping noise and then reaches out to Jessica. I think this is going to be a wonderful day.

Our morning is filled with fun. We swim for a couple of hours, and before we realize it, it is time to return to our little house for lunch. Fresh breads, cheeses and meats are scattered all over the table, so we can build our own "boterham" or open faced sandwiches.

After lunch, our son plays his portable video game, while Jessica and I lie on the couch together and read. In the afternoon, we go ice-skating and then for a very long walk. By the time we return home, we are exhausted from all of the activities. My bum is sore from falling on the ice, yet every time I sit down I am reminded of how much fun we had. It is real to me. I don't belong in the illusion. I am exactly where I am meant to be. The dragon is absent and I am at ease.

Plopping in a movie, our son jumps between us to relax before dinner. Jessica inches her way off the couch and announces she is going to shower and dress for dinner. Pulling me up, she hugs me tight. As she turns to go up the stairs, I give her a little pinch on her bum. She turns her head around and flashes me a playful smile.

Walking over to the counter, I pour a glass of wine then sit at the table to read through the brochures about other things to do in the area. We have another day left so we can still explore and have fun before returning home.

After a half hour, Jessica comes down in a beautiful multicolor dress. It is long, with flowing sleeves and it hugs every curve on her body. I glance up as she enters the room and find myself spellbound by her beauty. She has a look. It is *the* look that draws me to her. It shoots down deep inside of me, creating the ultimate penetration of my soul. I never want to run away from her again.

I have put on a pair of black pants and a black vest with only a thin black camisole under it. All the restaurants are so warm. I reach for a silver and black tie that I brought to wear around my naked neck, but decide to wear a necklace instead.

We go to a fancier restaurant tonight, that serves delicious fish dishes. During dinner, we repeat the previous night's activities. Our son finds a puzzle in his bag and becomes lost in it. Jessica sits across from me, our eyes flirting relentlessly. We are consumed with our happiness. It feels comfortable. I think Jessica is releasing her idea of having another child to complete our family, because I feel that empty gap between us closing. We are a perfect family unit just the way we are.

After dinner, we almost hurry back to the house. I think we both anticipate the moment we can once again be naked together. After giving our son a bath, his exhausted body falls into bed, and his breathing immediately grows deep and heavy. Standing at the doorway watching him escape to dreamland, we hold hands and just look at him. It still baffles me how such a perfect creation was made. I remember the joy I felt watching her give birth to him, and how much happiness this little boy has brought to both of us. We stare at him, as all parents do, in wonderment and feeling so lucky.

Downstairs Jessica and I listen to music as we talk about what we are going to do during the holidays. I welcome rediscovering the activity that had recently disappeared completely. I remember how frozen we were, even just a couple of days ago. Such a contrast to how we are now, the fire is burning again, and we are both absorbing its heat. There is a lull in the conversation as we both stare at the fireplace.

Jessica stands, pulls up her dress, and steps out of her sexy underwear. Moving forward, she straddles me. Slowly lifting it, she exposes a delicious red bra. Leaning over she offers her breast to my mouth as she moves her hips on top of me. I want her! She knows exactly how to turn me on. This combines with our intimacy and passion still left over from last evening, and drives me wild.

Rolling playfully across the couch, we knock over a lamp as we rip each other's clothes off. Our hunger for one another whips through our emotions. Finding our way to the big fluffy rug by the fireplace, we lay fully naked with our hands exploring each other's flesh eagerly. Reaching for her purse, Jessica pulls out the Feeldoe. She had been planning this all along.

I slip the smaller end inside of me. Turning the vibrator on, my body immediately responds to the tingling inside. On top of Jessica, I kiss her breasts, as she reaches down and pushes the dildo further inside of me. My desire for her lips below is uncontrollable, as I slowly move down, with licks and kisses until I am between her legs. Glistening and swollen, it is begging for attention. I lay down flat on my stomach, as the larger end of the dildo presses between the rug and my sweet spot, while the smaller end is buzzing away inside of me, searching for my g-spot.

Licking her softly, her lips continue swelling, as I breathe heavily onto them in between tongue tickles. Hips moving in synch with mine, it is incredibly sensual. We are entirely synchronized with our infatuation. This woman fills every desire I could possibly imagine.

With my hips pressing down against the dildo, my mouth continues to feast on her. Slightly moaning in ecstasy, she twists as my hot breath covers her. I feel her clit harden and a fast pulse pushes against my tongue. Cupping her bum and pressing her fully into my mouth, I suck on her sweet spot as she releases to me. I rub faster and press harder against the buzzing dildo, while her pulsing clit tempts my orgasm. The moment is so intense, so feminine, that I come loudly as my tongue continues to feel her last few throbs.

After a few moments, I turn my head and rest it beside where I had just been with my tongue. My cheek on her inner thigh and my hands still cupping her bum, my heart is brimful. My craving is completely satisfied.

By the light of the fire, we have made love. Grabbing the fluffy blanket, we cuddle in each other's arms by the fireplace. I caress her shoulder, slowly moving my hand down the side of her body. Our flesh is still warm and sticky as we fall asleep in each other's arms. Around midnight Jessica wakes me and we go upstairs. In a dreamlike state, everything else is far away. I am in the moment with my girl, my wife, my true love.

The next morning I lay awake enjoying the quiet room. Hearing Jessica's breathing lulls me back to sleep until 7:00am. Slipping out of bed unnoticed, I creep downstairs. I don't expect to hear from Emma, but unsure of her intentions, I had better check anyway. There is one new message waiting for me and it is from her...him. It has no subject line. It is odd because he always has a subject header.

Opening the message, I am horrified at the 5 words he has written.

Date: October 27, 2008   7:30AM
Subject: <no subject>

Beautiful, Sweet Jade,

I have found the box.

Your friend,
Emma

Reality sets in. The dragon must awaken again and this time be prepared for a fight.

16

Date: October 28, 2008   7:13AM
Subject: Betrayal

Dearest Emma or should I call you Erik?

You found the box.   Why are you telling me this?   Are you
threatening me in some way?   From where I'm sitting, I should be
the one that's angry.   I am the one that should be threatening to tell
your wife you have been fucking other women online and under
false pretenses.   Pretending to be a lesbian, it is disgraceful.   How
many others have their been?

Erik, I don't know you.   Emma is dead.   I am sorry you have lost
your sister.   It must have been very difficult.   I am really very sorry
to hear that.   However, I don't know you.
You have betrayed me Erik.   You have lied to me about everything.
Now confess to me.   Confess everything.   I deserve at least that
much and then, I am going to walk away.

The box with the address and the tie, get rid of it.   You no longer
have any need for it.   And all of my messages, erase them.   All of
them.   You owe me this.

Jade

Date: October 28, 2008   9:02AM
Subject: The Real Confession

Beautiful, Sweet Jade,

You are angry with me and you should be. I have been very

naughty. I am not good enough for you Jade. You are perfect and I am pathetic.

Do not misunderstand my email. I only wanted you to know I had found it. I would never hurt you or threaten you. I could never. I love you. I knew it was now time to tell you just how naughty I have been.

I knew you had come to my house. Eve told me. She also showed me the box. You dropped it in the street as you were running to your car. She opened it and was puzzled. She was worried about you and wanted to call. I told her no, let's not make matters worse.

She said you were an old girlfriend of Emma's and that you had no idea she died. That was very clever. I knew it! I knew you would be able to handle yourself in any situation! She felt very sorry that you had to find out that way and she still wants to contact you. But I will do as you say and get rid of the box and the phone number so she is unable to find you. I have also erased all of your messages as you have asked.

Eve has no idea about Emma, the Emma that I have created, that fell in love with you and is still in love with you. For me nothing has changed.

You tell me to confess everything to you and I will. Yes, you deserve to hear it, I will tell you the whole truth. Please know this, I did not lie to you about everything. I never, EVER lied about my feelings for you.

Here is my confession. You have told me your life story and now I will tell you mine starting from the beginning.

My father was American and my mother Dutch. They met in Amsterdam when my father was over from the US taking an art class. My mother was in the same class. They fell madly in love and married when they were 22, both the same age.

My parents were artists, but you probably know this already. That is how you found me. My father and mother traveled all over Europe making paintings and sculptures. My father became very famous in America and in Europe as well. My mother sold most of her sculptures to local art galleries in whatever city they were traveling in. This is how they spent their twenties, carefree.

Upon turning thirty, my mother got pregnant accidentally and this changed their life course. They had not planned on having children but there she was, pregnant with twins. Emma was born first. I came eight minutes later. I guess I did not want to come out. Maybe I knew then that my life would be difficult and have more tragedy than a person can handle.

Emma was older and that is the role she assumed with me. She was someone I looked up to, and she took care of me. She was my other half, in many ways my better half.

We grew up with a lot of very interesting people around us. All mostly were artists, writers or connected to the artistic world of Amsterdam. Many were struggling financially and my parents would take them in. They would stay on the top floor of our house that was like a small apartment. My parents called it their "Floor of Birth". My father was so inspired by Andy Warhol that he wanted his own "Factory" right in Amsterdam. And, in a way, it was. So many different people stayed there throughout the years and contributed to so many of my parent's projects.

My mom and dad were always nice to us, and we both loved them very much. My mom was outgoing like Emma but my dad was quiet like me. He wasn't as shy as I was back then, just introspective. More like I am now, I believe.

My parents lived in their own world though with a more bohemian philosophy of raising children and living life. I know they loved us, they showed in their own way. They needed space to be creative though, so they spent most of their time on the third floor of our home. Emma understood this better than I did because she was so independent. We were left to create our own world and in many cases take care of each other.

When we were young, we did everything together. She was always the one with the most talent and the one everyone liked the best. She was a talker. She could talk to anyone.

Many times she would entertain all the people that were in our house with dancing or singing, but her greatest talent was telling stories.

But I was very shy and would sit back and watch or listen to her. I felt invisible most of the time. Em would always sense when I felt that way. In the middle of her dance or story, she would always come to me and pull me up with her. She would give me something to do, like beat on a drum, or she would have me act out the story with her.

I could never go up in front of people on my own. She always had to come and get me, to make me feel safe. She believed in me. Without Emma's encouragement, I would have melted into the walls and no one would have noticed.

Sometimes at night when I was scared, I would crawl into bed with her. She would put her arms around me and tell me there was nothing to be afraid of. I would fall asleep in her arms knowing that my sister, my other half would always be there for me.

When we were older, in our teens, Emma started acting a little different. She was a bit more secretive. She didn't want to share everything with me. She would have her girlfriends spend the night and she did not want me around. Later, I found out why. For me, this time was so lonely.

I began to draw and do different things. I studied English obsessively. I always spoke it frequently with my father and with our visitors. I didn't have many friends, but Emma had loads. She tried to pull me into to her popular crowd, but I was not as cool as she was. Everyone loved her. They always did. I loved that about her. I was never jealous of her. She radiated energy. She had a way of making people feel like they were better than they actually were. She made them feel like the most important and accomplished individuals and she brought out the best in people. She had a way of making them feel so special and they flocked around her.

I told you that Emma started acting distant to me and to everyone. This is because she was finding out that she was a lesbian. She didn't tell me this until years later. Before I tell you about that, I need to disclose the day that changed everything.

One day my parents had an opportunity to go to India. A wealthy Indian man, who was a fan of my fathers work, asked him to come to India to do a portrait of him, and then another of his wife and daughters. My mother and father were both very excited at the thought of being inspired by India, the people, and a radically different way of life than they knew in Europe. Of course they decided to go. They also wanted to travel around after my father completed his work. In total they would be gone for three to four weeks.

There was a problem. What to do with us? Emma and I were sixteen and we were in school. They could not take us out for that long. So they had my Dutch grandmother, Oma Simone stay with us.

After finishing the paintings, they went to Goa to hang out on the beach with all the other artists that were there from Europe. They rented a scooter to travel around, which is very dangerous in India especially for foreigners, who were not used to the crowded confusion on the roads. Maybe they did not think about it. I will never know. The day before they were due to leave and return home, they were riding down a dirt road and got hit by a car. They were both killed. Their deaths were instant from what I understand. There was no suffering. But then, I will never really know what happened. That is hard to accept.

Emma and I were devastated. She was extremely close to both of them. I went to her every night because I could hear her crying. I would crawl into bed with her and she would cry on my shoulder. This went on for a very long time. I cried too but not in front of Emma. I wanted to be strong for her, because she needed me to be. This was the most important thing I could give back to her, for all the times she took care of me.

Our grandmother sold her house and moved in with us. She didn't want to cause further tragedy by uprooting us to another house, or another school. It is big house and it is entirely paid for. It is the same house Eve and I live in now and the one that you came to.

Our grandmother was very nice to us and she did the best

she could. When we were 18, Emma and I went to university in Amsterdam. Around this time our grandmother passed away. She too was heartbroken having lost her daughter. She always said that she thought she would be the first to die, and that a child dying before their parents just wasn't right.

Emma and I stayed in the house, but she moved up into the apartment on the top floor. I moved into my parent's bedroom that had an on-suite bathroom. So it was almost like we had separate apartments with the same living area. We needed each other because we could not get over the devastation of unexpectedly losing both parents.

I studied all the time while Em was exploring her freedom. She came out as a lesbian when she was 19 or 20. She told me that she had crushes on girls when she was younger. That is why she was so distant to me during that time. She was trying to figure it all out.

Emma was beautiful. Well, you saw a picture of her and that really is her. My wife looks a lot like her. As I was saying, Emma was beautiful but rebellious, maybe a little like Gia. She went through a period of dating a lot of women. They all wanted to date her. They wanted to own her.

None of them were good enough for her though. Except for one, but I will tell you about that in a minute. She dated both very feminine and very butch women. They all fell in love with her. Men fell in love with her too. But Emma was never interested in men. Never.

Emma was a very difficult one to catch. She would go out to the bars, to parties, and she was always on the go, traveling everywhere. Always moving faster and faster.

She sounds a little bit like you don't you think? I do.

On the weekends, she would always come home very early in the mornings, after having been out all night. Sometimes she would bring women home, sometimes not. No matter how late or how early, she would always crawl in under the covers with me and tell you stories of what had happened

233

that night.

I lived vicariously through her. I really did. I did not have any friends, all I did was go to school and study. I was a social outcast. Emma brought forth a whole other life in my imagination with her stories, and I loved that about her very much.

After university, I went on to further my education and I studied engineering. I dated a few women during this time. But none that were interesting to me. I was beginning to come out of my shyness and women were starting to notice me. I wasn't the skinny quiet boy anymore. I guess you can say I developed into a pretty smart guy with a lot to say.

I dated one woman who was very beautiful. She was a tall blond. She had a nice smile and she was also pretty smart. She was the woman I lost my virginity to. She was not a virgin. We dated for about 3 or 4 months and then I told her we could not see each other anymore. She wasn't what I was looking for. I am very picky.

You see, I will tell you that Emma was the ideal woman and strangely all the women I met, had to live up to her. And the truth was, no one could.

This first relationship opened me up sexually and I dated and had sex with a few other women. These were not women of substance. They were easy and one night stands mostly.

After university, Emma kept on with her carefree life. She kept going out and traveling around Europe with different friends. She started writing and painting as well, she was pretty good. She wasn't home a lot during that period and the house was very lonely. I told you this is the time that I started going out and meeting women. I was never very good at it though. It always felt uncomfortable and pushed. I never was the one-night-stand kind of guy.

You might wonder how Emma could afford all the traveling. I told you our parents were famous artists. They left us a lot of money. Their investments did well and with the insurance

234

from their deaths, we were able to live quite well without having to work much. I always wanted to, I had to work. It occupies the mind you know. And it is what I am good at. I eventually became a very successful businessman.

When Emma and I were 30, Emma was living in Paris for a few months. She met another Dutch woman who was on vacation there and started dating her. The woman was bi-sexual. Emma sent me emails from Paris telling me all of her secret thoughts, all kinds of stories. She always emailed me two or three times a day. She told me about this woman and how she liked her but was not really very interested in her. But that there was just some reason she could not quit seeing her.

The woman returned back to the Netherlands after a three-week vacation. Emma came home too. I was so happy and I'd hoped she would stay because I missed her.

The woman she was dating came over to our house one day. She walked through the door and I thought she was the most beautiful woman I had ever seen. Her name was Eve. Yes, this is the Eve that I am now married to.

Emma noticed right away that I was infatuated with Eve. Eve would come over and we would all hang out. Emma was not really that into Eve, maybe because she looked like her? But do you know what? One night Emma told me something. You see with Emma around I could be myself with Eve. Eve was the first woman that got to see the real me. Emma had a gift of always getting me to open up and one night she saw in my eyes that I had fallen in love with Eve. She said to me "Erik, do you remember when I was in Paris, I wrote you that I was not sure why, but I could not give her up just yet? Well, I know now. I was meant to bring her to you."

Do you see why I loved my sister so much? She was always doing things like that for me. She took such good care of me.

Emma started dating another woman. Eve was okay with that, because she was starting to fall in love with me. Em told me she thought that Eve and I would be very happy together. Eve and I married a few years later. We don't have children. We are unable to have kids. We had thought about adoption but the process was so long, so we decided against it.

Eve and I were very happy together, I believe. Emma lived upstairs in the apartment on the top floor. By this time, she had a girlfriend who was a lesbian named Saskia. Emma fell in love with her. They were good together. Saskia was a very tall woman with short black hair. She was muscular because she was a fitness trainer. Emma was crazy about her. I think it was the first time I ever saw her really in love.

Em moved out of the apartment and in with Saskia. Eve and I missed having her around, but it was time for her to move on. So I encouraged my sister to move in with Saskia. Something was wrong though. I didn't know what, but I sensed something was wrong with Emma.

She was having headaches for a couple of days. They were unbearable, she could not email me or even call me. She laid in the dark for two days according to Saskia. Saskia called the doctor and made an appointment for the next day. She was very worried. Emma died that night in bed next to Saskia. She died of a brain aneurysm.

I never spoke to her before she died. The last conversation that I had with her was about buying a computer and downloading music. Did I tell her I loved her? I don't remember. It was such a random conversation. The kind that after you hang up the phone, you cannot imagine life any other way. You assume that person will always be there for you.

Emma's death devastated me. I didn't know if I would survive it. I had lost so many people in my life and now the one that was the most important, my better half, was dead.

All that was left was half of a person. You know they say when someone loses a limb they can still feel it. That is how I felt about Emma. Although she was gone, I still felt her.

236

Eve tried to comfort me, but I was not the same person any longer, I was unreachable, an empty shell. Our relationship started to struggle. I kept dreaming of Emma coming into our room telling me stories as she always had. I guess I just always lived through her and now that part of me was dead too. It felt like my life had stopped.

I missed her so desperately that I was unable to cope. I noticed though, that as time passed, I couldn't feel Emma as strongly and it began to worry me. What if I woke up one day and could not feel her at all?

That is when I overheard a colleague telling another about MyLIFESeeker. I started thinking about going on the site as Emma. It would be a way to keep her alive and to revive a part of myself. I could go on MyLIFESeeker and tell stories just like Emma would. I know it sounds fucked up. But her death really did fuck me up.

So I created a profile that Emma would create. The dominant submissive thing was not Emma. That was my imagination. You see I was always submissive to Emma. Part of me craved having a dominant woman in my life again. One like Emma. One that could tell me stories.

I found a lot of women (and men posing as women) on MyLIFESeeker, who wanted to dominate Emma. They wanted sex. None were of interest to us. None, that is until we met you.

You, my beautiful, sweet Jade, you began to tell me stories like she used to tell me. You brought Emma back to life. You made me feel whole again. I wanted to actually BE my sister so I could be with you. I wanted to tell you the truth. I let it go on far too long.

I hurt you. I hear the hurt in your last two emails. That is the very last thing I ever wanted to do. I didn't expect to fall in love with anyone online. I just wanted to keep my sister alive. And then you came along and I fell in love with you. Before I knew it, I had gone too far.

I was selfish and I could not let you go. We could not let you go. Just when I found the one person that changed everything for me, I feared I would lose you if I told you the truth. I am so sorry for hurting you Jade. I love you. Believe me when I say the last thing I ever wanted to do was hurt you.

I am crawling on my hands and knees, kneeling before you. I am begging for your forgiveness. My feelings for you are real. There were no others that I have fallen in love with. Only you.

Jade you are the only woman for me. I would have met with you, and I would have left my wife for you. But I know that you do not want me, because I am a man. My sister was a lesbian, so I get this and respect it.

This I am certain. I have fallen in love with you so deeply. If only I could see you. I am not even sure you will respond to this. I feel like I need to see you and talk to you.

I am so sorry.

In regret, your friend,
Erik

Date: October 28, 2008 7:54PM
Subject: Re: Confession

Erik,

You have confessed to me. I admit it has been a difficult confession to read. I believe you are telling me the truth; however, you must understand it is difficult, almost impossible, to trust you.

I believe, that in your confession, you are not playing games with me. That you genuinely somehow found comfort and completion by bringing Emma alive again for yourself. Maybe I am naive for saying that, but I try to believe the best in people.

Erik, you say that you love me and you never lied about that. I do believe this too. Although, when you love someone you do not lie to them. Learn from this Erik.

I am sorry that you have lost everyone that means something to you, aside from Eve. Erik, she seems like such a good woman. She is beautiful and she loves you. You have said nothing but kind words about her, and I believe you should concentrate on making things better between the two of you.

I am left in a very strange position. Emma has broken my heart. Now she is dead. Someone that only lived in my imagination is dead, and I am trying to replace her face with yours. It is difficult. It has totally fucked me up because somehow you both mesh into one person. I am recovering and I am focusing on making my life better as well, but it is really messed up.
I genuinely believe you are a good person who made a very big mistake. People make mistakes, and I feel sorry for you. I do. Everyone you have ever loved has been taken from you. Including me.
You want to meet? I am sorry Erik. I simply cannot meet you.

Xoxo
Jade

I write the last line of my message "I simply cannot meet you," but as I write it, something deep inside contradicts me and whispers in a quiet voice, "I simply *have* to meet you."

17

We arrive home late morning from our four-day adventure. I love coming home after a little vacation. Cherishing the first few moments of stepping into our house, I look around. It is quiet and still, just waiting for our return. I always miss it and find comfort in my favorite things that surround me, even the way it smells like home. It is our home that we have built together. My son loves returning as well. He rushes around playing with the toys that he has missed. While unpacking, I can hear him talking to himself and his best-loved toys.

This time is slightly different though. I keep thinking of Erik, of Emma, and of his confession. I feel angry. He created someone that I fell in love with, and then he took her away. I am plagued by the simple fact that I allowed him to use me. I understand now what this means. I feel stupid. I got caught up in my passion for improving my writing and it evolved into an obsession that I still struggle to control.

There is still something tugging at me. I am afflicted. Do I feel sorry for him? I do not want to. I want to walk away and forget this entire nightmare ever happened. I am surprised at my reaction, but I feel genuine compassion for his situation. He seems like a decent guy that had a lot of bad things happen to him. The tragedies really messed with his head and his existence. He made some mistakes, but at the end of the day, he is a guy who desperately misses his twin sister and who has lost a part of himself. The death of a twin, I cannot imagine. I appreciate he has told me the truth. It takes a lot of courage, assuming it is the truth. It must be difficult to admit that you are psychologically traumatized and capable of such things.

I wonder in a weird way, if Erik was also in love with his sister. Is this why he fell in love with me, he see's some of Emma in me? His wife is even connected to Emma. She must have had a sexual relationship with her as well, which makes this all the more incestuous.

For some reason, I feel drawn by the need to meet with Erik. Perhaps it is closure for me, so I can get rid of Emma's ghost that still haunts me. Once I see in the flesh that he is, in fact, a man, I can move on. I feel I need a glimpse of reality.

But what if he is a weirdo or a stalker? I don't think he is, my gut tells me he is not, yet I am not certain. I don't think he is capable of harming me. If he were, he had my address and he would have used it by now, to find me. But what if he is waiting, building courage?

I feel I need to do this, to find my way completely back to Jessica. Otherwise, this will always remain a hole between us. Knowing how my mind works, it isn't always logical. I have to know the end of a story to begin another one, regardless the price of getting there. Sometimes, I have to create the end to move on. Other times, I force the end. It is a catharsis. But on occasion, it scares me.

I struggle with demons. My inner dragon is constantly forcing me forward faster and faster. SHE pushes the boundaries of my passions. I become so strong in HER presence, yet SHE presses. I am forced to walk the line. Passion or obsession? Self-fulfilling prophecy or self-destruction? Dangling my feet over the edge, fearlessly challenging the abyss to swallow me, I enjoy it.

Most people would just walk away from the situation, but my heart is involved which even further complicates everything. It is devastated, confused and fucking with me. This is a person who knows me, who I have confessed to. I have given him insight to some of my innermost thoughts about myself, my life. Part of me is curious to meet him, a man who knows so much about me, while a piece of me still thinks of him as Emma.

And then the other part wonders how this story will end.

Date: October 29, 2008 6:45AM
Subject: Meeting

Beautiful, Sweet Jade,

241

Yes, you are right that what I have given you is the truth. It was difficult to put it on paper. I have never told anyone my story. Eve knows it to a certain extent but not all of it.

Even though I expected it, I have to tell you that it is hard for me to hear that you will not meet with me. But I understand it. I do. I have hurt you and you need to leave me.

You say that you cannot distinguish between Emma and me. Maybe meeting would help. Jade, I don't want anything from you and the last thing I would ever do is hurt you. I would like to talk to you and tell you more about how you have helped me. I understand if you cannot.

I will make it easy for you. You have been to my house. If you continue down the road to the north on the corner, there is a place where I go to have coffee. There is a booth that looks out onto the street and I always sit there. I will be there tomorrow night (Thursday) at 19:00. If you change your mind I will be there until 20:00. I will bring my favorite picture of Emma.

I would like to meet you if you can make it. If not I understand.

Your friend,
 Erik

_____

Date: October 29, 2008   10:43 PM
Subject: RE: Meeting

Erik,
I will meet you, for one hour. I will be there at 7:00pm.

xoxo
Jade

_____

I cannot believe I clicked "send". I have agreed to meet him. There is no turning back now. In the car, I am lost in my thoughts.

242

I had a meeting late this afternoon in Amsterdam anyway, and it was by coincidence, or by fate, that he asked me to meet him on this day.

I don't know what I am doing. It feels natural, but guided by an unnatural force. I have no idea what I want to get out of this meeting, other than the need to separate Emma and Erik. I want Emma out of my mind. Needing her story to end, I do feel like afterwards I will be able to get on with my life.

He chose someplace near his house that he often goes to. I believe that this is his way of proving to me that I can trust him. He also knows that I can walk back to his house and tell his wife everything. He is relinquishing all of the power to me.

Arriving on time, I drive around looking for an empty space. It is now ten minutes past seven o'clock and finally, I have found a spot. I get out of the car, look down and realize that I am wearing a tight skirt, tall boots and a suit jacket. My appearance is a mix between the dominant side of myself and my GG. I didn't plan on that, I didn't even think about it, did I? Colder than it should be this time of year, I throw on a scarf and black leather gloves to shield the crisp air.

Parking several streets away, I quickly retrace back through the winding streets until I can see the corner and the café. My heart drops. I realize there is no turning back now. I am about to come face to face with the person I have been communicating with every day. It is odd thinking of meeting someone for the first time and realizing they already know most of your secrets. Someone I have been so intimate with, yet have never seen.

Glancing up, I see a man sitting in the booth that is facing the window. Recognizing me immediately, he smiles a big friendly grin, and he moves his fingers in a quick little wave. Carefully crossing the street, I reach the sidewalk and I stand in front of him. Seeing him through the glass, his smile is selfless, genuine and I react with a soft smile.

The moment is broken as my phone startles me with a loud ring. I motion to him with one finger in the air, signaling I will be right in. Answering the phone, I hear the voice of the client I just met with, who called to say that he had made a decision. He would like to move forward with the opportunity we discussed earlier to grow his business and we have a short discussion. I am visibly excited because this is a very big opportunity I have been working on for almost a year.

All the while I am talking, I can feel Erik watching me. He is intrigued and I sense no creepiness by his stare. He is observing my expressions. Glancing over at him a few times, his kind eyes continue to smile back at me. My senses tell me this is a nice man, but my head proceeds with caution. After scheduling a follow up meeting, I hang up the phone and go inside. It is now 7:30pm, and I am a half hour late.

As I approach Erik's table, he stands awkwardly and smiles broadly. He reaches out to shake my hand, but I grab his hand and pull him closer to me, as I offer him my cheek. Habitually, I always offer my cheek to those I am close with. In the Netherlands, when greeting someone, it is with either with three kisses or a handshake. A handshake is formal and meant for someone you have never met. Kisses are for someone who is more familiar.

He is tall, 6'1" I guess, and has the most beautiful clear blue eyes. They are Emma's eyes from the picture, the exact ones, which catch me off-guard. He has a medium muscular build and is in good shape. His blond hair is a little longer and messy in a trendy way. Wearing a pin stripped suit, a white shirt and a white satin tie, I can tell he is a successful businessman. I did not expect him to have such a normal appearance or to be so attractive. My mother would call him dashingly handsome, and my straight friends would all drool over him. I imagined he would be shy, introverted and well, not necessarily into the latest fashion and hair trends. Most of my Dutch colleagues are all pretty trendy though, rather than conservative, but I just thought he would be a little more...well, mousey. He is full of expression and I am a bit intrigued that he is exactly opposite of how I had pictured him.

Erik seems moved by my gesture of offering him my cheek and after he kisses me three times, he stands in a daze. Looking at my hair, face, and eyes, I sense that he wants to also look at my breasts, but he does not. He stops at my lips and then snaps into awareness.

A little embarrassed he says, "Jade, I am so sorry," he chuckles a little, "I am staring aren't I?"

"Yes, you are, but it is okay." Looking directly into his eyes as I sit down, "I am sorry I am late, but you know...parking."

"Oh yes, in Amsterdam, parking *is* the illusion," he says playfully.

"You know how I am fond of illusions," I say flippantly. I order a cappuccino and Erik orders another espresso.

"I was beginning to think you had changed your mind. I'm so glad you didn't." He then grows very serious. "Jade, I am really, really sorry about everything, and I hope you can one day forgive me."

His clear blue eyes are tender and glossy. He doesn't waste time and gets right to the point. The waitress delivers our coffee and there is a pause in the conversation, as I take a sip and look over at him.

"Thank you Erik, for apologizing. I believe we all make mistakes in our life. You admitted yours and you told me your story. I am working on forgiving you, but you understand...it takes some time."

"I know," he says, "I hope you can. I really didn't mean for this to happen. You've taught me a lot. You taught me about building friendships, about making love, about a lot of things. You trusted me completely and were so open to me. I want to be open with you, now that I can."

"You took advantage of my heart Erik," I say directly.

"I know, but I promise you, I will NEVER do that again...not ever! I do cherish your heart... more than you know."

"But you must realize it isn't the same. Emma had my heart, not you. You stole it. I could only love you as a friend. I could never be *in* love with you, we could never be lovers," I say.

"Yes," he says looking down and then back up contemplating what I just had said. "Yes, I know." He pauses and attempting to break the tension he teases, "But did you have to be so sexy?"

I raise my eyebrow, shake my head as if scolding him and change the subject, "Now, where is the picture of Emma?"

He smiles acceptingly and says, "Thank you." Reaching in his coat pocket, he pulls out three pictures.

"This one was taken when we were six and Emma was entertaining everyone with a song. I am pretending to play the guitar on a tennis racket. I was so awkward back then."

I look at the picture and notice a very shy boy. Long, curly blond hair, he is strumming on the tennis rack while looking over at Emma. It is the same look that my son gives the boys that are older than him, when they are teaching him something, or he is trying to copy what they are doing. I grin warmly.

Reaching for the second picture, sadness emerges in his voice and expression. "This is when we were sixteen, it was taken the day my mom and dad left for India. It's the last picture that was taken of the four of us." He studies it for a long moment and then hands it over.

"You look remarkably like your father, except your eyes. Both you and Em have your mother's eyes."

"Yes, you know my mother and father both used to say if all they could see were our eyes, they would never be able to tell us apart. Our eyes are identical…were identical."

"I would have to agree," I say slightly lost in looking in Erik's windows, longing for Emma.

Erik hands me the third picture. "This was taken just after Eve and Emma returned from Paris. I took it holding the camera up high."

The three of them were crammed together on the couch, legs intertwined, arms around each other. You could almost hear the echo of their laughter. I studied Emma very closely. She was so breathtakingly beautiful. Those eyes, of course, and her lips were full even when she smiled. Oh, those were the lips I dreamt of kissing. Longing for her to be alive, I wished she would walk through the door any moment.

Looking at Eve, the resemblance between the two is extraordinary. Eve's eyes have a similar shape and color. Their bodies are almost a reflection of one another, and their smiles identical. They could easily pass as sisters. A strange feeling chose this moment to present itself. Knowing that although Emma is dead, Eve is still here, and it torments me. The moment I met her, I thought she was Emma.

"Erik, doesn't Eve remind you of Emma? I mean just seeing Eve everyday, doesn't that remind you of your sister?" I ask openly.

"It used to. Yes, she looks like Em, but she is nothing like her.

246

Eve could never tell a story if her life depended on it and she is quieter like me. As outgoing and exciting as Emma was, Eve is completely opposite. She doesn't have a spark to her, not like Em," he paused and lowered his voice. "Not like you."

"Erik I..."

"Look, hear me out. Jade, I respect that you are a lesbian. I do! But when I saw you, the way you smiled at me, watching you talk on the phone... It validated that what I feel for you is real. I am in love with you. And I would be lying if I said that you didn't remind me of Em. You don't look anything like her. It's all the other things. When she talked on the phone, she would raise her hands in the air, raise her eyebrows, and use all sorts of expressions. Sometimes she would even knock people on the side of the head because of her dramatic gestures." He laughed out loud.

"You do that too. But even more, when you walked in here tonight and sat down, I was speechless. You are very dominant, Jade. You are smart and witty. And yes you are very pretty, but your whole package makes you completely desirable, in every way. You are more than what I imagined you to be, if that is possible." He pauses and collects himself. "But I respect you. If we can only be friends...if there is anyway, I would be happy just with that. Friendship."

Erik looks at me with such innocent eyes. Oh god, those eyes. They are Emma's eyes and entirely distracting me.

"Thank you, I'm flattered, really, I am. I am sure every woman in this café would love it if you said those things to her. But I am not every woman."

"No, you're certainly not every woman. You're like Emma in that way."

"Erik, you realize that I am not Emma, right?"

"Of course! I'm not crazy, although you can't tell by my recent behavior. The way you are like her makes me feel so... comfortable around you. Don't you have that too? You meet people that remind you of someone else that you are fond of? It's the same thing."

"Yes, I guess I do. Maybe Erik. Maybe one day we can be friends. Let's just take it one day at a time okay? So do you have

247

any more pictures of Emma?"

"No, but I do at the house if you would like to come to see them? Eve is working late tonight so she isn't there. Don't worry. I will be a perfect gentlemen, you have my word."

I look at him for a very long time and hear myself saying, "Okay." Dangling my feet over the abyss, challenging it.

Erik stands and goes to pay the check as I gather my scarf, gloves and purse. He opens the door and we walk straight into the October wind. It knocks me to the side and he grabs my arm to steady me.

"Still not used to the Dutch wind I see?"

"Or I am always fighting the height of my heels." I banter. "Thank you for the coffee."

"It's the LEAST I could do." He pauses, "Hey Halloween is tomorrow. Do you celebrate it?"

"Yeah, we are having friends over with their children for a dress up dinner party. We do it every year. Did you ever celebrate it with your dad?"

"Of course! It was a big deal at our house. Every year my mom and dad threw a Halloween party. It was my favorite holiday because I could dress up as someone else. We would have their friends over, everyone would dress up and we would sing and dance all night long." Erik reflected while smiling off into the distance.

"You don't celebrate it anymore?"

"No, there is no one else to enjoy it with." He looks down watching our footsteps.

Walking together on the small sidewalk towards his house, I remember all the times I walked with Emma in my imagination, her hand to my breast. It was odd to think of holding a man's hand that way. The story I made up for Emma begins to dissolve in my head. I see her fading beside me, hand to breast, she disappears.

Erik opens the door to his house and motions for me to walk in first. He takes off his coat and then takes my scarf and hangs it up next to his. Looking around the very large living room, the furniture is all big, fluffy and white. There is some artwork on the walls, but not much for someone with a father that was a famous artist. At the end of the living room is a large fireplace. Above the fireplace is a painting of a naked woman standing on the streets of Paris, holding one red rose. I immediately recognize it is Erik's mother, and it is the only painting Christopher kept.

Seeing my reaction he says, "Yes, that is the only one we have left of my dad's work."

"I read about it online. It's amazing," I say, standing in front of it, lost in the sentiment that crashes through. It is obvious that he loved her. It is extraordinary.

"I thought you would like it, it was created in Montparnasse."

"Was it really?" I say baffled at all of the coincidences, one after the other that keep surfacing and unveiling.

"Yeah, that is why Emma went to Paris. In a way she was looking to be closer to our mother and father. She wanted to go to all of the places they had been to." He looks at me for a very long time and then turns to the kitchen.

"Do you want a glass of wine?"

"Maybe just one but I am driving so make it a very small one."

Erik opens a bottle of red wine and pours two glasses. He comes to the couch carrying the wine and two picture books. Handing me a small glass, he sits down.

"A toast, to new friends, I hope," he winks in a non-threatening way. Our glasses clink.

Opening the first book of pictures, he scoots close to me so I am able to see. It is not uncomfortable, actually it seems like we have been friends for a long time. It is easy to talk to him and I find myself enjoying his company.

The first book is older and has pictures of when they were younger. Telling me story after story, he is really very funny, charming even. I can see a glowing on his face as he remembers each little detail. I laugh at his jokes, as I feel the wine warming me. They were so cute and in every picture their closeness is obvious. After finishing the first book, he takes out the second one that is more recent. There are pictures of Emma and Eve in it.

Erik has a few stories for each of the pictures and they look like a very close family. Erik laughs heartily telling stories of their adventures. He talks about the time they got locked out of the house and had to break in the bathroom window. He had lifted Emma up, she crawled through and ended up stepping directly in the toilet. He said she was laughing so hard with her foot stuck in the toilet. Her laugh was contagious. She took off her shoes and just threw them in the wastebasket.

"They were her favorite shoes, they must have cost 300 euro, but that was Em. Once something was ruined for her, it was out with the old and in with the new," he chuckles. "I loved that about her. Me, I keep everything. I want everything just as it always has been."

Then he tells me about the time that Emma got trapped out on her upstairs balcony in her underwear and a little tank top. She had gone out to sit in the morning sun and had closed the sliding glass door. The bar that they used for an additional lock, slid down in the locked position, so she was unable to get back inside again. The sun faded and it grew pretty chilly. It rained all day long. When he and Eve came home she was outside shivering and whimpering. The neighbors were all at work so no one could hear her when she yelled for help.

"She was sick for two weeks after that, and after a few days she could actually laugh about it. It was just another Emma adventure," he laughed hard and out loud.

Seeing her pictures and hearing the stories makes me want to know her. It is as if her ghost is haunting me, and each time I look up at Erik, I see Emma's eyes. This is such a foreign feeling. I mean, he is a man but his eyes are those of my imaginary lover, whose real life is being revealed to me. Everything is so jumbled up inside of me.

I want Jessica. I want my life back. Yearning to get up and walk away, I cannot leave Emma behind. Not yet. I am trying and I had hoped this would help, but so far it is not. It is actually making me more confused.

We come to the last picture in the book. Erik becomes visibly upset. The smile leaves his face and he loses all expression as his eyes begin to tear. "This is the last picture of Em."

I look down. He had taken the picture of her. Standing in a pair of jeans and a black bra, she is trying to put her hand in front of the camera. She is looking directly into the camera with a playful smile and everything else aside from her perfect face is blurry. I barely notice in the background, you can see Eve, also in jeans and a bra. It is so blurry but it is definitely Eve.

250

Looking up at me with sad, almost desperate eyes, he is embarrassed. "I'm sorry but I forgot the last picture I ever took of her was still in here. I thought I'd put it away. This is the first time I've seen it since she died." He looks down at the floor devastated. I can feel his deep sadness and I see a tear flow down his face. He wipes it away quickly. Without thinking, I put my arms around his head and draw him close to me.

"It's okay." Caressing his head while growing very emotional, my heart still aching from my loss of Emma and seeing his pain, allows me to submit to my feelings for her too. Erik looks up and grabs my face. "Jade, you have tears in your eyes."

"I know," I say trying to look away.

Holding my face gently in both hands, he wipes them away very tenderly with his thumbs. Instinctively, I grab his face and do the same. Our eyes connect. They are my Emma's eyes and I can see nothing but her. Erik responds to my look immediately. He leans over and kisses me.

Closing my eyes, I kiss him back. My heart begins to swell, aching for my Emma. She is in the room with us. She is inside of Erik and I can sense her all around us.

My eyes remain closed and the kisses grow more passionate. I feel myself move from my seated position, pulling up my skirt and crawling on top of him, straddling him, as he sits on the couch. My eyes remain closed. His hands are all over my back and wander down to my bare legs. I feel Emma below me. Responding to me, she pulls my jacket off and kisses my chin, my neck and the top of my breasts that are peaking out of my low cut shirt. Rubbing my hands through her hair and pressing her face into my breasts, my Emma is touching me.

She lifts my shirt as I put my arms in the air. I feel the shirt slipping over my head as she takes it off and throws it aside. Sticking her hands up under my bra, she caresses my breasts. Licking and sucking my nipple, I hear her breathe heavily. She pulls me down, and I can feel the dildo hard and ready for me. The wetness between my legs pours, as my panties rub on the hard dildo hidden underneath of her zipper. She unzips her pants and pulls it out. Rubbing myself against it, she could feel the wetness of my panties, a small layer of fabric that separates us. She lets out a very loud, deep, manly moan, breaking the spell.

Opening my eyes, I look down. There is no dildo. Instead, I see a penis, bulging and throbbing. Where did my Emma go? Oh my God, she is a man. She is Erik! Pulling back, I stand up, disgusted and distraught. I step back and fall into a chair that almost appears out of nowhere. I look at Erik, his penis exposed and his eyes full of desire, waiting for me to tell him what to do.

Something takes over my body, and I cover my naked breast with my bra. A fire ignites in my eyes and I am angry, at everything. What am I doing? What about Jessica? How could I do this to her? And Emma, there IS no Emma. Why will she not leave me alone! There is no Emma and there isn't even an illusion. It was a story, made up by him. There is no way I am going to let him fuck with my head again! Someone breaks through and a new person emerges, I am dominant Jade magnified, and I am pissed off!

I hear my voice, but do not know who is speaking. "Down on your knees and masturbate," I command.

Erik responds, looking at me in surprise. He quickly slides off of the couch to his knees. He begins caressing himself. His eyes wonder up my legs to my breasts as he works his penis in his hands. I can see he is about to climax.

"Stop," I say sternly.

He stops immediately. Standing, I walk over to him. "Bend over on all fours," I demand. "You have been very naughty." I spanked him, much harder than I would ever spank Emma, as I see the red mark of my hand on his ass.

Leaning over, I tug on his tie, much harder than I imagined with Emma. I can see the spark in his eyes from the spanking I just gave him, as my anger begins to build. Raising my eyebrow to him, I hear myself continue.

"Now take me to the box with my tie and my address," I say.

Erik does not look up at me, but instead obediently hangs his head. Crawling a few meters over to his desk, he takes a key out of his pocket and unlocks the bottom drawer. Carefully placing his hands around my box as if it were a treasure, he hands it over to me.

I remembered he said that he saved everything. He said that he had taken the box so Eve could not call me, but he never said anything about himself. I will not allow him to get the best of me again. Seeing his computer on his desk, I realize he probably didn't delete my messages either.

"Now log on to MyLIFESeeker and show me the Inbox, Outbox and Trash."

He obeys without uttering a word, continually hanging his head but now in embarrassment. I was right; he has not erased my messages after all. Everything is still there. And in a moment, CLICK, they are all gone. I look down at him with a stern look. He is still on his knees looking at the floor and for the first time he cannot look at me.

"Did you save them to your hard drive?"

He shakes his head, "No."

"Search your hard drive for my name."

He does and file pops up containing all of the messages that have transpired between us. "Erase it and delete the trash." Obediently he erases everything, and in a flash and it is gone.

I pull hard on his tie. "You lied to me Erik, again."

"Yes." He shakes his head continuing to look down. I take my hand to his chin and raise his face so he is looking up into my eyes. Humiliation. Something I said I would never do to Emma. Why am I doing it to Erik? Has my dragon completely overtaken me, where all of my morals are compromised? What have I become? I stare blankly. What the fuck have I become!

Snapping back into reality, I turn to the entryway. Erik sees this and jumps up, covering himself and zipping his pants.

"Jade, are you okay? Please don't go! I am sorry!"

Keeping my back turned to him so he can no longer see my breasts, I put on my shirt and then my jacket.

"I want you, you are perfect and I love you! I have never known love like this. I want to make love with you right now. Please, my beautiful, sweet Jade," he pleads.

Turning around, I look right through him. "Erik, I thought you were Emma." Our eyes meet and I begin to soften. "For a minute I thought you were Emma. I feel her here Erik. I thought that after seeing you, she would go away. But the truth is, I feel her more. She is with you, Erik, and she wants me too. When I opened my eyes, I saw you. You were not Emma and my reaction...my God Erik, who the fuck have I become? I humiliated you!" I say raising my voice.

Pausing to gather myself, I say in a low voice, "I cannot be with you. Ever. It was a mistake. Even though you remind me of a woman, you are a man. Everything has been such a mistake."

I rush for the door and grab my scarf, gloves, and my purse. With the box in my other hand, I have everything this time. Nothing is left behind except my scent. Erik is behind me and I can feel him coming toward me, trying to speak. I turn and look at him. He is speechless.

"I have to go," I say. Turning to leave, he grabs my shoulder firmly.

He looks at me and I see a fire in his eyes. "You cannot leave."

18

Pulling myself away from him and spinning around, I open the door and throw myself through it. I am outside. Glancing back, I catch his estranged stare and a chill runs through me. Immediately, I turn and run down the stairs. His eyes are burning in my back as he watches me flee. I walk quickly down the road back to the café where we began. Crossing the street, I weave back to my car. He will not follow me. It is just something that I know.

Driving home I wonder how I let this go so far. We were having such a good evening. I really enjoyed his company. I found him to be very funny, charming even, polite and respectful. He was sensitive and honest, but I could not get past his eyes. Identical, they further linked him to Emma and made her real to me. So real, that I almost made love to him. He *was* Emma to me. It was as if she was commanding both of us. I felt her in the room with us, summoning me. How could I let myself be so stupid? My imagination got away from me and I almost made the biggest mistake of my life.

And I am still thinking of a picture, by the couch, that I kept glancing at all evening. It was of Eve. She looked so much like Emma that it became difficult for me to distinguish them as two separate people as well. So now there are three of them, Erik, Emma and Eve, all in my head and fucking with my mind. What am I going to do? I cannot befriend him. Several of my closest friends are men and I am capable of friendship, but we crossed a line and nothing can change that. Intuition warns me.

My shirt was off and he was kissing my breasts. Even though I imagined he was Emma, he was not. He had his tongue deep in my throat and I saw his penis, enlarged, throbbing, and wanting me. It made me angry and disgusted. I hated him for what he did to me, and I lashed back by humiliating him. My words echo in my head, what the fuck have I become?

I arrive home at 11:00pm. The house is dark and my nerves are still frazzled by what had just occurred. Carefully opening the door I creep through the entryway and cross the living room to the kitchen. Grabbing a beer, I sit dazed by the table. The cold bottle freezes my fingers. I sit still, determined to force the unsteadiness away. Opening my laptop to check my messages, the shining bright screen reflects on my face, making me look like the undead. I know there will be a message from him, and I am ready for it.

The beast is no longer behind me. My eyes are now HERS, glowing, WE have become one.

Date: October 30, 2008 10:33PM
Subject: Caught in the Moment

Beautiful, Sweet Jade,

What just happened? I swear to you I had not intended on that to occur. I did not. I am so sorry. Have I crossed the line and ruined everything once again?

Jade, I don't want to lose you. I was very caught up in the moment and there you were. You were sitting beside me comforting and holding me. I could smell your perfume and feel the softness of your skin. All night you were so wonderful and yes, very sexy too. I have to admit my attraction to you was unlike I have ever felt before. You showed me love and tonight is the very first time I have ever physically experienced it. It was even more than I had imagined. But I must not say that to you.

I kissed you. That was wrong and I should not have. You were crying, and so was I. And yes, Emma was there too. It surprised me how strongly she was there with us. You felt it too. I knew it! Has she brought us together for a reason? You say you humiliated me Jade. You did not. I deserved it.

I have to say something. There are more things that I want to tell you in person. Things that I did not get to say, and I want

256

to see you again. I need to see you again because there is something I need to ask you.

Do you trust me enough to see me again? Please give me another chance. I had a really great time with you tonight, you did too I think. Let's not lose this friendship.

Your friend,
Erik

_____

Date: October 30, 2008 11:57PM
Subject: Goodbye

Dearest Erik,

I am sorry too. It was as much my fault as it was yours. Yes, right, you kissed me, but I climbed on top of you. I let everything happen and I wanted it to happen, because my eyes were closed and you were Emma, in my mind. You really were.

Looking into your windows I saw her. She was there. I thought by seeing you I would eliminate Emma, and perhaps you and I could be friends. You are right we had a wonderful time, and I believe very much that we would make great friends.

But, what I did not count on was not only did Emma not go away, as I had hoped, but instead she magnified inside of you and became real. She was living and breathing through you and I kept seeing pictures of Eve, who looks exactly like Emma. So instead of walking away with one friend, I walked away with three people who in some strange way were all my lovers and who are now haunting me. Erik, you were my lover virtually under false pretenses. We could never be lovers in real life. I could never be with a man again. It would never work and I have no desire to try. I am not attracted to men in that way, you know that.

So you must understand that I cannot possibly see you again. I choose my family. I want to be with my wife. I love her so deeply and she is my reality. I have been caught way too long in this fantasy. This situation, instead of helping me release Emma, has become very dangerous. I cannot be in this situation, nor do I want

257

to. I did humiliate you Erik, something I promised Emma I would never do. I did, because I was angry and that was not right. I am sorry for that.

I do forgive you Erik. I do.

I wish you the very best, but this is where we must say goodbye.

And Erik, I want you to know that this experience has brought something to my life. I think I always knew that you were not who you said you were. Something told me inside, but you were giving me something that I needed. Friendship yes, and other things. You brought me back to life. You made me rediscover my words and want to write again. For that gift, I say thank you.

Know I will miss you. I will miss Emma, and in a strange way I will miss Eve too.

I must say goodbye. It is time.

xoxo
Jade

  I close my laptop and I realize that no matter what he replies, it is all over for me. What I didn't know was that even though it was over for me, it was not over.

19

It is Halloween night. We are having a few friends and their kids over for a spooky dinner party. Dressing up in costumes is always a big hit with our Dutch friends, and they also look forward to the Halloween games, like bobbing for apples. We have done this every year since having a child. Our son adores Halloween.

Jessica and I are dressed as mimes, in all black with white faces. Our son is a dressed like a Storm Trooper from Star Wars. He has been a little jumping bean, waiting for everyone to get here. Halloween decorations cover every bare spot in our house. I also bought dry ice to put in the toilet. With the lid closed, it appears to be steaming, and this is always a favorite. Cobwebs, ghosts, witches and jack-o-lanterns are sprinkled throughout the house. We do have some scary monsters, mainly for the adults to see. And Jessica's grandfather lent us one of his old sickles that he collects. He keeps it very sharp. Even though it has a self-made blade protector, I admit it is disturbing. But it was his proud contribution to our big day, so we have hung it up in the hallway, very high, far out of reach from the children.

Scary music plays in the background, but not too scary, we do want the kids to be able to sleep tonight. Otherwise, we will have some angry parents on our hands. Jessica and I are busy preparing the food and running around getting ready. As we pass each other in the hallway or in the kitchen, I grab her face and kiss her. Or she grabs my bum playfully. It is our way of never being too busy for each other.

Tonight is a welcomed distraction from Erik, who lingers in the back of my mind. Although, he is slowly disappearing, and I feel relieved. When I think of Emma, my heart still aches, but I have some consolation knowing that she never really existed. I believe I knew all along that Emma was hiding something. I thought perhaps her picture wasn't real or that maybe she wasn't as attractive as she claimed to be, but I never really truly believed she was a man. I suspected it early on, but her words grew so feminine that the thought had escaped me.

Erik has not responded to my email and I am glad. I think he will respect the situation and not contact me again. I am so happy to be fully present in my own home again, and to be celebrating Halloween with our friends.

Two couples arrive simultaneously with their children. They are our closest friends that we have known for many years now. Our children are all around the same age. The kids play and pretend to trick or treat upstairs while we fix blood soup, which is really red pepper soup with crusty bread, for the first round. We are all laughing and poking at each other's costumes.

Opening the full trash, I remove it from the bin and take it outside. The night air is crisp and the wind is howling through the trees. The men come outside with me to cool off because we keep our house pretty warm. Standing outside, Pieter is telling me a story of taking his children to look at Halloween decorations.

Halloween is something new for the Netherlands, so not many people really understand what it is. This is the first year some of the stores have set out decorations, costumes, wigs etc... Pieter said he and his wife and kids were trying on wigs and laughing at each other. The passersby watched and then joined in too, as others stood by, speechless. They were curious and were laughing, while watching Pieter try on a wig. I laughed at his story. One thing I know is that Dutch people are rarely speechless, and secondly, they are rarely surprised by anything.

It feels so good to be around friends that are familiar to me, yet I notice being outside, that something is distracting me. Maybe it is the creepiness of the evening, with all the scary sounds in my head, as the wind whips through the trees. This coupled with the strange things that happened yesterday makes it all a bit surreal. And I have a very strange sensation that someone is watching us.

Jessica breaks the moment by opening the door and singing, "Soup is ready." I glance around our very large backyard before going inside. There are so many shadows from the trees, and it is impossible to see the entire yard. Shivering as a chill runs up my spine, I sense someone is hiding in the shadows, waiting. I glance at both neighbors' houses and the lights are dark. It is a Friday night, so they are most likely out to dinner. Perhaps it is the cat next door. He loves to observe us, and often I see his eyes shining in the dark under the trees that separate our property from the neighbors. Most likely it is my overactive imagination.

We sit for hours at the long dinner table that overlooks the back yard. The kids are playing and having fun running around in their costumes. The night passes quickly and by eight o'clock, we have eaten and had several glasses of wine. Cheerful and open, we are all enjoying a perfect evening. The children are bouncing off of the walls, too much chocolate and excitement for one night. So after coffee, we decide it is time to end the evening so our friends can get home and put the kids to bed at a decent hour.

The children gather their bags with candy, and everyone begins to shuffle out the door. Jess and I stand in the doorway waving, as our friends pack up their kids and disappear into the darkness. Jessica goes in the living room, undresses our son and put his pajamas on. Turning on the computer, I pop open iTunes and search for some happy, dance music. I love to sing and dance around as I clean the kitchen. The dishes are stacked high so this will take a while.

Jessica shouts at me that she it taking our son upstairs to bed. I look outside and can only see my reflection in the window with a background of darkness. I don't feel like someone is out there anymore, but I do feel a presence. As I turn around to look behind me, I see Erik standing in the living room, watching me dance.

Startled, I drop the dish that I was holding and it shatters on the floor. He sees a look of fright and uncertainty in my eyes. His expression changes as Jessica enters the room.

"Jade, your colleague has stopped by." She looks at me and notices the apprehension. "Are you okay?"

"Yes baby, I am fine. I just turned around and saw him standing in the living room and it startled me. I didn't hear him come in."

"Turn down the music silly! It is a good thing I heard the knock at the door, you never would have." Jessica pats me playfully on the shoulder and walks over to Erik.

"I am off to put our son in bed. It is always nice meeting Jade's colleagues. I haven't heard her mention you. You must be new?"

"Yes, I started about a month ago."

"Well, if I don't see you before you leave it was nice meeting you," she says matter-of-factly.

"Thank you, it was nice meeting you too, Jessica." Watching her leave, he turns to me and approaches with a concerned look on his face. "Before you get angry, I did not keep your address. I remembered your last name and I looked you up in the directory."

I walk over to him and closely stare into his eyes, searching for intimidation. "Erik you should not be here. How could you come here," I whisper angrily. "Why do you continue to fuck with me and create problems?" I am visibly angry and in disbelief that he actually showed up at my home.

"I needed to speak with you. I thought if I wrote it in a message, you would not respond to me. You said it was goodbye and this is the only way I knew to be able to talk to you. I knew you would never come to me again."

"You are right about that Erik. I have nothing left to say. I've told you everything. We cannot continue as friends...we crossed a line that wasn't meant to be crossed!"

"I know. I've come to talk to you about something else. There is something that I want to tell you."

"I don't want to hear it, I mean it. You shouldn't be here. You have to leave! How dare you come to my house? I'm so angry that you have specifically done what I have asked you never to do. Do you understand the risks for me? Do you want me to come to your house when Eve is home?" I whisper a little louder.

Entirely unintimidated, Erik grows frustrated, as he steps closer to me and raises his voice, "I'm sorry. What you're doing is not fair. You can't just end this. I need you in my life. I need you, and I want to tell you why."

Stepping back, I shake my head and say in a threatening tone, "Erik, leave or I will call the police!"

His face grows very red, and I can see his anger rising to the surface. It begins to scare me. My wife and son are upstairs, and I am not sure what this guy is capable of. I don't think he will hurt me, but then I didn't think he would come to my house either.

He approaches me looking down and then up at me. He is looking obsessively at all of my body parts that I shared with Emma, shaking his head and saying over and over, "You don't understand."

I back up further and smack against a tall table behind me. He quickly moves over to me, grabs my arms and presses my back

262

against it hard. Physically blocking me from moving, I become hyper-aware of his strength. His shirt is tight and I can see the veins in his chest and arm muscles bulge while pushing against me. I try to move, but he has me pinned to the table.

"Stop, you're hurting me." I need to stop fighting him and maybe he will release me. My body goes limp, as I soften my voice and my eyes turn sad. Trying to reach his emotional side I whimper, "Erik, don't hurt me...please."

Instead of releasing me, he continues to press his body against me. I can feel his hard penis on my hip. He thrusts forward slightly. Then gaining control of himself, he releases my arms and put his hands around my face.

"I could never hurt you," he whispers, and I can see the emotion in his face. Clearly, he is in love with me.

"What is going on?" I hear Jessica's voice behind him. Startled, Erik backs up away from me, and looks over at Jessica with surprise.

"Get the fuck out of my house!" Jessica says in a voice that I have never heard. I hear rage building in her throat, but she is fully in control of her tone.

Erik glances over at me. I don't know this look. It is despairing, yet something behind his eyes frightens me. He is possessed with Emma's ghost and both of them crave me. I see the hunger grow, and now he is ravenous. He is obsessed with me, and Jessica is his rival.

After a long look at me, he turns, walks past Jessica, and out the front door. My entire body is shaking as I feel the hot tears streaming uncontrollably down my cheeks. Putting my face in my hands, I finally release all of my emotion. I weep, as my body falls limp and crumbles onto the floor.

Jessica rushes over to me, crawls beside me, and puts her arms around me. She holds me tight, caresses my head and says, "Don't worry, no one is going to hurt this family."

Calming down, I look at her completely confused. "Don't you want to know who he is?"

"I already know. I have known something was going on for a long time. I didn't know exactly...I knew you found a fuck-buddy. But a man, your fuck-buddy is a man," she says in disgust.

"No, Jessica. No!" Looking her in the eyes then lowering my head, I reply in guilt, "It is a long, incredibly fucked up story. I thought he was a woman…remember Emma?"

"THAT was Emma?"

"Yes. At first we were friends and I was writing stories to her. I wanted to improve my writing and also I'd hoped to make a friend. But after you told me to get a fuck-buddy, I did, virtually. She was there. Then she fell in love with me and I began to fall in love with her, or at least I thought I did. Maybe my imagination did. The joke was on me though, because I found out Emma was a man. I was having sex online with Erik. I was so scared to tell you, Jess, I was afraid you would leave me." My eyes move to the ground as I confess.

"I want you to tell me everything, and I mean *everything*. I'm not going to leave you. If that were the case, I would have left you a long time ago. But first, tell me what you have learned," she says.

I look up into her eyes with surprise. They are beautiful, and I am not worthy of her reaction. I respond immediately and respectfully, "I thought that I wanted another life, but once I realized that I didn't, I was in too deep. What a mess I made. I realized that everything I ever wanted was not in a new life or with a new person. Everything that I wanted and needed was right before my eyes. This is my home Jessica. You and our son are my home."

Jessica hugs me, takes my hand and leads me to the couch. Sitting down she looks at me for a very long moment. "Your confirmation hurts, but I knew something was going on. I am very, very hurt, but we have to deal with that later."

I look to the ground, embarrassed that I disappointed her and filled with the guilt of my betrayal. She grabs my face and forces me to look at her. "I would do anything to keep this family safe. In order to do that, I need to know everything. We'll fix this together."

I told her everything, but maybe I should not have told her *everything*.

20

I cannot sleep. It is four o'clock in the morning, and I am fully awake. Thinking of what happened last night, I am still in disbelief that Erik came to our house. He physically restrained me, yes, and also the look that was in his eye is unsettling. I am afraid he might try to come back and hurt us.

Earlier in the evening, when I felt someone watching me, I bet he was in the back yard, hidden between the trees. The thought of him standing there, visually following us throughout the evening while studying every gesture that I made, repulses me. I felt him. He was there almost all evening, I was sure of it.

I wonder if he saw me dancing while I was preparing the meal and Jessica was upstairs. Windows cover the entire backside of our house. It is a private yard, so unless you are actually standing in it, you cannot see in. I often bring my clothes down when we are having people over. After I cook, I change my shirt to a nicer, dressier one. If I cook in my nice clothes, I always spill something on them and have to change anyway.

Last night after I cooked, I was standing facing the sink. I took my shirt off and I had no bra on. If Erik had been outside, he would have seen my naked breasts while I put on my red and black strappy bra.

I had called for Jessica to bring down a shirt for me. So I stood there in my bra, getting out the silverware. The music was up loud and I was dancing around the kitchen shaking my bum. The thought of him standing outside, wanting me, sent cold chills up my spine.

Staring at the ceiling, I think about Jessica's reaction to what I told her. In all of the years we have been together, she has never been jealous. After I told her about Erik and Emma, I could see it covering her, fierce and barely under control.

I found it odd was that she was not mad. She had me back. She was angry with Erik. Was she though?

Seeing him pressing against me, holding my arms. She had

walked in just as I released my resistance and asked him not to hurt me. She saw him release and touch my face. He was in love with her wife. As she broke the moment and spoke, her eyes were raging and her body tense. I feel sure that my very feminine wife could have taken Erik down at that very moment.

Jessica's back is to me, so I spoon up next to her and put my arm around her. I stick my hand up her shirt touching her warm skin. I can feel her breathing and I feel safe.

Last night, after telling Jessica everything, she had said we would discuss it tomorrow and figure out a way to fix it. She also said that we needed to protect ourselves. This keeps echoing in my mind. Jessica always has been able to foresee things. Even with the most insignificant situations, she has been able to predict the outcome. It is a sixth sense.

In the Netherlands, if someone breaks into your house you do not have the right to defend yourself. Well you do, but not like in the US. The Dutch call it "eigen rechter spelen". It means playing your own judge, and you must never do that. Restraining the culprit is okay, but you cannot hurt them. Often you hear stories of someone breaking into a home, and the homeowner goes to jail for hurting the offender.

Pepper spray is illegal, and so are guns (I am all for that). I wonder how two women are supposed to protect themselves against an intruder, and especially one that is there to hurt them.

We thought maybe we should call the police, but that would be bringing something quite embarrassing into the public eye. Everyone knows us and before long, our entire community would be meddling in the fucked up situation.

Jessica said she thought Erik was obsessed with me, and that he wanted to have sex with me very badly. She thought he wanted to make all of those messages a reality. She said that he might come back to hurt me, rape me, or maybe both.

A friend of mine had a lesbian sister in California. She and her girlfriend took their car in to be repaired. Not thinking, they also left their house key along with the car key. This was a trusted establishment that had been servicing their car for years. They knew everyone there. The mechanic ended up breaking into their house, holding them against their will and raping both of them.

266

I told Jessica that I really didn't think Erik had it in him. Even though he got physical with me last night, I was not sure he could ever do that, but then... When I replayed his actions, it was clear that I wasn't sure. So we decided to send our son to grandpa and grandma's house for a couple of days while we found a solution. We will take him there as soon as everyone is up, fed and dressed.

It is 6:30am as I drift off to sleep. An hour later, I can hear noises downstairs. Looking over, the bed is empty. Dragging myself into the shower, I dread the day ahead. The warm water awakens my body as the morning chill dissipates. Washing over my face, it cleanses me from the residue of last night, of the last month.

I dress, dry my hair and put on my makeup. After packing an overnight bag for my son, I go downstairs to send Jessica up to get ready. Opening the door to the living room, my little jumping bean is bopping up and down, happy to see me. I give him a hug and kiss as his smiling eyes brighten my world. Helping him dress he is telling me a joke. Even though it doesn't make sense, I giggle at his very cute attempt.

After making a cup of tea, I check my email, but I do not log on to MyLIFESeeker. I've promised Jessica we would check it together from now one. We have agreed that we will jointly read all communication moving forward. In case there are little hints in them, predicting Erik's next move. It feels good having her on my side, working to help me figure this out. I surrender access to my once hidden life, allowing me the ability to regain my strength and prepare for what might come next.

As we drive our son to his grandparent's house, I hold Jessica's hand as I guide our car through all of the traffic. "Where is everyone going on a Saturday?" I say, breaking the silence. Glancing over at Jessica, she is lost in thought. I can feel her hand tense and see her lips are tight. She seems worried and preoccupied. Noticing my concern, she squeezes her hand in mine.

"Don't worry, it will all be fine," I say. She smiles uneasily and tightens her grip.

After dropping our son off, we return home to discuss what we are going to do if Erik does come back. Jessica makes some tea and we sit down by the kitchen table. I am prepared to face this head on, with her by my side.

"If he knocks on the door we shouldn't let him in. He might keep coming back...or maybe even try to hurt us...we don't know. I think we should agree to both meet him someplace public. We'll talk to him through the closed door, and ask that he meet us somewhere in town," I say assertively.

"That's a good idea" she replies, "but what if he only wants to meet with you?"

"I'll tell him the only way I will meet him, is if you can come with me."

"Then threaten him, threaten telling Eve or better yet, threaten going public with your story. He is a businessman, he couldn't afford that."

It is a good point. "Yes, I need to let him tell me whatever else he needs to say and then, to make sure he will stay away, I will threaten him."

"Have you checked your messages yet today?" she questions.

"Not yet." I stand, go to the computer and log on, but there are no new messages.

"This is really unusual. He writes every day. I expected a message, and it is very strange there isn't one there."

"He will come tonight," Jessica says, staring out the window.

"Should I message him and agree to meet?"

"No, let's not write anymore messages. Maybe he will just go away...but I would not count on it."

"I have pepper spray someplace upstairs that we brought over from the US when we moved here. It probably would not hurt to get that out."

"It couldn't hurt. So now what?" Jessica's blue eyes are searching for me to take control.

"Well, I doubt he will come during the day today, so why don't you go out and get movies for us to watch and some food for tonight. I will stay here and look for the pepper spray and clean up upstairs. When you get back we can start taking down all of the Halloween decorations."

Jessica nods her head. She puts her shoes on, and gathers her purse and keys. She is entirely distracted and moving in a confused manner. "I'll be back in a half hour or so." She comes over and kisses me for a very long time. "I love you baby."

268

"Do you forgive me Jessica?"

"Yes I do. We all make mistakes. You realized what was important, and that is what I needed to hear," she smiles, gently pushing back the hair out of my face. Then her expression turns serious and I see the look of jealously and betrayal.

"But don't let it happen again." Looking at me for a very long time, she then turns and walks into the kitchen. I know she means it.

Running up stairs, I start sifting through the very full drawers, searching for the pepper spray. About ten minutes later, I hear Jessica close the door and her car drive off, as I begin digging through the third drawer. I find it at the bottom. It is eight years old so it probably isn't any good anyway. I need to check online to see what the lifetime of pepper spray is. I'll do that later. First, I need to clean, it will be a good distraction.

Our bedroom is in the back of the house, and I love the windows that cover this room overlooking the pool. Gazing out at our backyard, my mind flashes to last night. I think of how it looked in the dark. All of the trees created so many shadows anyone could hide in several places in our yard and never be seen, even in daylight.

Then I hear the sound of our drapes closing downstairs. Jessica must have forgotten something and has come back. The drapes are attached to the ceiling so whoever is upstairs can clearly hear as they open or close. Moving to the top of the stairs, I can hear Jessica walking about in the living room.

Without thinking I yell, "Jess, did you forget your movie pass?" Just before speaking I noticed the footsteps were unusually heavy. They sound strange and immediately stop after I speak. Everything falls silent. I didn't hear the front door buzzer that goes off each time it opens. Sheer terror shoots through my body, as I realize, it isn't Jessica.

He is back!

21

Frozen at the top of the stairs, I dare not move. My mind races along with my heart, as I think of what I can do to stall him from coming up the stairs. I hear myself say, "Honey, I will be right down. I think I put the movie pass in the bookcase, I'll help you look for it."

I step slowly backwards from the hallway, into the bedroom, and I grab the phone. Holding it in my hand, I am shaking uncontrollably. My mind is blank. 911? What is the fucking number in the Netherlands for emergency services! My memory is frozen, and I cannot think clearly. My son just got a toy rescue boat for his birthday with the number on it. What is it? I dial 1211 and I realize this is not the right number. Shit! I am trapped!

Unable to believe this is happening to me, I search for clarity and try to suppress my panic. I know this is the only way forward. Think clearly, act intelligently, I want to live and I will not let him hurt me. I breathe in and exhale long twice. I need more time, but don't have it. Looking over at the picture of my family at Disneyland, I stand at the stairway determined. I am ready to face this.

I listen. Complete silence. He is waiting for me to come down the stairs. The heavy footsteps are gone and he is lurking, waiting to pounce on me. I sense it. If I do go down, he will physically overpower me. I have to remain upstairs; there is no choice. There is only one weapon to threaten him with from afar, the phone.

Looking down at it, my fingers are white from the death grip I have on it. I hear myself yell loudly, channeling my dominant voice, "Erik, get the fuck out of my house! I am calling the police. I have the phone in my hand and I am calling the fucking police!" Pretending to dial, I say loudly, "Hello, there is an intruder in my house. My address is..."

Stopping midsentence, I look down at the bottom of the stairs. Complete fear, like I have never experienced, penetrates my body, as my determination is suffocated. Erik is standing there, looking up at me. He is holding my other phone and I can hear the dial tone. He knows that I am bluffing. Smiling absently, he tilts his head and states articulately, "Now Jade, you are fibbing."

He swiftly jumps up the steps, moving with intention. He has an estranged look in his eyes, more intense than the previous evening. My knees feel like they will buckle underneath of me. It is a familiar feeling, like when in a dream and something scary is happening. You cannot move, your knees become weak and everything is in slow motion. I am paralyzed with fear, and very aware that this is certainly not a dream.

Managing to move backwards into the bedroom, I close the door as I hear him getting closer. I try to turn the lock, but it is missing. My son had accidentally locked himself in this room when he was little and could not get out. Jessica and I pounded on the door in a panic, without success. We ended up breaking the lock with a crowbar. We never replaced it, why would we need it?

Frustrated, I pound hard on the door with my fist. Fuck! I lean over, look through the missing lock hole and see him reaching the landing. His face is smug and he is entirely in control. Who is this man?

The top of the stairs is directly across from the bedroom so there is no way to go to another room. I am really trapped now and in an unlocked room. Heartbeat racing, I am completely outside of my body watching this happen in disbelief. How did I end up here?

"Jade, open the door, or get back because I am busting it down!" I try to hold the handle, but he is stronger than I am. He realizes there is no lock, so he easily turns the handle and pushes his way in. Using such force, he knocks me back against the window that overlooks the backyard. For a moment, I think of jumping through it.

I remember the pepper spray across the room. I need to get to it. Will it even work? Erik thunders through the door. His face is red and he seems more frustrated than the other night.

"Will you stop acting like a crazy person!" he says as he reaches out for me.

"A crazy person? You motherfucker! You broke into *my* house. FUCK YOU!" I scream. I am enraged. As he reaches for me, I start to hit him in the chest. He grabs my arm and throws me easily aside and onto the bed.

271

"Jade, stop it! Listen to me, would you just stop. I just want to talk to you."

Scrambling across the bed, I reach for the pepper spray, while he grabs my feet and pulls me back towards him. Kicking him in the chest, I attempt to again reach for it. He yanks me backwards and restrains my legs as my fingers brush the pepper spray. It tumbles off of the table and slides across the floor, completely out of sight. I am defenseless.

"Stop struggling!"

He flips me over, spreads my knees, and he is now lying on top of me. His full body weight presses against me. Holding down my arms so I am completely immobile, his face is just above mine. My eyes are full of hate. Damn it! I don't want him to see me cry, so I suppress my tears with anger. "Get off of me!" I scream. I cannot move my arms, and I know that I am panicking.

"Stop it!" Erik raises his voice and presses harder on top of me. I can feel his penis on my leg. Again, it is rock hard and I am disgusted. All of this is exciting him? I cannot move my legs enough to knee him in the groin.

"Jade, I love you. Stop struggling! I love you!"

My body stops hoping this will make him release too. He bends down and kisses me romantically on the lips. I do not kiss him back, but I stare at him, at Emma's eyes, with intense hatred.

His hands move down my body, reaching for something. Is he reaching for a knife or a weapon? Will he kill me now? I am breathing hard as he pulls his hand out of his pocket. He puts the object beside my neck. Oh my God, he has something. It is a knife, and he is going to kill me!

"Erik please don't...don't kill me," I plead.

Thrusting his hard penis in between my legs harder and harder, he caresses my forehead. His eyes are crazed and I do not recognize him. Lifting up high, he opens his mouth. I expect to hear those words again. He is going to say he loves me, rape me and then kill me. I know it.

Suddenly, I see a flash of an object appear from nowhere. I hear him grunt, as a strange mixture of love and pain comes over his face. What? What the fuck is going on?

Looking directly at me, he opens his hand to reveal not a knife or

272

a gun but a small box. I thought he had a knife? Where is his knife? Looking at him in confusion, the box falls out of his hand and against my cheek. What is happening? He reaches down to his chest and I see the sickle lodged deeply in it.

Loosing consciousness, he collapses. His full body weight on top of me presses the sharp sickle further into his heart, as it crushes my arm. I see Jessica at his side, standing in shock.

He is dead.

22

Jessica stands frozen in disbelief, entirely out of her element. She thought he was raping me or going to kill me. She saved me, didn't she?

"Get him off of me!" I began to panic as my body moves in a frenzied rush to escape. My legs that were pinned break free, but his weight makes it impossible to completely escape from underneath of him. Jessica revives back into the moment and helps lift him, as I crawl out from under him.

Wiping my face, I look down to see blood all over my hands. Looking past my hands, my shirt is bloody. Am I bleeding as well? Lifting it up, I see my tummy and chest, uninjured. I look down at him in disbelief, and then I glance over to Jessica. She is back in her same position, staring at him. She is a statue. We both gaze in shock at the body for what seems an eternity.

His body is still, and he is not moving. My two fingers slide around his neck to check his pulse. Come on Erik, you need to have a pulse, please have a pulse! Nothing. I can't believe it. She killed him. I turn and look at her in despair. What have we done?

"Jess, Jessica...you are going to have to look at me. Look at me!" She turns to me and her face is filled with confusion. "Jess, we cannot call the police. You will go to jail. He didn't have a weapon and we have played our own judge. You will go to jail."

Realizing the magnitude of the consequences, it hits me with the power of a hurricane, as I struggle to remain standing. We are at a crossroads and I will not let her go to jail. She saved my life and now I will protect hers.

"We have to clean this up. Help me put him onto the floor," I say.

Sitting on the bed, we struggle to flip him over. Finally, he rolls off and lands on the floor with a very loud thud. Our son had been sleeping with us the past couple of nights. We had put two plastic covers over the mattress in case he had an accident, something that still sometimes happens even at five yrs old. I pull the sheets and the plastic off of the bed and lay it over Erik's face covering his eyes. Taking a moment to collect my thoughts, my body is shaking and my mind is retreating.

Everything is running in reverse. He was thrusting against me, hurting me. Annoyed that I would not listen to him, yet hard and excited, I knew he was enjoying it. There was something in the way he looked at me that warned me, he was still playing a game, one that he intended on winning. I run to the bathroom and throw up twice.

What have we done? Would he have raped me? There was no weapon so I don't think he would have killed me, but I am not sure. My instincts tell me he would, but I have no idea what he was *really* thinking or what he might have done. What would have happened had she not come home? We will never know.

I have to stop thinking about it. More immediately, I need to concentrate on what we are going to do. Everyday in my business negotiations, I disconnect my emotion, focusing only on mental. I must now too. Channeling this side of me, I close my eyes and concentrate on my breath. It slows as I isolate the muscles in my face and lips, consciously working my way down to my feet, while releasing some of the tension from my body. Though not fully relaxed my thoughts become crisp again. We have to get him out of here, but the blood, we need to contain the blood.

"We have to clean this up and I need you to do exactly what I say. Don't think of anything else okay? Look into my eyes Jessica. Okay?" Jessica blinks, looks down at the sickle in his chest, and then to me. She nods slowly.

"Okay, good. Now go downstairs. Grab scissors, electric tape, towels, wipes, paper towels, a bucket and all the garbage bags you can find. Make sure all the doors are locked and the curtains are closed. Do you understand?" She nods again, this time a little more quickly.

Jessica pauses, then turns quickly and she disappears. Walking over to the sink, I look up at a stranger staring back at me. Whose face is underneath all of the blood? I don't recognize her anymore. My fiery eyes that have been burning for the last several months have now dimmed. Erik's are black.

Spreading soap all over my face, neck and arms, I scrub hard and quick, needing to remove some of the blood. It is in my hair and my shirt, but at least I get the majority of it off of my skin. I need to recognize myself.

Jessica arrives with everything that I have asked her to get. I need to remove the sickle. Shuddering at the thought of it, I squat down and place my hands over the end and pull. Surprisingly, it slides out easier than I expected. Stuffing tissues around and inside the wound, I tape over it. As we wipe the floors clean with the white paper towels, they transmute into red handkerchiefs. I pick one up and it has a large tear in it. I think of Emma, and the last adventure with the red handkerchief. Torn, dying of heartache.

After wiping up the majority of the blood, we cover his head and shoulders in a doubled garbage bag. I reach into his pockets and pull out keys and a wallet. We continue to cover the rest of his body with garbage bags cut open. We piece them together like a quilt and seal them with electrical tape. After we have wrapped and bound him we stand back and stare at the large package. I shake my head and feel tears welling up inside of me. I push my emotion back down inside of my tummy. Focus, I must stay focused.

Downstairs we roll up the large black rug that is in our living room. Carrying it upstairs, we lay it flat on the bedroom floor. Pulling the bundle by the legs onto the rug, we roll him up in it. His feet and lower legs are extending out of the end of it, but they are covered and sealed, unidentifiable to the naked eye. Wrapping the entire mass again with another layer of garbage bags, we secure it again with electrical tape.

Underneath of our bed is a long wooden board, left over from some of the repairs that we had done in the upstairs before we moved into the house. Remembering it, I slide it out. We push his body to one side and slide it underneath him.

Pulling him from the ankles, the board slides across the laminated floor to the top of the stairs. We push him over the landing and down the stairway. The heavy wrapped corpse, resting on the board, quickly slides down. Stepping around the edges of the rolled up carpet as we creep down carefully, we manage to reach the bottom. We pull him the rest of the way down and into the garage that is next to the stairway. No blood seeping out, we have managed to contain it pretty well.

Jessica is waiting for me to speak, revealing our next steps. I look

276

down and everything around me begins to shrink. My world and all of its possibilities seem to absorb into the self-constructed body bag.

"I need to go shower. Will you finish cleaning up the bedroom? I need to think." Jessica nods. "Then you'll need to shower. We will take our clothes and put them in a plastic bag. Then I'll figure out what we will do next. Okay?" Jessica hugs me tight. "What have I done?" she whispers. "I didn't think I would kill him. He was hurting you and I didn't know what else to do. The sickle was the first thing I could see. I heard him yelling at you...and...then you begging him not to kill you. I was so scared he would hurt you. I should never have left you here. I didn't know...I didn't mean to..." she begins to cry hysterically. Her body is shaking uncontrollably. I hold her and let her try to release some of the negative energy that has now become part of both of us.

"You saved us, that is what you did. That would have been me in this body bag had you not come in, Jess...and maybe you too. It's going to be okay. I'll figure this out, but I need you to try to get it together." She began to calm down.

"Okay, I am going to take a shower, while you get started on the bedroom."

I climb up the stairs while she walks to the kitchen to get a drink of water. Entering the bedroom, I see the box. I had almost forgotten about it. Standing above it, I wonder, what could be inside?

Opening it slowly, a key reveals itself. Underneath of it is a card with a number scribbled on it. I have no idea what it is and there are no hints as to what this obviously very important key unlocks. I put it back in the box and set it on the dresser.

I undress slowly, aware of how my muscles are sore from struggling with Erik. His eyes were crazed and his actions had become so unfamiliar to me. The typically safe, predictable person, that I had initially met, was erratic.

Time is critical and I need to keep moving. I carefully place my clothes in a garbage bag, while Jessica enters the room and begins to clean up. "Everything must go in the bag Jess."

"I know," she stammers. I notice her movements are robotic. She is never robotic. When she is working on a task she is usually singing or humming and enjoying the moment.

Standing in the shower, the temperature of the water is high, raining down hot on my skin. There is no way to make it scalding enough to cleanse me from what has just occurred. So, I scrub my skin and my hair madly, but the harder I scrub the more polluted I feel. It is no use. I am contaminated. The bloody water is dripping down from my hair, and my skin in blotchy red from the friction of the washcloth. Placing my hands on my face, the tears begin to well up. I pinch myself hard. Get it together.

Turning off the shower, I dry off and then walk into the bedroom. I am surprised by how far Jessica has gotten. She finishes putting the mop head in a dirty bucket, and all other towels and wipes are in the garbage bag.

I look at her compassionately as I see her fright, "Baby, go shower. Get clean. We both need to be clean."

"What are we going to do?"

"I'm not sure yet, I am still figuring it all out, just go shower. I'll have a solution soon."

She gathers the trash bags filled with bloody rags and puts them in the hallway for us to take downstairs. I grab a clean towel out of the closet and hand it to her. She walks blankly into the bathroom. This is too much for her. I know my girl. It is too much for both of us. This is not where we were meant to be, and it is my fault.

Opening the box again and picking up the key, I wonder what it could open? Maybe Erik's desk drawer where he kept my box? His house? What? Well this I will need to come back to, first I need to prioritize the package in our garage. I have to pretend it is a package. I cannot cope with acknowledging there is a dead body in it. I cannot.

Walking stiffly down the stairs, I habitually am drawn to my computer. I should recheck my MyLIFESeeker account for messages just in case I received something from him. To prevent any further link to one another, I must delete him from my friends list. Later tonight, I need to try to see if I can figure out his password and log on to his account and deactivate it.

I have one new message and it is from Emma, Erik. My heart sinks. It was sent at 11:45am. That was just after I checked my account this morning, and I missed it by only minutes. It must

278

have been sent just before he left to come to my house. It was possibly the very last thing he did before coming to me. The timing of our messages feels like fate is driving this mess. But why?

Staring at his message, I am reluctant to open it. This is the last one I would ever receive from her, my Emma. From him. My hands tremble and guilt sweeps over me. Oh Emma, what have I done? I am so sorry we killed your brother.

Opening the message, I begin to read:

Date: November 1, 2008   11:45AM
Subject: The final truth

Beautiful, Sweet Jade,

This is the last time I will be writing to you. I am going to come to your house to tell you this story and I hope you will see me. If not you will have to read this message one day. Maybe not now, but I hope that you will forgive me enough to open this and read it.

I gave you my story and now I want to give you the full story. This is the story I tried to tell you when I came over to see you Halloween night. I wanted to tell you this, but you would not listen to me. I think that I scared you, Jade, am I right? I love you and I mean it when I say, I will not hurt you.

Let me be clear, I love you more than you will ever know. I love you because you have set me free. You have released me from the prison of guilt that I have lived in for many years. You have released me from my sister Emma. Let me tell you more about my relationship with her. Everything I have told you is true, everything. But there is more, something more private. Something I have told no one until now.

When I was a teenager, I was like all teen boys, hormonal and going through puberty. I was about fourteen and I started having these thoughts about Emma. I was having sexual thoughts about women, yes, but I was beginning to translate those to my sister. She was the only girl in my life that would even speak to me. I felt disgusted with myself. I knew it was wrong. Nothing ever happened, it was my secret.

After mama, dad and Oma died, we were even more tightly linked because there was only the two of us. She and I took care of one another. My feelings for her began to grow but I never told her.

We went to university but continued to live together. I used to become so jealous of the women she brought home. I imagined them making love to my sister. I am so embarrassed to even write this to you. I thought that I was in love with her. I wanted to be the one making love to her.

So I hated those women, all of them that she brought home. She used to come into my room before she had sex with them and tell me stories. She was laughing and relaxed. She would sit beside me or sometimes lay with her head on my feet. She had no idea how lovely she was. She had no clue how much that I wanted her. She would lay there in the dark telling me these stories. I would be still, listening, while trying to deny that I wanted her. After she would leave my room I would be so angry with those women, with anyone that could have Emma. I hated them all. Except Eve, she was different, at first.

I had a crush on Eve. She looked like Emma, as you know. At night after she and my sister would make love she would sneak downstairs for a cup of tea. We would stay up all hours of the evening talking as Emma slept. I was jealous of her, but I liked her. I started thinking that Eve could release me of my sister. That I would no longer be in love with her and that I would be in love with Eve.

Emma told me that she wanted me to be with Eve. The first night that Eve and I slept together Eve didn't replace Emma as I hoped. I was even more connected to her. For the first time, I was touching someone Emma had touched and was making love to someone that had made love to her. I was still in love with Emma. And then I was in love with Eve too. At

280

least I thought I was.

There were always three of us in the bedroom. Not physically, but in my head. Emma never knew, although I am sure Eve suspects it. This is so embarrassing for me. But it is important that you know this to understand what you have brought to me.

After Emma died, I was devastated. I lost a sister and also someone who I thought was the love of my life. Making love with Eve became empty. My sister had filled all the missing parts, the gaps that Eve did not have. When Emma was gone so was my love for Eve and I began to resent her and began treating her badly. She was not my lover. Not the one that I really wanted to have. And I began resenting the fact that she was living, looking like Emma, and Em was dead. I realized she could never be Emma. Never.

I was so lonely and so lost. I was trying to keep Emma alive when I started the account on MyLIFESeeker. I really was. And somehow by having sex online as Emma, she was still my lover as well as my sister. She was the best part of me. I know it all sounds so incestuous and incredibly fucked up. I have hated myself many years for these feelings, but then I met you and I realized something.

You taught me about love. You showed me making love and I felt it. I really did for the first time. You showed me that what I felt for my sister was lust. She was the only woman in my life for a very long time. I did not have any friends or girlfriends. And the lust made me feel so guilty that I obsessed about it. I made a bigger issue out of it than really was there. I thought I was in love with Emma, but I fell in love with YOU. I found out what being in love really is. There is only one woman I have ever been in love with. You.

You released me from the guilt and from my sister. I have decided to close down the MyLIFESeeker account. I will no longer use it. I don't need it. I am a free man now, except for one problem. The woman I love actually made love to my sister, not to me. You can never love me back.

There is something you should know. I love you enough to

free you, which is what I am going to do. If you ever change your mind and think you could have a relationship with a man, I hope you think of me. Or if you think we can be friends, I can handle that too. Although I don't think your wife will let us.

My beautiful sweet Jade, you have allowed me to hope that I can find true love again. Do you think it is possible to find true love twice in your life? I am going to ask you when I see you. I want to know. I hope so.

I am also going to give you something when I see you. It is a box. In it you will find a key to a safety deposit box in Amsterdam. At the bottom of the box is an address. Here you will find the safety deposit box and in it you will find some things. I have put some very important material in this box about Emma. There are some pictures and several other items you might find interesting. I want you to go to this box and use this key. Take what you want from it. All of it if you need to, it is yours. There is no one else that I would ever give this key to. Only you.

I have the only other copy. Eve knows nothing about this and I appreciate your confidence. So for the gift of releasing me, I want to give you two in return, the gift of freedom from me, and the gift of closure with Emma. Maybe this key will help set you free as well.

I love you Jade. I hope one day you can find it in your heart to forgive me, and all of the terrible things I have done to you. I want to see you one last time in person so I can tell you this. I can help free you as well.

Your friend,
Erik

_____

I realize tears are streaming down my face. Guilt and regret well up and pour out of my windows, burning like acid down my cheeks. What have I done? Why did this come only minutes after checking my messages? We might have been able to prevent all of

282

this. The guilt and regret are stifling.

Grand gestures, he has made two of them. I knew he was not capable of hurting me, in my heart I knew this. Now, instead of letting him talk to me, I killed him. Jessica physically killed him, but I am the one who really killed him. I brought him here in the first place and drove him to threaten our family. Jessica protected me, and now I will protect her by not telling her about the message. The self-condemnation would be unbearable for her.

Yet, it still does not make sense. Why did he enter my house without my knowledge? He must have used the back door. Why didn't he ring the bell? Why did he wait for me after I called out to him? He could have responded to me. He had the chance at the bottom of the stairs. Why did he not talk to me? Did I back up and show fear again, is that why? He could have still said something. He had me trapped, but he didn't have to chase after me? Why did he? Did the moment just escalate like on Halloween night? His eyes were so estranged and it scared me. My instincts warned me. Would he have raped me? Did he plan to kill me all along? It doesn't make sense. The more I try to remember exactly what happened and decipher his actions, the more confused I get.

Jessica comes downstairs, showered and clean. She sees me behind my computer. "Any messages?"

"No, no important ones." I log off the computer quickly, go to the refrigerator and pour us both a glass of juice. Our hands are shaking as we drink.

"We can't carry him to the car, we aren't strong enough. So, we'll bury him in our backyard just beyond my office in between the trees. There is a bare spot that is not viewable by anyone. No one can see us digging. Let's hope the neighbors will not hear."

Jessica remains silent and is looking at her empty juice glass. "Whatever you think is best. Let's just do what you think is best. I trust you."

It rains all night long. As soon as darkness hits, hidden in our secret spot in the shadows of the trees, Jessica and I dig for what seems an eternity. We are both wearing black clothes. Concealed by the darkness, we work steadily. Robots programmed to complete a task; we do not speak, but quietly dig. After two hours we are growing so tired that we need to alternate turns. My hands and feet are bruised from the shovel but we continue. I am possessed with a familiar force. By HER. The hole is deep. It must be five or six feet.

The rain has created puddles in our yard. We slide him across the wet grass, into the hole and cover it up. As each shovel of dirt is thrown on him, my conscience feels its weight. When the grave is filled, the pressure is unbearable. I will carry the full burden.

At 5:00am we finish and it is still raining. This has worked to our advantage because it has prevented the neighbors from wondering outside and it allowed us to make noise without being heard. Jessica looks over at me. "Jess, I just need a few minutes okay. I will be in, in a minute. Go wash up and lay down."

She kisses me and grabs my face, "I love you. I know what you have done for me. We'll always protect each other and our family. Whatever it takes."

After watching her walk inside the house, I turn and look at the ground at the freshly covered grave. Before I know what I am doing, I find myself crawling on top of it. I lie down, with my arms spread so my body is the shape of a cross. Hugging the ground, I imagine Emma just below me. She is under me, and I am pressing against her with six feet of dirt between us. She is not Erik. She is Emma. I can feel her cold body whispering to me. Unable to hear the words, I only hear a muffled voice. Tears flowing down my cheeks I speak softly, "Secretly bound." Forever.

Then a flash of Erik comes to me. I think of him in the bag beneath, suffocating. I stand up frantically and wipe my tears. Turning to walk away, I stop and turn back around.

I silently speak to him, "Just when you thought you were released, I've taken you back to her. At least now she is only your sister. I'm sorry...and yes Erik, it's possible to find true love more than once in a lifetime."

Walking into the house, I shut the door. The dragon lifts off and flies away. SHE is gone.

23

It has been almost eight months since Erik's death. Jessica and I chose to never speak about it again. Erik had closed Emma's MyLIFESeeker account down before he had come over. Emma disappeared from my friend list that day so when I woke up, she no longer existed.

The following afternoon I took the keys that we removed from his pocket and disposed of his car. I drove it to Brussels, and left it at Midi Train Station, abandoned and unlocked, with the keys still in it. I have no idea whatever happened to it.

I never showed Jessica that email from Erik. I didn't want her to feel guilty. I would take all of it on for both of us. She had made peace with it, knowing she prevented him from raping and killing me. It was justifiable in her mind and she slept at night because of it.

In my mind, I still have so many unanswered questions. Sometimes, I think he could never rape or kill me. Most of the time, I know he was so obsessed, and that he was no longer aware of his actions. It is easier to think that, than to think I misinterpreted it all, and we killed a potentially innocent man.

I don't know if Erik intended to keep his word on going on with his life. He was now released from Emma. I guess I was able to do that for him. I don't think he initially planned to hurt me, but I think his obsession drove him to act in ways he normally would not have. I wonder what he meant by "freeing me" of her. Was he so obsessed that he was capable of actually killing me? Is that what he meant? Ultimately, I am responsible for his death. I know this. Regardless of what the truth may be, I am the one that drove him to his actions.

I have nightmares. At first, I had them every night, then it was twice a week and now it is two or three times a month. I dream of him coming out of the grave and watching me through the windows, waiting for me to come outside, so he can pull me into the hole with him. Those dreams have become so real, that I have to close every curtain in the house after dark. Always, there is never an exception, and I never go in the back yard after dark. I think of him there, waiting for me.

What do I believe? Do I accept he was going to hurt me? When I think back to the moment I thought he was reaching for a knife, the look in his eye...I know he was there to hurt me. I was certain. But I am lost somewhere between reality and fantasy, between waking and nightmares. Somewhere in a world where the guilt has eaten me, and I am no longer alive.

My fiery dragon left me the night, after we buried Erik. I feel dead. I have tried to hide this from Jessica and our son, but they see it, when I am quiet and lost in my thoughts. The passion from my eyes has gone, and I have been struggling to recapture it. But how can it survive something like this? Is there room?

Jessica and I are bound forever with this secret. We have been working on our relationship and I feel that it is my responsibility to protect her. I want to be there for her, but there is one thing that stands in the way.

Emma. Oh, Em. I look out at the garden and the grass is growing over the grave. There lies the ghost of Emma too. We are also bound together forever. I know that I need to release myself from her. I have tried, but I cannot, she still haunts me.

I think of her wondering in the yard during the day looking for me. Sometimes, I find myself outside working in the garden, and I sense her, just over my shoulder. Catching a glimpse of her smile, she is still with me. Even though her face has faded in my mind, her ghost is alive and feeding off of my energy. Erik was right. She penetrates my mind in a way that makes it almost impossible to release her. Without letting her go, I cannot fully recover from all of this. But how? There is only one way.

I know that no one will ever make the connection between Erik and I. Now it is safe to go to the safety deposit box. Maybe this is where I will find peace and where I will fully release Emma's ghost. I *must* go.

It is June and such a beautiful day. It has rained for the last three weeks so on this sunny day the Netherlands has come alive. People are everywhere outside riding their bikes, playing in the parks, walking and enjoying life. Cars are piled up for miles heading for the beach.

My son is in school today, and his grandpa and grandma will pick him up and bring him home with them for the weekend. Jessica and I have a date weekend planned. We will shop and go out for dinner, just be with each other. I thought this would be the perfect chance to drive into Amsterdam and to have a look at the secret box. I have to release the ghost of Emma, so I can move on entirely and put all of this behind me.

The streets of Amsterdam are so full of people, everyone enjoying the beautiful day, shopping or sitting on terraces. There are street performers and tourists wondering about. I feel clarity, ready to face her ghost.

The safety deposit box is housed in a very old, beautiful building. I walk in and show my key to the tall man behind the counter. He gives me a slightly confused look, shrugs and asks for the code. I quietly reveal the secret set of numbers. Handing me back the key, he says, "You will have company. I guess you know that already." Assuming he means there will be other people in the room as well, I smile and reply, "Of course, why would that be a problem?" He smiles back and says, "Oh good, I just wanted you to be aware in case you were not."

I am escorted through a heavy door into a small area with another open door in the back. It leads to another small room with many safety deposit boxes. Following the guard, we walk across it to yet another door. He takes out his keys, unlocks it and reveals a very exclusive space. "I guess you know your box is in there. Just ring the bell when you are ready to leave."

I nod as if I know what I am doing. Inching my way into the dimly lit space, I look around as the door closes and locks behind me. There are not very many boxes in here. It must cost a fortune to keep such a secret, housed in such a beautiful building, where the rent must be rather high. It makes me curious to see what could be so precious.

Faintly, I see another woman in the back of room, whose back is to me. Scanning the number on the key, I begin to search for the matching box. Moving closer and closer toward the other woman, I am almost to the number that corresponds with my key. Now shoulder-to-shoulder, I glance over and I gasp! Feeling a sense of panic, my breath stops momentarily. The woman looks over at me, and I immediately see recognition.

"What are you doing here?" she says inquisitively, "I thought I would never see you again."

Looking into her eyes, I find myself speechless, lost in their beauty. I study her face and lips. She is conscious that I am looking at her in a very sensual way, as I step back to see her more clearly.

"Eve, right? Your name is Eve?" I hear myself say in a strange voice.

"Yes, that's right." She smiles big, and then it fades as she studies my face closely, returning the sensual stare I had just given her.

"Jade," she says, "I remember from the box you dropped." She pauses and looks down searching for the right words.

"Actually, I think about you a lot. I mean...I felt so bad about how you found out about Emma. How surprised and sad you were. I guess you were hoping to reconnect with her, maybe start seeing her again? I'm sorry...I'm being too personal." She glances up at me, waiting for me to speak. I feel butterflies begin to dance in my tummy. Oh no.

She is slightly taller than I am and has on a short, white skirt and brown, strappy sandals. Her shirt is a brown, white and black dressy tank top made of silk. The print is very unusual, almost psychedelic. Her arms are feminine but toned. She has on light make-up and a thick layer of lip-gloss. Long and blond, her hair is pulled back in a thick twist. Her eyes, oh, Emma's eyes. I am clearly startled by her beauty and find myself unable to speak. She is ravishing.

"No, its okay," I say finding my words. "I was just coming to see Em. I wanted to see how she was doing." I lie. "I wanted to reconnect with her, it had been a long time." I curl my lips in a flirtatious smile.

"That is nice of you to worry about her."

She flashes an enticing smile back. Butterflies are unifying in my tummy, coaxing and prodding the sleeping dragon. I am entirely lost in her stare. She is inviting me just the way that I pictured Emma would, without words. She looks so much like her. It is almost supernatural, as that familiar feeling rises inside of me.

Emma's ghost stands and watches us. Desperately wanting to kiss her, I look up at the video cameras in each corner.

"We are being watched," she says motioning to the camera.

"Yes." We are being watched like in my last adventure with Emma.

"So Jade, what brings you here?" she says with a tilt of the head. Her eyes big and curious, she takes me off guard, but my reply comes naturally.

"I have a friend who is sick and needed me to pick something up for her." Immediately changing the subject I continue, "So, how about you?"

"Well, not so good, you could say."

"Do you want to talk about it?"

She pauses, looks down shyly and up again. She is diving into my windows. "Well you know my husband Erik, Emma's brother, I told you about him? He has been missing for the past eight months. I have no idea where he is. Maybe he left me. Maybe he killed himself. He just disappeared, no reason." She looks down.

I touch her shoulder tenderly, "I am so sorry. It must be very difficult for you." I say it sincerely, yet feeling guilt digging at me.

"Well, we had not been getting along for a long time, not since Emma's death. It changed him. He has never been the man he publically appeared to be. He was a master at fooling people. After her death, he became mean. He...scared me." Hesitating, she looks at me in despair and then continues. "I was getting ready to call an attorney to draw up divorce papers, and he just disappeared. Maybe he knew it and left me instead. I think he was having an affair. I'm not sure, and I'll never know." Her voice is low.

"What makes you think he was having an affair?"

"He worked late and spent a lot of time in his office." Again pausing, then further revealing, "He was horrible to me."

"Here, sit down by the table", I say. Seeing she is clearly distraught, I pull out a chair for her. Sitting beside her, I grab her hand, and hold it in both of mine. Her head is tilted down and she is shaking it slightly. I lean forward, lowering my head under hers, to connect with her eyes again. She looks at me and I raise my head back up, as she keeps contact with me. Looking deeply, so vulnerably, I see tears well up in her eyes. I respond by touching her cheek.

"How was he mean to you Eve?" I say, needing to know the answer to this question.

She pauses, wanting to speak but unable. "It's okay...it's okay," I say squeezing her hand tight.

"It started with resentment...and...then silence. It grew from there."

"Did he physically hurt you?" I could tell, by her facial reaction, the answer to the question. Bastard. That fucking bastard!

"I can't talk about it here, I'm a mess...I'm sorry, I should not be...why am I telling you all of this?"

I reach up, holding my hand to one side of her face, and I smile reassuringly. "You know, talking about it is the most difficult thing. Look at you. You're okay...you will be just fine."

Her lips curl slightly. I have said the perfect words. She closes her eyes, finding comfort in my touch, while I am lost in her face and the sensitivity of the moment. She grabs my hand that is resting on her cheek and squeezes it. She is almost clutching me. And I want to protect her and love her the way she deserves to be loved. My Dragon is yawning. SHE is stretching and opening HER eyes.

Her beauty is astonishing. Gentle and soft, I feel her submitting to me. I sense she wants me to hold and kiss her, as I feel every nerve enliven in my body. I begin to ache for her. In a flash, I envision our two bodies naked. I long to caress her soft skin and inhale her scent. I see myself on top of her, spreading her legs, running my hands over her hips, her tummy, and gently finding her breasts. I imagine kissing those beautiful lips for the first time.

Looking at me intensely, she is reading my thoughts. There is no hiding my feelings, as my eyes are growing dark with desire. They begin to become fiery and commanding, and before I know what I am doing I am pulling her towards me. A familiar wetness emerges between my legs.

Pulling her in close and putting my arms around her, I am intoxicated. Her head resting on my shoulder, she is facing me, and I can feel her warm breath on my neck. Aware that her lips are just centimeters away, my heart is pounding simultaneously with

290

the pounding of my clit.

I feel her face move closer to my neck as she nuzzles up to me. My body tenses and she responds to this by moving even closer. I begin to rub her back, as my touch is growing more and more intense. I hear her breath begin to grow heavy, as she is pulling more and more towards me.

She leans up to my ear and whispers "I have been thinking about you since you came to my house. I told Erik I wanted to call you, but he wouldn't let me. I think he knew that I was interested in you. The truth is, I still think about you and the way you looked at me, when I opened the door that night. Isn't it strange? Someone I don't know. There's something about you, I feel like I know you. You are familiar to me." She leans even closer to my ear. Her hot breath is driving me crazy and I am exploding inside.

"The way you looked at me that night. You undressed me with your eyes. I felt such passion coming from you. It's the same way you are looking at me now." She pauses and then says the words that reveal everything, "If you want me, I am yours."

I hear the submissive Emma. I hear her very words! Erik had not used Emma's actual words when writing to me. He had used Eve's! Is Eve really the Emma that Erik wrote about? Is she the one that I fell in love with?

The real Emma was not submissive. Erik had to find his words somewhere because he was not submissive either. He was a manipulator. He had said Eve was always his link to the real Emma, but that they were completely opposite. If Emma was dominant, was Eve submissive? Had he used Eve's words? Emma wrote that Eve "scared her". And Eve just told me the same about Erik. Was *he* really the Eve he wrote about?

Her lips are just before mine. They are swollen and I want to kiss them softly, lick them and suck on them. I raise my eyebrow, put my hand on her neck and pull her closer, as I inch forward and open my mouth. I run my hand slowly down the side of her body, enticing her. She responds by lifting up a little and releases a soft sigh. As soon as I hear this, I am pouring. I gently brush her breast, moving up over her neck and resting my hands on her soft cheeks. Her skin is creamy. I have almost lost consciousness to the fantasy that has now become real. She moves her mouth almost on mine. Suddenly, another person enters the room.

Tormented, we pull back from one another.

Eve looks over and smiles shyly. I think she quite likes getting caught. We are still seated at the table as the man enters and turns his back to us. Looking down, I see Eve's short skirt, pull it up and grab her knee moving my hand upwards to her mid thigh. I think of her upper inner thigh hidden under her skirt. Eve presses her leg against mine and spreads them slightly. She wants me too.

The much older man turns and comes to the table and proudly places his box down. He looks at us with a genuine smile and says, "I must be so lucky to be in a room with such exquisite women. Yes, this is certainly my lucky day." He starts digging through his box.

"Eve, I have to go."

"Wait, I found this key to a safety deposit box. I opened it, but decided I didn't want to look at it. It is filled with Emma's things and I feel guilty going through someone else's private information. Would you like to clean it out with me? We can bring the contents with us and you can help me go through them. I don't live too far from here."

If I follow her, I know what will happen. Eve is the Emma I fell in love with. It wasn't the real Emma. It was Erik's Emma who wrote to me, and she is alive. His Emma, that he created, is really Eve. I am tempted, tortured, but I need to think this over before making any rash decisions. Trying to control my dragon, I fight my instincts. SHE is breathing fire, commanding me to release HER

"I can't. I have run out of time and am going away for the weekend. You know what Eve? I am over Emma. There is nothing else that I need to see." I pause and notice her disappointment. Pulling myself very close to her face, the heat between us is smoking. The man across the table is staring at us, but the passionate connection is so intense, that I don't care.

"If I come with you now, I know what would happen." Looking at her and longing for her, I brush away a piece of hair that has fallen down into her face. Gently pushing it aside, I can see her windows.

"I am with someone Eve. But I have to admit, I have not been able to release you from my mind either." Placing my cheek on hers, I whisper in her ear, "God, I want to make love to you. I want you so badly. But, I... I need to go now."

I close my eyes, trying to resist her softness. Moving back reluctantly, I stand up. She copies my movement. The man across the table is still staring in disbelief. I see the disappointment in her face, but she smiles a little and touches my arm softly. She needs me and instinctually I want to take care of her.

"I understand. At least let me walk out with you, I'll deal with this another day." Her touch burns my skin, and her words revive me. She picks up the box, locks it and carefully puts it back in its place. She can see that I am torn, so she smiles in a soft caring way.

Grabbing her hand and bringing it to my breast, we walk over and ring the bell. A guard comes and escorts us out. She seems uncomfortable as the men watch us leave. I pull her closer. You are safe with me, Eve. I will protect you.

Standing outside we are lost in one another. She is waiting for me to say something to her, but I am quiet. We are both in an uncharted territory, wanting to release to our desire, but stagnated by our morals.

"Can I ask you a question?" she breaks the silence. "Were you in love with Emma?"

I look at her and can see this is a very serious question for her. "No. I thought I was once, but I wasn't. I was never in love with her." A look of relief comes over her face.

"I don't think I could ever date someone again that had been in love with Emma."

"You dated someone who was in love with her?"

"Yes, I married him. But that is a long story."

I nod my head. "You said 'date someone again'." She shrugs and tilts her head with a smile. She is so fucking cute! Already, I adore her.

"Maybe if you are ever on your own again, maybe we could...?" Taking a piece of paper and a pen out of my purse, I write my MyLIFESeeker account down and hand it to her.

"Are you on MyLIFESeeker?" I ask.

"I have heard of that, actually I was thinking about creating an account. I hear it is a good way to meet people."

"I'd like to talk to you more, get to know you a little better. It's all I am capable of right now. But Eve, if you need to talk, I am a good listener. Send me a friend request after you have created an account."

"Okay, I will!" She smiles big then surprises me. She leans over and whispers "Jade, you are the kind of woman that could handle a woman like me." My heart grows.

I kiss the top of her hand. I am reluctant to dive into my feelings for her, but she is ready. I turn and walk away. After a few steps, I feel her undressing me from behind. Stopping and looking back, she is still watching me. She waves and then turns in the direction of her house.

I retreat knowing I am free of the ghost of Emma, but what have I gained? All along Eve's picture was calling me. She was the submissive Emma. And she is a real person. She exists! What Erik did to her, that motherfucker! What exactly *did* he do to her? It drives me crazy to think of him hurting her, all the while emailing with me. What a bastard!

I must hear more of her story. The guilt I felt for Erik now transforms. I feel compelled to help Eve, to protect her and help her get back upon her feet. She doesn't deserve to feel this way. It is partially my fault.

On the drive home, I re-enact what happened with Eve in my mind. My body is still filled with desire for her. I cannot deny my thoughts of her and equate them to every burning touch that had existed in my head with Emma. It is now a possibility. The question is what am I going to do with it? My dragon sits in my backseat, breathing down my neck.

Returning home, I walk in and Jessica kisses me long and passionately. "Twenty minutes before we leave, okay?"

"Okay," I say a bit distracted.

I log on to MyLIFESeeker. I am surprised to find a message and a new friend request.

Date: June 1, 2008   11:45 AM
Subject: My First

294

Jade,

Hi. I started a MyLIFESeeker account as you asked me to do. This is really a lot of fun. I found a few of my friends on here. You are my first friend request and first message.

It was strange that we ran into each other. Fate maybe? I hope so. I felt such a connection with you, like we have known each other before, perhaps in another lifetime? Thank you for listening to me. I still can't believe I told that to you. Thank you. You were a good friend to me today.

I hope to hear from you. I have been thinking of you all day, but I mustn't say such things. You seem like a very wonderful person.

xxx
Eve

I feel a twinge of excitement and a familiar wetness. A friend request, should I click "Accept" or "Reject"? I hover for a moment. I click on "Accept". Then I click "Reply" and start typing.

The dragon is fully awake and SHE is very hungry.

The End

Epilogue

I watch them. They are holding hands as they leave the building, and she has her hand to her breast, where my hand should be. Jade has found Eve. She has finally figured out that Erik's real Eve is actually the submissive Emma he wrote about. Didn't she know that? Didn't she see that all along like I did?

I had Jade's password to MyLIFESeeker from the very beginning. I was watching when she created the account. I read everything. *Everything*. I suspected there was something else behind Emma all along. After Erik revealed himself and wrote about his sister Emma, I knew that she was not the submissive one Jade craved. I knew it was Eve. It had to be, because after seeing Erik with Jade, I knew he wasn't submissive. And I see now, I was right.

I thought Jade had figured it out and came into Amsterdam to meet Eve, but after reading the message Eve just sent to her, I see it was unplanned. Fate. The inevitable has finally happened. Jade is now fiery again behind her eyes. I see it in her. I love when she is fiery. She used to be that way with me, and she will be again.

I will stop this. Just like I stopped Erik.

On Halloween night, I knew who he was when I opened the door. It took everything I had not to crush him with my words. Jade needed to figure it out for herself, in order to come back to me. I left the room, but stood outside the door, waiting for Jade to tell him to go away. I could not hear all that was said, but I heard the tension and came into the room. I saw then, he was in love with my wife.

I left the door open that afternoon, accidentally. I knew he would come back; otherwise, he would not have messaged her. Yes, I read his message. While Jade was upstairs looking for the pepper spray, I logged into her account. I read his message and I knew he would come. Jade never noticed that the last message he sent her was marked "read". She missed that I had already read it. She never told me about that message either. I know she wanted to protect me. She has proven that she loves me so deeply. And I will protect her, from herself.

I saw him waiting in his car, so I drove around to the other side of the playground and parked where he could not see. I got out and hid between the cars. I thought he would ring the doorbell and confront Jade. She would never let him in the house. I planned to sneak up closer behind a wall and watch her speak with him. I needed her to finish this story with him. She had to do it herself. I wanted her to realize the consequences of her bad choices. She needed to see how wrong she really was, and this was her opportunity to finally stop what she had started. Her closure.

But then I saw Erik get out of his car and he immediately went around to the back of the house. I panicked as I remembered the back door was unlocked. I was so distracted that I forgot to lock it. I ran to my car to get the keys so I could set off the wireless alarm system when I got to the house. But I had accidentally locked them in my car. I ran across the playground, in a panic. I would not let him hurt her. I came through the back door as he was running up the stairwell. Standing at the bottom of the stairs, I was terrified. I could hear him yelling at her and she was begging him not to kill her. I never imagined he would get inside without her knowing. Looking around, I remembered my grandfather's sickle and pulled it down from the wall, removing the blade protector.

I never expected to find him on top of her. He was going to kill her. There was no doubt in my mind. So, I did it.

I knew he was still playing Jade, and that there was much more to his story. He wanted to break up our family, and he had to have her. I never suspected he would actually try to kill her. So, I did the only thing I could have done. I killed him.

I will keep Jade and she will keep me. She belongs to me and I am hers. There is nothing and no one that will come in between this family. I will make sure of that.

A Message from Jade

There is more to my story. I have more to confess and many more secrets. I know you want to know what was in Emma's box. Only I know right now. And what exactly were Erik's intentions? What is his real story? What will happen between Eve and I? Should I continue to reveal?

The dragon is resting…

If you would like for me to write a sequel, let me know.
infopursuitpub@gmail.com

I look forward to hearing from you.

xoxo,
Jade

Acknowledgements

I would like to take the opportunity to thank some very important people that made this book possible, and whose individual talents and support all contributed to this book. You graciously gave your time and helped me realize my dream. You took this journey with me, and I am forever grateful to all of you.

I would like to thank my first editor, Anne Reed, who saw my very first rough draft and encouraged me to keep going, even though it was shit. You are such an inspiration to me, and you helped me have the courage to continue with this book, as you know. I cherish our friendship and our long, passion-filled, cryptic discussions.

I would like to thank my second editor, Catherine Whitebread, who poured over every word and sentence in this book with so much energy and enthusiasm. Brainstorming with me on numerous and very long phone conversations, you helped me find my words when I felt underwater. Thank you for putting so much heart into it. You are so special to me, and I love that you shared this experience with me. You're the best Billy.

Laura Bartick, who did the cover of this book, you are amazing. You are unbelievably creative and took a few simple ideas that I had and created something far better than I ever imagined. You are a dear friend, who always connected with me at so many levels. Your loyalty and encouragement helped plant the seed for this creative endeavor. Thanks B, for everything.

To Blue Sleighty, my mentor, thank you for your inspiration, advice, and friendship. Your ideas and suggestions completely transformed my writing, and you have also prepared me for what might come. An incredible motivator, Blue, you are amazing. Thank you, did I say that already? It could never be enough.

I would like to thank my family and friends for all of your support. I told some of you I was writing an erotic novel (that was also a thriller). Yes, some of you were shocked, but most of you embraced the journey I was taking. I am so lucky to have so many wonderful people in my life that love and support me.

Thanks to Houghton Mifflin Harcourt Publishing Company, publishers of Anais Nin's *Henry and June,* for allowing me to include so many passages from one of my very favorite books. I only wish I could thank Anais Nin personally for her inspiration. Her words changed me, beyond comprehension, and inspired me to search for my own.

I would also like to thank Ridderprint. The Mac loving family of creativity that worked so hard to deliver the first edition of this book. Thank you.

I would like to thank my mother, who always believed in me. Mom, you gave your time to me, so much of it. As a mother, I now understand how precious that gift is. I can say nothing more than you are such a wonderful woman and mother. You bring light into my day, even when the clouds hover above me. I adore your eccentricities, your courage, and your zest for life. I love you.

And finally I would like to thank the most important contributor to this book, my beautiful, amazing wife. You have supported me through every moment. This has been a very long and exhausting process, but you have encouraged me, stood by me and contributed to this project in so, so many ways. I think of all the nights we brainstormed in the kitchen, and you came up with the best ideas and twists to the storyline. The editing process was brutal, pouring over one more chapter after the other, without complaining. This book exists because of you and your support of my dream. Our relationship drips with passion, and our lives are full of love. I strive every day to be the woman and companion that you are to me. You are my home and always will be. I still don't know how you put up with me. I am so lucky. I love and cherish you more every day. And will forever.

How to Order

This book is available to order online.

If you are a business that would like to sell this book, please contact us at infopursuitpub@gmail.com

Thank you for your interest and support!

PURSUIT publishing

About the Author

Jade is a first time author, who remains anonymous. She is an international woman of mystery.